DIANA
PALMER

CARLA
NEGGERS

EMILIE
RICHARDS

AND

BRENDA NOVAK
SUSAN MALLERY

HARLEQUIN®

TORONTO • NEW YORK • LONDON
AMSTERDAM • PARIS • SYDNEY • HAMBURG
STOCKHOLM • ATHENS • TOKYO • MILAN • MADRID
PRAGUE • WARSAW • BUDAPEST • AUCKLAND

ISBN 0-373-83619-8

MORE THAN WORDS

Copyright © 2004 by Harlequin Books S.A.

The publisher acknowledges the copyright holders
of the individual works as follows:

Susan Kyle is acknowledged as the author of *The Greatest Gift*.
Carla Neggers is acknowledged as the author of *Close Call*.
Emilie Richards McGee is acknowledged as the author of
  Hanging by a Thread.
Brenda Novak is acknowledged as the author of *Small Packages*.
Susan Mallery is acknowledged as the author of *Built to Last*.

This edition published by arrangement with Harlequin Books S.A.

® and TM are trademarks of the publisher. Trademarks indicated with ® are registered in the United States Patent and Trademark Office, the Canadian Trade Marks Office and in other countries.

www.eHarlequin.com

Printed in U.S.A.

CONTENTS

THE GREATEST GIFT   7
Diana Palmer

CLOSE CALL   85
Carla Neggers

HANGING BY A THREAD   145
Emilie Richards

SMALL PACKAGES   209
Brenda Novak

BUILT TO LAST   316
Susan Mallery

Dear Reader,

As you may know, Harlequin has been a longtime
supporter of women's causes. Recently though, we
decided that our impact could be much greater if we
reimagined our program—and Harlequin More Than Words
was born. Harlequin More Than Words is dedicated to
celebrating the lives of ordinary women who have made
an extraordinary contribution in their community.

We always knew that Harlequin readers cared for those
around them, but this was proven over and over again as
the nominations came streaming in. The first five recipients
of the Harlequin More Than Words awards, each of whom
has a description in the pages that follow, are truly inspiring.

We also believe that the impact these women have on their
communities can truly inspire others if we share their stories
with the millions of women who read our books.

What you currently hold in your hands is the first book
in the Harlequin More Than Words program. Five of our
most acclaimed authors have written wonderful fictional
stories that are inspired by the lives of our award winners.
Diana Palmer, Carla Neggers, Emilie Richards, Brenda Novak
and Susan Mallery all gave their time and energy to creating
stories that we hope will inspire you. All of the proceeds
from this book will be reinvested in the More Than Words
program, further supporting causes that are of concern to
women.

Please visit www.HarlequinMoreThanWords.com for more
information, or to submit a nominee for next year's book.
Together we can make a difference.

Sincerely,

Donna Hayes
Publisher and CEO
Harlequin Enterprises

CHEFS TO THE RESCUE
SUE COBLEY

Most people, if they think about it at all, just shake their heads at the food wasted in restaurants and grocery stores. Eight years ago, Sue Cobley decided to do something about it. That would be remarkable enough in itself, but Sue was no well-heeled suburbanite or high-placed executive with a mission statement and plenty of backing. In 1996, just divorced from an abusive husband, evicted from their rented property and living in a borrowed car with her five children, Sue embarked on a course of action that would literally move mountains of food—and change her community of Boise, Idaho.

To anyone else, just keeping body and soul—and the family—together would be challenge enough, yet despite her own daily struggle for survival, Sue made what would turn out to be a life-changing decision: to be a link between surplus food and the many people who needed it. She didn't have to know the statistics—over 33 million Americans, 12.7 million of them children, living with hunger or on the edge of it, according to U.S. Department of Agriculture estimates, and a staggering 96 billion pounds of food wasted each year in the United States—to be aware that there were people going hungry in her own community. She began calling local grocery stores and restaurants for donations of surplus food to distribute to shelters and needy families. The response was encouraging. "Restaurants hate to throw away food they've prepared," Sue says. "They were happy to be able to help." From this humble yet bold beginning, Chefs to the Rescue was born, though it didn't yet have a name.

It started as a family project, one that Sue now sees as key in shaping her family's future. "I didn't want our experience to hurt my kids for the rest of their lives," she says. When the idea for redistributing food came to her, "It was like it was meant to be—helping other people empowered the kids. They have come out of the experience with a positive outlook, and I hope that when they have to go through hard times, they'll be able to draw on that."

Maintaining a routine was important in keeping the family together through these hard times. The two eldest children, then twelve and thirteen, were in school during the day; the other three, the youngest a baby, accompanied Sue when she cleaned houses, her only means of support. The older children helped the younger ones, baby-sitting, reading to them, assisting with homework—and all of them did chores. "They're awesome kids," Sue says.

Most nights the family stayed in motels when they could afford it, and Sue did her best to make it seem like camping out, an adventure. Cole and Chase, then three and five, loved being able to use the swimming pool, but for Sue, frightened and at times on the edge of despair, keeping up a cheerful façade required all her resourcefulness. Sometimes after she was sure the children were asleep, she would cry, and she remembers all too clearly sitting in a park one day and coming to the realization that she might have to turn them over to welfare. "But we had a family meeting about it," she says, "and they voted to stay together." During the two years it took to save enough money to rent a house, they continued to deliver food donations to soup kitchens, homeless centers and shelters. "I'm so glad we were busy," Sue says. "It took our minds off our situation."

What motivates such generosity of spirit? Sue's own particular inspiration was her grandmother, the first female officer in the Boise prison—dubbed "Feeder" by Sue's brother because of her habit of generously sharing food, even though she had little money. She also taught female prisoners how to sew. It was only later, however, that Sue became fully aware of her grandmother's influence. Though she'd studied social work in college, Sue knew nothing about homelessness and says she probably shared most people's attitude of indifference. Her personal experience taught her what it means to be homeless, hungry and abused, and now, in her work with the Idaho Foodbank, she says, "Every day I learn something from somebody else. I meet people who are priceless."

One such person was Roger Simon, executive director of the Idaho Foodbank. Sue met Roger a year or so after starting her project. At that time, having caught the attention of the local media, she was doing a TV appeal for volunteers. "I didn't know who he was and I tried to recruit him," Sue laughs. Instead he persuaded her to come work with him. Today, what began as a part-time job is full-time, and Chefs to the Rescue, the program Sue initiated and now heads, is an important part of the food bank's work. Roger, Sue maintains, is "the reason Chefs to the Rescue has grown. He has been instrumental in getting funding, grants, a vehicle…" Although, she adds, he jokes that he knows he could get her to do all this for free—and he's right.

"How many people get paid to do a job they love?" Sue asks. "It's a gift to be able to go to work and help people." She expresses the hope that through the experiences she encounters daily, she has become a more compassionate and understanding person. Roger Simon has no doubt about that. "Sue's heart is what drives her," he says.

Having personally delivered hundreds of thousands of pounds of donated food, Sue is currently working toward helping other cities and food banks adopt the same food-rescue policy that last year alone was instrumental in acquiring 187,000 pounds of surplus food. If that sounds like a challenge, Sue is ready to hear from you!

More Than Words

DIANA PALMER
THE
GREATEST
GIFT

DIANA PALMER

Today the bestselling author of over one hundred novels, Diana Palmer is renowned as one of North America's top ten romance writers. When she published her first novel in 1979, fans immediately fell in love with her sensual, charming romances. A diehard romantic who married her husband five days after they met, Diana admits that she wrote her first book at age thirteen—and has been hooked ever since. She and her husband, James Kyle, and their son, Blayne, make their home in northeast Georgia, with a menagerie of animals that includes three dogs, five cats, assorted exotic lizards, a duck, one chicken and an emu named George.

CHAPTER
ONE

THE CAR LIGHTS passing by the side road kept Mary Crandall awake. She glanced into the back seat where her son, Bob, and her daughter, Ann, were finally asleep. Sandwiched between them, the toddler, John, was sound asleep in his little car seat. Mary pushed back a strand of dark hair and glanced worriedly out the window. She'd never in her life slept in a car. But she and her children had just been evicted from their rental home, by a worried young policewoman with a legal eviction notice. She hadn't wanted to enforce the order but had no choice since Mary hadn't paid the rent in full. The rent had gone up and Mary could no longer afford the monthly payments.

It was Mary who'd comforted her, assuring her that she and the children would manage somehow. The order hadn't mentioned the automobile, although Mary was sure that it would be taken, too. The thing was, it hadn't been taken today. By tomorrow, perhaps, the shock would wear off and she could function again. She was resourceful, and not afraid of hard work. She'd manage.

The fear of the unknown was the worst. But she knew that she and the children would be all right. They had to be! If only she didn't have to take the risk of having them in a parked car with her in the middle of the night. Like any big city, Phoenix was dangerous at night.

She didn't dare go to sleep. The car doors didn't even lock....

Just as she was worrying about that, car lights suddenly flashed in the rearview mirror. Blue lights. She groaned. It was a police car. Now they were in for it. What did they do to a woman for sleeping in a car with her kids? Was it against the law?

Mary had a sad picture of herself in mind as the police car stopped. She hadn't combed her dark, thick hair all day. There were circles under her big, light blue eyes. Her slender figure was all too thin and her jeans and cotton shirt were hopelessly wrinkled. She wasn't going to make a good impression.

She rolled the window down as a uniformed officer walked up to the driver's window with a pad in one hand, and the other hand on the butt of his service revolver. Mary swallowed. Hard.

The officer leaned down. He was clean-shaven, neat in appearance. "May I see your license and registration, please?" he asked politely.

With a pained sigh, she produced them from her tattered purse and handed them to him. "I guess you're going to arrest us," she said miserably as she turned on the inside lights.

He directed his gaze to the back seat, where Bob, Ann and John were still asleep, then looked back at Mary. He glanced at her license and registration and passed them back to her. "You can't sleep in a car," he said.

She smiled sadly. "Then it's on the ground, I'm afraid. We were just evicted from our home." Without knowing why, she added, "The divorce was final today and he left us high and dry. To add insult to injury, he wants the car for himself, but he can't find it tonight."

His face didn't betray anything, but she sensed anger in him. "I won't ask why the children have to be punished along with you," he replied. "I've been at this job for twenty years. There isn't much I haven't seen."

"I imagine so. Well, do we go in handcuffs…?"

"Don't be absurd. There's a shelter near here, a very well-run one. I know the lady who manages it. She'll give you a place to sleep and help you find the right resources to solve your situation."

Tears sprung to her light eyes. She couldn't believe he was willing to help them!

"Now, don't cry," he ground out. "If you cry, I'll cry, and just imagine how it will look to my superiors if it gets around? They'll call me a sissy!"

That amused her. She laughed, lighting up her thin face.

"That's better," he said, liking the way she looked when she smiled. "Okay. You follow me, and we'll get you situated."

"Yes, sir."

"Hey, I'm not that old," he murmured dryly. "Come on. Drive safely. I'll go slow."

She gave him a grateful smile. "Thanks. I mean it. I was scared to death to stay here, but I had no place I could go except to a friend, and she lives just two doors down from my ex-husband...."

"No need even to explain. Let's go."

He led her through downtown Phoenix to an old warehouse that had been converted into a homeless shelter.

She parked the car in the large parking lot and picked up the baby carrier, motioning to Bob and Ann to get out, too.

"Dad will probably have the police looking for the car by now," Bob said sadly.

"It doesn't matter," Mary said. "We'll manage, honey."

The police officer was out of his own car, having given his location on the radio. He joined them at the entrance to the shelter, grimacing.

"I just got a call about the car..." he began.

"I told you Dad would be looking for it," Bob said on a sigh.

"It's all right," Mary told him. She forced a smile. "I can borrow one from one of the ladies I work for. She's offered before."

"She must have a big heart," the policeman mused.

She smiled. "She has that. I keep house for several rich ladies. She's very kind."

The policeman held the door open for them as they filed reluctantly into the entrance. As she passed, she noticed that his name tag read Matt Clark. Odd, she thought, they had the same initials, and then she chided herself for thinking such a stupid thing when she was at the end of her rope.

Many people were sitting around talking. Some were sleeping on cots, even on the floor, in the huge space. There were old tables and chairs that didn't match. There was a long table with a coffee urn and bags of paper plates and cups, where meals were apparently served. It was meant for a largely transient clientele. But the place felt welcoming, just the same. The big clock on the wall read 10:00 p.m. It wasn't nearly as late as she'd thought.

"Is Bev around?" the policeman asked a woman nearby.

"Yes. She's working in the office. I'll get her," she added, smiling warmly at Mary.

"She's nice people," the policeman said with a smile. "It's going to be all right."

A couple of minutes later, a tall, dignified woman in her forties came out of the office. She recognized the police officer and grinned. "Hi, Matt! What brings you here at this hour?"

"I brought you some more clients," he said easily. "They don't have anyplace to go tonight. Got room?"

"Always," the woman said, turning to smile at Mary and her kids. She was tall and her dark hair was sprinkled with gray. She was wearing jeans and a red sweater, and she looked honest and kind. "I'm Bev Tanner," she said, holding out her hand to shake Mary's. "I manage the homeless shelter."

"I'm Mary Crandall," she replied, noting the compassionate police officer's intent scrutiny. "These are my children. Bob's the oldest, he's in junior high, Ann is in her last year of grammar school, and John's just eighteen months."

"I'm very happy to have you here," Bev said. "And you're welcome to stay as long as you need to."

Mary's lips pressed together hard as she struggled not to cry. The events of the day were beginning to catch up with her.

"What you need is a good night's sleep," Bev said at once. "Come with me and I'll get you settled."

Mary turned to Officer Clark. "Thanks a million," she managed to say, trying to smile.

He shrugged. "All in a night's work." He hesitated. "Maybe I'll see you around."

She did smile, then. "Maybe you will."

Phoenix was an enormous city. It wasn't likely. But they continued smiling at each other as he waved to Bev and went out the door.

An hour later, Mary and the children were comfortably situated with borrowed blankets. She realized belatedly that she hadn't thought to take one single piece of clothing or even her spare cosmetics from the house. There had hardly been time to absorb the shock and surprise of being evicted.

Mary looked around, dazed. The homeless shelter was just a

little frightening. She'd never been inside one before. Like many people, she'd passed them in her travels around Phoenix, but never paid them much attention. The people who frequented them had been only shadows to her, illusions she remembered from occasional stories on television around the holiday season. Helping the homeless was always a good story, during that season when people tried to behave better. Contributions were asked and acknowledged from sympathetic contributors. Then, like the tinsel and holly and wreaths, the homeless were put aside until the next holiday season.

But Mary was unable to put it aside. She had just sustained a shock as her divorce became final. She and her three children were suddenly without a home, without clothes, furniture, anything except a small amount of money tucked away in Mary's tattered purse.

She was sure that when they woke up in the morning, the car would be gone, too. The policeman, Matt Clark, had already mentioned that there was a lookout for the car. She hoped she wouldn't be accused of stealing it. She'd made all the payments, but it was in her ex-husband's name, like all their assets and everything else. That hadn't been wise. However, she'd never expected to find herself in such a situation.

She'd told Bev that they were only going to be here for one night. She had a little money in her purse, enough to pay rent at a cheap motel for a week. Somehow she'd manage after that. She just wasn't sure how. She hardly slept. Early the next morning, she went to the serving table to pour herself a cup of coffee. The manager, Bev, was doing the same.

"It's okay," the manager told her gently. "There are a lot of nice people who ended up here. We've got a mother and child who came just two days before you did," she indicated a dark young woman with a nursing baby and a terrified look. "Her name's Meg. Her husband ran off with her best friend and took all their money. And that sweet old man over there—" she nodded toward a ragged old fellow "—had his house sold out from under him by a nephew he trusted. The boy cashed in everything and took off. Mr. Harlowe was left all on his own with nothing but the clothes on his back."

"No matter how bad off people are, there's always someone worse, isn't there?" Mary asked quietly.

"Always. But you see miracles here, every day. And you're welcome to stay as long as you need to."

Mary swallowed hard. "Thanks," she said huskily. "We'll find a place tomorrow. I may not have much money or property, but I've got plenty of friends."

Bev smiled. "I'd say you know what's most important in life." She followed Mary's quick glance toward her children.

With the morning came hope. They'd had breakfast and Mary was working on her second cup of coffee, trying to decide how to proceed. Mary watched her brood mingling with other children at a long table against the wall, sharing their school paper and pencils, because they'd had the foresight to grab their backpacks on the way out, smiling happily. She never ceased to be amazed at the ease with which they accepted the most extreme situations. Their father's addiction had terrorized them all from time to time, but they were still able to smile and take it in stride, even that last night when their very lives had been in danger.

One of the policemen who came to help them the last time there had been an incident at home, an older man with kind eyes, had taken them aside and tried to explain that the violence they saw was the drugs, not the man they'd once known. But that didn't help a lot. There had been too many episodes, too much tragedy. Mary's dreams of marriage and motherhood had turned to nightmares.

"You're Mary, right?" one of the shelter workers asked with a smile.

"Uh, yes," Mary said uneasily, pushing back her dark hair, uncomfortably aware that it needed washing. There hadn't been time in the rush to get out of the house.

"Those your kids?" the woman added, nodding toward the table.

"All three," Mary agreed, watching with pride as Bob held the toddler on his lap while he explained basic math to a younger boy.

"Your son already has a way with kids, doesn't he?" the worker asked. "I'll bet he's a smart boy."

"He is," Mary agreed, noting that Bob's glasses had the nose-piece taped again, and they would need replacing. She grimaced, thinking of the cost. She wouldn't be able to afford even the most basic things now, like dentist visits and glasses. She didn't even have health insurance because her husband had dropped Mary and the kids from his policy once the divorce was final. She'd have to try to get into a group policy, but it would be hard, because she was a freelance housekeeper who worked for several clients.

The worker recognized panic when she saw it. She touched Mary's arm gently. "Listen," she said, "there was a bank vice president here a month ago. At Christmas, we had a whole family from the high bend," she added, mentioning the most exclusive section of town. "They all looked as shell-shocked as you do right now. It's the way the world is today. You can lose everything with a job. Nobody will look down on you here because you're having a bit of bad luck."

Mary bit her lower lip and tried to stem tears. "I'm just a little off balance right now," she told the woman, forcing a smile. "It was so sudden. My husband and I just got divorced. I thought he might help us a little. He took away the only car I had and we were evicted from the house."

The woman's dark eyes were sympathetic. "Everybody here's got a story, honey," she said softly. "They'll all break your heart. Come on. One thing at a time. One step at a time. You'll get through it."

Mary hesitated and grasped the other woman's hand. "Thanks," she said, trying to put everything she felt, especially the gratitude, into a single word.

The worker smiled again. "People give thanks for their blessings, and they don't usually think about the one they take most for granted."

"What?"

"A warm, dry, safe place to sleep at night."

Mary blinked. "I see what you mean," she said after a minute.

The woman nodded, leading her through the other victims of brutal homes, overindulgence, bad luck and health problems that had brought them all to this safe refuge.

★ ★ ★

John curled up next to Mary while she sat at the long table with Bob and Ann to talk.

"Why can't we go back home and pack?" Ann asked, her blue eyes, so like her mother's, wide with misery. "All my clothes are still there."

"No, they aren't," Bob replied quietly, pushing his glasses up over his dark eyes. "Dad threw everything in the trash and called the men to pick it up before we were evicted. There's nothing left."

"Bob!" Mary groaned. She hadn't wanted Ann to know what her ex had done in his last drunken rage.

Tears streamed down Ann's face, but she brushed them away when she saw the misery on her mother's face. She put her arms around Mary's neck. "Don't cry, Mama," she said softly. "We're going to be all right. We'll get new clothes."

"There's no money," Mary choked.

"I'll get a job after school and help," Bob said stoutly.

The courage of her children gave Mary strength. She wiped away the tears. "That's so sweet! But you can't work, honey, you're too young," Mary said, smiling at him. "You need to get an education. But thank you, Bob."

"You can't take care of all of us," Bob said worriedly. "Maybe we could go in foster care like my friend Dan—"

"No," Mary cut him off, hugging him to soften the harsh word. "Listen, we're a family. We stick together, no matter what. We'll manage. Hear me? We'll manage. God won't desert us, even if the whole world does."

He looked up at her with renewed determination. "Right."

"Yes, we'll stick together," Ann said. "I'm sorry I was selfish." She looked around at the other occupants of the shelter. "Nobody else here is bawling, and a lot of them look worse off than us."

"I was thinking the same thing," Mary confided, trying not to let them all see how frightened she really was.

She left them near Bev, who promised to keep an eye on them while she went to make phone calls.

Fourteen years ago, she'd had such wonderful visions of her future life. She wanted children so badly. She'd loved her husband dearly. And until he got mixed up with the crowd down at the local bar, he'd been a good man. But one of his new "friends" had introduced him first to hard liquor, and then to drugs. It was amazing how a kind, gentle man could become a raging wild animal who not only lashed out without mercy, but who didn't even remember what he'd done the morning after he'd done it. Mary and the children all had scars, mental and physical, from their experiences.

Bob understood it best. He had a friend at middle school who used drugs. The boy could be a fine student one day, and setting fire to the school the next. He'd been in and out of the juvenile justice system for two years. His parents were both alcoholics. Bob knew too much about the effects of drugs to ever use them, he told his mother sadly, both at home and school. She hoped her other children would have the same stiff common sense later down the road.

First things first. She had a good job. She had clients who were good to her, often giving her bonuses and even clothing and other gifts for the children from their abundance. Now that they knew her situation, she knew this would increase. Nobody she worked for would let Mary and her children starve. The thought gave her hope and peace. A house was going to be impossible, because rents were high and she couldn't afford them yet. But there were small, decent motels where she could get a good weekly rate. It would be crowded, but they could manage. She could borrow a car to take them to and from school from one of her employers, who had a garage full and had often done this for her when her own car at home was in the shop. Clothing she could get from the local Salvation Army, or from the thrift shops run by the women's abuse shelter and the churches.

Her predicament, so terrifying at first, became slowly less frightening. She had strength and will and purpose. She looked around the shelter at the little old lady who was in a wheelchair and thin as a rail. She was leaning down on her side, curled up like a dried-up child, with one thin hand clutching the wheel, as if she were afraid someone would steal it. Nearby, there was a black woman with many fresh cuts on her face and arms, with a baby clutched to her breast. Her clothes looked as if they'd been slept in many a night. Against the far wall, there was an elderly man with strips of cloth bound around his feet. She found that she had more than the average guest here. She closed her eyes and thanked God for her children and her fortitude.

Her first phone calls were not productive. She'd forgotten in the terror of the moment that it was Sunday, and not one person she needed to speak to was at home or likely to be until the following day. She asked Bev if she and the children could have one more night at the shelter and was welcomed. Tomorrow, she promised herself, they would get everything together.

The next morning she was up long before the children. The shelter offered breakfast, although it was mostly cereal, watered down coffee and milk.

"The dairy lets us have their outdated milk," the woman at the counter said, smiling. "It's still good. We have a lot of trouble providing meals, though. People are good to help us with canned things, but we don't get a lot of fresh meats and vegetables." She nodded toward some of the elderly people working their way through small bowls of cereal. "Protein, that's what they need. That's what the children need, too." Her smile was weary. "We're the richest country in the world, aren't we?" she added, her glance toward the occupants of the shelter eloquent in its irony.

Mary agreed quietly, asking for only a cup of coffee. The young mother, Meg, sat down beside her with her baby asleep in her arms.

"Hi," Mary said.

The young woman managed a smile. "Hi. You got lots of kids."

Mary smiled. "I'm blessed with three."

"I just got this one," Meg said, sighing. "My people are all in Atlanta. I came out here with Bill, and they warned me he was no good. I wouldn't listen. Now here I am, just me and the tidbit here. Bev says she thinks she knows where I can get a job. I'm going later to look."

"Good luck," Mary said.

"Thanks. You got work?"

Mary nodded. "I'm a housekeeper. I work for several families, all nice ones."

"You're lucky."

Mary thought about it. "Yes," she agreed. "I think I am."

The elderly man, Mr. Harlowe, joined them at the table with his cup of coffee, held in unsteady old hands. "Ladies." He greeted in a friendly tone. "I guess poverty's no respecter of mothers, is it?"

"You got that right," Meg said with a faint smile.

"At least we're in good company," Mary added, glancing around. "The people here are nice."

"Noticed that myself." He sipped his coffee. "I retired two years ago and had all my money in a corporation money market fund. Last year, the corporation went belly-up and it came out that we'd all lost every penny we had in our retirement accounts." He shrugged. "At least the top scalawags seem headed to prison. But it turned out that I was related to one. My nephew talked me into giving him power of attorney and he took it all. I lost my house, my car, everything I had, except a little check I get from the veterans' service. That isn't enough to buy me a week's groceries in today's market. I was going to prosecute him, but he went overseas with his ill-got gains. No money left to use to pursue him now."

"Gee, that's tough," Meg said quietly.

The elderly man glanced at her, noting the cuts on her face and arms. He grimaced. "Looks like you've had a tough time of your own."

"My man got drunk and I made him mad by being jealous of his other girlfriend. He said he'd do what he pleased and I could get out. I argued and he came at me with a knife," Meg said simply. "I ran away with the baby." She looked away. "It wasn't the first time it happened. But it will be the last."

"Good for you, young lady," he said gently. "You'll be okay."

She smiled shyly.

"What about you?" the old man asked Mary. "Those kids yours?" he added, indicating her small brood.

"Yes, they are. We lost our house and our car when my divorce became final." She gave Meg a quick glance. "I know about men who drink, too," she said.

Meg smiled at her. "We'll all be all right, I expect."

"You bet we will," Mary replied.

The old man chuckled. "That's the spirit. You got a place to go after here?"

"Not just yet," Mary said. "But I will soon," she said with new confidence. "I hope both of you do well."

They thanked her and drifted off into their own problems. Mary finished her coffee and got up with new resolve.

It was Monday, and she had to get the kids to school. She used the shelter's pay phone and called one of her friends, Tammy, who had been a neighbor.

"I hate to ask," she said, "but the kids have to go to school and Jack took the car. I don't have a way to go."

There was an indrawn breath. "I'll be right over," she began.

"Tammy, I'm at the homeless shelter." It bruised her pride to say that. It made her feel less decent, somehow, as if she'd failed her children. "It's just temporary," she added quickly.

"Oh, Mary," she groaned. "I noticed the For Rent sign on your place, but I didn't know what to think. I'm so sorry."

"The divorce became final Friday. Jack is failing to pay alimony or child support…and we were evicted." She sighed. "I'm so tired, so scared. I've got nothing and three kids…"

"You could stay with us," came the immediate reply.

Mary smiled, seeing the other woman's quiet, kind smile in her mind. "No, thank you," she added gently. "We have to make it on our own. Jack might track us down at your house, you know. I don't want the children close to him. We'll find a place. I'll get the loan of a car later, but right now, I have to have the kids in school before I go to work. I can take John with me, but the others must be in school."

"I'll come and get you," Tammy said. "Be five minutes."

"Thanks," Mary choked.

"You'd do it for me in a heartbeat," she replied. "And you know it."

"I would." It was no lie.

"Five minutes." She hung up.

Sure enough, five minutes later, Tammy was sitting in front of the shelter, waiting. Mary put the kids in the back of the station wagon, with John strapped securely in his car seat.

"I can't thank you enough," she told the woman.

"It's not a problem. Here. Give this to the kids." It was two little brown envelopes, the sort mothers put lunch money in. Mary almost broke down as she distributed the priceless little packets to the children.

First stop was grammar school, where Mary went in with Ann and explained the situation, adding that nobody was to take Ann from school except herself or her friend Tammy. Then they went to middle school, where Mary dropped off Bob and met with the vice principal to explain their situation again.

Finally they were down just to John.

"Where do you go now?" she asked Mary.

"To Debbie Shultz's house," she said. "She and Mark have about eight cars," she said fondly. "They'll loan me one if I ask. They've been clients of mine for ten years. They're good people. They don't even mind if John comes with me—they have a playpen and a high chair and a baby bed, just for him."

"You know, you may not have money and means, but you sure have plenty of people who care about you," Tammy remarked with a grin.

"I do. I'm lucky in my friends. Especially you. Thanks."

Tammy shrugged. "I'm having a nice ride around town, myself," she said with twinkling eyes. "Before you go to work, want to try that motel you mentioned?"

"Yes, if you don't mind."

"If I did, I'd still be at home putting on a pot roast for supper," Tammy said blandly. "Where is it?"

Mary gave her directions. Tammy was dubious, but Mary wasn't.

"One of my friends had to leave home. She went to the women's shelter first, and then she came here until she got a job. She said the manager looks out for people, and it's a good decent place. Best of all, it's not expensive. If you'll watch John for a minute…"

"You bet!"

Mary walked into the small office. The manager, an elderly man with long hair in a ponytail and a young smile, greeted her.

"What do you rent rooms for on a weekly basis?" she asked after she'd told him her name. "I have three children, ranging in age from thirteen to a toddler."

He noted the look on her face. He'd seen it far too often. "Fifty dollars a week," he said, "but it's negotiable. Forty's plenty if that's what you can manage comfortably," he added with a grin. "You can use the phone whenever you like, and there's a hot plate in the room where you can heat up stuff. We have a restaurant next door," he added, "when you want something a little hotter."

"I couldn't afford the restaurant," she said matter-of-factly, but she smiled. "I'll have the money tonight, if I can come after work with the kids."

"They in school?"

"Two are."

"Is one old enough to look after the others?"

"Bob's thirteen, almost fourteen. He's very responsible," she added.

"Bring them here after school and pay me when you can," he said kindly. "I'll check on them for you and make sure they stay in the room and nobody bothers them."

She was astonished at the offer.

"I ran away from home when I was twelve," he said coldly. "My old man drank and beat me. I had to live on the streets until an old woman felt sorry for me and let me have a room in her motel. I'm retired military. I don't need the money I make here, but it keeps me from going stale, and I can do a little good in the world." He smiled at her. "You can pass the help on to someone less fortunate, when you're in better economic times."

Her face brightened. "Thank you."

He shrugged. "We all live in the world. It's easier to get along if we help each other out in rough times. The room will be ready when you come back, Mrs. Crandall."

She nodded, smiling. "I'll have the money this afternoon, when I get off work. But I'll bring the children first."

"I'll be expecting them."

She got back into the car with Tammy, feeling as if a great weight had been lifted from her. "They said he was a kind man, not the sort who asked for favors or was dangerous around kids. But I had no idea just *how* kind he really is until now." She looked at Tammy. "I never knew how it was before. If you could see the homeless people, the things they don't have…I never knew," she emphasized.

Tammy patted her hand. "Not a lot of people do. I'm sorry you have to find out this way."

"Me, too," Mary said. She glanced back at the motel. "I wish I could do something," she added. "I wish I could help."

Tammy only smiled, and drove her to her job.

Debbie was aghast when she learned what had happened to Mary in the past twenty-four hours.

"Of course you can borrow a car," she said firmly. "You can drive the Ford until the tires go bald," she added. "And I'll let you off in time to pick up the kids at school."

Debbie's kids were in grammar school now, so the nursery was empty during the morning. Mary had made a habit of taking John to work with her, because Jack had never been in any condition to look after him.

Mary had to stop and wipe away tears. "I'm sorry," she choked. "It's just that so many people have been kind to me. Total strangers, and now you...I never expected it, that's all."

"People are mostly kind, when you need them to be," Debbie said, smiling. "Everything's going to be fine. You're a terrific house-keeper, you always keep me organized and going strong. You're always smiling and cheerful, even when I know you're the most miserable. I think a lot of you. So does Mark."

"Thanks. Not only for the loan of the car, but for everything."

Debbie waved a hand. "It's nothing. If I were starving and in rags, then it might be, but I can afford to be generous. I'll get you up some things for the kids, too. Please take them," she added plaintively. "You of all people know how choked my closets are with things I bought that the kids won't even wear!"

Mary laughed, because she did know. "All right then. I'll take them, and thanks very much."

"Have you got a place to stay?" was the next question.

"I have," Mary said brightly. "That was unexpected, too. It's a nice place."

"Good. Very good. Okay. I'll leave you to it. Just let me know when you're going after the kids and I'll watch John for you."

"Thanks."

Debbie just smiled. She was the sort of person who made the most outlandish difficulties seem simple and easily solved. She was a comfort to Mary.

The end of the first day of their forced exile ended on a happy note. From utter devastation, Mary and the kids emerged with plenty of clothing—thanks to Debbie and some of her friends—sheets and blankets and pillows, toiletries, makeup, and even a bucket of chicken. Not to mention the loaned car, which was a generous thing in itself.

"I can't believe it," Bob said when she picked him up at school, putting him in the back with John while Ann sat beside her. "We've got a home and a car? Mom, you're amazing!"

"Yes, you are," Ann said, grinning, "and I'm sorry I whined last night."

"You always whine," Bob teased, "but then you're a rock when you need to be."

"And you're an angel with ragged wings, you are, Mama," Ann said.

"We all have ragged wings, but I'll have a surprise for you at the motel," she added.

"What is it?" they chorused.

She chuckled. "You'll have to wait and see. The manager is Mr. Smith. He'll look out for you while I'm away. If you need to get in touch with me, he'll let you use the phone. I'll always leave you the name and number where I'll be, so you can reach me if there's an emergency."

"I think we've had enough emergencies for a while," Bob said drolly.

Mary sighed. "Oh, my, I hope we have!"

She loaded up the car with all the nice things Debbie had given her, and put the children in the car. Debbie had a brand-new baby car seat for John that she'd donated to the life-rebuilding effort as well. When he was strapped into it, Mary impulsively hugged Debbie, hiding tears, before she drove away. The old seat was coming apart at the seams and it couldn't have been very safe, but there had been no money for a new one. Something Debbie knew.

Bob and Ann met her at the door with dropped jaws as she started lugging in plastic bags.

"It's clothes! It's new clothes!" Ann exclaimed. "We haven't had new clothes since…" Her voice fell. "Well, not for a long time," she added, obviously feeling guilty for the outburst. They all knew how hard their mother worked, trying to keep them clothed at all. She went to her mother and hugged her tight. "I'm sorry. That sounded awful, didn't it?"

Mary hugged her back. "No, it just sounded honest, honey," she said softly.

The other two children crowded around her, and she gathered them in close, giving way to tears.

"What's wrong?" Bob asked worriedly. "Is there anything else you're not telling us?"

She shook her head. "No. It's just that people have been so good to us. Total strangers. It was such a surprise."

"My friend Timmy says we meet angels unawares when we don't expect to," Ann said in her quiet, sensible way.

"Perhaps that's true, baby," Mary agreed, wiping her eyes. "We've met quite a few today." She looked around at her children. "We're so fortunate to have each other."

They agreed that this was the best thing of all.

"*And* chicken," Bob exclaimed suddenly, withdrawing a huge bucket of it from the plastic bag.

"Chicken…!"

Little hands dived into the sack, which also contained biscuits and individual servings of mashed potatoes and gravy and green beans. Conversation abruptly ended.

Life slowly settled into a sort of pattern for the next couple of days as the memory of the terrifying first day and night slowly dimmed and became bearable.

The third night, Mary walked gingerly into the restaurant Mr. Smith had told her about, just at closing time.

"Excuse me," she said hesitantly.

A tall, balding man at the counter lifted his head and his eyebrows. "Yes, ma'am?" he asked politely.

"I was wondering…" She swallowed hard. She dug into her pocket and brought out a five dollar bill left over from the weekly rent she'd paid in advance. "I was wondering if you might have some chicken strips I could buy. Not with anything else," she added hastily, and tried to smile. "It's so far to the grocery store, and I'd have to take all three children with me…" She didn't want to add that they had hardly any money to buy groceries with, anyway, and that Mr. Smith was at his poker game tonight and couldn't watch the children for Mary while she drove to the store.

The man sized up her callused hands and worn appearance. Three kids, she'd said, and judging by the way her shoes and sweater looked, it wasn't easy buying much, especially food.

"Sure, we have them," he said kindly. "And we're running a special," he lied. "I'll be just a minute."

She stood there in her sensible clothes feeling uncomfortable, but it only took a minute for the man to come back, smiling, with a plastic bag.

"That will be exactly five dollars," he said gently.

She grinned, handing him the bill. "Thanks a million!"

He nodded. "You're very welcome."

She took the chicken strips back to the motel and shared them around. There were so many that they all had seconds. She was over the moon. But there was always tomorrow, she worried.

She needn't have. The next afternoon, when she dragged in after work, she found the man from the restaurant on her doorstep.

"Look, I don't want to insult you or anything," he said gently. "But I know from your manager here that you're having a rough time. We always have food left over at night at our restaurant," he said kindly. "You see, we can't carry it over until the next day, it has to be thrown out. I could let you have what there is. If it wouldn't insult you. If you'd like it?"

"I'd like it," she said at once, and smiled. "Oh, I'd like it so much! Thank you."

He flushed. "It's no problem. Really. If you don't mind coming over about ten o'clock, just as we're closing?"

She laughed. "I'll be there. And thank you!"

She went to the restaurant exactly at ten, feeling a little nervous, but everybody welcomed her. Nobody made her feel small.

The restaurant assistant manager went to the back and had the workers fill a huge bag full of vegetables and meats and fruits in neat disposable containers. He carried it to the front and presented it to Mary with a flourish. "I hope you and the children enjoy it," he added with a smile.

She started to open her purse.

"No," he said. "You don't need to offer to pay anything. This would only go into the garbage," he said gently. "That's the truth. I'd much rather see it used and enjoyed."

"I'm Mary Crandall," she said. "My children and I thank you," she added proudly.

"I'm Cecil Baker," he replied. "I'm the assistant manager here. It's nice to meet you."

"Thank you," she said huskily. "Thank you so much."

"It's my pleasure. I hate waste. So much food goes into the trash, when there are people everywhere starving. It's ironic, isn't it?"

"Yes, it is," she agreed.

"Here. I'll get the door for you."

She grinned up at him as she went out. "I can't wait to see the children's faces. They were only hoping for a chicken finger apiece," she added, chuckling.

He smiled, but pity was foremost in his mind. He watched her walk back the way she'd come, to the small motel.

Mary walked into the motel with her bag. Bob and Ann looked up expectantly from the board game they were playing. The toddler, John, was lying between them on the floor, playing with his toes.

"More chicken strips?" Bob asked hopefully.

"I think we have something just a little better than that," she said, and put her bag down on the table by the window. "Bob, get those paper plates and forks that we got at the store, would you?"

Bob ran to fetch them as Ann lifted John in her arms.

Mary opened the bag and put out container after container of vegetables, fruits and meats. There were not only chicken strips, but steak and fish as well. The small refrigerator in the room would keep the meats at a safe temperature, which meant that this meager fare would last for two days at least. It would mean that Mary could save a little more money for rent. It was a windfall.

She held hands with the children and she said grace before they ate. Life was being very good to her, despite the trials of the past week.

CHAPTER
TWO

MARY TOOK THE CHILDREN with her to the grocery store on Friday afternoon. It was raining and cold. Trying to juggle John, who was squirming, and the paper bag containing the heaviest of their purchases, milk and canned goods, she dropped it.

"Oh, for heaven's sake!" she groaned. "Here, Ann, honey, take John while I run down the cans of tuna fish…!"

"I'll get them," came a deep voice from behind her. "I'm a fair fisherman, actually, but catching cans of tuna is more my style."

Mary turned and saw a police officer grinning at her. She recognized him at once. "Officer Clark!" she exclaimed. "How can I ever thank you enough for what you did for us?" she exclaimed. "Bev has been wonderful. We have a place to stay, now, too!"

He held up a hand, smiling. "You don't need to thank me, Mrs. Crandall. It was my pleasure."

In the clear daylight, without the mental torment that had possessed her at their first meeting, she saw him in a different way. He was several years older than she was, tall and a little heavy, but not enough to matter. He was good-looking. "You seem to have your hands full as it is," he added, scooping up the cans and milk jug. "I'll carry them for you."

"Thank you," she said, flustered.

He shrugged. "It isn't as if I'm overwhelmed with crime in this neighborhood," he said, tongue-in-cheek. "Jaywalking and petty theft are about it."

"Our car's over here. Well, it's not really our car," she added, and then could have bitten her tongue.

"You stole it, I guess," the policeman sighed. "And here I thought I was going to end my shift without an hour's paperwork."

"I didn't steal it!" she exclaimed, and then laughed. "My employer let me borrow it…"

"On account of Dad taking our car away after he left us," Bob muttered.

The policeman pursed his lips. "That's a pretty raw way to treat someone."

"Alcohol and drugs," she said, tight-lipped.

He sighed. "I have seen my share of that curse," he told her. "Are all these really yours?" he added, nodding toward the kids. "You didn't shoplift these fine children in the store?" he added with mock suspicion.

The children were laughing, now, too. "We shoplifted her," Bob chuckled. "She's a great mom!"

"She keeps house for people," Ann added quietly.

"She works real hard," Bob agreed.

"Have you got a house?" the policeman asked.

"Well, we're living in a motel. Just temporarily," Mary said at once, flushing. "Just until we find something else."

The policeman waited for Mary to unlock the trunk and he put the groceries he was carrying into it gingerly. Bob and Ann added their packages.

"Thanks again, Officer Clark," Mary said, trying not to let him see how attractive she found him. It was much too soon for that.

"Do you have any kids?" Ann asked him, looking up with her big eyes.

"No kids, no family," he replied with a sad smile. "Not by choice, either."

He looked as if he'd had a hard life. "Well, if you haven't stolen the car, and you need no further assistance, I've no choice but to go back to my car and try to catch a speeder or two before my shift ends. I hope I'll see you around again, Mrs. Crandall…. Mary."

"Are you married?" she blurted out.

He chuckled. "Not hardly. I entered the divorced state ten years ago, and I heartily recommend it. Much better than verbal combat over burned potatoes every single night."

"Your wife couldn't cook?" Mary asked involuntarily.

"She wouldn't cook and I couldn't cook, which led to a lot of the combat," he told her with a chuckle. "Drive safely, now."

"I will. You, too."

He walked off jauntily, with a wave of his hand.

"And I used to think policemen were scary," Bob commented. "He's really nice."

"He is, isn't he?" Mary murmured, and she watched him as he got into his squad car and pulled out of the parking lot. She found herself thinking that she had a very odd sort of guardian angel in that police uniform.

Mary went to her jobs with increasing lack of strength and vigor. She knew that some of the problem had to be stress and worry. Despite the safe haven she'd found, she knew that all her children had only her to depend on. Her parents were dead and there were no siblings. She had to stay healthy and keep working just to keep food on the table and a roof over their heads. In the middle of the night, she lay awake, worrying about what would happen if she should fail. The children would be split up and placed into foster homes. She knew that, and it terrified her. She'd always been healthy, but she'd never had quite so much responsibility placed on her, with so few resources to depend on. Somehow, she knew, God would find a way to keep her and the children safe. She had to believe that, to have faith, to keep going.

Somehow, she promised herself, she would. After all, there were so many people who needed even more assistance than she did. She remembered the elderly gentleman at the homeless shelter, the mother with her new baby. The shelter had a small budget and trouble getting food.

Food. Restaurants couldn't save food. They had to throw it out. If the restaurant near Mary's motel room had to throw theirs out, it was logical to assume that all the other restaurants had to throw theirs out, too.

What a shame, she thought, that there were so many hungry people with no food, where there were also restaurants with enough leftover food to feed them. All people had to do was ask for it. But she knew that they never would. She never would have, in her worst circumstances. People were too proud to ask for charity.

She put the thought into the back of her mind, but it refused to stay there. Over the next few days, she was haunted by the idea. Surely there were other people who knew about the restaurant leftovers, but when she began checking around, she couldn't find any single charity that was taking advantage of the fact. She called Bev at the homeless shelter and asked her about it.

"Well, I did know," Bev confessed, "but it would entail a lot of work, coordinating an effort like that. I've sort of got my hands full with the shelter. And everybody I know is overworked and understaffed. There's just nobody to do it, Mary. It's a shame, too."

"Yes, it is," Mary agreed.

But it was an idea Mary couldn't shake. Maybe nobody else was doing it because it was *her* job to do it, she thought suddenly. She'd always believed that people had purposes in life, things that they were put here on earth to do. But she'd thought hers was to be a wife and mother—and it was, for a time. But she had more to give than that. So perhaps here was her new purpose, looking her in the face.

When she got off from work, she went to the restaurant where the assistant manager had given her the leftovers, and she spoke to him in private.

"It's just an idea," she said quickly. "But with all the restaurants in the city, and all the hungry people who need it, there should be some way to distribute it."

"It's a wonderful idea," Cecil replied with a smile. "But there's just no way to distribute it, you see. There's no program in place to administrate it."

"Perhaps it could start with just one person," she said. "If you'd be willing to give me your leftovers, I'll find people to give them to, and I'll distribute them myself. It would be a beginning."

He found her enthusiasm contagious. "You know, it would be a beginning. I'll speak with the manager, and the owner, and you can check back with me on Monday. How would that be?"

"That would be wonderful. Meanwhile, I'll look for places to carry the food. I already have at least one in mind. And I'll get recommendations for some others."

"Do you think you can manage all alone?" he wondered.

"I have three children, two of whom are old enough to help me," she replied. "I'm sure they'll be enthusiastic as well."

They were. She was amazed and delighted at her children's response to the opportunity.

"We could help people like that old man at the shelter," Bob remarked. "He was much worse off than us."

"And that lady with the little baby. She was crying when nobody was looking," Ann told them.

"Then we'll do what we can to help," Mary said. She smiled at her children with pride. "The most precious gift we have is the ability to give to others less fortunate."

"That's just what our teacher said at Christmas," Bob said, "when he had us make up little packages for kids at the battered women's shelter."

"That's one place we could check out, to see if they could use some of the restaurant food," Mary thought aloud. "I'm sure we'll find other places, too," she added. "It will mean giving up some things ourselves, though," she told them. "We'll be doing this after school and after work every day, even on weekends."

Bob and Ann grinned. "We won't mind."

Mary gathered them all close, including little John, and hugged them. "You three are my greatest treasures," she said. "I'm so proud of you!"

Monday when she went back to the restaurant, Cecil was grinning from ear to ear. "They went for it," he told her. "The manager and the owner agreed that it would be a wonderful civic contribution. I want to do my bit, as well, so I'll pay for your gas."

She caught her breath. "That's wonderful of you. Of all of you!"

"Sometimes all it takes is one person to start a revolution, of sorts," he told her. "You're doing something wonderful and unselfish. It shames people who have more and do less."

She chuckled. "I'm no saint," she told him. "I just want to make a little difference in the world and help a few people along the way."

"Same here. So when do you start?"

"Tomorrow night. I'm already getting referrals."

"I'll expect you at closing time."

"I'll be here."

Mary was enthusiastic about her project, and it wasn't difficult to find people who needed the food. One of the women she cleaned for mentioned a neighbor who was in hiding with her two children, trying to escape a dangerously abusive husband who'd threatened to kill her. She was afraid to go to a shelter, and she had no way to buy food. Mary took food to her in the basement of a church, along with toys and clothes for the children that had been provided by her employer. The woman cried like a baby. Mary felt wonderful.

The next night, she took her box of food to the homeless shelter where the elderly man was staying. The residents were surprised and thrilled with the unexpected bonanza, and Bev, who ran the shelter, hugged her and thanked her profusely for the help. Mary made sure that Meg, the young woman with the baby, also had milk, which the restaurant had included two bottles of in the box. The elderly man, whom Bev had told her was called Sam Harlowe, delved into the food to fetch a chicken leg. He ate it with poignant delight and gave Mary a big smile of thanks.

On her third night of delivering food, after the children had helped her divide it into individual packages, Mary decided that there might be enough time to add another restaurant or two to her clientele.

She wrote down the names and numbers of several other restaurants in the city and phoned them on her lunch hour. The problem was that she had no way for them to contact her. She didn't have a phone and she didn't want to alienate her motel manager by having the restaurants call him. She had to call back four of them, and two weren't at all interested in participating in Mary's giveaway program. It was disappointing, and Mary felt morose. But she did at least have the one restaurant to donate food. Surely there would be one or two others eventually.

She phoned the remaining four restaurants the next night after work and got a surprise. They were all enthusiastic about the project and more than willing to donate their leftovers.

Mary was delighted, but it meant more work. Now, instead of

going next door to get food and parcel it up, she had to drive half-way across town to four more restaurants and wait until the kitchen workers got the leftovers together for her. This meant more work at the motel, too, making packages to take to the various shelters and families Mary was giving food to.

It was a fortunate turn of events, but Mary was beginning to feel the stress. She was up late, and she was tired all the time. She worked hard at her jobs, but she had no time for herself. The children were losing ground on homework, because they had less time to do it.

What Mary needed very much were a couple of volunteers with time on their hands and a willingness to work. Where to find them was going to be a very big problem.

She stopped by the homeless shelter to talk with the manager and see if they could use more food, now that Mary was gaining new resources. Bev was on the phone. She signaled that she'd be through in a minute. While she waited, Mary went to talk to Mr. Harlowe, who was sitting morosely in the corner with a cup of cold coffee.

"You still here?" Mary asked with a gentle smile.

He looked up and forced an answering smile. "Still here," he replied. "How are you doing?"

She sat down. "I've got a place to live, clothes for the children and this new project of distributing donated food in my spare time."

He chuckled. "With three kids, I don't imagine you've got much of that!"

"Actually, I was hoping to find a volunteer to help me."

He lifted an eyebrow and took a sip of coffee. "What sort of volunteer?"

"Somebody to help me pick up and deliver the food."

He perked up with interest. "The last time you delivered food here, Bev said something about what you've been doing. But she didn't go into specifics about how all this came about. Tell me more."

"I've discovered that restaurants throw out their leftover food at the end of the day because they can't resell it the next day," she explained. "I found five restaurants that are willing to let me have what they don't sell." Her eyes brightened as she warmed to her subject. "And now I'm looking for places to donate the food and people to help me carry it and sort it into parcels."

"You're almost homeless yourself, and you're spending your free time feeding other people?" He was astounded.

She grinned. "It helps me to stop worrying about my own problems if I'm busy helping others with theirs. Feeding the hungry is a nice way to spend my spare time."

"I'm amazed," he said, and meant it. "I don't have a way to go…"

"I'll come by and pick you up in the afternoons before I make my rounds," she promised, "if you're willing to help."

"I've got nothing else to do," he replied gently. "I don't have anything of my own, or any other place to go except here," he added, glancing around. "They haven't tried to throw me out, so I suppose I can stay."

"Don't be silly," Bev laughed as she joined them. "Of course you can stay, Mr. Harlowe!"

"Sam," he corrected. "Call me Sam. Do you know about Mrs. Crandall's new project?"

"Mary," she corrected. "If you get to be Sam, I get to be just Mary."

"And I'm Bev," the older woman laughed. "Now that we've settled that, what's this project, Mary?"

"Remember I told you I discovered that restaurants throw away their food at the end of the day," Mary said.

"And they don't save the leftovers…." Bev said with a frown.

"They can't. It's against the law. So all that food goes into the garbage."

"While people go hungry," Bev mused.

"Not anymore. I've talked five restaurants into giving me their leftover food," Mary said. "I'm carrying some to a lady who's in hiding from her husband."

"Doesn't she know about the battered women's shelter?" Bev asked at once.

"She does, but she can't go there, because her husband threatened to kill her, and she doesn't want to endanger anyone else," Mary said. "She's trying to get in touch with a cousin who'll send her bus fare home to Virginia, before her husband catches up with her. She's got two kids. So I'm taking her food. There's an elderly lady staying in the motel where we are, and I take some to her.

But there's still so much food left over. I thought you might like some for the shelter," she added hopefully.

Bev smiled from ear to ear. "Would I!" she exclaimed. "Have you thought of the men's mission and the food bank?" she added.

"Men's mission?" Mary asked blankly.

"It's another shelter, but just for men," Bev said. "And the food bank provides emergency food for families in crisis—where one or both parents are sick or out of work and there's no money for food. Or disabled people who can't get out to shop, and elderly people who have no transportation and no money."

Mary started to feel a warmth of spirit that she'd never had before. Her own problems suddenly seemed very small. "I've heard of the food bank, but I never knew much about it. And I didn't know we had a men's mission."

"There's a women's mission, too," Bev told her. "We have a Meals-On-Wheels program with its own volunteers who take hot meals to elderly shut-ins. There's quite an outreach program, but you wouldn't know unless you'd been homeless or badly down on your luck."

"I'm ashamed to say I never knew much about those programs, and never noticed them until I got into this situation," Mary confessed. "But now I'm wondering if there wasn't a purpose behind what happened to me. Otherwise, I'd never have been looking into the restaurant food rescue."

"It's nice, isn't it, how God finds uses for us and nudges us into them?" Bev teased.

Mary's eyes shimmered. "I don't think I've ever thought of that before, either," she said. "But whole new avenues of opportunity are opening up in front of me. You know, I never knew how kind people could be until I lost everything."

"That's another way we fit into the scheme of things, isn't it?" Bev said. "Until we're caught up in a particular situation, we never think of how it is with people in need. I was homeless myself," she said surprisingly, "and I ended up in a women's mission. That opened my eyes to a whole world that I'd never seen. When I got involved trying to better the situation of other people in trouble, my own life changed and I found a purpose I didn't know I had. I became useful."

Mary grinned. "That's what I'm trying to become. And so far, so good!" She glanced at Mr. Harlowe. "I've just found a willing volunteer to help me parcel up and pass out food."

Bev's eyebrows lifted. "You, Sam?"

He nodded. "I do think I've just become useful, myself," he said with a chuckle. "I can't lift a lot of heavy things," he added hesitantly. "I had a back injury from service in Vietnam, and it left me unable to do a lot of lifting."

"The food parcels the children and I have been making up aren't heavy at all," Mary was quick to point out. "We try to make sure we have bread, vegetables, fruit and meat in each one. And dessert, too. But that was only from the one restaurant. With the four new ones added, we can make up larger ones."

"You'll need containers," Bev said. "I know a woman at one of the dollar stores who's a good citizen. She contributes paper plates and cups to our shelter, and if you go and see her, I'll bet she'd contribute those plastic containers for your project."

Mary, who'd been buying such things herself, was surprised and delighted at the suggestion.

Bev had a pen and paper. "Here. I'll write down her name and address for you. And I'll see if I can find you one more volunteer with a car and some free time."

"That's great!" Mary exclaimed.

"You borrowed a car, didn't you?" Bev asked. "Does the person who loaned it mind if you use it for this?"

That was something Mary hadn't asked about. She bit her lower lip. "I don't know," she confessed. "I'll have to go and see her and ask if it's all right."

"That may not be necessary. We have a patron who has an old truck that he's offered to donate to us," Bev volunteered. "I'll ask him if he's still willing to do that. You might talk to one of the independent gas stations and see if they'd donate gas."

"Bev, you're a wonder!" Mary exclaimed.

"I've learned the ropes," Bev said simply, "and learned how to get people to follow their most generous instincts. After you've been in the business for a while, you'll be able to do that, too."

"I never knew how many people went to bed hungry in this country," Mary commented. "I've learned a lot in a few days."

"Welcome to the real world."

Sam sighed. "Well, then, when do we begin?"

"Tonight," Mary said enthusiastically.

"Wait just a minute," Bev said, and went to the phone. "I want to see if I can get in touch with our patron before you go."

Amazingly she did, and he promised to have the truck at the shelter promptly at 6:00 p.m. that evening.

"Thanks a million, Bev," Mary said.

"We're all working toward the same goal," Bev reminded her. "Go see that guy about the gas, okay?"

"I'll do it on my way back to the motel."

Mary stopped by the gas station, introduced herself, mentioned Bev, and outlined her new project. "I know it's a lot to ask," she said, "and if you don't want to do this, it's okay. I've been paying for the gas myself…"

"Hey, it doesn't hurt me to donate a little gas to a good cause," he told Mary with a chuckle. "You bring your truck by here before you start out tonight, and I'll fill it up for you. We'll set up a schedule. If I'm not here, I'll make sure my employees know what to do."

"Thanks so much," Mary told him.

He shrugged. "Anybody can end up homeless," he commented, "through no fault of his or her own. It's the times we live in."

"I couldn't agree more!"

Mary told the children what was going on, and how much work it was going to be. "But we do have a volunteer who's going to help us with the deliveries," she remarked. "It will mean getting up very early in the mornings to get your homework done, or doing it at school while you're waiting for me to pick you up."

"We could stay at the homework center until you get off work, instead of you coming to get us as soon as school's out," Bob suggested.

"Sure," Ann agreed. "We wouldn't mind. There's a boy I like who's explaining Spanish verbs to me," she added shyly.

"This will work, I think, until we get some more volunteers," Mary said with a smile.

"We want to help," Ann said. "It's not going to be that much work."

"It's sort of nice, helping other people. No matter how bad it is for us, it's worse for many other people," Bob agreed. "I like what we're doing."

Mary hugged them all. "When they say it's better to give than to receive, they're not kidding. It really is. I feel wonderful when we take these packages out to people who need them."

"Me, too," Ann said. "I'm going to do a paper on it for my English class."

"Good for you!" Mary said.

"We're doing okay, aren't we, Mom?" Bob asked gently. He smiled at her. "Dad didn't think we could, I'll bet."

The mention of her ex-husband made Mary uneasy. She'd been afraid at first that he might try to get custody of the children, just for spite. But perhaps he didn't want the aggravation of trying to take care of three of them. Mary had never minded the responsibility. She loved her children, she enjoyed their company. As she looked at them, she felt so fortunate. Things got better every day.

That evening, she and the children went to the homeless shelter to pick up the donated truck.

"Can you drive it?" Bev asked worriedly, when she noted petite Mary climbing up into the high cab of the big, long bed, double-cabbed vehicle. It was red and a little dented, but the engine sounded good when it was started.

"I grew up on a farm," Mary said with a grin. "I can drive most anything, I expect. I'll bring it back, but it will be late, is that okay?"

"If I'm not here, George will be," Bev assured her. "You keep the doors locked and be careful."

"Don't you worry," Sam Harlowe said as he climbed up into the passenger seat. "I may be old, but I'm not helpless. Mary will have help if she needs it."

"Sure she will," Bob added, chuckling. "I play tackle on the B-team football squad."

"Good luck, then," Bev called to them as Mary put the truck in gear and pulled out into the street.

Mary stopped by the gas station. True to his word, the manager filled up the tank and even checked under the hood to make sure the truck was in good running shape. He checked the tires as well.

"Thanks," she told him.

He grinned. "My pleasure. Drive carefully."

"I will," she promised.

She pulled out into the sparse traffic and headed toward the first of the five restaurants. "We'll probably have to wait a while at first, until we get into some sort of routine."

"No problem," Bob said. "We all brought books to read."

Sam laughed. "Great minds run in the same direction." He pulled out a well-worn copy of Herodotus, the Histories, and displayed it.

"I've got my piecework, as well," Mary said, indicating a small canvas bag with knitting needles and a ball of yarn. "I'm making hats for people in the shelters. I can only knit in a straight line, but hats are simple."

"I wouldn't call knitting simple," Sam assured her.

She laughed. "It keeps my hands busy. Okay, here we are," she added, pulling into the parking lot of the first restaurant.

The waiting was the only bad part. They had to arrive at or near closing time in order to gather the leftovers. On the first night, the last restaurant was already closed by the time they got to it.

"We'll have to do better than this," Mary murmured worriedly. "I hadn't realized how long it would take to do this."

"First times are notoriously hard," Sam said. "We'll get better at it. But perhaps we can find one more volunteer to go to the last two restaurants for us and pick up the leftovers."

"There aren't a lot of volunteers who can work at night," Mary fretted.

"Listen, if things are meant to happen, the details take care of themselves," Sam said. "You wait and see. Everything's going to fall into place like clockwork, and you'll wonder why you ever worried in the first place."

Mary glanced at him and was reassured by his smile. She smiled back. "Okay. I'll go along with that optimism and see what happens."

Sam glanced out his window confidently. "I think you'll be surprised."

CHAPTER
THREE

As the days passed, Mary and her helpers got more efficient at picking up the food and parceling it out. The truck ran perfectly, and Mary got better at managing her finances. She picked up two more cleaning jobs, which was the maximum she could fit into the week.

Debbie, who'd loaned her the car, also suggested that a slight raise in her hourly rate would provide her with more money. Mary was hesitant to do that, for fear of losing customers.

"You just tell them that I raised you two dollars an hour and they'll be ashamed not to follow suit," Debbie said firmly.

"What if they let me go?" Mary worried.

"You've come a long way in a short time," Debbie said. "You're much more confident, more poised, and you're a whiz at organization. I'm amazed at the change in you."

"I've changed?" Mary asked hesitantly.

"You've taken charge of your own life, and the lives of your children. You've organized a food rescue program to benefit needy people, you've kept the children in school and up with their homework, you've found a decent place to live and you're on your way to financial independence." Debbie grinned. "I'm proud of you."

Mary smiled. "Really?"

"Really. You just keep going the way you've been going. You're going to make it, Mary. I'm sure of it."

That confidence made Mary feel on top of the world. "You're sure you don't want the car back now?"

"When you can afford one of your own," Debbie said, "you can give mine back. Listen, honey, it sits in the garage all day and hardly ever gets driven. You're actually doing us a favor by keeping it on the road, so that it doesn't gum up and stop working."

"You make things seem so easy," Mary said. "You've done so much for us. I don't know how to repay you."

"I'm doing it for selfish motives," Debbie whispered conspiratorially. "If you leave, my husband will divorce me when the dishes and the laundry pile up and start to mold."

Mary knew that wasn't true. Debbie did, too. But they both smiled.

The food rescue program was growing. Mary now had ten restaurants on her list, and two more volunteers who helped to gather the food and make it up into packages. One of the new volunteers had a car. And his identity was a shock.

It was Matt Clark, the policeman they'd met their first night in the car. He was wearing a neat new sports shirt and khaki slacks with a brown leather bomber jacket. He'd had a haircut and he looked younger.

"I've never seen him look so neat off duty," Bev whispered wickedly as Mary entered the shelter with armloads of packaged food. "I think he's dressing up for somebody. Three guesses who."

"Hush!" Mary exclaimed, blushing.

"Well, hello," Matt greeted her, taking some of the containers from her arms. "I had some free time and I heard you were looking for help. So here I am."

"We're happy to have you here," Mary replied breathlessly. "There's so much food to pick up and deliver, and it takes a lot of time."

"I don't see how you managed, when you were doing it alone," Matt remarked as they put the food parcels on the long table.

"I'm beginning to wonder that, myself," Mary had to admit. She smiled shyly at him. "This is just the first load. There are two more in the truck, at least, and the other volunteers will be along soon with even more."

"Where do all these go?" Matt asked.

"There's a list," Sam volunteered as he joined them, grinning, with an armload of food. "How's it going, Matt?"

"Fair to middling, Sam," came the reply. The two men smiled

and shook hands, and then Sam went back to collect some more food packs.

"You know each other?" Mary asked Matt curiously, in a low voice.

"Before he retired, Sam worked for the city as a building inspector," Matt told her. "I had to rescue him from an irate client once. We had a beer together and discovered we had a lot in common. We were having lunch once a month until Sam's bad luck." Matt shook his head. "Pity about what happened to him. I remember a time when ethics were the most important part of business. Now it seems to be that only the corrupt prosper."

"I know what you mean," Mary agreed. "It's nice of you. Helping us make the deliveries, I mean."

He smiled at her. "It isn't as if I have a hectic social life. Mostly I work."

"Same here!" she laughed.

He hesitated, his dark eyes quiet and searching. "You're an amazing person," he commented quietly. "Most people would be thinking about themselves in your position, not about helping others."

"I wasn't always like this," she said. "I can remember a time when I was afraid of street people. It makes me a little ashamed."

"All of us have to learn about the world, Mary," he said gently. "We're not born knowing how hard life can be for unfortunate people. For instance, Sam there—" he nodded toward the elderly man "—was a decorated hero in Vietnam. He's had a bad shake all the way around. His wife left him while he was overseas and took their daughter with her. They were both killed in a car wreck the week after Sam got home from the war. He remarried, and his second wife died of cancer. Now, his retirement's gone with his thieving nephew, after he worked like a dog to become self-sufficient. The nephew was only related to him by marriage, which makes it even worse." He shook his head. "Some people get a bad shake all around. And Sam's a good man."

"I noticed that," she said. "He's proud, too."

"That's the problem that keeps so many people out of the very social programs that would help them," he said philosophically. "Pride. Some people are too proud to even ask for help. Those are the ones who fall into the cracks. People like Sam. He could get assistance, God knows he'd qualify. But he's too proud to admit that he needs relief."

She smoothed over a food package. "Is there any way we could help him?"

He grinned. "I'm working on something. Let you know when I have any good ideas, okay?"

She grinned back. "Okay."

Sam returned with four more big containers of food. "Been talking about me behind my back, I guess?" he asked them.

"We don't know that many interesting people, Sam," Matt pointed out.

Sam shrugged, shook his head and went back inside with the packages.

Matt drove the truck, giving Mary a brief rest. It had been an especially long day, because one of her employers wanted to take down and wash and press all the heavy curtains in the house. It had been a backbreaking job, although the house certainly looked better afterward. Bob and Ann had stayed after school for their individual sports programs. The extracurricular activities were important to them and Mary was going to make sure that they had as normal a life as possible, even with all the complications of the moment.

"Where are the kids?" Matt asked, as if he'd sensed her thoughts.

"At sports and band practice," she said. "I arranged rides for them back to the motel, and the manager's promised to keep an eye on them."

"And the youngest?"

She grinned. "My friend, Tammy, is keeping John tonight until we get through. I have to pick him up at her house."

"I'll drive you," Matt offered. "Don't argue, Mary," he added gently. "I wouldn't offer if it was going to be an imposition. Okay?"

Sam glanced at her. "I'd give in, if I were you. He's the most persistent man I ever met."

She laughed. "All right, then. Thank you," she told Matt.

Their first stop was at the men's mission. Mary had passed by the building many times in the past, and never paid it much attention. She'd had a vague idea of the sort of people who stayed there, and not a very flattering one.

But now she took time to look, to really look, at them. There were several sitting in the lobby watching a single television. Two were paraplegics. One was blind. Five were elderly. Two were amputees. She could understand without asking a single question why they were here.

"We brought you some food," Mary told the shelter's manager, a portly gentleman named Larry who had a beard and long hair.

"This is a treasure trove!" Larry exclaimed. "Where did you get this?"

"From restaurants in town," Mary said simply as Matt and Sam started bringing in the parcels. "They have to throw away their leftovers, so I've asked for them. Now I'm finding more places to donate them."

"You can put us on your list, and many thanks!" Larry exclaimed, lifting the lid on one of the plastic containers. "Good Lord, this is beef Stroganoff! I haven't had it in six years!"

Mary grinned. "There's a price," she told him. "You have to wash the containers so that I can pick them up when I bring your next delivery. I thought maybe Monday, Wednesday and Friday?"

"That would be great," Larry said enthusiastically. "Thanks. What's your name?"

"Mary Crandall," she said, shaking hands.

"I'm Larry Blake," he said, "and I'm very happy to meet you. Thanks a million!"

One of the men, a paraplegic, wheeled over to ask what was going on. He took a sniff. "Is that lasagna?" he queried hopefully.

"It is," Mary said. "And there's tiramisu and cake and all sorts of pastries for dessert, too."

"I think I have died and gone to heaven," the man in the wheelchair said with a sad smile. "Thank you."

She noticed that his wheelchair had no footrests and that it squeaked terribly. One of the tires was missing part of its rubber tread. She wished with all her heart she had a little extra money so that she could offer it to him for a newer chair.

He saw her sad glance and he smiled. "I can see what you're thinking, but I don't want a new chair. This is my lucky one. That sticky wheel kept me from going off the edge of a building when I got lost. I wouldn't trade it for the world."

She smiled. "So much for women's intuition," she said.

He chuckled. "Never you mind. Thanks for the food!"

"My pleasure," she replied.

Their second stop was a small village of tents and boxes that moved from time to time when the authorities made halfhearted efforts to clear away the homeless people. It was a temporary measure at best, because the homeless had no place to go except shelters, and most of the people in the moveable village didn't like being shut up inside.

"These are the real hard cases," Matt said quietly as they stopped. "They don't want to be subject to rules of any kind. Periodically the police are asked to break up these camps, but they just set up across town all over again."

"Why are so many people homeless?" Mary asked absently.

"Thousands of reasons," Matt told her. "Some are mentally ill and have no family and no place to go. Some are alcoholics. Some are drug users. A few have relatives who are trying to forget all about them. Society today is so mobile that extended families just don't exist in one town anymore. This never happened a century ago, because families stayed put and were required by morality to take care of their own and be responsible for them. These days, morality is very widely interpreted."

"In other words, everybody's looking out for number one," Sam murmured.

Matt nodded. "In a nutshell, yes."

"I think the old way of taking care of one's own was better," Sam said with a sigh.

Several people from the camp came close, hesitantly, looking around suspiciously. "What do you want?" a man asked.

"We brought you some food," Mary said, indicating the boxes in the bed of the pickup truck.

"That don't look like cans," the man commented.

"It isn't." Mary took down one of the bags, opened it, took out a plastic container and opened it. "Smell."

The man sniffed, stood very still, then sniffed again. "That's beef. That's beef!"

"It is," Mary said. "In fact, it's beef Stroganoff, and you should eat it while it's still warm. Do you have something to put it in?"

The man went running back to the others. They came back with a motley assortment of plates and cups and bent utensils. Mary and the men filled all the plates and cups to capacity, adding a bag of bread and another with containers of fruit and vegetables.

A ragged old woman came shyly up to Mary and took her hand. "'Ank oo," she managed to say.

"That's old Bess," the man introduced the little woman, who took her plate and waddled away. "She's deaf, so she don't speak plain. She said thank you."

Mary had to bite back tears. "She's very welcome. All of you are. I'll come back Friday with more, about this same time."

The man hesitated. "They're making us move tomorrow," he said dully. "We never get to stay noplace long."

"Where will you go?" Mary asked.

He shrugged.

"When you have another place, get in touch with the shelter on Blair Street, can you do that? They'll get word to me," Mary said.

He nodded slowly, then smiled. "Thanks."

She sighed. "We're all victims of circumstance, in one way or another," she told him. "We have to help each other."

"Good!" An unshaven man with overlarge eyes was tugging on Mary's sleeve. "Good, lady, good!" he said, pointing his spoon at the food in his cup. "Good!"

He turned away, eating hungrily.

"That's Billy," the man said. "He's not quite right in the head. Nobody wanted him, so he lives with us. My name's Art."

"I'm Mary," she said. "Nice to meet you."

"I'll get word to you," he said after a minute, nodding politely at Matt and Sam. He went back with the others into the darkness of the camp.

The three companions were very quiet as they drove toward the nearby women's mission.

"That hurts," Sam spoke for all of them.

"Yes," Mary agreed. "But we're doing something to help."

"And every little bit does help," Matt added quietly. He glanced at Mary. "I'm glad I came tonight."

"Me, too," Sam said. "I'll never feel sorry for myself again."

Mary smiled tiredly. "That's exactly how I feel."

The women's mission was very much like the men's mission, but the women seemed a little livelier and more receptive to the visitors.

Three of them were doing handwork in the lobby, where an old movie was playing on a black-and-white television. Two others were filling out forms.

The mission was run by a Catholic nun, Sister Martha, who welcomed them, surprised by the food and its quality.

"I would never have thought of asking restaurants for leftover food!" she exclaimed, grinning at Mary. "How resourceful of you!"

Mary laughed. "It was a happy accident, the way it came about," she said. "But I feel as if I have a new lease on life, just from learning how to give away food."

"Giving is a gift in itself, isn't it?" the sister asked with a secretive smile. "I've learned that myself. No matter how hard my life is, when I can help someone else, I feel as if I've helped myself, too."

"That's very true," Mary said.

She introduced Sam and Matt, and they unloaded the last of the food. The women gathered around, impressed by the fancy food and anxious to taste it. When Mary and the men left, the women were already dishing it up in the small kitchen.

"That's all I have tonight," Mary said. "I'll call some more restaurants, and maybe Bev can suggest another volunteer or two."

"You know there's a food bank around here, too," Matt suggested. "They might like to have some of this restaurant chow."

"Already got that covered," Mary murmured. "I'm planning on giving them a call tomorrow."

"If you'll give me some names," Matt said, "I'll make some calls for you."

"So will I," Sam volunteered. "I'm sure Bev won't mind letting me use the phone."

"But how are we going to manage this?" Mary wondered aloud worriedly. "It's taken us two hours to give away what we had, and that's just from five restaurants. Besides that, the truck was full when we started."

"We'll need another truck," Matt said. "Maybe a van."

"Where are we going to get one?" Mary asked.

"I'll make some arrangements," Matt said.

She smiled at him. "You're a wonder."

"Oh, I'm in good company," he replied, glancing from Mary to Sam with a grin.

When they dropped Sam off at the shelter, along with the truck, Matt put Mary into his sedan and drove her to Tammy's house. Mary was uneasy until they were back in the car with John strapped in his car seat in the back of Matt's car, and on their way out of the neighborhood.

As they passed Mary's old house, she noticed that there were two cars in the driveway and that the For Rent sign had been removed.

"What is it?" Matt asked, sensing that something was wrong.

"I used to live there before I was evicted," she commented sadly as they passed the old house. "Those must be the new tenants."

"I don't know how you're handling all these changes," he said with admiration. "You have three kids to support, a full-time profession and spending all your nights handing out food to people." He shook his head. "You're an inspiration."

"I'm getting an education in the subject of people," she told him. "It's a very interesting subject, too."

He smiled in the rearview mirror at the baby. "You have great kids," he commented.

"Thanks," she said shyly. "I think they're pretty terrific. I could be prejudiced," she added with a grin.

He laughed. "No, I don't think so. Where are we going?" he added.

She realized that he didn't know where they lived. "It's that old motel next to the new Wal-Mart superstore," she told him.

He glanced at her. "Al Smith's motel?"

She laughed. "You know Mr. Smith?"

"Do I," he laughed. "We were in the military together, back when the Marines were stationed in Lebanon and the barracks were car-bombed. Remember that, in the eighties?"

"Yes, I do," she said.

"Two of my friends died in the explosion," he said. "Smith was in my unit, too. He's good people."

"I noticed," she said, and explained how kind he'd been to her family while they were adjusting to the new uncertainties of their lives.

"He's that sort of person," he agreed. "He's done a lot of good with that motel, taking in people who had nowhere else to go and trusting them for the rent. I don't know of one single person who's skipped without paying, either."

"He's been great to us," she said.

"So it would seem."

He pulled up at the door of their room and got out, opening Mary's door for her with an old-world sort of courtesy. He helped her get John out of his car, and carried the car seat into the room for her as well.

"Hi!" Bob called, bouncing off the bed to greet Matt. "Did you bring Mom home?"

"I did," he told the boy with a smile. "We've been handing out food all over town. How was football practice?"

"Pretty good, if we could teach Pat Bartley how to tackle," he said with a wistful smile. "He won't wear his glasses and he can't see two feet in front of him. But the coach is working on him."

"Good for him. Who's in band?"

"Me," Ann said, grinning. "I play clarinet. I'm good, too."

"I used to play trombone in band," Matt volunteered.

"You did?" Ann exclaimed. "That's neat!" She looked up at Matt curiously. "You look different when you aren't wearing a uniform."

"I'm shorter, right?" he teased.

She smiled shyly. "No. You look taller, really."

"We've got leftover pizza. Want some?" Bob offered. "Mr. Smith brought it to us. It's got pepperoni."

"Thanks, but I had egg salad for supper. I'm sort of watching my weight." His dark eyes twinkled at the boy. "New uniforms are expensive."

"Tell me about it," Mary sighed. "I'm trying to keep my own weight down so mine will fit."

"You wear a uniform?" Matt asked.

"Just for one lady I work for," she said. "She's very rich and very old, and traditional. When I work for everybody else, I just wear jeans and a T-shirt."

"Amazing," he mused.

"Look, Mom, there's that movie Bob wants to see!" Ann enthused, pointing at the small television screen.

It was a promo for a fantasy film with elves and other fascinating creatures.

"I want to see that one, myself," Matt commented. "Say, you don't work Sunday, do you?" he asked Mary.

"Well, no, but there's still food to pick up and deliver—"

"There are matinees," he interrupted. "Suppose we all go?"

Mouths dropped open. None of them had been to a movie in years.

"I guess I could ask Tammy to keep John…" Mary thought out loud.

"Wowee!" Bob exclaimed. "That would be radical!"

"Sweet!" Ann echoed.

"I need a dictionary of modern slang," Matt groaned.

"We mean, it would be very nice," Ann translated. "We'd like very much to go, if it wouldn't be an imposition."

Matt glanced at her and then at Mary. "We don't need a translator," he pointed out.

They all laughed.

"Then, that's settled. I'll find out what time the matinee is and call Al and have him tell you when I'll be here. Okay?"

"Okay," Mary said breathlessly.

Matt winked at her and she felt suddenly lighter than air. Worse, she blushed.

"She likes him!" Bob said in a stage whisper.

"Think he likes her, too?" Ann whispered back, gleefully.

"Yes, he likes her, too," Matt answered for them. "See you all Sunday."

"I'll walk you out," Mary said quickly, with a warning look at her kids, who suddenly assumed angelic expressions.

On the sidewalk, Mary wrapped her arms around her chest. It was cold. "Matt, thanks so much, for everything. Especially tonight."

He paused at the door of his car and looked back at her. "I like your kids," he said. "I really like them. They're smart and kind-hearted and they're real troopers. Under the circumstances, I wouldn't be surprised if they were sad and miserable. But they're so cheerful. Like you."

She smiled. "We've been very lucky, the way things have worked out for us," she explained. "But the kids have always been like this. They get depressed sometimes. Everybody does. But they're mostly upbeat. I'm crazy about them."

"I can see why." He gave her a long, quiet look. "You're one special lady."

She stared back at him with a racing heart and breathlessness that she hadn't felt since her teens.

He bent, hesitantly, giving her plenty of time to back away if she wanted to. But she didn't. He brushed his mouth tenderly across her lips and heard her soft sigh. He lifted his head, smiling. He felt as if he could float. "Dessert," he whispered wickedly.

She laughed and blushed, again. He touched her cheek with just the tips of his fingers, and the smile was still there.

"I'll look forward to Sunday," he said after a minute, and grinned as he got into his car. "Don't forget," he called before he started the engine.

"As if I could," she murmured to herself.

She stood and watched him drive away. He waved when he got to the street.

Mary walked back into the room. Three pair of curious eyes were staring at her.

"He's just my friend," she said defensively.

"He's nice," Bob said. "And we like him. So it's okay if you like him, too. Right?" he asked Ann.

"Right!" she echoed enthusiastically.

Mary laughed as she took little John from Ann, who was holding him. She cuddled the little boy and kissed his chubby little cheek.

"I'm glad you like him," was all she said. "Now, let's see if we can get our things ready for tomorrow, okay?"

CHAPTER
FOUR

MARY FELT LIKE A NEW WOMAN as she went to her job the next day. It was too soon to become romantically involved with any man, at the moment. But Matt was a wonderful person and she was drawn to him. Her children seemed to feel a connection to him as well, which was terrific.

One of her employers, a middle-aged society hostess named Billie West, was married to old money and dripping diamonds. She was particularly interested in Mary's project.

"You mean these restaurants are actually willing to just *give* you food?" she exclaimed.

"At the end of the business day," Mary replied with a smile. "It's only the leftovers, not the full meals."

"Oh. I see." The woman shook her head. "And you call them up and they give it to you."

"Well, I do have to pick it up and deliver it to people."

"Deliver it? Hmm. Is Chez Bob one of your clients?" she persisted.

"No, ma'am. I asked, but they weren't interested."

The older woman smiled. "Suppose I ask the owner for you?"

Mary was surprised. The elderly woman wasn't usually talkative. Often, she wasn't at home when Mary cleaned for her, using a key that was kept in a secret place. "You would do that?" Mary asked.

"There are two others whose owners I know, Mary's Porch and the Bobwhite Grill. I could ask them, too."

Mary just stared at her.

"You're suspicious," the blonde replied, nodding. "Yes, I don't blame you. I'm filthy rich. Why should I care if a lot of society's dropouts starve. That's what you're wondering, isn't it?"

Mary perceived that only honesty would do in this situation. "Yes, ma'am, that's what I'm wondering," she said quietly.

Billie burst out laughing. "Honey, I grew up on the back streets of Chicago," she said surprisingly. "My old man was drunk more than he was sober, and my mother worked three jobs just so my brothers and I could have one meal a day. She could barely pay the rent. When I was sixteen, she died. It was up to me to take care of Dad, who had liver cancer by then, along with three young boys and get them and myself through school." She sat down on the sofa and crossed her long legs. "I wasn't smart, but I had a nice figure and good skin. I had a friend who was a photographer. He shot a portfolio for me and showed it to a magazine editor he did layouts for. I was hired to be a model."

That was news. Mary had never heard the woman speak of her background at all.

"Overnight, I was rolling in money," her employer recalled. "I got the boys through school and never looked back. Dad died the second year I was modeling. The third, I married Jack West, who had even more money than I did. But I never forgot how I grew up, either. I donate to the less fortunate on a regular basis." She stared at Mary curiously. "Your other client Debbie and I are friends. She said that after your divorce was final, you were on the streets with three kids to raise. And despite that, you were out begging food from restaurants and delivering it to people in shelters. I must admit, it didn't seem possible."

Mary smiled. "You mean, because we were in such bad shape ourselves?"

"Yes."

"I never learned how kind people could be until I hit rock bottom," Mary explained patiently. "Or how much poverty and need there is out there, on the streets. There are disabled people, handicapped people, paraplegics and diabetics and people dying of cancer who have nothing." Mary took a long breath. "You know, handing out a little good food might not seem like much to do for people in those situations. But it gives them hope. It shows them that they're important, that they're valuable to someone." It

helps them to see that everyone doesn't turn away and avoid looking at them."

"I know what you mean," the woman said quietly as she got to
her feet. "I'll make those calls. Have you got a way to pick up the
food? What am I saying? You must have, or you wouldn't be adding restaurants to your list."

"The shelter where I started out was given a pickup truck. We
use that."

"We?"

"I have a few volunteers who help me," Mary said. "And my
children, of course."

"How do you manage to do that and keep your children in
school?"

"Oh, not just in school," Mary assured her. "One of them plays
football and one is in band. I think it's important for them to learn
teamwork."

The other woman smiled. "Smart. I've always said that baseball
kept my younger brothers out of jail. One of them plays for the
Mets," she added, "and the other two are assistant managers on different ball teams."

"You must be proud of them," Mary commented.

"Yes, I am. I helped keep them out of trouble. Could you use
another volunteer? I don't just have sports cars in the garage; I've
got that huge SUV out back. It will hold a heck of a lot of food."

"You mean it?"

"I'm bored to death, alone with my fancy house and my fast
cars and my money," Billie said blandly. "I don't have any kids and
my husband is working himself to death trying to enlarge a company that's already too big. If I don't find some sort of useful purpose, I'll sit here alone long enough to become an alcoholic. I saw
my Dad go out that way. I'm not going to."

Mary grinned, feeling a kinship with the woman for the first time.
"We all meet at the 12th Street shelter about five in the afternoon."

"Then I'll see you at five at the shelter," Billie said, smiling back.

"Thanks," Mary said huskily.

"We all live on the same planet. I guess that makes us family,
despite the ticky little details that separate us."

"I'm beginning to feel the same way."

The two women shared a smile before Mary got back to work. It was so incredible, she thought, how you could work for somebody and not know anything about them at all. So often, people seemed as obvious as editorial cartoons. Then you got to know them, and they were really complex novels with endless plot twists.

Not only did Billie show up with her SUV at the shelter, but one of Matt's colleagues from the police force, a tall, young man named Chad, drove up in another SUV and offered to help the group transport the food.

It was getting complicated, because there were now so many restaurants contributing to the program. Mary had been jotting down everything in a small notebook, so that she could refer back to it, but the notebook was filling up fast.

"We've got a small laptop computer with a printer that was donated last week," Bev mentioned. "We really should get all this information into the computer, so that you can keep up with pickup and delivery locations and the time frames."

Mary agreed. "That would be nice. But I don't know how to use a computer," she added with a grimace. "We were never able to afford one."

"I work with them all the time," Matt said with a lazy smile. "Suppose I come over an hour before we start tomorrow and key in the data?"

"That would be great, Matt!" Mary exclaimed.

"It shouldn't be too difficult," he added. "If I can read your handwriting, that is," he mused.

"Well," Mary began worriedly.

"Could you get off an hour early and have Smith watch the kids for you?" Matt persisted.

"She works for me tomorrow, and sure she can get off early," Billie volunteered, stepping forward. "Hi. I'm Billie West. Don't let the glitter fool you," she added when the others gave her odd looks. "I came up in Chicago, on the wrong side of the tracks."

The odd looks relaxed into smiles.

"I'm Bev, I run the shelter. Welcome aboard," Bev said, shaking hands. "That's Sam Harlowe over there, and this is Matt Clark. Matt's a police officer."

"Nice to meet you," Billie said. "Thanks for letting me and my SUV join up."

"You and your SUV are most welcome," Mary replied. "And thanks in advance for the hour off."

"Where do we start?" Billie asked.

Now that they'd added three restaurants to the ten they already had, Mary realized the waiting time and the packaging of the donated food once it was picked up was going to pose a problem.

"This isn't going to work," she told Matt while they were briefly alone in the shelter's kitchen, finishing up filling the last containers of food. "We really need one more vehicle so that we can split the list three ways and each truck will have a third of the restaurants to pick up from."

"Bev said that she's already had calls from six more restaurants that heard about your project and want to contribute," Matt told her. "Your little project is turning into a business."

"But there aren't enough people," Mary said worriedly. "Not nearly enough."

"You need to talk to someone about the future of this project," Matt pointed out. "You can do a great job if you just have more volunteers. It's a wonderful thing you're doing. You can't let it overwhelm you."

"It already has," she said with a husky laugh.

"It shows," Matt said with some concern. "You look worn-out, Mary, and I know you can't be getting much rest at night. Not with a toddler."

"John's a good boy, and the kids are great about helping look after him," Mary said defensively.

"Yes, but you still have to be responsible for all of them. That includes getting them to and from practice and games, overseeing homework, listening to problems they have at school," he said gently. "That's a heck of a responsibility for one woman, all by itself. But you've got a full-time job, and you're spending every night running around Phoenix to restaurants and then distributing food until late. Even with your energy and strength of will, you must see that you can't keep this up indefinitely."

Until he said it, she hadn't realized how thin she was spreading herself. She was beginning to have some chest pain that was unexpected and alarming. She hadn't mentioned it, thinking that perhaps if she ignored it, it would go away. But that wasn't happening.

"I can do it as long as I need to," she said firmly.

"You're like me, aren't you?" he mused, smiling. "You're stubborn."

"Yes, I think I am," she agreed, smiling back. He made her feel young. He was like a sip of cold water on a hot day. He was invigorating.

"I have ulterior motives, you know," he commented. "I'm fond of you. I don't want you to keel over from stress."

She was touched. "I promise not to keel over," she told him.

He signed. "Okay. That will have to do for now. But you really should think about delegating more. And eventually, you're going to need some agency to help you oversee the project. It's outgrowing you by the day."

"I don't even know where to begin," she said.

"Talk to Bev," he told her. "She's been in this sort of work for a long time, and she knows everybody else who's involved in it. She may have some ideas."

"I'll do that," Mary promised.

"Meanwhile," he drawled, "don't forget Sunday."

She had forgotten. Her wide-eyed stare made him burst out laughing.

"Well, that puts me in my place," he said with a grin. "I'll have to stop strutting and thinking I'm God's gift to overworked womanhood."

She smiled at him. "You're a nice guy, Matt. I'd only forgotten today. I'd have remembered when I went home, because it's all the kids talk about."

"So I made an impression, did I?"

"A big one," she agreed. "They like you."

"I'm glad. I like them. A lot."

"Speaking of the movies, it turns out Tammy has a prior commitment and can't watch the baby after all. Looks like he'd be joining us. Hope that's okay."

"No problem," Matt reassured her.

"Hey, are you guys coming, or what?" Sam called from the parking lot. "We're running behind schedule."

"Sorry, Sam," Mary said at once, preceding Matt out the door. "Let's go!"

They had a routine of sorts by now, through the various shelters and homeless camps. People came out to meet them when they saw the headlights, and there were beaming faces when the smell of food wafted out of the containers that were presented to the staff for their residents.

"We never had stuff like this to eat before," one disabled young woman commented to Mary at the women's shelter. "You sure are nice to do this for us."

"You're very welcome," Mary said, searching for the right words.

The young woman smiled and walked away to the kitchen as quickly as she could with her crutches.

"That's Anna. She has multiple sclerosis," the shelter manager told Mary quietly. "Usually she's in a wheelchair, but it got stolen two days ago when she left it outside the stall in a rest room a block away." She shook her head. "Imagine, somebody stealing a woman's wheelchair and nobody noticing!"

"How did she get here?" Mary wondered.

"One of our regulars saw her holding on to walls trying to walk. She came back here and borrowed our spare crutches that I keep in the office for Anna. She's been using them ever since, but it's hard for her to walk with wasted muscles."

"Is there some sort of program that could get her a wheelchair?"

The woman grimaced. "She'd probably qualify if she could get into the system. That's the problem. We have to have a caseworker come here and fill out forms, then there's a waiting period, and she might or might not get accepted on the first try. Bureaucracy is slow."

Mary sighed. "If I had the money, I'd buy her a wheelchair," she said.

"Me, too," the shelter manager said quietly.

They exchanged glances.

"No matter how much we do, it's like filling up a barrel with a teaspoon, isn't it?" Mary asked. "There's so much need, and so few people trying to meet it. Federal and state and local programs do what they can. But there are limits to any budget, and so many people fall through the cracks."

"That's true."

"I found that out the hard way," Mary said.

"You?" the manager exclaimed.

"I'm living in a motel room with three kids, holding down a full-time job, six days a week, sometimes seven, and I do this after I get off, every day," Mary told her. "Because no matter how bad things are for me, everybody I meet in these shelters is so much worse off."

"My dear," the manager said, lost for words.

"It's been a learning experience for all of us," Mary told her. "We've learned so much about human nature since we began this project. And despite our own circumstances, people have just been so kind to us," she emphasized. "I never knew how kind total strangers could be until we ended up like this."

"I like the feeling I get when I know I've helped someone out of a particularly bad spot, given them hope," the manager said with a warm smile.

"I do, too. It makes it all worthwhile."

"And you have three kids." She shook her head. "I only had one, and he's got a wife and three kids of his own. We had a good home and a comfortable income." She glanced at Mary. "You're unbelievable."

Mary laughed. "Maybe I'm just out of my mind," she suggested.

The other woman laughed, too. "If you are, I wish we had a hundred more just like you. Thanks, Mary. Thanks a million."

"It's my pleasure. And I mean that." Mary smiled.

The next day Billie let Mary off an hour early with no argument at all. "And I'll see you at the shelter in an hour," she added. "You know, this has given me a new lease on life. I've been so depressed lately. It was time I stopped feeling sorry for myself and started being useful for a change. I'm very grateful to you for helping me."

"We're all grateful to you for helping us," Mary replied. "And I'll see you at the shelter at five."

She was still driving the car that Debbie had loaned her, and Tammy had demanded that Mary let her keep John during the day.

"I have all this room and only two kids," Tammy had argued.

"And both of them love having John around to play with. Besides, I heard from a reliable source that Jack left town so there's
no danger that he's going to track the kids down anytime soon.
It's only for a couple of weeks, until you get some sort of system
worked out. So humor me!"

Mary had, with more gratitude than she could express.

She picked up John at Tammy's and went with him to the
shelter where Matt was ready to feed information into the
computer.

Two of the shelter workers came right up to take John.

"Let them," Bev coaxed when Mary started to protest. "We all
love kids, you know that. You just help Matt get that schedule on
a disk and we'll take care of John."

"Thanks," Mary said, smiling.

She sat down beside Matt at the long table. The computer was
an old one, but it seemed to be workable.

"The one I have in my squad car is older than this," he pointed
out as he opened a file in a word processor. "It's going to be a piece
of cake, getting your schedule fed into this thing. Okay. I'm ready.
Let's see that notebook."

She produced it and opened it to the appropriate page.

He glanced down and his eyes widened. "Good Lord, woman,
you call this handwriting? I'm amazed you didn't fail first grade!"

She burst out laughing. "You listen here, I got awards for my
penmanship in high school!"

"From doctors, no doubt," he drawled.

She gave him a restrained glare. "So I was in a little bit of a hurry
when I scribbled these things down," she confessed finally.

He chuckled. "Actually, I had a partner whose handwriting was
even worse than yours. Every time he wrote out a traffic citation,
we got a call from the clerk of court's office asking us to translate
for them."

"That makes me feel a little better," she replied with a laugh.

It was incredible how often she did that with him. Her blue eyes
swept over his rugged, lined face. He put on a good front, but she
could see the inner scars he carried. His whole life was there, in
those deep lines.

"Have you ever had to shoot anybody?" she asked involuntarily.

"Not yet," he replied. "But I've threatened to shoot a few people who robbed banks or abused helpless people."

"Good for you," she said.

His hands paused over the keyboard and he glanced up at her. "Could you ever date a cop?"

She was suddenly flustered. "Well…well, I never thought about it."

He pursed his lips. "Wow. That puts me in my place."

"It does not," she retorted. "You're a terrific person. The job wouldn't bother me, really. I mean, I don't think it would matter so much if you cared about somebody." She ground her teeth together. "I can't put it into words."

"Oh, I think you did a pretty good job of expressing yourself," he drawled, and wiggled his eyebrows.

She chuckled. "You're a character, you are."

"Takes one to know one. I think you'd better read me that list along with addresses and phone numbers. It will save hours of time trying to read your handwriting."

"Hold your breath until you ever get a letter from me," she teased.

"I like cards. Funny cards. My birthday is next month," he hinted. "You could send me one, and I'd put it on my mantel beside the pictures of my mother and father."

"I'll consider it seriously," she promised.

"You do that."

They joked back and forth as they went through the list and put all the necessary information into the computer. It wasn't as time-consuming as Mary had thought it would be. She had to admit, she enjoyed Matt's company. He was a complex person. She really wanted to get to know him. But it was much too soon for anything serious.

By the time Sunday arrived, Mary was so tired that she almost thought of backing out of Matt's generous offer to take them all to the movies.

She had some uncomfortable palpitations, and she felt sick in her stomach. It was frightening. She knew it probably had something to do with the stress, but for the moment, she had no idea how to get out from under it.

More importantly, she didn't want to frighten the children. Bob and Ann were already giving her curious looks. They began to notice that her mother was pale and listless when she wasn't working.

"Don't even think about trying to back out," Matt told Mary when he was standing in the motel room, comfortable in jeans and a long-sleeved blue checked shirt with a leather jacket. "You're going to enjoy today. I promise. Won't she, kids?" he asked the others.

"You bet!" they chorused.

"A movie and a few hours of being away from work, from any work at all, will rejuvenate you," Matt promised as he smiled down at her. "We're going to have a ball!"

Mary wasn't so sure, but she got her old coat on, put the kids in theirs, and all of them went out the door to pile into Matt's sedan.

CHAPTER
FIVE

THE THEATER WAS CROWDED, even at the matinee, but most of the audience was made up of children. Bob met one of his friends, and went to sit with him. Ann sat on one side of Matt, and the baby, John, curled into Mary's shoulder and promptly went to sleep.

"He really is a good baby," Matt whispered, watching the little boy with a tender smile.

"He always has been," she whispered back.

Matt glanced toward the other kids, who were engrossed in the movie. "Were the others like this?"

She shook her head. "Bob was a live wire, always in trouble for being mischievous. Ann refuses to show her work in math, which gets her into lots of trouble with teachers. She's very intelligent."

"I noticed," Matt agreed.

People in the seats ahead were glaring back at them. They exchanged wry glances and paid attention to the movie.

"That was just great!" Bob enthused when the movie was over and they were back in the car, heading for a fast-food restaurant that served chili dogs—the children's favorite food. "Thanks a lot, Mr. Clark."

"Matt," the older man corrected lazily. "I'm glad you enjoyed it, Bob. So did I. I think the last movie I went to see was the second of the new Star Wars films."

"That was ages ago," Ann exclaimed.

Matt shrugged, smiling. "My social life is mostly work."

"Join the club," Mary had to agree.

"We need to do this more often," Matt said. "At least a movie a month. If you guys would like to do that," he added.

There was a loud chorus of assents and excited smiles all around. "You're terrific, Matt," Ann said. "Thanks."

"My pleasure," he replied, with a smile in Mary's direction. "Now, for chili dogs!" he added as he pulled into the fast-food restaurant.

Mary and Matt had shared the cost of the outing, because she insisted. It had made a hole in her meager savings, but as she looked at the radiant faces of her children, she couldn't regret doing it. Sometimes in the struggle just to survive, she forgot that the children needed more than school and work in order to thrive. They needed a little breathing space from the problems of everyday life. In fact, so did she.

"That was really great, Matt," Mary told him as he deposited her and the children at the motel. "I enjoyed it. So did they," she added, nodding toward the children filing into the room with Ann carrying little John carefully in her arms.

He smiled. "That was obvious. I'm glad, because I had a good time, too. I haven't been out on a date since my wife left me."

She gave him a wry glance. "Some date," she mused. "Me and three kids."

He chuckled. "I was an only child. It was sort of a dream of mine to have a big family." He shrugged. "My wife hated kids. She didn't like my job, either. She wanted to party all the time, and I came home dead tired at night. We were doomed to failure, I guess. Neither of us was any good at looking ahead. We married on an impulse. It was a really bad impulse."

She sighed. "I had those same ideals myself. I did, at least, get the big family," she said with a smile. "But I never expected that I'd have to raise it all by myself. It's a big responsibility."

He touched her hair gently, just a gesture without any demands or insistence. "Listen, if you ever need somebody to look after your brood in an emergency, I've got a big-screen television and lots of G-rated movies. They'd be company for me."

Her face became radiant. "Wouldn't you faint if I said yes?"

"Try me."

She hesitated. "I might do that one day, if you mean it."

His dark eyes swept over her face. "You've got guts. You never complain, no matter how hard your life is. You love those kids and it sticks out like a neon light. You've got a good sense of humor and you don't back away from trouble. I think you're an exceptional woman. Having got that out of the way," he continued when she tried to speak, "I'll add that I think your sons and daughter are the nicest children I've ever met, and some of the most unselfish. It wouldn't be any chore to look after them, as long as I'm not on duty. I don't think you'd like having me take them on a high-speed chase or to make a drug bust."

She laughed. "No, really I wouldn't. But if I get in a tight spot, I'll remember you. I will."

"Good. I'll see you at the shelter tomorrow afternoon."

"Thanks again, Matt."

"I'm lonely," he said simply. "It was fun."

She watched him walk away. Her heart felt warm and safe. She sighed like a girl. Perhaps, someday, she thought to herself.

The routine was more fulfilling than Mary had ever dreamed it might be. She really enjoyed her trips to the restaurants and then to the shelters and homeless camps. It was the first time in her life that she'd ever felt she was making a difference. It was more than just feeding the hungry. She felt a sense of self-worth, of responsibility and pride, that she hadn't ever known.

To her surprise, her work was sparking comment in the community, to the extent that the shelter Bev ran got a call from a daily newspaper reporter. She wanted to do a feature article on Mary.

At first, Mary thought about refusing. She didn't want people to think she was doing the work just for publicity. But Bev assured her that this wasn't going to be the case. The reporter was a vivacious young lady who sat down with Mary for half an hour and wrote a story that sounded as if she'd known Mary her whole life. Best of all, people called the shelter and volunteered their time, and money, to help the needy.

Mary's kids were also learning a lot about the world through helping their mother with the project. Their own generosity in helping with their mother's routine without complaint said a lot for their unselfish natures.

"You know," Bob commented one evening when they'd just dropped off several containers of food at the women's mission, "I didn't understand how people could lose their homes and end up in places like this. I mean, not until we started taking them food." He frowned. "There are a lot of desperate people in the world, aren't there, Mom?" he added. "I guess what I mean is, when we're doing this stuff for other people, it kind of helps me forget how scared and uncertain I feel myself."

Mary reached over and hugged him. "That's a good feeling, too, isn't it?"

"It is," Ann joined in.

But despite the pleasure it gave Mary to pursue her project, she was feeling the pressure of trying to hold down several physically demanding jobs and look after the children's needs, as well as drive around most of the night picking up and delivering food. She had several volunteers, and she was grateful for every one of them. But her list was growing longer and the demands were increasing.

"You really are going to have to have help," Bev told her firmly. "You need someone to help you coordinate all this."

"Matt made a computer program," Mary began.

"You need an organization to sponsor what you're doing, Mary," came the quiet reply. "You're going to fold up if you keep trying to do it all by yourself."

"But I don't know any organizations," she said heavily.

"I do," Bev replied. "The head of the local food bank has been in touch with me. That article they did about you in the morning paper has gained some interest from some important people around the city. I've been asked to introduce you to the food bank manager tomorrow. Can you get off an hour early and meet me here?"

Mary was dumbfounded. "He wants to meet…me?"

Bev smiled. "You're an inspiration to all of us, a woman in your circumstances who's willing to give time and money she doesn't have to help people less fortunate than she is."

She shook her head. "Anybody else would have done the same thing."

"Not in a million years," Bev said quietly. "Will you come?"

Mary sighed. "Okay. I'll be here at four, is that all right?"

Bev grinned. "Just right!"

★ ★ ★

The manager of the City Food Bank, Tom Harvey, was tall and elegant, a soft-spoken gentleman with a warm smile and kind dark eyes.

"I'm very pleased to meet you, Mrs. Crandall," he said when he shook Mary's hand. "I must say, you've come as a surprise to all of us. I didn't really believe the story in the paper until I talked to Bev. So many times, reporters exaggerate the truth. But in your case, I think the story was actually an understatement. I'm amazed at what you've done on your own initiative."

"It's tiring, but it's the most rewarding thing I've done in my life," Mary told him. "I enjoy every minute of it."

"So I've been told." He frowned. "But your list of participating restaurants is growing bigger by the day, and even with your volunteers, you're not going to be able to keep up this pace."

"I'm beginning to realize that," Mary had to admit. She looked up at him curiously. "Do you have any suggestions?"

"Yes, I do. I'd like to consider adding your project under our program and putting you in charge of it. You'd work part-time, but it would be a paid job."

Mary felt the blood drain out of her face. It seemed almost too good to be true. "You're joking."

He shook his head. "I assure you, I'm not. Your program is unique, and it's doing a lot of good. I want to see it continue. I want to see you continue," he emphasized with a smile. "With three children to support and your full-time cleaning job, and this, I feel that you must be stretched pretty thin."

"I'm almost transparent," she confessed with a smile. "But that wouldn't stop me from doing it."

He nodded. "I thought you were that sort of person. There's a pilot program in California which does much the same manner of food rescue that you're doing. I'd really like to fly you out there and take a look at it, and see what you think. If you like it, we can expand your project and put it in place here."

Mary was thinking. Her mind was whirling. She could do this with professional help on the organizational level. She could do it part-time as a salaried employee and cut her cleaning jobs in half. She'd be able to spend more time with the children. They might be able to afford to rent a house, even buy a car. It was overwhelming.

"You haven't answered," Tom Harvey said gently.

She smiled from ear to ear. "I'm speechless," she admitted. "I'd like very much to see the California program and make my decision afterward."

"Great!" he exclaimed. "Then we'll get the ball rolling!"

Mary took Matt up on his offer to keep the children over a weekend, while she flew to San Diego. Although money wasn't an issue since the City Food Bank covered all her travel expenditures, she was nervous about the trip. However, Matt assured her that she was going to do just fine. The kids kissed her goodbye and told her not to worry. Matt gave her a speaking look, because he knew she'd worry anyway. He'd given her both his home and cell phone numbers, to make sure she could reach him whenever she wanted to check on the children. It made her feel better.

When she got to San Diego, she checked into the nice motel they'd put her up in and took a cab to the food bank office. There, she met a live wire of a woman named Lorinda who ran the food rescue program for the food bank there. It was similar to Mary's, except that it was much more efficient. There was a special unit of volunteers who made the rounds of the restaurants to pick up food, and a separate unit that had panel trucks with which to make the deliveries. It worked like clockwork, and served many shelters.

"We're adding to our suppliers all the time," Lorinda said with a contagious smile. "It's time-consuming and we spend a lot for gas, but the program is very successful. It's lucky that we have plenty of volunteers. I'm amazed at what you're able to do with so few people."

"Yes," Mary agreed. "Imagine what I could do with a setup like yours!"

The other woman just smiled. "We have the advantage of a comfortable budget and people with great organizational skills."

"I've been offered both," Mary said thoughtfully. "And I believe I'm going to accept them."

★ ★ ★

Two weeks later, Mary was officially on the staff of the food bank as a part-time employee in charge of food rescue.

She sat at a desk in the shelter and used the phone excessively in the first week on the job, setting up even more restaurants to be clients of the food bank. She was also trying to keep the cleaning jobs she'd had for so many years. The stress of it all suddenly caught up with her early one morning after she'd dropped the kids off at school and John at a nearby day-care center with a woman she trusted.

She was walking into the food bank office when she felt something like a blow to her chest. She saw the floor coming up to meet her. Everything went black.

She came to in a hospital bed with Matt sitting beside her in full uniform, except for his hat, which was on the floor beside him. He looked worn and worried.

Her eyes opened slowly and she blinked. "What happened?" she asked weakly. She looked around. "Where am I?"

His eyebrows lifted above wide dark eyes. "Apparently you decided to take a sudden nap on the floor of your office."

She smiled weakly. "Bad decision."

"Very bad." He reached over and stroked her cheek. "How do you feel?"

"Odd. Floaty. Disconnected."

"That would be the sedative kicking in," he assessed.

"Have I had a heart attack? Has a doctor been in?"

"A few minutes ago," he said. "But it wasn't a heart attack. The palpitations were induced by stress and you collapsed from exhaustion. I told him what you'd been doing, and he asked if you had a death wish."

She laughed softly. "I guess I need a vacation."

"You're having one," he pointed out. "All meals included."

"This is much too expensive a vacation," she argued. "I have minimal insurance coverage and it's brand-new."

"It's quite enough, as you'll find out," he replied. "I checked."

"The children…!"

"I picked them up from school, and John from day care and brought them here with me. They're with your friend, Tammy. I phoned her and she came straight over to pick them up. I would have been glad to keep them," he added at once, "but I'm on duty and I can't get anybody to cover for me. I took my lunch hour early to come and see about you."

"Thanks, Matt."

"No problem," he said gently. "I don't mind looking after people I lo…people I care about," he corrected abruptly, afraid that he'd gone too far too fast. She was fragile enough already without having to carry the burden of his feelings for her.

But Mary had caught his slip of the tongue, and even through the fog of the sedatives, she felt exhilarated. "You're a wonder, Matt. I don't know how to thank you…"

"I don't need thanking," he replied gently. "I'm glad to do it. Thank your friend, Tammy. She didn't even have to be coaxed into baby-sitting—if that's the right word to use."

"Are my babies all right?" she whispered.

They were terrified and half out of their collective minds with worry, he thought, but he wasn't about to tell her that. He smiled convincingly. "They're doing great. I'm going to bring them to see you when I get off duty tonight."

"I'll try to look better so that I don't scare them."

He reached out and took her hand gently in his. Her fingers were like ice. "Listen, you're going to have to make some hard decisions, and soon. The doctor said you'll make a speedy recovery—provided that you slow down. If not for your own sake, then for the children's. What are they going to do without you, Mary?"

She winced. "I've tried so hard to give them everything I could. Life is so hard sometimes, Matt."

"I may not look as if I know that, but I do," he said, curling her small hand into his big one. "Nevertheless, you're going to have to slow down."

"Where do I start?" she worried. "I can't give up my cleaning jobs, they're all I have to support me."

"You have a part-time job at the food bank that will help a lot. That should allow you the luxury of cutting down on your cleaning jobs, at least. And you'll have more volunteers to help with the pickups and deliveries of your program. Who knows, Mary, it might someday work into a full-time job. All you have to do is hang in there for the time being. But the pace is going to kill you if you don't put on the brakes." His eyes lowered to her hand. He brought it gently to his lips and kissed the palm hungrily. "I've suddenly got a family of my own," he added huskily, and without looking at her. "I don't want to be left alone."

Her heart skipped wildly. "Matt!" she whispered huskily.

His dark eyes lifted to hers. He searched them slowly, and her face began to grow radiant with faint color.

"I know," he murmured. "It's too soon after your divorce for this. You don't really know me yet, or trust me. But I'm going to be around for a long time, and I can wait until you're comfortable with me."

She laughed a little shyly. "I don't think I'll ever be that, exactly. You're…sort of an electrifying personality. You make me feel as if I could do anything."

"Same here," he replied, his lips tugging into a tender smile. "So don't skip out on me, okay? You have to get better. A lot of us can't go on without you."

She smiled up at him with her heart in her eyes. She drew the back of his big hand to her cheek and held it there. "I'm not going anywhere. Honest."

He stood up, bending over her with his heart in his eyes. "I'll hold you to that," he whispered, and, bending, he touched his lips tenderly to her forehead.

She sighed with pure bliss.

He lifted his head, dropped his eyes to her mouth, and bent down to give her a real kiss that took her breath away. When the door opened and a young nurse came into the room, she noted how quickly the policeman stood up, and how flushed he and the patient looked.

"Uh-huh," she murmured dryly. "I can see that I'll have to keep a closer eye on you two!" she teased.

The tension broke and they both started laughing.

"He's the one you have to watch," Mary said with a possessive smile in Matt's direction. "But not too closely, if you don't mind," she added with a wink at the pretty nurse. "I can't stand the competition."

"That's what you think," Matt drawled.

Mary sat up in bed. "Oh, my goodness," she exclaimed. "Who'll do my pickups and deliveries tonight? You can't do it all, not even with the children helping."

He held up a hand. "Already taken care of," he said easily. "I phoned Bev and she phoned a few people. Tonight, even if you could get out of that bed, you'd be superfluous. So you just concentrate on getting your strength back. Okay?"

Mary felt as if she had a new lease on life, as if tomorrow and all the tomorrows to come would be worth waking up for. The look in Matt's eyes made her tingle like an adolescent with her first crush.

He seemed to understand how she felt, because his eyes darkened and a faint ruddy flush darkened the skin on his high cheekbones.

"I really have to go," he bit off.

Mary was watching him hungrily while the nurse checked her blood pressure, and then her temperature, with her high-tech arsenal of diagnostic tools.

"You'll be back tonight, with the kids?" Mary added.

He nodded, and smiled. "Around seven."

"I'll expect you," Mary said huskily. "I'm going to phone Tammy and thank her."

"Good idea." He winked again. "Stay out of trouble."

"Look who's talking!" Mary exclaimed, and smiled back at him.

"See you." He went out with a quick wave of his hand. Mary stared after him until the door closed.

"Handsome guy," the nurse murmured dryly. "I gather he's spoken for?" she asked.

"Oh, yes, indeed, he is," Mary replied with a becoming blush.

"No wonder you're improving so much," the nurse laughed. "If you need me, just buzz. You're doing great."

"Thanks," she said.

The nurse smiled and went to her next patient down the hall.

Her family doctor, Mack Barker, stopped by just at suppertime to check her over. He dropped into a chair by her bedside after he'd checked her chart and taken her vitals himself.

"I suppose you know now that you can't go on burning the

candle at both ends," he told her. "You were pushing yourself too hard. Something had to give."

"I suppose I just went on from day to day without thinking about how much stress I was under," she had to admit.

"You're going to have to learn how to delegate more," he warned her. "Or this may not be the last trip you make to the hospital."

She drew in a lazy breath. "It's just that I've got three kids to look after, and now I'm doing this food rescue program…"

"Which is a very worthwhile thing," the doctor admitted. "But if you don't slow down, somebody else is going to be doing it instead of you. Or maybe nobody else will be able to do it at all, and it will fold. Either way, you're going to destroy your health if you don't find a way to curtail your work. I'm sorry. I know how much it means to you. But you can't possibly keep it up any longer."

"I can't give up what I do at the food bank," she said miserably. "You can't imagine how many people depend on those food deliveries—"

"Yes, I can imagine," he interrupted. "It's a tremendously worthwhile and unselfish thing you've been doing." He smiled quietly. "It's just that I'd like you to be able to continue it. This is going to require some compromise. But you can salvage some of your charity work and keep your job at the food bank as well. You only need to cut your housekeeping duties in half. Believe me, your clients will understand."

"It's the money," Mary argued. "I have to be able to keep the kids in clothes and food and pay my bills. We're living in a motel room, we can't even afford to rent a house!"

"Do you believe in miracles?"

Mary looked up as Bev stepped into the room with a big smile on her face.

She blinked. "Well, yes. Of course."

"Your hard work hasn't gone unnoticed. I know someone who has a house for rent, at a price you can afford."

"You're kidding!" she exclaimed.

"I'm not. And my friend knows where you can get some good used furniture and appliances to go in it."

"I can't believe it," she exclaimed.

When the doctor left the room a few minutes later, Bev filled her in on the details. "It gets better. The house is half a block from the shelter, so that you could walk to work."

She just stared at Bev, dumbfounded.

"I know you can afford the utilities on your salary. You could probably even afford to make payments on a good used car, since you won't have rent to worry about."

Tears stung her eyes and rolled down her pale cheeks. "I just can't believe it!"

When Matt returned that evening with the kids, she filled him in on her wonderful news.

He smiled. "It's amazing how kind people can be," he remarked. "I see a lot of cruelty in my line of work. Sometimes it really gets me down, seeing the dark side of human nature. But then, some-body like you comes along and renews my faith in mankind. Womankind, too. People who give always get repaid for it, Mary."

She wiped away the tears. "Bev went out of her way looking for that house, didn't she?"

He nodded.

"What a kind thing for her to do."

"I'll tell her," he said with a laugh. "For now, you just concentrate on getting better, and out of here."

She let out a long breath, thinking what an odyssey her life had become. It was a journey, an adventure, an obstacle course. But she'd become strong and self-sufficient and independent because of the hardships and challenges.

"Deep thoughts?" Matt probed.

She looked at him. "I was thinking that it's not the destination, it's the journey. I've heard that all my life. I never really understood it until I ended up in a shelter with my kids."

He nodded. "The journey is the thing. Not to mention the exciting and interesting people you meet along the way." He gave her a devilish wink and brought her hand to his lips.

Warmth flooded through her. "I never expected that people would be so kind to me, when I was about as low on the social ladder as a person could get. Even the people I work for have been supportive and generous. And you were the best surprise of all," she said softly.

"Right back at you," he said gruffly.

She laid back on the pillows. "Thank you, Matt, for everything. And you'll be happy to know I'm listening to the doctor. I'll speak with my employers when I get out of here. And I will slow down."

"That's a really good idea," he mused. "I'll be back with the kids first thing tomorrow."

After Mary kissed the kids good-night and exchanged a highly charged look with Matt that was ripe with possibilities of what the future could hold, she was left alone to rest. Closing her eyes, she thought about the changes she was going to have to make. Perhaps it wouldn't be so bad after all, slowing down. Well, slowing down just a little, she amended.

CHAPTER
SIX

MARY HAD A LONG TALK with three of her employers about giving up her work. They were nice, but she knew they didn't really understand why Mary had to quit working for them.

One asked if the money wasn't enough, and offered a substantial raise if Mary would stay on.

That was just too hard to turn down. Mary agreed to stay, but she was adamant about the other two jobs. She explained that if she had another stress attack, it could be much worse, and she had her kids to think about. She had to stay healthy so that she could get them all through school. Her doctor had insisted that she had to give up some work. In the end, they accepted her decision and even gave her severance pay.

Matt was delighted that she was following doctor's orders. "We get to keep you around for a while, right, kids?" he asked them when they were all enjoying hamburgers after a particularly great fantasy movie on their Saturday out.

"Right!" they chorused.

"It's been a super evening, Matt. Thanks again."

He smiled warmly at her. "It's only the second of many," he said easily, finishing his hamburger. "I see a pleasant future for us."

"Us?" she teased lightly.

"Us," he agreed. "We'll be best friends for a couple of years and then I'll follow you around Phoenix on one knee with a ring in my hand until you say yes."

She laughed delightedly. "I just might hold you to that," she murmured.

"We can carry your bouquet," Ann enthused.

"And tie tin cans to the bumper of the car we haven't got yet," Bob added, tongue-in-cheek.

"We can take care of him when he's sick," Ann added in her sensible way.

Matt gave Ann a beaming smile. "And I can take care of all of you, when you need it."

"I might be a policeman one day myself," Bob mused.

It was nice to see that the children liked Matt as much as she did. It wasn't wise to look too far down unknown roads. But she felt comfortable and secure with Matt. So did the children. He was truly one of a kind. She had a feeling that it would all work out just perfectly one day.

"Deep thoughts?" Matt mused.

"Very nice ones, too," she replied, and she smiled at him.

Her new job was more fulfilling than anything she'd done in her life. She felt a sense of accomplishment when she and her volunteers—many of them, now—carried food to the legions of hungry people around town.

More newspaper interviews had followed, including stories about her co-workers, which made her feel like part of a large, generous family. Which, in effect, the food bank was.

"You know," she told Tom one afternoon, "I never dreamed that I'd be doing this sort of job. It's like a dream come true."

"I understand how you feel," he replied, smiling. "All of us who became involved in this work are better people for having been able to do it. The more we give, the more we receive. And not just in material ways."

"Yes," she said. "There's no greater gift than that of giving to other people."

He nodded.

She glanced at her watch and gasped. "Goodness, I have to get on the road! Mr. Harvey, did I ever tell you how grateful I am to have this job?"

"Only about six times a day," he murmured dryly. "We're happy to have you working for us, Mary."

"I'll get on my rounds. Good night, Mr. Harvey."

He smiled. "Good night, Mary."

She went out the door with a list of her pickups and deliveries in one hand, her mind already on the evening's work. Matt was on duty tonight, Bob and Ann were at sports competitions, John was with Tammy, who'd agreed to pick up Bob and Ann at the games—her kids were playing, as well. Mary could pick them up on the way home.

Home. She thought of the neat little house she was now living in with her kids, rent free, and of the nice used compact car she'd been able to afford. It didn't seem very far away that she and the children had been living on the streets, with no money, no home, no car and no prospects. Life had looked very sad back then.

But now she was rich, in so many ways that had little to do with money. She waved to the volunteer staff standing by their own vehicles, waiting for her to lead the way. How far she'd come, from taking a little leftover food from a restaurant and delivering it to one or two clients.

Her heart raced as she climbed in behind the wheel. She started the car and drove off, leading the others out to the highway. There would be a lot of deliveries tonight, a lot of people to help. She felt as if she could float on air. She'd not only survived life at the bottom, she'd bounced back like a happy rubber ball to an even better place.

The future looked very bright. Life was good.

SHELTERNET
JAN RICHARDSON AND KATHRYN BABCOCK

*Never doubt that a small group of thoughtful committed citizens can
change the world: Indeed it's the only thing that ever has.*
                                                —*Margaret Mead*

Jan Richardson and Kathryn Babcock took Margaret Mead's inspiring words to heart when they first set out to create a safe Internet site to link abused women with local shelters. From the very
beginning, Jan and Kathryn envisioned a site that would help
women across Canada—truly working locally and thinking glob-
ally. That vision led to the founding of Shelternet. Today, women
and children, no matter where they live in Canada, can connect
with the shelter closest to them through Shelternet.

Kathryn and Jan first met by chance when a group of women
gathered to discuss philanthropic strategies. At the time, Jan was a
director of a London, Ontario, women's shelter, and Kathryn was
a Toronto-based corporate fund-raiser for charitable organizations. They were next to each other in the lineup for the buffet,
and the outgoing Kathryn began to chat to Jan as they waited. The
conversation turned to the Internet and the glaring absence of resources out there for women in crisis. In a desperate need to find
help, abused women were searching for information in unregu-

lated chat rooms, and shelters were receiving crisis e-mails from women without knowing how to safely respond. Shelters needed to increase their online presence in a way that would offer information and anonymity. Jan and Kathryn agreed something needed to be done. This casual meeting led to the dream of connecting all shelters for all women across Canada, and after three years of hard work and perseverance, the dream came true.

Jan has always believed a lot of important work comes into being through women's vision and passion—women dreaming the impossible and making it into a reality. "That's how women do business," Jan says. "Women network through their relationships with other women. And women show great strength in making things happen. They're undaunted—they'll champion monumental goals, and have a way of overcoming any obstacles in their paths."

With Shelternet, Jan and Kathryn had that kind of vision—to do something that had not been done before—and they had the courage and determination to realize that vision. Neither Kathryn nor Jan had a background in Web site design or technology, and they had no financial backing. But from her front-line experience, Jan knew what the site should look like and feel like to make it work for the women who needed it. The creation of the site became a collaborative effort as individuals, organizations and corporations came on board with technical and financial support.

Shelternet was successfully launched in August 2002 as the first site of its kind in the world, receiving international and national acclaim. Shelternet's interactive map connects women with the shelter closest to them. The site provides links to local helplines, information on developing a safety plan, and stories of inspiration from other women who have left abusive relationships. Shelternet also reaches out to children and teens who have witnessed the abuse of their mothers, with special resources for them about where they can get help. So often it is children who find the information for their mothers.

The children are Kathryn's motivation for her involvement

in Shelternet—and in all her work to end violence against women. It's unimaginable to Kathryn the level of fear a child would feel at seeing his mother being abused. Yet in Canada alone, more than 100,000 children witness the abuse of their mothers every year. More than half the women come into shelters with children—many under five years of age. The feisty part of Kathryn can't stand women being abused and children being scared. "I wish I could be twenty-five-feet tall and get the women and children out of there," she says. "I look at my relationship with my husband, how gentle and loving it is, and I want that for every woman. To never be afraid in an intimate relationship. True partnership is worth fighting for. Children raised in a loving home is the greatest gift we can give."

Jan was another motivator and inspiration for Kathryn as they worked together on Shelternet. As Kathryn describes Jan, "She had a huge history and significant experience in the shelters. She's incredibly well-versed in the issues. She's extraordinary."

Ever since she was a little girl, Jan wanted to help—wanted to work at making the world a better place. She's motivated by the possibility that a woman can be anything she wants to be, and she's dedicated her entire adult life to the experiences women have in the world. But as Jan says, "That means violence. Men violate women because they can—they're allowed to in our laws and culture." Besides being a director of a women's shelter since 1985, Jan has served as an advocate, teacher, writer and community builder—all as part of her ongoing commitment to one day eradicating violence against women and children. Jan's work with Shelternet has been an inspiration to continue her commitment. "I've been humbled by the incredible efforts of others," she says, "particularly the rural women and shelters that have so few resources and real hardships. Yet these communities have real heart."

Jan and Kathryn believe that the spirit of collaboration can make anything possible. But as Kathryn emphasizes, "There are so many issues that need help. Don't be afraid if you're just one person. Two is better—" she laughs "—but even one is okay. Any passion can be an issue you can volunteer for—and every skill is needed. You just have to reach out."

Reaching out is the first connection to making a real difference in a community. And in the words of Margaret Mead, it's the only thing that can change the world.

More Than Words

CARLA NEGGERS

CLOSE
CALL

CARLA NEGGERS

A respected member of the literary community, this award-winning author has written more than 40 novels, including mainstream fiction and series romance. She is a past president and member of the Advisory Council of Novelists, Inc., and is a mentor to a number of aspiring writers. A native New Englander, Carla studied music at the Boston University School of Fine Arts, but writing has always been her first love, and she ended up graduating, magna cum laude, with a degree in journalism. She and her husband, the parents of two, live in Vermont, where they are almost finished the renovation of their "house on a hill."

CHAPTER
ONE

A DIRT-ENCRUSTED mountain bike. A battered kayak. Free weights loose on the floor. Gym clothes and squash rackets hanging from a pegboard. Street and ice hockey sticks leaned up against the wall.

Brendan O'Malley's idea of how to welcome guests to his place.

As she stepped into the foyer, Jessica Stewart told herself there were no surprises. It wasn't as if she'd expected feng shui or something out of a decorating magazine. She loved the guy. She really did. She didn't know if she was *in* love with him, but that was a problem for later—right now, she had to fight her way into his apartment and find out what he was up to.

Jess stuffed the key that O'Malley's brother Mike—the firefighter brother—had loaned her. Brendan was one of the cop brothers, a Boston homicide detective. The other cop brother, the youngest, was just starting out. There was also a carpenter brother and a marine brother. Five O'Malley brothers in all. At thirty-four, Brendan was smack in the middle. A guy's guy.

There was, in other words, no logical reason Jess should have expected anything but hockey sticks in the foyer.

Brendan and Mike owned the triple-decker and were renovating it as an investment property. Brendan had the first-floor apartment to himself.

Jess had rung the doorbell. She'd pounded on the door.

Taking Detective O'Malley by surprise wasn't a good idea under any circumstances, but today it was really a bad one.

He'd almost been killed yesterday.

She hoped the kayak and mountain bike were a sign that he was still in town. Even his brothers didn't want him going off on his own so soon after a trauma.

Using the toe of her taupe pumps, Jess rolled the dumbbells aside and entered the living room. It was her first time inside his apartment. Their on-again, off-again relationship over the past two months had been at theaters, restaurants and her condo on the waterfront. They hadn't had so much as a candlelight dinner at his place.

No wonder.

It wasn't that it was a pigsty in the sense of trash and garbage all over the floors and furniture. He didn't live like a rat—or *with* rats. His apartment simply reflected his priorities. He had a flat-screen television, stacks of DVDs, an impressive stereo system, a computer, shelves of books on the Civil War and more sports equipment. In the living room.

He wasn't much on hanging up his clothes, either.

Mike had warned Jess when she talked him into giving her the keys to his younger brother's apartment. Brendan had lived on his own for a long time. His apartment was his sanctuary, his world away from his work as a detective.

Inviolable, and yet here she was.

She walked into the adjoining dining room. The table was stacked with car, sports and electronic gaming magazines and a bunch of flyers and guidebooks on Nova Scotia—another sign, she hoped, that he hadn't already left.

He needed to be with his family and friends right now. Not off on his own in Nova Scotia. Everyone agreed.

Jess continued down the length of the apartment to the kitchen. A short hall led to the bathroom and bedroom. The bedroom door was shut, but she knew she'd never have gotten this far if he were on the premises. It was only five o'clock—she'd come straight from the courthouse—but he'd taken the day off.

No dirty dishes in the sink or on the counter, none in the dishwasher.

Not a good sign.

The house was solid, built about a hundred years ago in a neighborhood that wasn't one of Boston's finest, and had a lot of character. Brendan and Mike were doing most of the work themselves, but they were obviously taking their time—both had demanding jobs. They'd pulled up the old linoleum in the kitchen, revealing narrow hardwood flooring, and scraped off layers of wallpaper. Joe, the carpenter brother, had washed his hands of the place.

Jess peeked out onto the enclosed back porch, stacked with tools and building materials, all, presumably, locked up tight.

Brendan had mentioned, over a candlelight dinner at *her* place, that a couple of jazz musicians lived in the top floor apartment, a single-mother secretary with one teenage daughter in the middle floor apartment. He and Mike had fixed up the upper-floor apartments first because they provided income and allowed them to afford the taxes and mortgage.

Taking a breath, Jess made herself crack open the door to his bedroom.

It smelled faintly of his tangy aftershave. The shades were pulled.

The telephone rang, almost giving her a heart attack.

So much for having a prosecutor's nerves of steel.

She waited for the message machine.

"Stewart?" It was O'Malley. "I know you're there. I got it out of Mike. Pick up."

No way was she picking up.

"All right. Suit yourself. I'm on my way to Nova Scotia. I'm fine."

She grabbed the phone off his nightstand. "You left your bike and kayak."

"Don't need them." She could hear the note of victory in his tone now that he'd succeeded in getting her on the line. "Place I'm going has its own bikes and kayaks."

She noticed his bed was made, not that neatly, but he'd put in the effort. "Why sneak off?"

"I didn't want a lot of grief from everyone."

"Brendan—come on. You had a bullet whiz past your head yesterday. You need to be with family and friends."

"The bullet didn't whiz *through* my head. Big difference. It just grazed my forehead. A little blood, that's it. I get banged up worse than that playing street hockey. A couple days' kayaking and walking on the rocks in Nova Scotia, and I'll be in good shape."

"Did you bring your passport? You know, they don't just let you wave on your way across the border these days—"

"Quit worrying. I'm fine."

"You don't sound fine," Jess said. "You sound like you're trying to sound fine."

"What are you now, Stewart? Ex-cop, hard-ass prosecutor, or would-be girlfriend?"

She stood up straight, catching her reflection in the dresser mirror. Chestnut hair, a little frizzed up given the heat and humidity. Pale blue suit in an industrial-strength fabric that didn't wrinkle, repelled moisture, held its shape through the long hours she put in.

Definitely a former police officer, and now a dedicated prosecutor.

How on earth had she become Brendan O'Malley's would-be girlfriend?

"Don't flatter yourself, Detective. Just because we've seen each other a few times doesn't mean I'm mooning over you—"

He laughed. "Sure you are."

"I've known you forever."

"You haven't been sleeping with me forever."

True. She'd slept with him that one time, two weeks ago. Since then, he'd been acting as if it had been a fast way to ruin a perfectly good friendship. Maybe she had, too. They'd known each other since her days at the police academy, when O'Malley had assisted with firearms training. He was only two years out of the academy himself, but even then everyone knew he was born to be a detective. She'd been attracted to him. What woman wasn't? They'd become friends, stayed friends when she went to law school nights and then took her job as a prosecutor. She'd never even considered dating him—never mind sleeping with him—until two months ago.

She could feel the first twinges of a headache. "Some crazy fairy with a sick sense of humor must have whacked me with her magic fairy wand to make me want to date you."

"Honey, we haven't just dated—"

"Don't remind me."

"Best night of your life."

He was kidding, but she knew what had happened that night. Brendan O'Malley, stud of studs, had gone too far. He'd been tender and sexy and intimate in a way that had scared the hell out of him. Now he was backpedaling. Pretending it was her chasing him and it was all a game.

"O'Malley—Brendan—"

"I'm losing the connection. I'm up here somewhere in moose country. Quit worrying, okay? I'll call you when I get back."

"I might never make it out of this damn apartment of yours. I'll need a compass to navigate through all your stuff."

But he wasn't making up the bad connection, and his cell phone suddenly blanked out altogether, leaving Jess standing there in his bedroom, his phone dead in her hand.

She cradled it with more force than was necessary.

Bravado. That was all this was about.

O'Malley was shaken by yesterday's close call. He and his partner had entered a seedy hotel to question a possible witness in a murder, only to have the guy throw down his backpack, turn and run. An ancient .38 fell out of the backpack, hit the floor and went off.

The bullet just barely grazed O'Malley's forehead.

It could have killed him. It could have killed anyone in the vicinity.

O'Malley was treated on the scene. He wasn't admitted or even transported to the hospital. As he'd said, he was fine.

Physically.

It was his third close call that year. The sheer randomness of this latest one had gotten to him. He wasn't a target. The witness wasn't a suspect in the murder, wasn't trying to kill him or anyone else, said he had the .38 for his own protection—never mind that he was now charged with carrying a concealed weapon, possession of a weapon in violation of his probation, and assault with a deadly weapon.

Over dinner with Jess last night, after he'd been debriefed, Brendan had admitted he didn't think he'd get this one out of his mind that easily. He kept seeing the gun fall out of the backpack. He kept feeling himself yell, "Gun!" and jump back, an act that had saved his life. The heat of the bullet, the reaction of his partner, the paramedics—he remembered everything, and it played like a movie in his head, over and over.

"In the blink of an eye," he said, "that would have been all she wrote on the life of Brendan O'Malley."

He'd wanted to be alone that night.

When Jess called to check on him in the morning, he blamed his moroseness the evening before on the shrinks and too much wine and said he was heading off on his own for the weekend.

She'd talked to a few people, who all agreed it might not be a good idea for him to be alone right now. He needed his support network. Family and friends. Time to process what was, after all, a scary incident, no matter that it had a happy ending.

Not that Detective O'Malley would listen to her or anyone else.

Jess wandered back out to the dining room and flipped through the brochures and guidebooks on Nova Scotia. She'd never been to the Canadian Maritime Provinces—she'd only been to Canada a few times, including the usual high-school French-class trip to Montreal in Quebec.

The brochures were inviting. The pictures of the rocky coastline, the ocean, cliffs, beaches, kayakers, fishing boats, harbors, quaint inns and restaurants. The Lighthouse Route. Cape Breton Island. The Evangeline Trail.

So many possibilities.

How would she ever find him?

No one had shot at her lately, but Jess could feel the effects of her months of nonstop work. She'd just finished a major trial and could afford to take a few days off. She knew better than to get in too deep with O'Malley, but she had to admit she'd fantasized about going somewhere with him. She kept telling herself that she was well aware he wasn't the type for long-term commitments—she had her eyes wide-open. She didn't mind if they just had some fun together.

He'd mentioned getting out of town together for a few days. Casually, not with anything specific in mind, but it at least suggested that the only reason he hadn't invited her to go with him to Nova Scotia was the shooting. It had only been a day. He wouldn't want to inflict himself on her.

She noticed that he'd circled a bed-and-breakfast listed on a Web site printout.

The Wild Raspberry B and B.

Cute. Cheeky, even. Jess smiled to herself and, before she could talk herself out of it, dialed the Wild Raspberry's number.

A woman answered.

Jess reminded herself she was a prosecutor accustomed to delicate situations. For the most part, it was best to come to the point. "Hello—a friend of mine has a reservation with you this weekend. Brendan O'Malley."

"Right. He's not due to arrive until tomorrow."

"Thanks," Jess said, hanging up.

Of course.

He was in moose country. That meant he'd gone farther north than Portland, Maine, and wasn't taking the ferry to Nova Scotia from there. He must have decided to drive up to Mount Desert Island and catch the ferry out of Bar Harbor. He had to be booked on one of the ferries, since it would take forever for him to drive all the way up through Maine and New Brunswick.

Jess dug some more on the dining-room table and found a printout of the ferry schedule from Bar Harbor to Yarmouth, Nova Scotia.

Bingo.

If she hurried, she could make the overnight ferry from Portland, about two hours north of Boston, and maybe even beat O'Malley to the Wild Raspberry.

After he checked into a small, tidy motel in Bar Harbor on Maine's Mount Desert Island, Brendan O'Malley walked over to the cheapest-looking restaurant he could find and ordered fried shrimp and beer. There was fresh raspberry pie on the dessert menu, but he passed. Once he got to Nova Scotia, he'd be staying at a place with a name like Wild Raspberry, so he figured he'd have another chance.

He touched the bandage on the left side of his forehead, just above his eyebrow.

Man. Talk about luck.

The graze didn't hurt at all. He could take the bandage off anytime. He figured he'd let it fall off in the shower.

His brother Mike had arrived at the scene. "Brendan—damn. You are one lucky cop. How many of your nine lives have you used up now?"

"Eleven."

Gallows humor, but Mike understood. He'd had his share of brushes with death in his work. They both counted on their training, their experience, the people who backed them up—they didn't want to count on luck.

Luck was unpredictable. Fickle.

And it could run out.

Brendan shook off any hint of encroaching self-pity and paid for his dinner. He'd have to walk all the way to Nova Scotia to burn off the fried shrimp, but he settled for an evening stroll along Bar Harbor's pretty streets, not overly crowded with summer tourists. He had a reservation on the morning Cat ferry, which shortened the normal six-hour trip from Bar Harbor across the Gulf of Maine to less than three hours.

Marianne Wells, the owner of the Wild Raspberry, had assured him he'd have peace and quiet at her B and B. She only had three guest rooms. One was free, one was occupied by a hiker, and then there was the room she'd reserved for him.

O'Malley had debated pitching a tent somewhere on the coast for a few days, but Jess would have regarded that as total nut behavior under the circumstances and hunted him down for sure—or, more likely, sent someone after him. There wasn't much that could pry her away from her job as a county prosecutor. She was a worse workaholic than he was.

A disaster in the making. That was what their relationship was.

Except he couldn't imagine not having Jess Stewart in his life. She'd been there so long—forever, it seemed.

He didn't want to screw things up by falling for her.

Mike had said she'd looked worried when she'd talked him into giving her the key to his place. Brendan doubted it. Jess had been a cop for five years, earning her law degree part-time. She wasn't a worrier. She just didn't like it that he'd skipped out on her.

What the hell, he didn't owe her anything. He didn't even know how they'd ended up dating. He'd always thought of her as a kind of kid sister.

Mike hadn't bought that one. "There isn't one thing O'Malley about her. You're in denial, brother."

Ten years Brendan had known Stewart, and not until two months ago had he seriously thought about sleeping with her. Maybe she was right, and they'd both been struck by some crazy fairy with a weird sense of humor.

They'd gone to dinner and the movies a few times. Jess had dragged him on a tour of the Old North Church because he was from Boston and he'd never seen it, and that just couldn't stand another minute as far as she was concerned. But she was a native Bostonian, and had she ever been to a Bruins hockey game? One time, when she was ten. It barely counted.

O'Malley found a flat stone and skipped it into the smooth, gray water of the harbor. He had to stop thinking about Attorney Stewart. Their relationship wasn't going anywhere. They'd slept together that one time a couple weeks ago, before the shooting, but that had just been one of those things. Spontaneous, unplanned, inevitable.

He'd been such a mush, too. He couldn't believe it.

He heaved a long sigh, feeling a headache coming on that had nothing to do with the bullet that had missed his brain pan by not very much at all.

Back at his motel, he flopped on his sagging double bed and stared at the ceiling.

Nova Scotia. He could just skip it and hang out on Mount Desert Island for a few days—except the same instinct that had prompted him to jump back a half-step yesterday, thus saving his life, told him to head east. He'd been gathering brochures on Nova Scotia for weeks, checking out the tourist sites on the Internet, poring over maps, all with some vague idea that he should go there.

Maybe it was karma or something.

With his head bandaged up last night and his brother's talk of using up his nine lives, he'd stared at the lodging list he'd printed off the Internet, picked out a B and B that looked good and called.

Now here he was, on his way. Alone.

Jess could have a point that he shouldn't be alone.

"Too late."

He hit the power button on the TV remote and checked out what was going on in the world, feeling isolated and removed and suddenly really irritated with himself. But he was nothing if not stubborn, and he needed a few days to pull his head together, not just about the shooting, but about Jess.

He thought of her dark eyes and her cute butt and decided the bullet yesterday was the universe giving him a wake-up call. What did he think he was doing, falling for Jessica Stewart?

He had no intention of tucking tail and going home.

CHAPTER
TWO

THE OVERNIGHT FERRY from Portland, Maine, to Yarmouth, on Nova Scotia's southwest shore, was surprisingly smooth—and fun. Jess hadn't been anywhere in so long, she made an adventure of it. When she arrived back on land, she followed the directions to the Wild Raspberry B and B, which, she soon discovered, was on Nova Scotia's South Shore, a breathtaking stretch of Canada's eastern coastline of rocks, cliffs, narrow, sandy beaches and picturesque villages.

"Forget O'Malley," she muttered to herself. "I want to go hiking!"

She'd at least had the presence of mind to pack trail shoes and hiking clothes on her quick stop back at her condo last night. Now it was a sunny, glorious morning, and she debated leaving Brendan to his own devices—his determined solitude—and finding another place to stay. He wouldn't even have to know she was there.

But she continued north along what was aptly named the Lighthouse Route and kept forcing herself not to stop, kept warning herself to stay on task. Finally she came to a small cove near historic Lunenburg, named a UNESCO World Heritage Site because of its pristine British colonial architecture and rich seafaring heritage, and found her way to the Wild Raspberry.

It wasn't a renovated colonial building like those in Lunenburg, which Jess had read about on the ferry. The Wild Raspberry was, fittingly, a small Victorian house, complete with a tiny guest cottage, that perched on a knoll across from the water.

A tangle of rose and raspberry vines covered a fence along one side of the gravel driveway. The house itself was painted gray and trimmed in raspberry and white, and had porches in front and back that were crammed with brightly cushioned white wicker furniture and graced with hanging baskets of fuchsias and white petunias.

Jess parked at the far end of the small parking area—so that O'Malley wouldn't spot her the minute he pulled into the driveway. As she got her suitcase out of the back of her car, she could smell that it was low tide.

And she could hear laughter coming from the back of the house, toward the guest cottage.

Women's laughter. Unrestrained, spirited laughter.

It was so infectious, Jess couldn't help but smile as she made her way up a stone walk to the side entrance, where an enormous stone urn of four or five different colors of petunias greeted her. There was also—of course—a Welcome sign featuring a raspberry vine.

She thought of O'Malley's rat hole apartment. How had he picked this charming, cheerful place?

She sighed. "Because he got shot in the head yesterday."

A forty-something woman in hiking shorts, a tank top and sports sandals came from behind the house. She had short, curly brown hair streaked with gray and a smile that matched the buoyant mood of the B and B. "May I help you?"

"I'm Jessica Stewart—"

"I thought so. Welcome! I'm Marianne Wells. Please, come inside. Make yourself comfortable. I can help you with your bags— I just need to say goodbye to some friends."

"Don't let me interrupt. I'm in no hurry."

"Oh, we were just finishing up. We meet every week."

As Marianne turned back to rejoin her friends, Jess noticed a faint three-inch scar near her hostess's right eye. A weekly get-together with women friends—it wasn't something Jess took the time to do. Given her busy schedule, her friendships were more catch-as-catch-can.

The side door led into a cozy sitting area decorated cottage-style, with an early-twentieth-century glass-and-oak curio filled with squat jars of raspberry jam, raspberry-peach jam and raspberry-rhubarb jam, all with handmade labels. There was raspberry honey in a tall, slender jar, and a collection of quirky raspberry sugar pots and creamers.

"I've told all my friends no more raspberry anything," Marianne Wells said as she came into the small room. "You should see what I have in storage. It can get overwhelming."

"I have an aunt who made the mistake of letting people know she collects frogs. Now she's got frog-everything. Frog towels, frog soaps, frog statues, frog magnets. Frogs for every room. She even has a frog clock."

Marianne laughed, the scar fading as her eyes crinkled in good humor. "I know what you mean. It's fun to collect something, though. You must want to see your room. Come on, I'll show you upstairs."

As she started down the hall, following her hostess, Jess noticed a bulletin board above a rolltop desk with a small, prominent sign on it:

The Courage to Click. Shelternet.ca.
Shelternet can help you find a link to a shelter or a helpline in your area.

From her experience both as a police officer and a prosecutor, Jess immediately recognized Shelternet as a resource for victims of abuse, one that Marianne Wells obviously wanted people coming through her B and B to know about.

Instinctively Jess thought of the scar above Marianne's eye and guessed she must have been a victim of domestic abuse at one time, then reminded herself that she didn't know—and shouldn't jump to conclusions.

But Marianne paused on the stairs and glanced back at Jess. "Clicking on Shelternet helped save my life."

"I'm a prosecutor in Boston. I didn't mean to make you uncomfortable. I just couldn't help noticing—"

"I'm not uncomfortable. If that sign prompts just one person to take action—well, that's why it's there. If a woman in an abusive relationship walks into this inn, I know that she'll walk out of here with that Web site address in her head. Shelternet.ca." Her smile didn't quite reach her eyes, but she seemed to mean for it to. "I don't mind that you noticed it. Not at all. I'm not ashamed of what I've been through. I used to be, but not anymore."

Jess smiled back at her. "I hope you'll tell me more about Shelternet while I'm here."

"Gladly."

They continued up the white-painted stairs to a large, airy room overlooking the water. The decor was Victorian cottage, with lots of white and vibrant accents, nothing stuffy or uptight. There was a private bathroom—with raspberry-colored towels—and upscale scented toiletries that surely would be a waste on O'Malley.

Marianne pointed out the television, how to work the windows, where to find extra linens. "My friend Pat comes in to clean every morning. Her grandmother lived in this house before I bought it. I've made a lot of changes, but Pat approves. You'll like her."

"I'm sure I will," Jess said.

"There's one other guest room on this floor and a room on the third floor in what was once the attic. A long-term guest is staying there. Brendan O'Malley will be staying on this floor. He's not here yet. I thought you two might have made arrangements to arrive together."

Jess felt a twinge of guilt. When she'd called back to make a reservation, Marianne had recognized her voice from her previous call about O'Malley. "Uh, no."

Marianne frowned. "But you *are* friends, right?"

"Yes. Yes, definitely." Which, Jess thought, didn't mean he'd jump up and down with joy to see her. But as a survivor of abuse, Marianne Wells would be sensitive to such matters—and properly so. "We've known each other since I was a police recruit."

"You're a former police officer?"

Jess nodded. "And O'Malley—Brendan is a detective."

Her hostess seemed satisfied. "Is there anything I can get you right now?"

"No, nothing. The room's lovely. Thank you."

"We serve afternoon tea at three, on the back porch if the weather's good, and a full breakfast in the dining room starting at seven. If there's anything special you'd like to request, please don't hesitate to let me know."

Jess debated warning Marianne that Brendan O'Malley wasn't expecting to find her here, but decided there was no point in complicating the woman's life just yet—or stirring up any old fears. O'Malley would behave. It wasn't as if he'd be really irritated that Jess had followed him.

On the other hand, he'd had a rotten week. Everything might irritate him.

After Marianne left her to her own devices, Jess unpacked, opened the windows and took a bath to the sound of the ocean, listening for O'Malley's arrival.

O'Malley waited in the hall while Marianne Wells pushed open the door to his second-floor room. The place was nice, a little quaint, probably, for his tastes, but maybe the bright colors would improve his mood. At least Marianne—she'd already told him to call her by her first name—was dressed for climbing on the rocky coastline. And the other guest, the one in the attic, was a guy.

The scar on Marianne's face looked like it was from a knife wound, but Brendan figured he was in a frame of mind to come to the worst conclusion. She could have slid off a sled as a kid and cut her face on ice.

He noticed the pink towels in the bathroom.

Pink. It was a grayed pink, but it was still pink.

He wondered if the guy in the attic got white towels.

"Your friend from Boston is in the room across the hall."

His experience as a detective kept him from choking on his tongue. "Jess?"

"That's right. You seem surprised."

And she didn't like his surprise. He could see it in her body language. She straightened, narrowing her eyes on him, and moved to the doorway, ready for flight.

O'Malley relaxed his manner, not wanting to get his hostess mixed up in whatever he and Jess had going on. "I'm just surprised she beat me here. I thought I had the head start."

"I don't want any trouble," Marianne said firmly. "If you don't want Ms. Stewart here—if she's stalking you—"

"Jess? Stalking me? No way. It's nothing like that."

"And you. You're not—"

"No, I'm not stalking her."

She seemed at least partially relieved. "I hope not."

He pointed to his bandaged forehead. "I was in a scrape at work a couple days ago. Jess is worried about me is all. She and I go way back."

"You're a police officer, aren't you? Were you—"

"It was nothing."

Jess had been talking. O'Malley had known her since she was a recruit. She'd gone through the police academy two years after him and had done a good job on the force, but her heart wasn't in it, not the way it was in her job as a prosecutor. She absolutely believed that the system could, should and most often did work, and that she was there to get to the truth, not advance her own career, change the world or pander to public opinion.

O'Malley wasn't that idealistic. Jess insisted it wasn't idealism on her part, but a serious, hardheaded understanding of her duties as a representative of the state's interests. She'd tried to convince him of that over one of their dinners together. But he wasn't convinced of anything, except she was a bigger workaholic than he was and needed to take a vacation once in a while.

And he'd wanted to make love to her.

He'd been very convinced of that.

After Marianne retreated downstairs, he stood out in the hall and stared at Jess's shut door. Damn. What was she doing here?

The three-legged puppy syndrome, he thought.

She must have been the kind of kid who brought home injured animals, and that was what he was at the moment.

Except he didn't see it that way.

He walked over to the door and stood a few inches from the threshold, wondering if he'd be able to figure out what she was doing in there. Sleeping? Plotting what she'd do once he got there? But he didn't hear a sound from inside—no radio, no running water, no happy humming.

No gulping.

No window creaking open as she tied sheets together to make good her escape.

She must have heard him talking in the hall with their hostess.

The door jerked open suddenly, and Jess was there in shorts and a top, barefoot, her hair still damp and her skin still pink from a recent bath or shower.

"O'Malley," she said. "What a coincidence."

"Like minds and all that?"

"Mmm."

"Sweetheart, there's nothing 'like' about our minds."

But she was unflappable—she'd had longer to prepare for this moment. "I saw all those Nova Scotia brochures on your dining-room table and couldn't resist. Funny we picked the same B and B."

"You're not even trying hard to sound convincing."

She ignored him. "It's adorable, isn't it? I love the cottage touches and the raspberry theme."

He had no idea what she meant by "cottage touches." He placed one hand on the doorjamb and leaned in toward her, smelling the fragrance of her shampoo. "How's your room?"

"Perfect."

He tried to peer past her. "I think it's bigger than mine."

She opened the door a bit wider. "See for yourself."

In her own way, Jessica Stewart liked to play with fire. O'Malley stepped into her room and saw that it was shaped differently from his, but about the same size. "I didn't see your car," he said.

"Really?"

All innocence. "Did you hide it?"

"I engaged in strategic parking. If you'd arrived with a woman friend, I'd have been out of here in a flash."

He smiled. "Don't want any competition?"

"I wouldn't have wanted to embarrass you. You deserve a break, you know, after the shooting. It's just that you also need to be around friends." She scrutinized his head as he walked past her. "How's the wound?"

"I've cut myself worse shaving." He peered into her bathroom. "Do you have pink towels?"

"They're a shade of raspberry. Don't think of it as a feminine color."

"It's a cheerful place. I'll say that." He stopped in front of Jess's bed and turned to her, noticing the color in her cheeks. It was more than the aftereffects of her shower. "Now that you see me, do you feel like a dope for following me?"

"It'd take a lot for you to make me feel like a dope, O'Malley. Everyone's worried about you. What did you think would happen when you snuck off like that?"

He shrugged. "I thought I'd get to spend a few quiet days on my own in Nova Scotia."

"No, you didn't. You thought I'd follow you. That's why you circled the name of the B and B—"

"You didn't have a key to my place."

"You knew I'd ask your brother. I'll bet he okayed it with you to give me the key. Am I right?"

"Hey, hey. I'm not on the witness stand, prosecutor."

She sighed, shoving her hands into her shorts' pockets. "O'Malley—" She broke off with a small groan. "You're impossible. I don't know why I ever slept with you. My first day at the academy ten years ago, I was warned about you."

He feigned indignation. "Warned in what way?"

"Every way."

"What, that they don't come any smarter, sexier, more hell-bent on catching bad guys—"

"More full of himself, more hell on women, more cynical—"

He shook his head. "I wasn't cynical in those days."

"You are now."

"Only a little."

He approached her, slipping his arms around her as she pulled her hands out of her pockets. She didn't stiffen. She didn't tell him to back off or go soak his head. Instead she met his eye and smiled. "You're more than a little cynical, O'Malley."

"It's to protect a soft heart."

"Ha."

But she had to know he had a soft heart—he'd exposed it to her when they'd made love. He'd never done anything like that before and wasn't sure he wanted to again. He didn't like feeling vulnerable—emotionally or physically.

She was still smiling when his mouth found hers, and he could taste the salt air on her lips, her tongue. She draped her arms around his neck and responded with an urgency that told him she'd at least thought about this happening on her trip up here. He lifted her off her feet. Why hadn't he asked her to come with him? Maybe she was right and it was some kind of test, some kind of sexy game between them.

"O'Malley." She drew away from him and caught her breath. "Brendan. Oh, my. I didn't mean—" She didn't finish. "Maybe we should take a walk."

"A walk?"

"It's a gorgeous day."

"Right."

He set her down and backed up a step, raking one hand through his close-cropped hair. She licked her lips and adjusted her shirt, which had come awry during their kiss.

"I'm on a rescue mission," she said. "I shouldn't be taking advantage of your situation."

"Why the hell not?"

But the moment had passed. She had something else on her mind besides falling into bed with him—not that it was easy for her, he decided. She just had a lot of self-discipline.

"I'll meet you downstairs," she said. "We can take a walk, then do afternoon tea."

That was it.

Jess made her way to the door and held it open for him as he strode past her back out into the hall. "Think Marianne Wells would have a ham sandwich or something at tea time?"

"I doubt it."

"Little scones, probably, huh?"

Jess smiled, looking more at ease, less as if she was afraid he'd go off the deep end at any moment. "I'd count on something with raspberries."

The afternoon stayed warm and sunny, and Marianne served tea on the back porch, laying out an assortment of miniature lemon scones with raspberry jam, tiny triangles of homemade bread, fresh local butter and watercress, and warm oatmeal-raisin-chocolate-chip cookies that one of her friends had dropped by that morning.

Jess couldn't have been happier, but O'Malley looked a little out of place sitting on a white wicker rocker with a watermelon-colored cushion as he negotiated a Beatrix Potter teacup and plate of goodies.

He'd gotten rid of the bandage on his forehead. His bullet graze looked more like a nasty cat scratch. Probably no one would guess what it really was, or even bother to ask. He'd had no trouble negotiating their hike along a stunning stretch of the rugged granite coastline. Whenever the afternoon sun hit his dark hair, his clear blue eyes, Jess was struck again by how really good-looking and madly sexy he was. She hadn't thought about his mental state—the possibility he was suffering from post-traumatic stress symptoms—at all.

Maybe it was being away from Boston—violence and his work seemed so far removed from Nova Scotia.

Or maybe it was the way he'd kissed her.

When a middle-aged man joined them on the porch, Jess forced herself to push aside all thought of kissing Brendan O'Malley.

The man introduced himself as John Summers, the Wild Raspberry's third guest. He had longish graying hair and a full gray beard and was dressed in worn hiking shorts and shirt, with stringy, tanned, well-muscled legs and arms. He looked as if he'd been strolling the nooks and crannies of Nova Scotia for months, if not years. His eyes were a pale blue, and he had deep lines in an angular, friendly face.

But something about him immediately set off O'Malley's cop radar. Jess could see it happening. He started with the inquisition. "How long have you been here?"

"A month. Gorgeous spot, isn't it?"

"Sure is. Spend the whole month here alone?"

Summers winced visibly at O'Malley's aggressive tone, then said coolly, "As a matter of fact, yes."

"Must be relaxing. Hike a lot? Or are you into sailing?"

"Hiking and kayaking, mostly." He sat on a wicker chair with his plate of goodies and a cup of tea and changed the subject. "What brings you to Nova Scotia? You're American, aren't you?"

"From Boston. Just taking a few days off." O'Malley didn't take the hint and back off. "Where are you from?"

"Toronto."

"That's a ways. You fly here or drive?"

Jess tried to distract O'Malley from the scent by offering him a warm cookie. He didn't take the hint. Summers, to his credit, just answered the question. "I flew into Halifax."

"I've never been to Halifax," Jess said.

Summers seized on her comment like a lifeline. "It's a wonderful city. I hope you'll have a chance to spend a day there, at least, while you're here. The entire South Shore is worth seeing. Lunenburg can occupy you for quite some time."

"What would you recommend I see?"

O'Malley scowled at her as if she'd interfered with a homicide investigation. He said nothing, just downed a final scone in two bites. Jess chatted with their fellow guest about South Shore sites, then got him to recommend hiking trails. O'Malley finally growled under his breath and excused himself.

Summers nodded at his retreating figure. "You two know each other?"

"We work together," Jess said vaguely. It was close enough to the truth. "He had a bad experience before coming up here."

"He reminds me of a cop. Are you two in law enforcement?"

Jess sighed, then smiled. "Caught. Brendan's a homicide detective. I'm a prosecutor."

He didn't seem pleased that he'd guessed right. "Have you prosecuted many domestic abuse cases?"

"Too many on the one hand, too few on the other."

"Meaning domestic violence shouldn't happen, ever, but it does and you want to get all the perpetrators." Summers nodded with understanding. "Our hostess left an abusive marriage two years ago. She's a very courageous woman. She's come a long way in a relatively short time."

Jess set her plate down, no longer hungry. "The scar above her eye?"

"Her ex-husband's handiwork. He was convicted. He's out of prison now. He was a businessman in Halifax, but he's relocated to Calgary." Summers's expression didn't change, but Jess could feel his sarcasm. "Apparently he said he needed a fresh start."

"Not for her sake, I'll bet."

"He's from western Canada originally. His reputation here was in tatters. People didn't want to believe he was capable of abuse, but the knife cut ended their denial."

Jess wondered why he was telling her all this. "It looks as if Marianne's built a new life for herself."

"She has. It wasn't easy. She told me she used to worry constantly that he'd come back. On some level, I think she still does."

"The emotional wounds of abuse can take a long time to heal."

He looked away. "Sometimes I wonder if they ever do, if someone who's been through that kind of horror can love and trust someone again—" He broke off, as if he hadn't meant to go that far, adding sharply, "Marianne has put all she has—her time, her money, her energy, her love—into getting this place up and running, into her life here. She has friends, she volunteers at a local shelter."

Something about his manner struck Jess as antagonistic, even accusatory. "Mr. Summers, we're not here to upset anyone—"

"What happened to your friend Detective O'Malley? He's had a recent brush with violence, hasn't he?"

"You're very perceptive. It wasn't a major incident, fortunately."

"But it wasn't the first. Men like him—" Summers paused, seeming to debate the wisdom of what he wanted to say. "They're magnets for violence."

"Not O'Malley," Jess said, although she didn't know why she felt the need to defend him.

Summers looked past her. "I've been her only guest on and off since I arrived, especially during the week. Weekends she's usually full." But he had a distant look in his eye, as if he wouldn't necessarily trust himself—or maybe Jess was reading something into his manner that wasn't there because of O'Malley's instant suspicion of him. Summers drifted off a moment, then smiled abruptly. "I'm sorry. I don't mean to be rude."

"You're not the one who was rude."

He almost laughed. "Well, I suppose we want a homicide detective to be of a suspicious nature. Does he give everyone the third-degree like that?"

"Actually, no. I think he's just on edge."

"It's taken a lot of courage and effort for Marianne to build a life for herself that's free of violence. See to it he keeps himself in check, okay?"

"Mr. Summers, Brendan has never lost control—"

"I'm sure he hasn't." He made a face, rubbing the back of his neck as he heaved a sigh. "And I'm sure Marianne would have a fit if she thought I was protecting her. She can take care of herself. She has a great group of friends. She's one of the most positive people I've ever met."

Jess smiled at him. "Smitten, are you, Mr. Summers?"

His cheeks reddened slightly. "I guess there's no point in hiding it."

"She's not interested?"

He shook his head. "I wouldn't know. I haven't—" He frowned suddenly. "You must be a hell of a prosecutor, Ms. Stewart. I didn't mean to tell you any of this."

"Call me Jess," she said. "And, yes, I do okay in my work."

She joined O'Malley in the English-style garden, filled with pink foxglove, purple Jacob's ladder, pale pink astilbe, painted daisies, sweet William, lady's mantle and a range of annuals. He looked as if he could stomp them all into the dirt. Jess inhaled deeply. "I could get into gardening."

"The guy's lying about something."

"Oh, come on. You don't know that."

He mock-glared at her. "Your gut's telling you the same thing."

"Maybe, but not all untruths are nefarious untruths. What set you off?"

"He's been here a month, shows up looking like he could scale the Himalayas. This isn't your 'outdoors guy' kind of place."

Jess smiled, amused. "Because of the pink towels?"

"You know what I'm saying."

"No, I don't. You're here—"

"That's karma or something. I can't explain it." He grimaced, as if the thought of trying to explain how he'd ended up at the Wild Raspberry made him miserable. "Whatever Summers is hiding, it's more than a social lie."

"Like telling me you're staying home in bed when you're actually packing for Nova Scotia?"

"That was a strategic lie. I knew you wouldn't leave me alone otherwise." He had a sexy glint in his eyes that he seemed able to produce at will. "You didn't, anyway."

"You can be alone after you're over the shooting."

"I was over the shooting once I knew the bullet missed."

Jess didn't argue with him and instead related her conversation with their fellow guest. O'Malley looked disgusted. "I hate wife-beaters. I knew a guy my first year on the force who beat up his wife and kids. He was a good cop. No one wanted to believe it, but it was true."

"What happened to him?"

"He went through anger management—after his wife packed up herself and the kids and got out of there before he could do more damage. He lost his job. He screwed up a lot of lives, including his own, before he figured out he was the one who had to change. Most guys don't ever figure that out. It was an eye-opener for the rest of us, seeing that a guy we respected was capable of beating up on his wife and kids."

Jess glanced back at the porch. "If Summers has a thing for Marianne and has lied—"

"She's not going to like it."

"He seems to admire her a great deal."

"Maybe." O'Malley tilted his head back and smiled. "The sun and sea agree with you, Stewart. You're looking good this afternoon."

"I wish I could say the same for you."

"I don't look so good?"

"No. You look like you had a bullet whiz past your head a couple of days ago."

He shrugged. "You still think I'm sexy."

"Where did you get the idea—"

"Uh-uh. You can't take it back. I heard you whisper it when we were in the sack—"

"Not so loud!"

He grinned broadly. "Shy?"

"I just don't need to be reminded. You're the lone-wolf type, O'Malley. Two seconds with you, and people know it."

"Lone-wolf type? What the hell's that? I like women."

"My point, exactly. Women. Plural."

He stared at her as if she'd just turned chartreuse.

"I don't want to fall for a guy like that," she told him.

"Hey. Lone-wolf. A guy like that. I think I'm being categorized here. You're not the only one who did some talking that night—"

"Yours was just of the moment. You were pretending to be what I wanted you to be."

He stared at her. "Stewart, where are you getting this stuff?"

But after his recent brush with death, Jess didn't want to get into an intimate, emotional talk with him. She didn't regret their night together, but she'd made the mistake of letting him know that she was attracted to him on a level that just wasn't smart. He'd responded in kind, but she knew better than to take what he'd said to heart.

No wonder he'd run off to Nova Scotia.

She squared her shoulders. "I followed you up here as a concerned colleague, nothing more."

"Uh-uh." He sounded totally disbelieving. "You didn't kiss me like a concerned colleague—"

"Well, you'd been shot at. I thought I could indulge you that once."

"It was a charity kiss?"

"Something like that."

He grinned at her. "Then I'll have to figure out a way to get another."

CHAPTER
THREE

O'MALLEY DRAGGED Jess out for dinner and a scenic drive through beautiful Lunenburg with its restored historic houses, narrow streets and picturesque waterfront, then on along the coast, past lighthouses and coves and cliffs. When they arrived back at the Wild Raspberry, Jess found a book in the library and settled on the front porch. She looked content, not so worried about him. O'Malley felt less jumpy, less as if he could—and should—run clear across Canada and not come up for air until he got to Vancouver.

Not that the dark-eyed Boston prosecutor on the front porch had a calming effect on him.

Suddenly agitated, he stormed down the steps and walked across the road to the water. The tide was going out, seagulls wheeling overhead, a cool breeze bringing with it the smell of the ocean. The sun had dipped low on the other side of the island, and dusk was coming slowly.

He spotted Marianne Wells sitting on a large boulder, her knees tucked up under her chin, her arms around her shins as she stared out at the Atlantic. Not wanting to disturb her solitude, he veered off in the other direction, heading down to a shallow tide pool forming amidst the wave-smoothed rocks as the water receded.

"Detective O'Malley?" Marianne jumped up off her boulder and trotted down to him, her agility on the rocky shore impressive. He paused, waiting for her to catch up to him. "I was wondering if I could talk to you about something."

"Sure. What's up?"

She didn't jump right in with what was on her mind, but nodded at the tide pool. "It's amazing—it never changes. I've come
out here every day since I got here. I had the house, friends—hope.
I'm one of the lucky ones."

"I understand you're a survivor of domestic abuse."

"My husband started out by isolating me from my family and
friends. He worked on my self-esteem, belittling me, telling me I
was ugly, stupid, going into rages when I made even the tiniest mistake—" She took a breath, but didn't look away from him. "He
didn't hit me at first. That came later."

"How long were you with him?"

"We met a year before we married. We were married for seven
years."

"No children?"

She shook her head. "That helped when it came to making a
clean break with my abuser. Visitation access often becomes another way for abusers to continue to control women. And children…what they see, their own lack of control…"

"It's a vicious cycle," O'Malley said.

"I gave up a lot when I decided to do something about my situation. There's no denying that I didn't. It's not just challenging
the violence that takes courage, but deciding to give up the status
quo and embrace an uncertain future."

"I've been to too many domestic-abuse crime scenes. Are you
worried this guy'll come back?"

"A tiny bit less with each day he doesn't. I'm prepared for that
fear to go on. I've found ways to live with it. I have a lot of support."

"You've done a good job with your place here."

She smiled, but without looking at him. "I didn't think I could
do it. I thought I'd fail. A part of me believed he was right about
me. But I got up each morning, and I did what I could. Then I
got up the next morning, and I did a little more. Bit by bit, it came
together."

"You deserve a lot of credit."

"Taking that first step was so scary and difficult. I was in the local library—I thought if I could go online and find some 'information, maybe it'd help." She crossed her arms on her chest, against the breeze. "I found the Shelternet Web site. It has a clickable map of Canada with links to local shelters, detailed information on how to make a safety plan, stories of other abused women. I sat there and read every word."

"How long before you went to a shelter?"

"A month. Abuse—it does things to your head."

"But you did it," O'Malley said.

She ran the toe of her sandal over a hunk of slimy seaweed. "My life was as big a wreck as this place was when I bought it. But I was living a violent-free life. That gave me such hope, such energy. It still does. I'm taking care of myself for the first time in a very long time. That matters."

"It matters a lot."

"I'd always dreamed of opening a bed-and-breakfast on the coast. I love it out here. I live in the guest house—it's perfect for me—and have the house for guests. That might change one day, or it might not. I'm just enjoying the moment. And I've done exactly what I want with the place." She let her arms fall to her sides. "I decided—I like pink. Raspberry, watermelon, orange-pink, petal pink. I didn't have to explain it to anyone or excuse it or pretend I liked chartreuse or rust when I like pink."

O'Malley smiled at her. "I'm not as big on pink as you are."

She laughed. "I appreciate your honesty. Anyway, I don't mean to bore you—"

"You're not boring me," he said sincerely.

She angled a look at him. "That's why you do police work, isn't it? Because you like people, you like to figure them out?"

"My father was a cop. I knew the work suited me."

"Jessica? She says she was a police officer, too."

"For a few years."

"Her father—"

"Investment banker. Very white bread. Her mother is a volunteer for a bunch of different charities. They almost had a heart attack when she got accepted to the police academy."

"But they supported her decision? They didn't try to stop her?"

"They were the proudest parents at her graduation."

"Good for them."

O'Malley knew Marianne hadn't joined him at the tide pool to chitchat. "Look—"

"I think someone's snooping on me," she blurted.

"What do you mean, snooping? Spying? Stalking you?"

She shook her head. "Nothing that overt. There've been these odd incidents." She took a breath, not going on.

"Like what?" he prodded.

She squatted down, dipping a hand into the cold water, her back to him. "I don't imagine things. I don't make things out to be worse than they are. The fears I have—they're real fears."

"You think your ex-husband is in the area?"

"Let's say I fear it."

But she didn't go on, seemed unable to. O'Malley walked around to the other side of the tide pool and squatted down, noticing that she had grabbed something from the bottom of the pool. "What do you have?"

"Starfish," she said, and smiled as she lifted it out of the water and showed it to him. "I used to love to collect things from tide pools when I was a little girl. I'd put everything back, of course. Once—once I forgot, and I was mortified for days."

A sensitive soul. "I understand."

Her eyes met his, just for an instant, and she replaced the starfish back in the water. "When I got up this morning, before you and Jessica arrived, I was positive someone had been through the Saratoga trunk in the living room during the night. It's an antique, from my great-grandmother."

"The living room's open to guests?"

She nodded. "But no one—it was just John Summers here last night. And he wouldn't be interested in the contents of an old trunk. He's a hiker. He goes out every day for hours. He pays me extra to load up his daypack with lunch and snacks."

"What's in the trunk?"

"Nothing of any value to anyone but me. Family photo albums

and scrapbooks of my life before I married." She spoke clearly, directly, without any hint of trying to hide something. "Some old books and diaries."

"Your diaries?"

"Oh, no. My great-grandmother's. She and my great-grandfather came to Nova Scotia from Scotland."

"Have you read her diary?"

"Bits and pieces. It feels like prying, frankly."

O'Malley shrugged. "That's half of what I do for a living. What made you think someone had been in the trunk? Was the latch open, something like that?"

"It was moved and—" She thought a moment as she got to her feet. "I'd draped a throw over it last night. It was on the couch this morning."

"Maybe Summers couldn't sleep and came downstairs to read for a while, get a change of scenery, and used the throw to keep his feet warm."

"It's possible." She smiled. "I like that theory."

"Any other incidents?"

"A few more like that."

"All with personal items?"

"Yes."

"Nothing that'd tempt you to call the police?"

"No, not yet. I just feel—I don't know how to describe it. Like somebody's looking for something, prying into my life, or if not my life, my family's past. It's a very strange feeling."

"Anything exciting about your family's past?"

She frowned at him. "What do you mean?"

"I don't know. Was one of your ancestors secretly married to the Prince of Wales or something?"

"Oh, no, no, nothing like that."

"But like something else?"

"Well—" She shook her head, laughing a little. "My great-grandmother lived in this area during a famous, tragic incident when a Halifax heiress ran off with a no-account foreign sailor. Irish, I think. Their boat went down in a storm just beyond the cove here."

"They were killed?"

"Drowned."

"Bodies recovered?"

Marianne nodded sadly. "There are rumors the heiress had taken gold coins and jewels with her, as a nest egg for her new life."

O'Malley watched her expression and, from long experience, knew there was more to the story. "No sign of them?"

"It depends on whom you believe."

Vague answer, but he didn't push.

"None of this is like my ex-husband. He's more the type to take a baseball bat to the kitchen because I left a coffee filter in the sink. But I haven't seen him in two years. I don't know—" She left it at that, then said abruptly, "I'll walk back to the house with you. Would you and Jessica care for some blueberry wine? It's made by a local winery. It's quite good."

O'Malley winked at her. "So long as it's not raspberry wine."

She laughed again, seeming more relaxed now that she'd told someone about her snooper. He wanted to know what she was holding back, but he doubted he'd get it out of her tonight. Marianne Wells was a direct, strong, self-contained woman, comfortable in her own skin. He wondered how much of that had been there before her husband went to work on her, and how much she'd had to get back, rediscover and build after she got him and his violence out of her life.

When they crossed the road, she paused at the base of the porch steps, then turned abruptly to him. "It's all too easy, isn't it?"

"What?"

"To hide yourself from the truth. I pretended for such a long time that I wasn't living the life I was living."

"Well, you know what they say."

"What's that?"

"Denial isn't just a river in Egypt."

"Oh, stop. Oh—oh, that is so lame!" She called up to the porch. "Jessica, your friend here is just *awful*."

Jess slid off her swing and stood at the top of the steps, the evening light catching the lighter streaks in her hair. O'Malley had tried to pretend she wasn't as beautiful as she was. Talk about hiding from the truth. She grinned at him and Marianne. "Is he telling you stupid jokes?"

"Close. Very lame pearls of wisdom."

Jess winced, still grinning. "That's our Detective O'Malley. He's got a saying for every occasion. His brothers are the same. They can reduce complicated issues and emotions to soundbites."

"Well," Marianne said cheerfully, "I guess it's a gift."

She trotted up the steps, a lightness in her gait that hadn't been there before, and went inside to fetch the blueberry wine.

O'Malley joined Jess on the porch. "Where's Summers?"

"He turned in early. What were you and Marianne talking about?"

"Violent men, snoops and treasure lost at sea."

"I hate the idea of violent men. Snoops can go either way. Treasure lost at sea—now, that could be fun."

"I'll tell you all about it. Speaking of snoops, how'd you like my apartment yesterday?"

"No vermin. That's something."

"No interior decorator, either." He moved in closer to her, smelling the scented soap she'd used in the shower. "It's a shame we're paying for two rooms."

"O'Malley—" She blew at a stray lock of hair that had dropped onto her forehead. "Damn."

"Hot all of a sudden, huh?"

"It's too late not to pay for both rooms…"

"We could do Marianne a big favor and pay for both rooms, but only actually use one. Save her on cleaning, anyway."

"You're just looking for distractions."

"It was your idea to come up here and become one."

But before she could respond, their hostess arrived on the porch with three glasses and an open bottle of blueberry wine.

Jess woke up very early and wandered outside to catch the sunrise, thinking of the rest of the continent still shrouded in darkness as the first morning rays skimmed the horizon and glowed orange on the ocean. Fishing boats puttered across the mirrorlike water, leaving a gentle wake, the quiet and stillness disturbed only by a few seagulls.

She'd never been anywhere more beautiful, and yet she couldn't relax.

It was O'Malley, of course. She'd dreamed about him.

Not good. An intelligent woman had no business dreaming about a Boston homicide detective with a penchant for getting himself shot at. Never mind all the other reasons. The tight-knit family where she would always be a stranger, the lone-wolf apartment that showed no sign of needing anyone to share it, the dedication to the job that bordered on obsession.

Then again, those could be the same reasons he was avoiding getting more involved with her. She thought of her own family, her own apartment, her own dedication to her job.

But she'd never been shot at, even during her five years on the police force.

She'd also never been more comfortable with anyone than she was with Brendan O'Malley.

Taking a deep breath, Jess pushed all thought of him out of her mind and focused on the sunrise as she walked down to the water's edge. It was just before low tide, which only added to the stillness, the sense of solitude and isolation.

When she returned to the Wild Raspberry, Marianne was up, humming as she worked in the kitchen. Jess called good morning, startling her. Marianne jumped, clutching her heart as she turned, recognized her guest, and collapsed against the counter. "I didn't realize you were up. Everything's all right? I'm fixing break-fast—"

"Everything's fine," Jess said. "Don't let me disturb you."

"It's no problem."

But Marianne's skin was pale—paler than it should have been. She must be used to guests getting up at different hours. Jess found herself lingering in the kitchen doorway. "Marianne? Are you okay? Is something wrong?"

John Summers appeared behind Jess in the hall. "What's going on?" he asked, immediately attuned to Marianne's tension.

"Nothing, I hope," Jess said. "I was out for a walk and startled Marianne when I came in."

Marianne turned quickly. "It happens sometimes," she mumbled, dismissing the subject as she busied herself pulling pots and frying pans out of a low cupboard.

Summers started to say something, then changed his mind and stalked out to the dining room. He sat at the smallest of three tables, snatched up a Halifax newspaper and held it up, a none-too-subtle way to cut off conversation. Jess didn't know if she'd annoyed him or he just wasn't a morning person.

She helped herself to a bowl of cut fruit—including raspberries—that Marianne had already put out on a sideboard. The breakfast room was as quirky and cheerful as the rest of the house, done in yellows and blues with raspberry accents. Summers's grumpiness was out of place.

Sitting at the farthest table from him, Jess decided to confront him. "Mr. Summers—"

He sighed audibly, folded his newspaper and set it on the table. "Something's wrong with Marianne. She's on edge. She wasn't like that when I first arrived."

Given Marianne's personal background and her talk of snoops and treasure with O'Malley, Jess was especially interested in Summers's observation. "How long has she been on edge?"

"A week or so." He eyed Jess a moment, as if she were responsible for their hostess's mood, then sighed again. "I'm sorry. I wanted to blame you and your cop friend, but she's been jumpy since before you two arrived."

Jess could understand his desire to blame her and O'Malley. A cop and a prosecutor could remind an abuse survivor of her past, dredge up fears and insecurities she thought she'd put behind her. It would make Marianne's uneasiness easier to explain. But it wasn't the case.

"You've been here a while," she said. "Any idea what's going on?"

Summers didn't answer at once, then lurched to his feet, muttering, "I hope it's not me."

Not one to let a comment like that go, Jess leaned back in her chair, chose a fat raspberry from the top of her fruit and watched Summers's stiff back as he grabbed a small glass bowl. "Why would it be you?" she asked.

He glanced over at her. "I've been here too long."

"Hiking?"

"I think of it as exploring."

He loaded up his bowl with fruit and took it out to the back porch without a word.

O'Malley came downstairs and sat across from Jess. He was showered and dressed, but he hadn't shaved, which didn't help her already supercharged reaction to him. The dark stubble on his jaw somehow made the scar forming on his forehead from the bullet graze stand out even more.

She pushed her bowl toward him. "Help yourself. I got too much."

"What's with Summers? Doesn't like to talk to people in the morning, or did you irritate him?"

"Perhaps both." But she told O'Malley about Marianne and Summers's reaction to her jumpiness, then added, "I wonder if something *is* going on around here. Do you think the ex-husband could be back? Abusers generally don't respect law and authority. And they don't like to give up. He could have got to thinking about her, found out what a success she's made of this place and decided to come back and resume control over her and her life."

"It's possible."

"But you don't think so." Jess sighed. "Neither do I."

"Maybe Summers and Marianne have a thing for each other and don't know what to do about it." His dark eyes lifted to Jess. "Sound familiar?"

"I don't have a *thing* for you, O'Malley."

"Uh-huh."

"Don't give me that dubious tone—and stop with the sexy twitch of the eyebrows."

"I had an itch."

"Ha."

"You just think everything I do is sexy."

It was true, but she wasn't about to tell him that. "We're friends. We let our friendship get out of hand. Insisting I'm falling for you is just another way for you to avoid dealing with the real issue."

"Which is what? That I almost got my head blown off the other day?"

She bit off a sigh. "Bravado, bravado, bravado."

"Yeah, yeah, yeah. Tell me more about Summers."

"He's tense, he's abrupt and he's more on edge than our hostess."

"Who is making up a hell of a breakfast this morning from the smell of it."

"Brendan—"

"I have no authority in Canada. Neither do you. If we have reason to suspect something's going on, we can call the local police, just like anyone else. That's it."

"You still think the guy's hiding something?"

"Yep." O'Malley held a raspberry up to one eye and examined it as if it were a diamond. "I think there's a worm in it."

"There is not—"

He popped it into his mouth and grinned at her. "Let's hope you're right. What do you want to do today? Go kayaking, or discuss my post-traumatic stress symptoms?"

"Both."

"Can't do both. What else?"

Jess lowered her voice. "I thought we might sneak up to the attic—"

"And search our fellow guest's room? You're going to get us arrested."

But she could tell he'd already thought of it, too. "Not if we're right and he's hiding something."

Summers returned from the porch in a moderately better mood, and Marianne set out an enormous breakfast of scrambled eggs, sausage, bacon, grilled tomatoes, corn muffins, streusel muffins and jam. Marianne's friend Pat, who also did the cleaning, had made the muffins. There was coffee, tea, juice and hot chocolate. Jess figured if she ate even a little of everything, she'd have to do a lot of kayaking to burn up the calories.

Hiking up the steep stairs to the attic wouldn't hurt, either.

When Summers retreated to his room after breakfast, O'Malley and Jess postponed checking out their fellow guest and instead went kayaking. Marianne provided all the equipment they needed—kayaks, paddles, life vests, emergency whistles, dry packs—and suggested several scenic routes that would take them anywhere from a couple hours to all day. O'Malley picked one that would have him in a restaurant, eating fresh scallops and drinking beer, by lunchtime.

After watching Jess drop her behind into the cockpit of her kayak and paddle two strokes, he forgot all about the scallops and beer and started looking for a secluded beach.

She seemed to sense his thoughts as they made their way along the shallow, rocky shoreline. "It's a romantic spot, isn't it?"

"Sure is."

"Is that why you picked it?"

"Jess, I came up here alone. I had lobster and scallops on my mind—a few days on my own, not romance."

She gave him one of her mysterious smiles. "I don't believe you."

"You think I had you in mind?"

But she stroked hard, pushing her boat ahead of him, and he cursed himself for being so obtuse. He held back, noticing the play of muscles in her arms and shoulders. She was strong. She worked hard, she was smart, she was dedicated.

He was all of those things, too. But that didn't make them right for each other.

After an hour paddling into the wind, they slid their kayaks onto a short stretch of beach and climbed out, sitting in the wet sand. Jess leaned back against her elbows. "This couldn't be any more perfect. What a day."

O'Malley gazed out at the sparkling water. "Pretty nice," he agreed.

She dug in her daypack and handed him a plastic bottle of water, then settled back into the sand with her own. She unscrewed the top, her eyes still on the view as she took a long drink, letting water drip down her chin and onto her T-shirt.

"Jess—hell, are you doing your best to torture me?"

She grinned at him. "This isn't my best. I can do a lot better."

"Try me."

Her eyes widened—she hadn't expected him to throw down the gauntlet—but she sat up straight. "Ah. A challenge. I'm an attorney, O'Malley. I love a good challenge."

He swallowed some of his own water. "You're stalling, buying yourself time while you try to think of something."

He'd barely finished his sentence when she was on top of him, straddling his lap, draping her arms over his shoulders, eye to eye with him. "There," she said. "I've thought of something. But we're exposed here. There's not much we can do without embarrassing ourselves."

"Kiss?"

"We could do that." She was a little breathless, and not just from kayaking. "But it might be worse than looking at wet spots on my T-shirt."

O'Malley decided not to let her off the hook. "Okay. Up to you. You're the one who loves a good challenge."

"You're just going to sit there, eh?"

"That's right."

She shifted on his lap. A provocative move. She leaned toward him and kissed him lightly on the mouth, then pulled back. He thought that would be it, which was a definite problem, but it wasn't. She kissed his nose, his forehead, then each cheek, until she found his mouth again, and this time, it was anything but a light kiss. He was trying to keep his hands off her, determinedly mashing them in the sand, just to amp up her sense of challenge, but it wasn't easy. His muscles were straining, his body responding to the play of her mouth on his, the touch of her fingers on his neck, in his hair.

Jess…

He didn't even know if he'd said her name out loud.

She broke off their kiss and tilted back from him. Her legs, he realized, were wrapped around his waist to anchor herself. "Oh, my." She took an exaggerated breath. "Wow. I did okay with that kiss, didn't I?"

"Jess—"

"I sort of like being bold like that. So much for the repressed New Englander."

O'Malley managed to clear his throat. "Jess—"

"I wonder if any fishermen saw us."

At that, he grabbed her by the hips, lifted her off him and sat her on the ground. He stood up and shook off the sand, resisting the temptation to howl at the ocean. Damn!

She smiled knowingly. "What, did you strain a muscle or something?"

"You're going to want to get your butt back in your kayak, because I'm not as puritanical as you are about who might see us making love on the beach."

"We could get arrested for public something-or-other." But she was scrambling for her kayak, grabbing her water bottle and dry pack. "You wouldn't want to get arrested in a foreign country."

He had her. She thought he'd do it. And it wasn't that he wouldn't take no for an answer. He would. But Jess wasn't so sure she could say no, that she wouldn't just take her chances and make love to him right there on a Canadian beach. For all they knew, a housing development was just over the knoll, or a group of bird-watching retirees was on its way there.

"You don't trust yourself to exercise good judgment in my presence," he said, amused.

She bent down to pick up her paddle, looking up at him, the sunlight catching those emerald eyes of hers. "You probably think making love on a beach is good judgment."

"Depends on the beach." He glanced around at the wet, fine sand, the protected horseshoe-shaped beach, the rise of sand and squat, gnarled evergreens that offered something of a screen to onlookers. Not that a passing boat wouldn't see everything. If the passengers were looking, of course. He shrugged. "This one seems fine."

But she wasn't taking any chances—with his power of persuasion or what the kiss had obviously done to her. She eased the kayak into the water and climbed in, shoving off with her paddle. "Coming?" she asked, looking back at him.

He grinned.

Then he wondered what her parents would do if he asked her to marry him. It popped into his mind as a joke, but it was like being sucker-punched.

Marry her.

His brother Mike had teased him on just that point for the past year, long before Brendan had ended up in bed with his dark-eyed prosecutor. He'd known Jess forever, it seemed. She'd always been there, frank, honest, idealistic, determined. Mike insisted she'd been half in love with Brendan for years.

"Fresh scallops," she said, as if she were snapping him out of a trance. "Iced tea. Fries. Coleslaw. Homemade pie. There has to be a place around here that serves homemade pie."

"Scallops aren't even a close second to sex."

She pretended not to hear him. Laughing, O'Malley shoved his kayak into the water and climbed in. Jess started paddling in steady, even strokes, and he noticed that her color was better. She didn't look as stressed out and overworked.

Must have been the bullet, him thinking about marrying her.

What he didn't want to do—never mind that Mike had vowed to flog him if he did—was to break Jess's heart.

CHAPTER
FOUR

SUMMERS HAD GONE somewhere, but now they had to wait for Pat to finish up in his room.

Jess had fresh doubts about the wisdom of what she and O'Malley were doing, but, on the other hand, she trusted his instincts—and her own. Something was up with their fellow guest and their spooked hostess. Jess didn't have the urgent negative reaction to Summers that O'Malley did, but she definitely had the feeling he wasn't telling the entire truth about his stay at the Wild Raspberry.

Marianne needed more to take to the police than a throw that was out of place and the suspicion that someone was snooping on her. She wouldn't want to tarnish the image of her B and B, or offend her guests by overreacting to an incident—even several incidents—that could have innocent explanations.

And focusing on Summers was easier than trying to figure out what she was going to do about Brendan O'Malley, Jess thought as she lingered in the second-floor hall.

He was right about her. She was falling for him.

She'd fallen for him a long time ago.

Refusing to admit she was in love with him was just a way of protecting herself. She didn't want to lose him as a friend. The thought of it made her sick to her stomach. He'd been a part of her life for ten years—why blow it now by telling him she was in love with him?

"Look at you," she whispered, "you're not even sweating."

He winked in that deliberately sexy way he had. "I'd have made a good criminal, don't you think?"

"Scary thought."

"Come on, you're a lawyer *and* an ex-cop. You've got nerves of steel."

She was surprised at how guilt-free and certain she was about what they intended to do. "If Marianne catches us, she'll probably throw us out."

O'Malley was unperturbed. "Then we take the ferry back to Maine together. Preferably the overnight ferry. Make a real night of it."

"O'Malley, do you ever think about anything except how to get me back into bed?"

"You bet. What to do when I've got you there." He pressed a finger to his lips and lowered his voice even more. "Here she comes."

They ducked to one side of a glass-fronted bookcase in the hall as Pat, a woman around Marianne's age, lumbered down the steep stairs with a lightweight vacuum cleaner and a canvas bag of cleaning supplies slung over her shoulder. She was high energy and good-humored—and obviously hard-working. Having already cleaned the second-floor rooms, she continued on down to the first floor without noticing Jess and O'Malley.

"I can go up by myself," O'Malley said. "You can stay down here and be the lookout."

Jess shook her head. "I'm not going to let you do this by yourself."

"Sweetheart, if I go down, you go down. You know the law. The guy driving the getaway car is just as culpable—"

"Quit arguing," she whispered, "and go."

Nothing about their escapade seemed to faze him. O'Malley was, without a doubt, Jess realized, a man who trusted his own judgment. He wasn't second-guessing himself now about his actions during the shooting because, fundamentally, he didn't question his instincts or his decisions that day.

So what about their night together? He was second-guessing himself all over the place about *that*.

He led the way up the stairs, which, unlike the stairs to the second floor, were carpeted. When they reached Summers's room, entry was no problem. O'Malley had "borrowed" the master key. If caught, he planned to explain himself to Marianne and ask for her indulgence. She'd probably let him off. Jess remembered Mike O'Malley telling her that his little brother Brendan had always been able to sweet-talk himself out of a tight spot.

Within thirty seconds, they were in Summers's room.

It smelled of cleaning products, and the streaks from the vacuum were still visible on the rug. The decor was quirky country cottage, but the colors were a bit more subdued than in her own room. The view of ocean and endless horizon through the floor-to-ceiling window needed no competition.

O'Malley immediately set to work, opening up the closet and rifling through their fellow guest's clothes. Keeping one eye on the door, Jess quickly checked the desk. She noticed a slim laptop computer, a stack of books on the history of Nova Scotia and a novel by an author named Alexander Crane.

"Well," Jess said, "nothing sensational in his reading habits."

"Hiking books?" O'Malley asked from the closet.

"Histories of Nova Scotia. Some of them look fairly old."

She opened the desk's center drawer and discovered a small basket of letters. Old letters, bundled together and tied with a grosgrain ribbon. Jess gingerly checked one of the dates.

August 1902.

"I think we're barking up the wrong tree, O'Malley."

He joined her at the desk. "Best we can do for loot is a stack of hundred-year-old letters?"

"They're not what you'd expect an avid hiker to have in his room," Jess said. "But this is an historic area. Maybe he's just interested in Nova Scotia's past."

O'Malley picked up the novel. "Even his reading material looks boring as hell."

"Alexander Crane—I've heard of him. He's a Canadian author. He's better known here than in the U.S., but he had a book a couple of years ago that was some kind of international bestseller. Remember?"

"No. Did you read it?"

Jess shook her head. "My mother's book club read it. They all liked it. He fictionalized some obscure but compelling Canadian historical event. I can't remember what it was."

"I guess it wasn't that compelling."

"No, it *was*." She tried to think. "I seem to remember it had a seafaring theme. It might have been about a Canadian ship that sank in the war. Something like that."

O'Malley frowned. "A ship sinking? You think that was it?"

"I'm not sure, but I know it had to do with the ocean. It might have been set on the west coast, though. I seem to remember something about Vancouver."

"Marianne told me something last night—" O'Malley broke off and flipped the book over, staring at the black-and-white photograph of the author. "I'll be damned. Look at this, Stewart. It's our guy."

"Summers?"

"Alexander Crane. Maybe it's a pseudonym and John Summers is his real name, but they're the same guy."

Jess looked at the photograph, and the resemblance was there, unmistakable if not striking. The man staying with them at the Wild Raspberry was the same man identified as Alexander Crane in the photograph on the back cover of his book.

O'Malley tapped the photo with one finger. "He's grown a beard, his hair's grayer and he's lost weight and dropped the pipe-and-tweed look for the middle-aged hiker—"

"But it's the same man," Jess said. "Why would he come here in disguise?"

"So he could research a tragedy and look for sunken treasure without drawing attention to himself."

Jess nodded. "It makes sense."

Leaving the room the way they found it, they took the Alexander Crane novel with them and headed back downstairs.

Marianne was setting out tea on the back porch, working quietly, obviously preoccupied. Jess hated having to tell her that one of her guests was, at best, staying there incognito. At worst, he was deliberately exploiting her and her friends for one of his books.

"Do you have a minute?" O'Malley asked softly.

Marianne didn't respond at first, then nodded, motioning to the wicker furniture. "Sit down, please."

Jess and O'Malley took side-by-side wicker chairs while Marianne sat on the very edge of a settee, her knees together, hands clasped in her lap as if she knew they were going to tell her something she didn't want to hear.

"How much do you know about John Summers?" Jess asked.

"Not much. He's been a good guest. Quiet. Friendly. Very intelligent."

O'Malley adopted the sensitive cop demeanor he used with traumatized witnesses. It was genuine, but he was also a professional. "How does he pay you?"

"Cash."

Jess said nothing, and neither did O'Malley as Marianne regarded both of them with fear and a measure of suspicion. "What is it?" she asked. "What's wrong?"

"Maybe nothing bad," O'Malley said. "We shouldn't jump to conclusions."

"He's not a friend of my ex-husband's. I'd know—" She took a shallow breath. "He'd never send a surrogate."

"Summers isn't who he says he is." O'Malley gave her the news about her guest in a straightforward manner, his tone gentle but not emotional.

"We're fairly certain that his real name is Alexander Crane," Jess added.

Marianne's eyes widened, not with fear or annoyance, but with tremendous relief and excitement, as if she were more than a little thrilled at the news. "Alexander Crane? You're kidding. Why, when John arrived here, my friends and I talked about how much he looks like Crane. We thought it was a coincidence. None of us looked into it. I mean, Alexander Crane is so well-known, and it just didn't occur to us—" She stopped a moment. "I never thought he'd lie about his identity."

"John, or Alexander Crane?" Jess asked.

Marianne understood what she meant. "I only know Crane by reputation. John—" Color rose in her cheeks, and she sat back, a touch of annoyance settling in. "Why would he lie? I don't understand. I would treat him like any other guest. I wouldn't care if he was a famous anything. He must know that by now, if he didn't at first."

O'Malley handed her the book, so that she could see the photo for herself. "Is Alexander Crane a pseudonym?" he asked.

"Not that I know of. No, I'm sure it's not."

"You never checked Crane's picture when you and your friends realized he resembled your guest?"

"No, of course not. I never for a second thought he and John really were one in the same, just that John resembled Alexander Crane." She rubbed the picture with two fingertips, as if she had to make sure it was real. Tears rose in her eyes. "I never—" She inhaled sharply. "Trust is a big issue with me. I don't like being lied to."

"He might have had valid reasons," Jess said quietly.

O'Malley shrugged. "I guess it's better to find a famous writer is hanging out in your attic than a bank robber."

"Or your abusive ex-husband," Marianne mumbled. "How could he let me think—"

She didn't finish, stumbling to her feet, shaken and upset, just as John Summers—aka Alexander Crane—walked out onto the porch. "Liar," she whispered, crying, and pushed past him.

He went white and glared at Jess and O'Malley.

But the glare didn't last. His shoulders sagged, and he shook his head, sighing. "I knew you were on to me. Did you search my room? I honestly don't blame you. I don't know why I just didn't tell you the truth. Or Marianne."

"Why the false identity?" O'Malley asked.

"Privacy. I'm researching a new book. It's a sensitive subject in this area. I thought it best…" He sank into a chair, looking miserable amidst the cheerful surroundings. "It seemed like a good idea at the time."

Jess could feel the guy's agony. "But you didn't expect to fall for Marianne."

He didn't raise his head. "Given her background, I don't see how she's going to understand."

"Don't sell her short, Mr. Crane," Jess said. "It could depend on your reasons."

O'Malley was obviously not that interested in the romantic undertones of what was going on. "What about the snooping?"

Crane raised his head, frowning. "What snooping? I've conducted all my research off the premises. Marianne... I suspect she has information I could use, but I was waiting for the right moment to tell her who I am and ask her indulgence. No, not waiting," he amended. "Postponing. I didn't want to face her sense of betrayal."

"You two have spent a lot of time together over the past month," Jess said. "You must have told her something about yourself."

"The surface stuff was all lies, but my thoughts and feelings—what matters most to me —" He broke off, exhaling loudly. "Damn it. I've blown it completely."

"Maybe you should talk to her," Jess suggested.

O'Malley got up, his cop radar obviously still pinging madly. "She thinks someone's gone through an old trunk of hers."

"That wasn't me! My God—you mean she thinks I've been sneaking around her house? I had no idea anything of the sort was going on. I knew she was upset about something, but it never occurred to me—" He seemed genuinely distraught. "I wish she'd told me about the snooping. I'd have told her the truth about me immediately."

"Then you didn't step over the line to research your book?" O'Malley asked.

"No. Absolutely not."

"What's it about?"

"I'd rather not say."

"You don't have to. I have a pretty good idea. An heiress and her Irish sailor boyfriend drowned just beyond the cove. Local legend says she had jewels and gold coins—"

"I'm not interested in treasure," Crane protested.

"Maybe not, but you're interested in their story. If Marianne decides to go to the police—"

"The police? For what? Operating under a false identity for research purposes may be a question of trust, but it's not that serious." He stopped, glancing from O'Malley to Jess and back again. "Tell me more about Marianne's suspicions."

"The contents of the trunk in the living room are from the early twentieth century," O'Malley told him. "Marianne's great-grandparents lived in this area. She says someone's been into the trunk." He regarded Crane a moment, then went on. "The letters in your room are from that same era."

"But I—" The writer seemed truly repentant, but also very unwilling to discuss his work. "I was waiting to ask her for information on her family's past. Her great-grandmother and Pat's great-grandmother were best friends when the *Osprey*—that's the name of the ill-fated boat with the supposed treasure—went down. Pat's great-grandmother lived here, in this house. Marianne's great-grandmother lived in the village."

Jess thought she could put the pieces together now. "So that's why you picked the Wild Raspberry. It wasn't just because it was in the area and had a room. It's because the women who own and operate it are descendants of characters in your book."

"It's not a book yet," he said, his voice barely audible. "So far it's just notes. The story's a mix of fact, fiction, myth and speculation. I'm not convinced the so-called treasure ever existed. I just wanted to get a feel for the area, the land, the air, the people."

"The treasure exists," Marianne said from the doorway, calmer now.

Crane surged to his feet, his anguish obvious. "Marianne, I'm sorry I didn't tell you the truth sooner—"

"You haven't told me the truth yet, Mr. Crane. I only know it from Mr. O'Malley and Ms. Stewart."

"I wanted to tell you. I must have started to a hundred times, but I knew that once I told you, I'd have to leave. And I didn't want to."

"Because of your book," she said stiffly.

"No. I'll burn every word I've written tonight if it'll help restore your trust in me."

O'Malley cleared his throat. "So about this treasure…"

Marianne smiled at him. "It's buried in the backyard."

Crane was stunned. "What?"

O'Malley turned to Jess and grinned. "I've never done buried treasure, have you?"

She hadn't.

"After I realized someone had been snooping around," Marianne went on, "I got out one of my great-grandmother's diaries and started reading it. There's a passage about the *Osprey*. Several passages, actually." She paused, pouring tea into a Beatrix Potter mug and staring at it, as if somehow it could help her to explain. "She and her friend Yvonne, Pat's great-grandmother, found the jewels and coins and buried them."

"Why?" O'Malley asked.

Crane didn't say a word. He was listening with intense interest, even fascination, as if all his research was making sense now as Marianne spoke about two long-dead friends.

"I think it was fear and a sense of romance that made them do what they did," she surmised. "They were ordinary women— they weren't heiresses. They were afraid they'd be accused of stealing or, worse, of having caused the *Osprey* to sink."

Jess tried to imagine two teenage girls from that era coping with such a tragedy so close to home. "And the romance? Where did that come in?"

"They didn't believe anyone should profit from such a tragedy," Marianne said with a touch of pride. "And they didn't want to give the jewels and coins back to the family. They blamed the family for what happened."

Crane shifted in his chair, some of his guilt and misery lifting. "The family was dead-set against the marriage, and not just the woman's parents. Her uncles and aunts, her grandparents, her older brothers and sisters—they all ganged up on her."

"So the girlfriends here in the sticks didn't want them getting back the loot," O'Malley said, and Jess knew he was trying to cut through some of the emotion in the room.

Marianne nodded. "If they'd tried to sell any of it themselves and were caught, they'd be rightly accused of stealing. It washed up on shore across the street from here, near the tide pool where you and I talked last night."

"Fate," Jess said. "What an amazing story."

O'Malley wasn't finished with it. "You said the treasure's buried in the backyard. Does that mean you know where?"

"It means I dug it up." Her eyes sparkled, and she let out a breath. "I can't tell you how relieved I am that my ex-husband hadn't somehow figured out that I might have buried treasure on the premises. I dug it up last night to check it was still there and reburied it immediately. It's under an old-fashioned pink rosebush that Pat's great-grandmother and my great-grandmother planted together to mark the spot. They're both still there—the rosebush and the treasure."

"Your friend Pat," Jess said. "Does she know?"

"No, I don't think so. I haven't said anything to her." Marianne dropped onto a chair, almost spilling her tea. "Oh. Oh, dear. Pat. She must have known our great-grandmothers' secret."

Jess exchanged a glance with O'Malley. "Pat cleans Mr. Crane's room," she said. "She could have figured out why he was here and been afraid he'd accuse your great-grandmothers of stealing the treasure."

"Poor Pat!" Marianne sighed. "She must have guessed there was something in the old photo albums and diaries in my trunk."

"Any indication she got to the rosebush before you did?" O'Malley asked.

Marianne shook her head. "I'm sure she just wanted to make certain there was nothing incriminating in the trunk. She must have been reading bits and pieces of the diaries at a time, when she could get to it. I have to find her and reassure her. I want her to read the diaries! There's so much about both our great-grand-mothers in it. It's inspiring."

Crane got to his feet, his earlier melancholy gone. He cleared his throat. "Marianne, if you'll allow me, I'd like to join you—as a friend—when you talk to Pat. The book I'm writing—" He smiled tenderly at her. "There'll be other books."

"Mr. Crane—"

"Alex."

She smiled then, her earlier tension and fear having disappeared, and set her tea down as she rose. "Thank you. I'm sure together we can convince her she has nothing to fear."

After Marianne and Crane headed out, O'Malley got up and dumped his tea over the porch rail into the grass. "What do you think was in it?"

"Tea leaves," Jess said.

"Nah. Something else. Tasted like someone put out a cigarette in it."

"It's Earl Grey tea, O'Malley."

He grinned at her. "I knew that."

"I know you did," she said. "You're just being obtuse on purpose."

"Had to break the spell before you got teary-eyed."

"Think Crane and Marianne are—"

"They're destined for each other," he said, finishing her thought. "It's like the muses drove the two of us here just to bring them together."

"Maybe so," Jess said. "What about us?"

"We didn't need the muses to drive us together, Stewart. We needed them to give us a swift kick."

"O'Malley—"

"I've been in love with you a long time, Jess. A long time."

"Me, too…with you. I just—" She quickly picked up the tea dishes, not knowing what else to do with herself. "I'm used to having you in my life, you know. As a friend."

"You're doing a pretty good job of getting used to me in your life as a lover."

She felt a rush of heat, then laughed. "I am, huh?"

He grinned at her. "I'd say so."

"I've been afraid of losing you altogether if the lover part didn't work out."

"I know."

"But friend *and* lover. That's the best of both worlds. I like that a lot. What about you?"

"Jess—damn. You've been in my life for ten years. I want you there for a hundred years. Hell, I want us to be together forever."

She believed him—he'd never been anything but straight with her. "What about the hockey sticks and the weights rolling around on the floor? And the way you've been living your life?"

"Ask the same questions about yourself."

She couldn't hold on to the tea dishes anymore and set them back on the table. "I'd say that I'm ready to make changes."

"So am I." He slipped his arms around her and kissed her, lingering close to her mouth, smiling. "I enjoy the hell out of kissing you."

"Your brothers—"

"Will be ecstatic. They like you. They think a lawyer in the family's just what we need. We've got everything else covered."

She smiled, feeling safe and warm and more content than she could ever remember. "They've been teaching me hockey on the sly so I'd know what to do with you."

He winked. "You know what to do with me."

"I have a mean slapshot."

"I can do a wicked body check."

She suddenly caught her breath. "I wonder how long Marianne and Crane will be gone."

"Not long enough." O'Malley pointed to the window, where their hostess, the author and Pat were making their way into the backyard. "The muses are having their fun with us now. It'd be rude to carry you upstairs when there's buried treasure to be dug up."

They decided to join Marianne, Pat and Alex Crane out at the rosebush. As she pulled herself together, Jess noticed the Shelternet sign again.

The courage to click.

Marianne Wells's new life—with all its challenges and rewards—had started with that first positive step of going to www.shelternet.ca and finding the help she deserved.

She was an inspiration, Jess thought. No question about it. Last night, after the blueberry wine, Marianne had shown her and O'Malley the Shelternet Web site. It had put Marianne in touch with a local shelter, just as it did thousands of women all across Canada. The site combined compassion and technology and provided a safe, anonymous environment for women to take those first scary, tentative steps into living a violence-free life.

As in the U.S., the Canadian statistics on domestic abuse were shocking. Each year, more than a hundred thousand Canadian children witnessed the abuse of their mothers. Worldwide, violence caused more deaths and ill health of women between the ages of fifteen and forty-four than malaria, traffic accidents and cancer combined.

Jess, who prosecuted such cases, welcomed the reminder of the positive message that Shelternet offered to abused women and their children.

The courage to click.

It was a beginning.

"Jess?"

She realized she'd been lost in thought and smiled at O'Malley. He was a strong, intense man in a sometimes violent profession, and he loved to banter and tease and play hard—but he respected her.

And he loved her.

"I'm fine," she said. "More than fine."

He smiled. "Me, too."

QUILTS FROM CARING HANDS
JUNE NIELSEN

June Nielsen wanted to reach out to children in crisis and wrap them in love, take away their pain and let them know there was someone who cared. That dream turned into a very tangible gift for her community—quilts. Now, as founder of Quilts from Caring Hands, June is wrapping an entire community in her love and compassion. Since its inception in 1990, Quilts from Caring Hands has made and donated over 3,200 quilts to more than a dozen social service agencies serving children in crisis in Oregon's Willamette Valley area.

Quilts from Caring Hands all began when June's two children were away in high school. June was part of a small quilting circle at the time. She had always sewn—from projects as a Girl Scout to making her own clothes in school, and came to quilting in 1970 when she and her husband were living in Wyoming. Pregnant with her son, June decided to try making a quilt, learning the craft through trial and error.

In 1989 June read an article about children born with AIDS and was deeply touched. "I couldn't cure AIDS or be a foster mother to a lot of kids," she realized. "I could, however, share a bit of TLC with them. Give them a quilt and let them know people care about them." Through local community groups and social services, June found there were many children-at-risk who could be helped—pediatric AIDS patients, the homeless, those in foster care, abused or emotionally ill children, infants of teenage moms and the visually impaired.

One of the women in her quilting circle was setting up a quilting shop and offered June space at the back of the store to work on the project. Four women with no money, no fabric—just an idea, and agencies who wanted quilts. "We began with the philosophy that we would make as many quilts as we could with the supplies and willing hands that came our way," June recalls. The fabrics were donated bit by bit, a few yards here, some batting there. They were literally making quilts out of whatever they could find.

Women coming into the quilting store heard all the noise and chatter in the back and, drawn by curiosity, came into the fold. By the end of the first year, the group had grown to fifteen women, and one hundred quilts had been made. Today the group numbers forty-five women, and they've expanded into a larger space in a local church. In the past few years, Quilts from Caring Hands has made and donated an average of three hundred quilts a year.

The women in the group range in age from forty to ninety. June describes the women as "energetic, interesting and vital." Some women who've joined have never sewn a thing, but June sincerely believes everyone has something to offer the group, and she encourages them to go as far as they wish in helping. June has been described as a master at encouraging others to stretch out and try something a bit more challenging than they thought they could.

The quilting circle itself is a very important part of Quilts from Caring Hands. Lots of sharing goes on in that circle—sharing of information about the community and about the craft of quilting…and a deeper level of sharing happens, too. Eyes focused on the work means less eye contact, and that makes it easier for the women to open up and confide in the group. That deep bond of friendship and support reaches out well beyond the regular Wednesday meetings.

The love, time and skill that go into making the quilts translate into love and caring for the recipients. June hears all the time from people in social service groups about how much the quilts mean. Many of these children have nothing at all—and they've never had something brand-new of their very own, something made just for them that will always be theirs. The children of women in crisis seem to find strength in being wrapped in a quilt, and find the courage to talk about what has happened to them. One victim of domestic violence received a purple quilt for her daughter. Purple was her daughter's favorite color—and the mother knew, in that moment, that everything would work out.

June gets so many words of gratitude from social agency workers, telling her that there's something indescribably comforting in quilts. It makes the stay in these social service facilities more comfortable for children. The quilts are for the children to keep, and become a symbol of their strength, of all they've survived. One front-line worker expressed to June how a child, wrapped in her very own quilt, is wrapped, too, in a work of art that means hope and peace. It's beauty where there has only been pain and loneliness.

June says she's motivated to continue her work by the idea that you never know what one event will turn a child around. Maybe it will be the fact that one person who didn't even know the child *cared*. And she's inspired by the women who bring their time and passion to Quilts from Caring Hands. "I'm just in awe of the women in the group," June says. "How they've immediately caught the spirit of what this is all about." She is overwhelmed at the way the group has grown, how doors have opened and little things have led to where they are today.

And as for her own work with Quilts from Caring Hands, June says, "My life is pretty ordinary. Being so blessed, I feel the need to give back. Volunteering gives me the opportunity to give back to the community…a way to say thanks."

June's life is far from ordinary. Her compassion for others and her heartfelt commitment to Quilts from Caring Hands is extraordinary…and an inspiration.

More Than Words

EMILIE RICHARDS

HANGING
BY A THREAD

EMILIE RICHARDS

With her background as a relationship counselor, and a thirty-four year marriage to her college sweetheart, Michael, it's no wonder Arlington, Virginia, author Emilie Richards consistently delivers richly textured family dramas that explore the human condition and earn high praise from readers and reviewers. Emilie began writing in 1983 after the birth of her fourth child. Now the award-winning author of more than fifty novels, she has appeared on national television and been quoted in Reader's Digest, right between Oprah and Thomas Jefferson.

CHAPTER
ONE

TRACY WAGNER pretended not to notice the baby girl in the pink striped coverall who was crawling determinedly in her direction. Little Liza Thaeler seemed to think that "Aunt" Tracy was the top pick in any room, the woman most likely to bounce a baby on her knee or play interminable games of peekaboo.

Tracy could only hope that as Liza grew, her instincts about people improved.

Janet Thaeler intercepted her daughter before she could reach Tracy, then immediately held her away. "Phew! Give me a break!"

"Don't look at me," Tracy said, although Janet never would have. She knew Tracy was not a baby person. Janet understood Tracy better than almost anyone in the world, except, of course, Graham, Tracy's husband. And even that was up for grabs sometimes.

"When was the last time you changed a diaper?" Janet checked to be sure her olfactory senses were working correctly. She screwed up her face at the evidence.

"Let me think." Tracy rested one sensibly manicured finger against her cheek. "I think it was the day I left home for college. By the time I went back the next summer, Mom had finally declared a childbearing moratorium, and my youngest sister was wearing ruffled training pants."

"Sometimes I'm surprised you even speak to me. I'm recreating your childhood." Janet abandoned the room with a giggling Liza tucked under one arm.

While she waited for her friend to return, Tracy gazed around. Janet was right. Tracy had grown up in a house like this one, if a shade more rustic. Toys piled in every corner. Building blocks and stuffed animals strewn across the floor. Strollers in the hallway, high chairs pushed against the dining-room table, shouts and squeals and demands rending the air.

Janet had four children and another—the last, she swore—due next spring. She claimed she was so used to being pregnant that morning sickness felt normal, and a visible belly button seemed grossly obscene.

Tracy was the oldest girl in a family of eight. She had grown up in Washington's Wenatchee Valley, the daughter of hardworking apple growers. Even now if she looked in the mirror, a farmer's daughter smiled back at her. A healthy round face with pink cheeks and clear blue eyes. Glossy dark hair that was bluntly cut to her collar. A little too plump, a lot too ordinary and much too busy to be worried about any of it.

Her role in the family had been clear as soon as she was old enough to hold a bottle. Tracy was in charge of the babies when her mother was called on to do other things, which was much of the time.

The family was a happy one, and her parents had been as fair as time allowed. But Tracy had gotten her fill of babies by the time she escaped to Oregon State. She loved her brothers and sisters, particularly now that they were more or less grown. But if she never opened a jar of baby food, washed a load of receiving blankets, or walked the floor with a feverish infant, it would be too soon.

Janet returned with a giggling, sweet-smelling Liza. "Thank heaven for Molly." She plunked Liza in the corner with a stack of blocks. "If she weren't here, we wouldn't be able to finish a sentence."

Tracy wasn't sure how many they'd finished anyway. "Molly Baker? The girl across the way?"

"I started paying her to come over every afternoon to play with the kids and keep them out of my hair for a while. They're wreaking havoc in the playroom right now. She's so good with them. She's a gem."

Janet's expression didn't match her enthusiastic words. An ebullient blonde, pixie-ish, freckled, Janet was almost always smiling. She wasn't smiling now.

"Some problem?" Tracy probed. "Don't tell me you're feeling guilty because you need a little help."

"Good grief, no." Janet frowned at her, as if Tracy had lost her mind. "I'm an earth mother, not a martyr. No, it's Molly I'm worried about. You know she's a foster child?"

Tracy knew that Molly had lived with the people across the street for most of a year. She was a quiet, self-contained teenager or preteen, Tracy wasn't quite sure which. She was a pretty girl, brown-haired, dark-eyed and slender, and showed the promise of greater beauty to come. During their few conversations, Tracy had been impressed with her manners and a little worried about the caution in her eyes. Molly seemed to weigh every word, as if she needed to be certain Tracy got exactly the right impression.

"What's the problem?" Tracy asked. "Some issue with the courts?"

"No. The Hansens are moving to Europe for a year, possibly longer. He's taking over his company office in Paris—or something like that." Janet lowered her voice. "They can't take Molly, or they won't. But I do know she's free for adoption, and for whatever reason, they've decided not to pursue it. So in three weeks, she'll have to move. And there aren't any foster homes available in this school district. At least not at the moment, and not one for a fourteen-year-old girl. And she's been at the same middle school since sixth grade."

Tracy tried to make sense of this. "So what happens to her?"

"The social worker's talking about placing her in a group home. In a different school district. From what I can tell, the other kids are there because they've had problems in traditional care. Molly's never caused anyone a problem."

"The foster parents told you all this?" Tracy was pretty sure that Molly hadn't confided these details. It was contrary to everything Tracy knew about her.

Janet inspected a fleck of lint. "A neighbor told me the family was moving without Molly. I called social services and talked to her social worker."

Tracy was surprised the agency would have confided so much in a phone call. Then her eyes narrowed. "You didn't call for information, did you? You called to volunteer to *take* Molly."

Her friend looked faintly chagrined. "She's such a great kid, Trace. And here we are, right down the street from her school."

"And?"

"The social worker visited. We have too many kids, and too few bedrooms. And with the new baby coming in the spring…" She shook her head. "I'm afraid she's right, as much as I hate to say it. At Molly's age, she shouldn't be sharing a bedroom with preschoolers, or competing for our attention with so many little children."

Tracy fell silent, mulling over this sad turn of events.

Molly chose that moment to appear in the doorway. She had a blond Thaeler girl on one hip and an even blonder boy in the crook of her arm. She was wearing faded jeans and a gold sweatshirt that was at least three sizes too large.

"We finished our third game of Chutes and Ladders," she told Janet. "Alex is still building a city out of Lego in the playroom. I have to get going. I have to practice saying the prologue to the Canterbury Tales in Middle English for extra credit."

"Still?" Tracy was surprised. "They still make you do that?"

Molly didn't exactly smile, but her expression lightened a little. "I chose it. We'll study it next year, and I kind of like it. It sounds so pretty."

"Whan that Aprill with his shoures soote, the droghte of March hath perced to the roote…" Tracy quoted.

"You remember that?" Molly sounded surprised.

"That's about it. And, hey, I'm not *that* old. I remember liking it, too. Maybe you can recite it for me once you have it all learned."

The girl tossed back a lock of her shoulder-length hair and looked appropriately embarrassed. "I'd better go."

The Thaeler kids began to chatter at the same time. Janet got up and took the girl in Molly's arms, soothed the boy, who was trying to tell her how he'd beaten Molly at their game, and simultaneously handed Molly some cash from her pocket.

"Can you come tomorrow?" she asked when there was a lull.

"Yes, but, Mrs. Thaeler, I won't be coming much longer. I'm going to be moving."

"I heard," Janet said, trying to shush her son for a moment. "I'm so sorry, Molly. We'll miss you very much. I hope you'll be close enough that we can still see you once in a while."

Molly didn't respond.

The children waved goodbye, and Molly did, too. Then she was gone.

Tracy thought back to her own middle-school years with a pang. The sense of never really belonging, the fear of being different, the spats with friends and the painful sputtering romances that never ended happily. She remembered a girl who had moved to her school, and the pleasure some of the other kids had taken in making her feel even more like an outsider.

Most of all she remembered that her own parents had guided her through the worst of times with wisdom and love. Who would guide Molly?

"Moving is going to be one huge disaster for her," Tracy said. The children had taken that one moment to fall silent, and her words, though softly spoken, rang in the narrow room.

"I'm afraid you're right," Janet said. "I hate it, but there's not a darned thing I can do about it."

Tracy and Graham's penthouse condominium in northwest Corvallis had walls of windows that overlooked the Cascades and Three Sisters, polished oak floors with expensive Oriental carpets, granite countertops and the chic, uncluttered appearance of a model home. When Tracy let herself in after her visit with Janet, the silence was both blessed and disturbing. Blessed because there were no shrieking children here. Disturbing because there was no one at all to greet her.

Graham wasn't home from his job as the vice president of a financial planning firm. He was often out in the evenings, visiting clients whose days were as busy as his. Tracy was often gone in the evenings, too. She was an interior designer who worked exclusively with a popular local developer. She consulted on the basics of his designs and dealt directly with his clients, helping them choose fixtures and draperies, floors and floor coverings. Tonight, the only reason she was home before six was that both her late-afternoon and early-evening appointments had canceled, giving her time to stop by Janet's.

She didn't kick off her shoes or throw her suit jacket on the back of the sofa. She was tempted, though. The condo would look more lived in if she did, and this evening the pristine beauty of the rooms was oddly unappealing.

She had spent a lot of time decorating their home. She had chosen just the right pieces for display, sculptures and pottery from local Oregon craftspeople, handwoven wall hangings and Indian ceremonial masks, carved candlesticks with hand-dipped candles.

Of course, Graham had provided the most important touches. He was an extraordinary woodworker. He had designed and crafted their dining-room table and chairs of natural cherry. The coffee table was bird's-eye maple, and the end tables beside their sofa—dotted with needlepoint pillows she had discovered on a shopping trip in Portland—were constructed from portions of a mahogany staircase he had salvaged with the help of a local wrecking crew.

Most of the furniture had been finished before they met, when he had dreams of opening his own custom cabinetry and furniture shop. They were display pieces, meant to entice new clients. After their marriage, Graham's dream had gently drifted away, and reality had intruded. Tracy, too, had stopped imagining new and fresher possibilities and settled for maintaining a comfortable lifestyle.

Neither of them despised their jobs. Both of them liked the financial rewards. When they could eke out the time, they had the money to travel anywhere they wanted to go. They drank excellent wines, ate at the best restaurants, gave each other extravagant gifts.

They were lucky. Tracy knew that. Nevertheless, tonight she wasn't feeling lucky. She was feeling lonely, out-of-sorts, unhappy with a world that would take a nice kid like Molly and throw her to the four winds. And there was nobody here to share that with. By the time Graham got home, she would probably be asleep.

She thought about calling her mother, but she didn't want to upset her with the vision of a homeless child. She considered calling one of her sisters, but wasn't sure which one would understand. None of them would ever meet Molly or have a stake in what happened to her.

She wandered into the master bedroom, which was dominated by a king-size bed with no headboard. For the ten years of their marriage, Graham had promised to build one from leftover mahogany but never found the time. She had solved the decorating dilemma by hanging a contemporary quilt of red, black and silver strips behind it and piling the bed with pillows of coordinating fabrics. The room seemed stark and empty anyhow, so she tossed her clothes on the bed as she undressed, just to liven it up.

As she was pulling on sweats, she heard the front door open. She slipped into sneakers and went to check. Graham was hanging up his all-weather coat in the hall closet.

"You're home so early."

He whirled, surprised. "Jeez, Tracy. You startled me. What are you doing here?"

"I live here. Remember?"

He laughed and walked over to her for a hug. "Well, I thought you did. At least I've seen your name on the mailbox and mortgage."

She sank into his welcoming arms. He smelled like the crisp fall air and she laid her head against his shoulder.

Sometimes she was overwhelmed by the knowledge that this man was hers. Graham Wagner had come into her life during her final year at Oregon State. He was broad-shouldered and lithe, with light brown hair and smoky green eyes. His smile could warm the coldest winter night; his generous heart was even warmer.

Sometimes she still wondered why a man with his background had fallen in love with a simple farmer's daughter. His parents were professors, his family as historic as the Oregon Trail. He had grown up a quiet only child in a household devoted to study and debate. The antics of her large, raucous family were as foreign to Graham as picking apples.

She stepped out of his arms after a moment. "Are you home for good? Or did you just stop by on the way to an appointment?"

"I had an appointment. I canceled."

Immediately she was worried. "You're sick. It's that virus that's going around."

"Nope." He loosened his tie, a conservative gray with a thin green stripe that went with the image, if not precisely the man. "I was just tired of being gone every evening. I need a night here with my feet up." He paused. "You're a huge bonus, you know that? And from the way you're dressed, you're not going back out. Right?"

"Right." She rested fingertips on his shoulders. "You're sure you're okay?"

He paused a moment. "Just tired. Really."

She sensed something else but knew better than to push. "Let's see what we have for dinner."

"I could take you out," he offered, although he didn't look enthused.

"No. You need to stay home. Besides, it sounds better. Let's see what we have."

He joined her in the kitchen after he'd changed into khakis and a polo shirt. Together they prepared a meal of jarred marinara sauce over linguine and canned green beans. She set slices of frozen cheesecake on the counter to thaw.

They sat in the cozy breakfast nook, and Graham poured wine from a newly opened bottle. "To being together for a change," he said as a toast.

Tracy tried to remember exactly how long it had been since they had eaten a meal together at home. She rarely needed to shop. She kept emergency supplies on hand, like those they were eating, but she couldn't remember the last time they'd had anything fresh to prepare or any reason to prepare it.

"Two weeks?" she said out loud. "Since we ate together here?"

"Something like that."

"We'd better be careful. Dining in could get to be a habit, although I'd like some mushrooms or peppers to put in the sauce."

"That would be a commitment." He smiled.

"I might be up to a mushroom commitment." She smiled, too, and asked him about his day.

His recital was short, and when it was her turn, she considered whether to tell him about her visit to Janet's. But Graham was too perceptive not to notice her hesitation.

"What's going on, Trace?" He sat back, most of his linguine untouched. She could hardly blame him.

She pushed a few green beans around her plate with a fork. "I went to Janet's today."

"And now you have a migraine."

She laughed a little. "That would be more likely than a sudden yearning to have a litter of tiny Wagners."

"Noisy and chaotic, huh?" He picked up his wineglass. At least the wine had flavor.

The two of them had agreed early in their marriage to delay the question of having children. Graham had had no experience with babies, and she'd had too much. Over the years he had shown no more desire to add one to their lives than she had. The issue had been sidelined indefinitely.

"Absolutely chaotic." She told him about Molly, finishing with a little grimace. "I'm not sure why it's bothering me so much, but it is. I know there are a lot of children out there who get shoved from pillar to post through no fault of their own. I just haven't seen it up close before. The way she looks at me when I talk to her, Graham... It's like she's trying to read what I want her to say. She must have picked that up along the way."

"Maybe that's how she survived the system. She figures out what people need, then she gives it to them. And in return they don't make her life any worse than it already is."

"I can't figure out why her foster parents don't want to adopt her. They could take her to France if they did."

He shrugged. "Maybe they just don't think it matters that much."

"Of course it matters!"

He stared at her.

"I'm sorry." She chased some more green beans with her fork. Her stomach was too knotted to eat them.

Graham sounded as if he were struggling to be patient. "I didn't say it *didn't* matter. I said maybe that's the way the foster parents think."

"It's just pretty screwed up, wouldn't you say? What chance will this kid have now? They're leaving her behind. She has to move to a group home and live with kids who can't get along in regular foster care. She has to change schools. And the social worker won't even let Janet take her."

"Does Janet really want her?"

Tracy considered, then shook her head. "No. She's overwhelmed. She wants to help Molly, but I suspect it was a relief when the agency said no."

"The social worker probably sensed her ambivalence and factored it in."

"I'm sorry," Tracy said. "This isn't your problem. It's not our problem. I shouldn't have brought it up."

He swirled the wine in his glass. "Why not?"

"Because this is our first night home together in ages."

"And the first time in a long time we've talked about anything really important."

She set her fork down. "You sound unhappy."

He reached over and took her hand. "I think I miss you. We're so busy all the time. It's just nice to be here talking to you, hearing you talk about something that matters. Feeling like it matters to me, too."

"Does it matter to you?"

"I like kids. I used to be one. I remember what it was like."

"I wish we could do something."

He waited. When she didn't say more, he cocked his head. "Trace?"

"Well, I'm not sure, but I think we're in the same school district as Janet. She's only a mile away."

"And?"

"Well, all they need is a *temporary* place for Molly to live until a real foster home opens up. I don't really need a study. I could move my desk into the bedroom. We could move in a dresser from our room, buy a twin bed. A daybed would be nice in there, anyway, even when it goes back to being my study. It wouldn't take much work to fix it up a little so she'd feel at home."

"We're never here. You want this girl to take care of herself?"

Tracy thought about that. "I could limit my evening appointments to two nights a week. Maybe even one. You could cover one night, couldn't you? You say you're tired. It would guarantee you a night at home. Maybe your clients could come here if you had to see them."

Graham was silent a moment. She watched his thoughts parade across his face. She was more than surprised he hadn't just said no outright, that it was impractical, not like her at all, a complete intrusion on two lives that were too busy already.

Then he squeezed her hand and dropped it. "Call the social worker. See what she says. We'll talk some more when you find out."

Panic filled her. It had only been an idea. "You're serious?"

"It would be nice to do something for this kid." He stood. "I'll clean off the table."

No matter what she learned from the social worker, she was suddenly, powerfully certain that she had married the best—not to mention the most attractive—man in the world.

"There's not much to clean." She stood, too. "But our room's a different story. I threw my stuff all over the bed when I got home. Did you notice?"

"I did. I think we need to go and clean it off. We can't have a mess in our house."

"It will definitely take two." She leaned against him and kissed him, tasting marinara sauce and wine. "It's a very *big* mess. A skirt, a blouse, a slip. It's possible there could be more soon."

"I'm glad I still have some strength left."

"Oh, so am I," she said with a little smile. "So am I."

CHAPTER
TWO

MOLLY HAD LEARNED a long time ago not to give in to panic when she woke up in a strange house. Through the years she'd taught herself that strange houses were normal, that if she lay in bed without moving and let the early-morning cobwebs drift away, she would eventually remember where she was, why she was there, and if she wanted to make the effort to stay a while.

This morning she remembered quickly. She was living with the Wagners now, Tracy and Graham, who didn't expect to be called Aunt Tracy and Uncle Graham, or worse—much, much worse—Mom and Dad. They were just Mr. and Mrs. Wagner, and this room that Mrs. Wagner had fixed up for her was really a study and would go back to being a study soon enough.

She had lived here three weeks. This was just one more stop until she made it to eighteen and said goodbye once and for all to life as an outsider. When she was eighteen she would get an apartment and she would never leave it. She didn't care how crummy or small it was, it would be her home forever.

She heard noises in the hallway, slippers scuffing their way toward the kitchen. Mrs. Wagner got up every morning to make Molly a hot breakfast before school. Molly figured that would stop soon enough. The woman was playing house, and once she got tired of making the effort, Molly would be rooting in the cupboards to find something to eat.

She'd been there before.

She got up and carefully made her bed, tucking the sheet in the way one foster mother had taught her. Mrs. Grey, two foster homes ago, hadn't been mean, exactly, but she had demanded that every chore be done exactly to her standards. She had stood over Molly, tugging the sheet out over and over again if there was a wrinkle or a sag. Molly had finally met the test just before moving on to a different home.

She showered quickly. She'd gotten in trouble with the last foster family because she used too much hot water. She wasn't sure if that had anything to do with their ditching her before they went to Paris, but she figured she'd better not take a chance. All she had to do here was stay out of the way, follow the rules, until real foster parents turned up to take her, people who needed the county's money and would have something to lose if Molly was moved again.

She knew she was skating on thin ice here. The Wagners didn't need the county's money. All Molly had to do was look around the condo to know that. She was just a good deed, something to do so they could feel proud of themselves, and Molly knew if she tried their patience even a little, she'd be packing her suitcase.

She dressed as quickly as she'd showered and made sure the room was tidy before she grabbed her book bag and headed for the kitchen to choke down eggs and bacon. She was a vegetarian, waiting for the moment when she could choose her own menu. Four years. Just four more years...

Pausing in her doorway, she went back to the bed and lifted the pillow. Her quilt was tucked carefully beneath. She fingered it a moment for good luck, closed her eyes and made a quick wish that she could keep the Wagners happy for a while, then tucked it back in and headed for the door.

Tracy was still surprised how easy it had been to become Molly's foster mother. She and Graham had received emergency training so the placement could be made without delay. Molly's social worker had been so thrilled to keep Molly in the school district that she had cooperated in every way.

Tracy was also surprised how easy it had been to change her schedule, and Graham's, too, so that Molly had the required supervision. Molly went to Janet's every afternoon to help with Janet's kids, and Tracy or Graham picked her up on the way home from work.

Not that the girl seemed to need adults. Tracy couldn't imagine a child with fewer needs than this one. She suspected that if Molly could learn not to breathe their air, she would permanently hold her nose. She asked for nothing and seemed worried about everything Tracy and Graham did for her.

This absolutely infuriated Tracy. Life had taught the girl this was what she had to do to survive. Some nights Tracy didn't sleep much just thinking about it and wondering how to help.

This afternoon Tracy got off early and went home alone. Molly wouldn't be finished at Janet's for another hour, and Tracy wanted to start a pot roast. The recipe was her mother's favorite, but it had been years since Tracy had used it. Neither she nor Graham really liked beef, but with a teenage girl in the house, a growing girl who needed iron, they were eating more of it.

When she unlocked the front door and stepped inside, she was greeted with silence. The condo seemed as empty as it had before Molly's arrival. As uncluttered, as perfect, as cold.

She resisted the impulse to drop her coat on the floor and went to change into jeans and a cotton sweater before she started the roast. On the way back toward the kitchen she stopped at the door to Molly's room and peeked inside. On one level she was pleased at what she saw. She and Graham had moved Tracy's desk to *his* study and replaced it with a dresser from their bedroom. Tracy had hung flowered curtains at the window and covered the daybed with a matching comforter and pastel throw pillows. She hadn't known what to put on the walls, so she'd left them blank. She hoped maybe she and Molly could buy a few posters, but Molly had resisted every invitation to shop. Still, at least the room was inviting and feminine. She hoped Molly approved.

Despite the cheery floral motif, the room seemed empty. Both Tracy and Graham had been astonished at how little Molly had brought with her. The most basic toiletries, one suitcase of clothing, a few books. Now Tracy stepped inside and looked around.

The room was painfully neat, with absolutely nothing out of place. Except…

A colorful scrap of fabric peeked out from under the pillow on the bed. Tracy knew she was snooping, and that snooping was a major offense to a girl Molly's age. Still, she felt justified. She wanted to know more about Molly. She needed to. Leaning over, she tugged. Out came a small quilt, larger than those made for infants, but still too small for a twin bed. The quilt was ragged, tattered at the edges, definitely not as clean as it should be. It looked as if it had been dragged around by a much younger child and nearly loved to death.

Tracy held the quilt at arm's length to examine it closer. It was made of two different types of blocks. Half the blocks were made of three equal fabric strips of different patterns and shades of lilac, sewn into about a six-inch square. The remaining blocks were made of yellow and white patches, four in each square. The pattern was simple, but charming. Or it would have been charming if the quilt weren't so ragged. The blocks in the middle were still in pretty good shape, but the rest of the quilt was hanging by a thread.

Tracy tried a deep breath and found that breathing was harder than she'd expected, because now there was a lump in her throat. The quilt said so much about her young charge. That there was still a little girl inside the self-possessed fourteen-year-old. That Molly had *something* left from her past to treasure. That Molly needed comfort, even if she didn't show it.

When she flipped the quilt to the other side, Tracy saw that the back was a flowered lavender and yellow calico, broken only by the knots of embroidery floss scattered over the surface to hold the quilt together. She almost missed the label in one corner. She was turning the quilt back over when a logo caught her eye—a hand with a heart on the palm.

"Quilts from Caring Hands, Corvallis, Oregon," Tracy read out loud. "This quilt belongs to Molly Baker."

Who had given Molly the quilt and why? Exactly what did it mean to the girl?

She folded it carefully again, lifted Molly's pillow and slipped it back underneath. She couldn't tell Molly she had seen the quilt, since clearly the girl had hidden it. But she was determined to find out more. This was a key, even if only a small one, to her foster daughter's heart.

Molly seemed to like the potatoes and carrots well enough, but her thin slice of meat had gone down quickly and largely unchewed, as if she was swallowing medicine. Graham's slice was every bit as thin, and now he chased it around his plate as if he were designing a still life: *American Pot Roast Supper.* Tracy half expected him to bring out an easel and canvas after dinner.

"Okay," she said, putting down her fork. "The pot roast was not a good idea."

"It's fine," Graham said. "Great. But I had a big lunch."

"Oh, I'll have some more," Molly said. "It's very good. I'm sorry."

Tracy covered the girl's hand as she reached for the serving fork. "You don't have to eat another bite, Molly. If you don't like something here, you never have to eat it."

"But I didn't say I didn't like it." For a moment panic flickered in her pretty blue eyes.

"Honey, everybody likes to eat different things. It's perfectly natural. Tell me what you do like."

Molly's eyes widened. "Oh, pretty much everything."

"Well, I don't really like pot roast," Graham said. "Or steak. Or black-eyed peas, or turtle soup. Or sweet potatoes with marshmallows on top. I particularly despise marshmallows unless they're covering a graham cracker and a square of chocolate."

"Turtle soup?" Tracy said. "Have I ever served you turtle soup?"

"And I don't like kale," he continued. "I *really* don't like mushy peas."

Tracy got into the spirit. "Okay, I don't like lima beans. We used to have them three nights a week when I was a little girl, and nobody wasted food in our house. And succotash. Who ever thought calling vegetables succotash would make *anybody* want to eat them?"

"I'm not that crazy about pork chops, either," Graham said. "I grew up reading *Charlotte's Web*. I practically memorized it."

"I really hate chicken nuggets," Tracy said. "Who are those fast-food people kidding? Like there's any real chicken in one of those things?"

Graham made a face. "You think chicken nuggets are a joke? Read the label on a pack of hot dogs."

"I don't like any kind of chicken," Molly said. Immediately she looked embarrassed and, worse, fearful that she'd just made an error.

"How about turkey?" Tracy asked, keeping her voice even, the question light. "Thanksgiving's coming up, you know."

"I eat turkey." She gave Graham the quickest of glances. "But mostly I eat the sweet potatoes with little marshmallows on them—if somebody makes them. They're my favorite."

He reached over and ruffled her hair. "You and I are a team, Moll. I'll eat your turkey, you eat my sweet potatoes. This is a match made in heaven."

Molly smiled, but she looked more relieved than happy. She hadn't made anyone mad. No one was going to criticize her for speaking her mind or having preferences.

She was safe.

They finished what was left of the meal in silence. When Molly got up to clear the table, Tracy stood, too. "Mr. Wagner and I'll take care of that tonight. Tomorrow's Friday. Don't you have a quiz in history?"

Molly looked surprised. "How did you know?"

"Well, you've had a history quiz every Friday since you came to live with us. I just assumed…"

"Oh." The girl looked flustered. "It's just that… Well, I do. It's just that…"

It was just that she was surprised that anyone had noticed. Tracy saw this as clearly as she saw that the new discovery worried Molly. She understood the girl's train of thought. People here paid attention. Attention meant expectations. Expectations were impossible to meet.

"It's nice to have a teacher you can count on, isn't it?" Tracy said. "I always hated the kind who popped quizzes any old time."

"I never count on anything," Molly said. "Just in case."

She was gone before Tracy could comment. She heard the door to Molly's room close quietly.

Graham's hands were a welcome weight on her shoulders. For a moment she couldn't speak.

"She needs more from us than we're giving her," he said at last.

"But she's only been here a few weeks. It takes time to develop trust." Tracy faced him, her expression pleading.

"Hey, did you think I meant we should pass her on to somebody else?" He smoothed Tracy's hair back from one cheek. "Don't you know me better than that?"

"Then what did you mean?"

"That we have to spend more time with her. Get to know her. Let her know she can speak her mind around here and not get in trouble. How about this weekend? What's on your calendar?"

Tracy's calendar was filled with new homeowners who couldn't see her any other time. Just this once she decided she didn't care. "I can cancel my appointments with the stroke of a pen, except for a couple. And I can finish those by noon Saturday."

"Me, too. Let's go out to Alsea and spend Saturday night. We can show Molly the sights, take her to Alsea Falls. The colors will be at their peak. Besides, now that the renters have moved out, we need to check the old place."

"The old place" was a run-down farmhouse in the picturesque Coast Range mountains that Graham's parents had used as a getaway during the years he was growing up. When his father took a position as a biology professor at the University of Miami, the senior Wagners turned over the house to Graham and Tracy. Graham was waiting for the right moment to sell it, when interest rates and property prices converged and he could make the biggest profit for his parents.

At first he and Tracy had hoped to use the house on weekends, as his parents had, but almost immediately it had become clear there was little point in keeping the house for themselves when they were both so busy. So they had rented it out, instead. Now that the latest renters had moved, it was time to either sell or rent again.

"Do you think she'd *want* to come?" Tracy asked. "She might have something planned with her friends."

"She hasn't had anything planned since she came to live here. If she has friends, she doesn't spend time with them on weekends."

"It's a good idea. A great idea." She rose on tiptoe and kissed him. "You're thinking like a father."

"As long as I don't have to give her a bottle or let her teethe on my finger."

She grinned and kissed him again.

CHAPTER
THREE

MOLLY COULDN'T BELIEVE that most of the time nobody lived in the old house in Alsea. The whole area was amazing, like something out of a picture book, with evergreens marching so high up the hill behind the house that they seemed to pierce the sky. She could almost touch the blue-green mountains. There was a creek not far away, and a stone path leading down to it. The kitchen was huge, with a table so large you could seat a dozen people around it without anyone tapping elbows. There were so many bedrooms on the second floor, she had been allowed to choose whichever one she wanted for the weekend.

Sure, the house wasn't up-to-date, like the Wagner condo. The porch sagged and the wood had weathered to the color of tarnished silver. She knew about tarnished silver. There'd been a lot of it in one of her foster homes, and Molly had volunteered to polish it. The foster mother hadn't let her. Molly figured that was because she didn't want to take it out of the locked cabinet. That family had watched her like she was a thief in training because her real mother had been arrested once and sent to jail.

The Wagners didn't watch her at all. They knew where she was, of course, but nobody paid attention to the little stuff. Their condo was filled with beautiful things, but nobody seemed to care if she looked at them or picked them up. On Thursday morning Mrs. Wagner had caught her looking at a pottery vase with the coolest metallic swirls all over it, and when Molly came home from the Thaelers's that afternoon, the vase was on the dresser in her room, filled with flowers.

Molly wasn't sure what this meant. The Wagners were just playing at being parents. Molly knew Mrs. Wagner wasn't all that fond of babies. Mrs. Thaeler made jokes about it. So maybe this was just their way of showing everybody they didn't *hate* children even if they didn't want any. Not that Molly was really a child anymore.

It was Sunday morning and late. For most of her life she'd been routed out of bed on Sundays to attend some church where nobody knew her. She'd watched foster parents tell pastors the sad story of her life, seen the pity in everybody's eyes, or worse, the distrust. The Wagners seemed too busy to go to church. She'd never seen busier people in her life. Even when they were home they were always working. She wasn't sure why they'd gotten married, since they never seemed to spend time together.

There was a lot to think about here. She was lying in the old double bed in the room at the end of the hall, her quilt against her cheek, sorting it all out, when someone tapped on the door. Before she could respond, Tracy opened the door and peeked inside. "You're awake?"

Molly didn't know what to say. She was always careful to put her quilt away where nobody could see it. It was in sad shape, and one foster mom had tried to throw it away. Molly had learned to keep it under her pillow or in a drawer covered with neatly folded clothing. She bolted up, thrusting the quilt behind her.

"Do you need me to do something?" she asked.

"Nope. Not a thing. I just wondered if you were ready for breakfast. Mr. Wagner's making his famous pancakes and I need reinforcements at the table." She lowered her voice. "They're as heavy as lead, and if I have to eat them all by myself, I'll sink right through the floor."

Molly giggled before she could stop herself. Tracy was pretending to sink right where she stood. "What are they made out of?"

"Some mix with every whole grain known to man. I think he adds ground-up rocks for flavor."

Molly made a face. "What do they taste like?"

Tracy smiled warmly. "Come and see. And after breakfast we're going over to Alsea Falls. You'll like it there. There's a great place to swim at the bottom, but it's probably too cold by now. Besides after these pancakes, you'd sink like a stone."

"I heard that!"

Tracy grimaced, as if someone had caught her doing something she wasn't supposed to. Hands appeared on her shoulders, then one masculine arm came round her neck in a pretend choke-hold.

"Just for that you'll have to do the dishes, woman. And I'm going to get every bowl in the place dirty, just to show you."

"There's, like, one bowl in the cupboards," Molly said.

"Well, there's a measuring cup and a spatula, and a frying pan."

Tracy rolled her eyes. Then she winked at Molly. "You'll be up in a little while?"

"Oh, I'll get up right now. No problem."

"Good. Sounds like I'll need help with *all* those dishes."

The Wagners left, arms around each other's waists. Molly watched them go. For just a moment she wished it was a threesome walking down that hallway, arms entwined. But wishes were pointless, and even worse, dangerous. She tucked her quilt out of sight under her pillow and made the bed before she headed for the kitchen.

By Sunday afternoon Tracy was feeling more relaxed than she had in months. She and Graham had decided—with Molly's input—to stay another night and drive back to Corvallis early enough in the morning to get Molly to school. Graham had gone to buy fresh salmon and vegetables to grill on the old stone fireplace in the backyard.

"Do you like fish?" Tracy asked Molly, who had just come inside from a walk to the creek. "How about salmon?"

"I like almost all fish," Molly said.

Tracy was getting good at interpreting the girl's responses. This one was said with some enthusiasm. "So you're an aquatarian," Tracy said.

"What's that?"

"A vegetarian who also eats seafood? Or maybe that's a vegequarian."

"I'm not a vegetarian."

"Maybe not, but only because you don't cook for yourself. Right?"

Molly smiled a little, but she still looked as if she wasn't sure she should.

"I could be a vegetarian easily. Mr. Wagner, too. Except for fish. I don't think I could give up salmon." Tracy waited, making a point of her silence.

"I don't really like meat that much, I guess," Molly said carefully. "But I'll eat it if you want me to."

"But why should you? We can fix other things. If you're all right with fish, we'll have that a couple of times a week. But we love pasta and vegetables."

"Except lima beans," Molly said.

Tracy felt her smile widening. "You have a great memory."

"I can cook. I learned how a couple of years ago. I like it okay."

"What do you like to make?"

"Cakes. Pies."

"Oh, good. A pastry chef. This is incredible news."

"You don't have any cookbooks."

Tracy was delighted that Molly had been doing some snooping. "I guess they're packed away. I don't do much cooking. I think I have one at home on the bookcase in our bedroom in case I can't remember how to boil water."

"There aren't any here. I was looking around—" Molly stopped and looked embarrassed.

"Had a sweet-tooth attack, huh? We should have told Mr. Wagner to get a cake mix or some ice cream for dessert."

"I like to make cookies."

Tracy tried to remember what was left in the pantry. The last renters hadn't bothered to pack any of their staples since they were moving across the country. And she'd bought essentials like eggs and butter for the weekend. "If we had a cookbook, we could probably put something together." She had a sudden inspiration. "The attic. Mr. Wagner's mother left a bunch of stuff up there for us to sort through. I've never really gotten around to it. But there were boxes of books, and I'm sure some were cookbooks."

She changed her tone to conspiratorial. "Mr. Wagner's mom is a chemist. Whenever we visit, she gives me lectures on proteins and carbohydrates. Every meal we eat is like a science experiment. But the food's pretty good anyway."

Molly looked interested. "Did Mr. Wagner ever really, you know, live here?"

"Just for summers and weekends. But I think this felt like his real home. His parents are pretty formal, but they relaxed more when they were here. He got to run around and be a kid."

"Was your life like that, too?"

"Mine?" Tracy laughed. "Good grief, no. My house was crawling with kids. Still is. There are grandkids now. I'm the only one who doesn't live nearby. I want you to meet everybody. They'll like you."

Molly looked wary.

"Not right away," Tracy assured her. Then she stopped. If she didn't take Molly to Washington right away, maybe Molly would be living somewhere else by the time she and Graham went to visit her family.

She changed the subject abruptly, not wanting to examine that thought too closely. "Let's go see what's in the attic, shall we?" She put her arm around Molly's shoulder. "Let's just hope there aren't any mice."

The fish was a success. The vegetables, although a little on the blackened side, were consumed with enthusiasm, and Molly's oatmeal cookies were a major hit. She went to bed on a sugar high, and high on praise, as well.

Tracy and Graham sat outside by the fireplace after Molly went inside, sharing the last of a bottle of wine they had brought from home.

"The more I get to know her, the less I understand all this," Tracy said. "She's a great kid. Maybe I could see passing her around the system if she was setting fire to mattresses or sticking pins in Barbie dolls. But she's just a normal teenage girl. Too worried about pleasing people. Too quiet and self-contained. But a great kid."

Graham swished the wine in his glass. "You spent a lot of time up in the attic with her. Did you learn anything new?"

Tracy thought about their conversation as she and Molly searched through boxes for cookbooks.

"We found your baby book, Graham. Apparently you were precocious even then. Walked at nine months, spoke in sentences by eighteen months. I'm impressed. Did you know the book was here?"

"I'm not surprised. Mom probably thought I should have it. She knew we'd go through all that stuff eventually."

"Molly was absolutely fascinated. She forgot to be a grown-up and turned into a kid again. I don't know if she's ever seen a baby book before."

"She certainly never had one of her own."

The two of them fell silent. They had learned the basics of Molly's past during their foster care training. Her mother was only sixteen when Molly was born. Molly's father was unknown. At first the mother tried, in her own limited way, to care for the infant, but she was a child herself, with little education and no support from her family.

Molly was removed from the home several times before she was two. When she was three, her mother was arrested, then briefly imprisoned for forging checks. Once released, she was investigated again for child neglect. By the time Molly was four, she went into foster care and never came back out.

The story might have ended happily if Molly's mother had been willing to relinquish her rights so that Molly could be put up for adoption. But even though she'd never made another serious attempt to get Molly back, she refused to give up her legal claim. By the time the courts terminated the woman's rights, Molly was so old she was considered a special needs adoption. And though there was always hope the right family would step forward to take her, so far no one appropriate had materialized.

"My mother was always too busy for baby books," Tracy said. "But she kept shoe boxes for each of us. Locks of hair, hospital bracelets, photographs, notes about the first time we walked, sat up, said 'Mama.' You know. Stuff that proves she was paying attention to all my milestones, even if it wasn't exactly organized."

"I'm guessing nobody cared enough about Molly to make notes."

"She told me about the first foster home she remembers. It was an older woman with a couple of other foster children—kind of a surrogate grandmother from what I can tell. She was good to Molly. I think she's probably the person who set her on the right path and taught her what it was like to be in a family. Molly was there until she was almost nine."

"What happened?"

"The woman died suddenly. The children all went to separate homes. Molly never saw any of them again." Tracy paused. "At least she had some good years when they really mattered."

"That was a lot of information for her to share."

"It came out in little tiny pieces. She'd say something, then she'd wait for me to respond. If I didn't jump on her or say something stupid, she'd tell me a little more. It was like walking through a minefield."

"And that's why nobody's adopted her," Graham said. "Maybe she's not sticking pins in Barbie or Ken, but she holds back so much that nobody can get to know her."

"So what do these idiots expect? A perfectly normal teenager after all these years in the system? Heck, do they even want a perfectly normal teenager? I mean, I remember what I was like at fourteen. Molly's easier to love than I was."

The words drifted heavenward with the smoke from their fire. Both of them waited for words and smoke to dissipate. But they were left with the residue.

"Be careful," Graham said at last.

"I know. This is temporary. She knows it. We know it. And it won't pay to get too close. Then she'll have trouble leaving us when a real family comes along." Tracy faced him. "This is a lot harder than I thought it would be. And I *thought* it would be hard. I know kids. I know it's never easy."

"You're doing a great job." Graham put his arm around her and drew her closer. "I like watching you with her. It's a side of you I don't get to see unless you're with your brothers and sisters."

She punched him in the arm. "Well, you're pretty squishy with her yourself, you know. Feeding her pancakes, taking her out back to see your old woodworking shop, teaching her how to skip rocks at the creek."

"She's a good kid. I like being with her. I like showing her things. It's nice to see her in this house. I had some good times here at her age. Being here brings them back, and I like sharing them."

Tracy was unexpectedly attracted to this side of Graham. She had always known he was a warmhearted, caring guy. So why was his concern for Molly such a surprise?

She tried to feel her way. "You were right that night we started talking about taking Molly. Suddenly we're talking about things that really matter again. Not just what we did at work or where we want to grab a quick bite for supper before we both go home and start working some more."

He didn't say anything for a while. When he spoke, it was clear he'd been thinking. "Trace, are you happy? With our lives? With who we've become?"

The fire was dying down, and she shivered. "I'm happy with *you*."

Graham squeezed her shoulder and drew her closer. "And I'm happy with you. But do you remember the dreams we used to have? Did they involve working so hard at jobs we don't love?"

"When did you start thinking about this?"

"When I started spending time doing other things again. Like coming home at a decent hour. Having family dinners with you and Molly."

"Working on your paperwork every night after dinner until midnight?"

"My job is never going to be nine to five."

"Mine, either."

"Which is one reason we haven't really gotten around to having children."

"One reason," she agreed. "But not the only one."

"I've missed you, Trace."

She sighed and turned her face up to his. The fire sputtered and died and the night grew colder. It didn't really matter. They went inside, and for the rest of the night they kept each other warm.

CHAPTER
FOUR

TRACY WAS SO BUSY for the next three weeks that the dinner hour was the only time in her day when she wasn't working. She looked forward to preparing the meal and spending time with Molly and Graham at the table catching up.

Molly still kept to herself too much, but she did answer when they asked questions about school. The picture of a girl with no close friends was emerging. She seemed to get along well enough, but she resisted any suggestions to have friends over to study with her or just to hang out on the weekends. And if *she* was invited anywhere, she was certainly turning down all the invitations.

On Friday night three weeks after their weekend away, Tracy knocked on Molly's door. She opened it when it was clear Molly couldn't hear her over the sounds of a voice wailing "I'm not a girl, not yet a woman" from the new portable CD player Graham had installed in her room.

"Molly?"

Molly looked up from the bed where she was reading, her quilt tucked under one arm.

"Dinner's almost ready. We're trying some new veggie burgers." Tracy spied the CD cover beside the player. "Hey, don't tell me that's Britney Spears?"

"Somebody at school loaned it to me. Is it too loud?"

"Not for me. I like the noise. But maybe not the way she dresses." She watched Molly stuff the quilt back under her pillow.

"You know, you can leave that out," Tracy said. "My younger brother took the few shreds that were left of his security blanket off to college. I understand. Nobody here's going to toss it, no matter what shape it's in."

Molly looked embarrassed, and for a moment Tracy was sorry she had spoken. But not speaking wasn't working any miracles. Molly was still too much like a shadow in the house.

She went to sit on Molly's bed. "Tell me about it. Are those your favorite colors?"

"They're all right."

"You've had that a long time, haven't you?"

"Uh-huh."

"May I see?"

Reluctantly Molly handed her the quilt. Tracy examined it, turning it over. "Quilts from Caring Hands."

"It's these ladies who make quilts for kids who have, you know…"

"Kids in foster care?"

"Kids who have messed up lives. All kinds of kids."

Tracy nodded, at a loss for words.

"It's falling apart," Molly said.

Sort of like the girl's future, Tracy acknowledged silently. No telling what the coming year was going to bring the girl or this well-loved scrap of fabric.

"I tried to fix it once," Molly went on, "but I don't sew."

"I sew, but I don't know a thing about quilts," Tracy said. "You know, though, if these people are still making quilts, I bet they could tell us what to do to fix it."

Molly's eyes brightened. "You think? I mean, I know it's silly—"

"It isn't silly. Molly, you haven't had an easy time of it, honey. It would be *silly* of us to pretend you had. And I think this quilt has helped you through the rough spots. It would be an honor to help you fix it up and preserve it. Will you let me?"

"You don't have much time."

Truer words had never been spoken. And wasn't that sad. That something as simple as repairing this quilt seemed impossible with her crowded schedule.

"The quilt's a priority," Tracy said. "Top of my list. Now come and try the veggie burgers and tell me what you think."

"You really won't, you know, decide it's no good and trash it?"

"There is no chance of it. None whatsoever."

Molly smiled for the first time since Tracy had opened the door.

Darla Chinn, Molly's Hawaiian-born social worker, had bone-straight black hair and blue eyes in a classic oval face. Her beauty was clearly noteworthy, but her strength and intelligence were even more so. She and Tracy were becoming friends, and formalized meetings between foster mother and social worker had turned into lunch dates.

On Wednesday they met at a restaurant near the university to munch their way down the salad bar.

"These women get together every Wednesday," Tracy told Darla once they had piled their plates and were back at the table. As they'd loaded up, she had started filling Darla in on her trip that morning to the Lifespring Foursquare Church to see the quilters of Quilts from Caring Hands in action. "And they've made literally thousands of quilts. But you probably know all that."

"We've given away a lot of their quilts," Darla said. "And I can tell you, they make a real difference to the children. The quilt's something to hold on to when there's not much else."

"They make quilts for a lot of different agencies. They even make tactile toys and quilts for blind children." Tracy was still impressed with everything she had seen that morning.

The church where the quilters met—she'd counted at least thirty—had once housed the YMCA. Their regular room was cheery with shelves nearly spilling over with fabric. Tables and ironing boards and sewing machines were set up everywhere. There was so much equipment, the church allowed them to put tables in the sanctuary, too, and the atmosphere in both rooms was charged with excitement and high spirits.

"Sounds like you had a good visit with them."

"It was great. One of the women took me around and showed me everything they were doing. Then she sat down with me and looked at Molly's quilt. Pretty soon a crowd gathered. Everyone oohed and aahed and gave me advice. They handled the quilt with the care I'd give a medieval tapestry."

"Women whose priorities are straight." Darla added sugar to her iced tea.

Tracy envied her thin friend that second packet of sugar and stirred artificial sweetener into her own tea. "The prognosis isn't good. The quilt's in pretty sad shape. The binding at the edges can't be salvaged. The border is threadbare. But most of the blocks in the middle are in good enough condition to save."

She set down her spoon. "The woman who gave me the tour suggested that Molly and I take it apart carefully, then remake it using the good blocks. We can add more—they're really simple, and we can probably find similar fabrics—then sew some borders around it to make it big enough for a twin bed. She said we could have somebody else quilt it if we want, or do that ourselves, too."

Darla stirred her tea. "It sounds like a big project, and one that will take some time."

"Uh-huh." Tracy knew just where Darla was going with that. "Having any luck finding a real foster home for her?"

"At this point it's you or the group home. Things are still going okay?"

Sometimes Tracy wondered if Darla was really looking for another home for Molly. "She's easy to have around."

"Until she starts testing you."

"I don't think that'll happen."

"And if she does?"

Although she wasn't a child psychologist or a real foster mother with a bag of tricks up her sleeve, Tracy wasn't without experience, either. Her brothers and sisters had been teenagers, and not that long ago. "We'll cope if that happens."

Darla reached for a second muffin. Tracy was still trying to rationalize a first. "I say go ahead with the quilt. It'll be a good memory for Molly once she gets another placement."

Tracy couldn't imagine herself as simply a good memory. The image was definitely unsettling. She wondered if Darla had known it would be.

Her cell phone rang. She apologized before she left to go outside and take the call.

Back at their table she scooped up her coat. "Remember that question you asked? The one about Molly testing us?"

Darla lifted one sculpted eyebrow in question.

"That was the school. They've scheduled a meeting in an hour with Molly's English teacher. Molly was caught cheating on a test."

"Why would Molly cheat? She's smart as a whip and her grades have always been excellent."

Tracy slung her purse over her shoulder. "That's what I'm about to find out."

Tracy had not spent much time in guidance counselors' offices. Her family had expected her to work as hard at school as she did at home. She had been an A student.

But then, until today, so had Molly.

Graham joined her in the reception area outside the door. She hadn't expected him to drop everything and come, but here he was. He took her hand and squeezed it in greeting.

There was another couple waiting, as well. The man, dark-haired and athletic, was dressed in a cashmere sweater and perfectly creased khakis. The blond woman looked as if she had just come from the spa, and although Tracy's suits and dresses were of excellent quality, she and this woman did not frequent the same department stores. For that matter, Tracy was fairly sure this woman did her shopping in San Francisco or Seattle. Or Paris.

The guidance counselor ushered the four of them inside her office. Molly and another girl were sitting on one side of a narrow table with an older woman. Molly was looking down at the table and didn't acknowledge them.

Once they'd all seated themselves around the table, the counselor introduced the other woman as Mrs. Oakley. Then she introduced the expensive-looking couple as Mr. and Mrs. Carvelli, the parents of Jennifer Carvelli, the curvy blond student sitting next to Molly.

Mrs. Oakley was middle-aged with a ruddy complexion and salt-and-pepper hair. The table didn't hide her expansive waistline. "I'll come right to the point," she said, twisting her hands as she spoke. "I graded my third-period test papers this morning.

There were a number of multiple-choice questions, about twenty blanks to fill in, and a short essay at the end. The test counts for one quarter of this term's grade. I graded Jennifer's and Molly's papers back-to-back. Maybe if I hadn't, I wouldn't have noticed the problem."

"What problem?" Mrs. Carvelli said. Her voice was low and husky, but she bit off her words, clearly annoyed.

"Jennifer and Molly sit next to each other, and their papers are identical. Except for the essays, that is, and even those are remarkably similar, with key phrases repeated in both. Unusual phrases. There's no way that these two tests could be so much alike unless one of the girls was cheating."

She handed sheets of paper to both sets of adults. Tracy saw that the papers were copies of the girls' tests. She set them side by side on the table, glancing at Molly as she did. Molly looked miserable. Their eyes met for a moment, then Molly looked away. Jennifer, on the other hand, was examining her nails, which seemed to be decorated with perfect little flowers. Her hair was professionally streaked, and her clothes looked like a hybrid of *Seventeen* magazine and *Playboy*.

Her expression said she had nothing to worry about.

As Mrs. Oakley had concluded, the tests were too much alike to be anything but cheating. Tracy noted that one answer was misspelled on both papers and the essays were phrased a little differently, but the information was identical. There were even a couple of multiple-choice questions where both girls had erased or scratched out one answer and chosen the other.

She looked at Graham. He shrugged.

"What do the girls say?" she asked the teacher after the Carvellis had finished examining the tests.

"Jennifer says that Molly must have copied her paper."

"Then it's clear who cheated," Mrs. Carvelli said.

Tracy wasn't sure which Carvelli female she disliked more at the moment. "I'm sorry, but just because your daughter says Molly cheated doesn't mean it's the truth. Molly?"

Molly looked as if she wanted to shrink and disappear forever. "What?"

"Did you copy Jennifer's paper?"

Jennifer spoke before Molly could answer. "She said she did. Right, Mrs. Oakley?"

"My wife asked *Molly*," Graham said pointedly.

"You don't want my help…" Jennifer shrugged. "Means nothing to me."

"Molly?" Tracy repeated.

Molly didn't answer.

After a tense silence, Mrs. Oakley said. "Molly did indicate she was the culprit. But frankly, I'm not sure she's telling the truth. Molly is a superior student and doesn't need to copy from anybody. Jennifer…" Her voice trailed off.

"That girl tells you she cheated, and you still want to blame my daughter?" Mrs. Carvelli demanded.

"I know your daughter's work, and she hasn't turned in a test paper anywhere near this perfect in all the weeks she's been in my class."

"Well, I—"

The teacher ignored her and went on. "I took the girls one by one out into the hallway and asked them questions on the material I had tested them on. Molly knew all the answers and Jennifer didn't. Then I asked Jennifer to repeat the written test after school today, and she refused."

"Why would Molly confess if she didn't do it?" Graham asked. He looked at the girl directly. "Why would you, Moll?"

Tracy noted that Jennifer was glaring at Molly now, and Molly was all too aware of it.

"I told the truth," she mumbled. "I…I copied Jennifer's paper. She's the one with the good test, not me."

Tracy was one-hundred percent sure Molly was lying, and she was ninety-nine percent sure why. Jennifer, from the looks of her, was probably one of the more popular students. Molly, judging from her lack of friends, was not. Jennifer had copied Molly's test paper, but Molly didn't want to turn her in. Tracy could only imagine how miserable a girl like Jennifer could make Molly's life.

"I don't know why you had to call us in here," Mrs. Carvelli said. "We're busy people. You have the cheater. She admitted it."

"I still believe Jennifer is the one who cheated," Mrs. Oakley said. "But since Molly is going along with it, I really don't have any choice here. Molly will receive the zero, but *both* girls will have to do a five-page essay on a subject connected with the test material. If either of them chooses not to turn it in, that will be another zero in my book."

"You have no right to punish Jennifer. I have close friends on the school board," Mr. Carvelli said. "I'll be talking to them."

Mrs. Oakley didn't dignify the threat with a reply. "Parents, I hope you'll talk to your daughters and try to get to the bottom of this."

"They're not my parents," Molly said.

Jennifer giggled. Tracy just wanted to cry.

Molly was staring out the window when Tracy walked into her room that night after a very quiet dinner. The girl didn't look at her when Tracy sat down on the bed.

"I have a bedtime story for you," Tracy said.

At her words, Molly turned. Her eyes were shining with tears, but her mouth was drawn in a determined line. The tears wouldn't be allowed to fall. "I'm not a little kid."

"I know you aren't. But I'm about to make up for some of the stories you didn't get to hear when you were."

Molly looked away.

"When I was fourteen, just coincidentally the same age you are, I had my first boyfriend. His name was Al, and I thought he was really hot. I thought I was really hot because he liked me, too."

"Hot?" Molly grimaced.

"I know. I'm trying to be fourteen again. Just temporarily. Play along."

Molly didn't answer.

"Anyway, let's just say that by my standards today, Al was a complete loser. But at the time, I thought he was everything good under the sun wrapped into one gorgeous fifteen-year-old body. One day Al and I were at this little shopping mall where our parents had dropped us off to see a movie. Afterward we went into a department store to look around, and Al saw a belt he liked. So he stuffed it under his coat. I couldn't believe it. I'd never seen anybody shoplift before. I told him he was crazy, but he just walked back into the mall, like he hadn't done anything. I went after him, trying to get him to take the belt back…"

Tracy waited. Molly turned around. "What happened?"

"A security guard at the store had seen him take the belt, so he came after us. When Al realized who the guy was and what he wanted, he shoved the belt at me and took off running."

"But the guard saw him steal it, right?"

"Right. The man knew it wasn't me. But when he finally caught up with old Al and dragged him back to the store, Al kept repeating it was my fault, that I'd taken it. And when that didn't work, he changed his story and said that I'd *made* him do it."

Tracy fell silent. She waited for Molly to speak, but the teenager said nothing.

"I didn't take the blame for him," Tracy said. "Because I knew, even then, that any boy who wanted me to take the blame for something he'd done wasn't worth much." She paused. "Which is not to say I wasn't devastated for days after we broke up."

"Why are you telling me this?"

"Because you took the blame for Jennifer today when you shouldn't have. And she's not worth it."

"You don't know anything about it."

"I know I care about you, Molly. And even worse than that zero is knowing that you're trying to protect somebody at the expense of your own integrity."

"Maybe it runs in my family."

Tracy's heart beat a dozen times before she trusted herself to speak. "I know about your mom. I know she was young, scared, confused and probably not very mature when she went to prison. But I hope if you blame her for the mistakes you make, you also give her credit for all the wonderful things about you. It's not fair to do one without the other." She took a deep breath. "Even more, I hope you don't blame *anybody* for your mistakes except yourself. But don't blame yourself too hard. You're a wonderful young woman."

"I'm going to sleep now."

Tracy wasn't sure what to do. So she did what seemed perfectly natural, perfectly right. She leaned over and kissed the top of Molly's head, then she ruffled her hair. "Sleep tight, honey."

She turned off the light and closed the door quietly behind her.

Graham was waiting in the living room. They had talked about which of them should speak to Molly tonight, and Tracy had volunteered. But she knew that he had been waiting for her, hoping it went well.

"Did she admit she lied?" he asked.

"She's not going to do that. She'll stick with that story until it comes up at Christmas dinner when she's twenty-eight or thirty-eight. Then she'll laugh about it and tell the whole thing the way it really happened."

"And we won't be there to hear it."

Tracy plopped down on the sofa beside him. Graham put his arm around her shoulder, and she nestled against him. "It's not *what* she said, it's whether she heard what *I* said," Tracy told him.

"Did she?"

"I don't know. I feel so bad for her. I remember how badly I wanted to be liked by the popular kids. We all did. Except you, of course. You were undoubtedly one of the popular kids, or one of the kids who was too mature to care."

"Maybe, but I was never as slick as Mr. Carvelli. Did you get a load of that sweater of his? And he was wearing $800 shoes. I wonder why Jennifer's not in private school?"

"She probably cheated her way out of a couple, which is why she's being educated with the huddled masses now," Tracy said with venom.

"Meow."

She punched him lightly. "What are we going to do?"

"You mean punish the kid even more? I'm against it."

"No, the school's taken care of that. I meant, what are we going to do to make her feel better about herself so she doesn't have to lie to make friends?"

"Short of vaulting her through time until she's twenty-one?"

"Short of that."

"Spend more time with her. We had so much fun that weekend in Alsea. I think about it a lot. We came home and went right back to being too busy. We sit down at dinner together, but that's about it. She's not getting much from us."

Tracy felt a little thrill of excitement. Graham sounded as lonely, as isolated, as she felt. They had begun making concessions in their schedule for Molly. Now suddenly those concessions weren't enough. She wanted more of Graham and less of her job. She wanted more of Molly, too. She loved having a career—that was never going to change—but she wanted more than work from her life.

"If we go to your folks' house for Thanksgiving, we'll hardly even see Molly," Graham said. "She'll be swallowed up by the thundering herd. Let's go back to Alsea. Just the three of us. We'll see your family at Christmas, instead. If my folks come to visit, we'll just take them along. Tell your mother why and she'll understand."

Tracy realized she hadn't been looking forward to the trip to Washington next week. She adored her family, but Graham and now Molly were her priorities. This felt new, even though she and Graham had been married for a decade. They were finding their way back to each other after drifting apart an inch at a time.

"Who's going to cook?" she asked.

Obviously realizing the answer to that question determined his future, Graham held up one hand as if swearing an oath. "All of us."

"Then I'm in," Tracy said. "But only if you agree not to take any work along. Just the three of us relaxing for four full days. Deal?"

He sealed the bargain with a kiss.

CHAPTER
FIVE

THE DAY BEFORE Thanksgiving, Janet brought Molly home from an afternoon of baby-sitting. Janet had promised to drive her if Tracy would let Molly stay longer than usual while she made preparations for the next day's dinner. Janet was entertaining all relatives west of the Rockies, and she was in panic mode.

Molly said hello to Tracy, then scooted through the house to her room. The door shut and seconds later the music went on. Tracy smiled at her friend. "You need a cup of tea. Sit. I'll get it for you."

Janet did just that, perching on a stool at the kitchen island as Tracy put the kettle on. She looked absolutely exhausted. "I don't know what I would have done without Molly today. I got the pies baked and the casseroles made."

"I hope other people are bringing things tomorrow. If they aren't, there's a problem in your planning."

"Everyone's bringing something, and my sister's bringing the turkey. I just wanted to finish all my cooking so I could spend tomorrow morning setting up. That'll take three times as long as it should since all the children will be helping."

Tracy made a face. "Sounds like fun."

"You're sure you don't want to come?"

"I appreciate the invitation, but we're looking forward to going out to the country, just the three of us. Graham's going to smoke a turkey. Molly's going to make a pumpkin cake—she doesn't like pumpkin pie. I'm making my mother's sausage and apple stuffing, minus the sausage, and lots of sweet potatoes with marshmallows.

We had a family vote on the menu." Belatedly, Tracy realized what she'd said.

Janet noticed it, too. "Molly's starting to feel like family, isn't she?"

"That's a loaded question."

As if to fill in the resulting blank space in the conversation, the volume from Molly's bedroom went up an audible notch.

"How do you stand that?" Janet asked, putting her hands over her ears.

Tracy checked the hot water. "I like it. The house was pretty quiet before she got here. And you'd better get used to it, kiddo. With five kids it will be twice as noisy once they're teenagers. Dueling stereos."

Taking pity on her friend, Tracy went down the hall to ask Molly to turn the volume down a notch. When she returned, Janet was leaning on the island, head in hands.

"Hey, you really need that cup of tea, don't you?" Tracy gave Janet's back a brief rub as she passed.

"I'm just having one of those moments of self-doubt," Janet said. "Ever have them?"

"At least ten times a day. What gives?"

"I'm trying to remember why I wanted five kids."

"Bad day with the tribe?"

"No. I love them to death. I love every little thing they do."

"So?" Tracy poured the boiling water into a sleek black teapot and pulled two matching cups from the cupboard.

"I don't think I'm going to like them as much when they're teenagers." Janet lifted her head. "Convince me."

"Teenagers are great."

"That's all you have to say?"

"Janet, you don't want kids who cling to you the rest of your life. Teenagers are fun to talk to. They finally have interesting things to say. They experiment with clothes and hair, and it's great to watch. You're the original earth mother. You'll love it."

"You're nuts. I'm not going to love it. I'm going to wake up every morning and wish I had my babies again. You're the exception to the rule."

"Me?"

"You. Look, I've been watching you with Molly. She's fine with me, but she treats you worse every time I see you together. She's surly and prickly—and listen to that music! And you don't seem to care one bit."

"Don't you get it?" Tracy said. "Every time she's a little gruff with me, that means she trusts me more. She knows I won't over-react. Of course, she also knows she can only go so far or I'll crack down on her. But it's a balancing act and she feels comfortable enough to experiment."

"You make it sound easy. I don't think you get it. You don't un-derstand—teenagers aren't easy for everybody. I'm just glad you'll be around to hold my hand when mine are that age."

Tracy poured the tea and they talked of other things, but even after Janet was gone, her words lingered behind. Tracy thought about them well into the evening.

Molly was so glad to be back in the country. The house was creaky and old, and it took a few minutes for the hot water to reach the shower. But Molly's room had two windows side by side that looked out to the mountains and a big soft bed that sank around her at night and kept her warm.

And on the Friday after Thanksgiving, her room also had a sew-ing machine.

"Okay, here it is. What do you think?" Tracy came through the door lugging an old black machine with spidery gold lettering. "I told you I'd find it. I just had to look behind every blasted box and trunk in the attic."

Molly had been busy clearing a space on a small table that had held a clock with huge glow-in-the-dark numbers and a collec-tion of silly ceramic dogs.

"Oh, good, you got rid of the dogs." Tracy plunked the old ma-chine where the dogs had stood. "I hope you pitched them out the window."

"I just put them in a drawer. They're pretty dumb, but I kind of like them. I like dogs."

"I like real dogs. I don't know who left those. One of the renters."

"I think the house gets lonely without people living in it.

Maybe the dogs keep it company." The moment she uttered the words, Molly was sure this was probably the dumbest thing she'd ever said.

Tracy just smiled. "I like that idea. It makes me feel better. I don't like to see the place standing empty."

"How come, like, you know, it's not rented now?"

"Graham…Mr. Wagner's looking into the local real estate market. This might be the right time to sell it."

"Sell it?" Molly couldn't imagine such a thing. The house was perfect. Old, but perfect. If it was her house, she'd live here all the time and never, never leave.

"I know exactly what you mean. I like it, too. But it seems unfair just to let it sit here and wait for us to visit when there are people who could live here year-round. It needs fixing up. I used to think…" Tracy's voice drifted off.

Molly normally didn't prod people to talk. Most of the time she preferred not to hear what they had to say, since the news was rarely good. But this time she couldn't help herself. "What did you think?"

"Well, I thought it might make a nice craft gallery."

"What's that?"

"A shop where people come to buy local handiwork. There are a lot of wonderful artists and craftspeople in this area. Potters, sculptors, weavers. There's a stained-glass artist just down the road who makes the most gorgeous windows. I try to get my clients to buy local pieces for their homes, but it's tough because people are busy and there aren't enough galleries for them to make selections without tramping from studio to studio. I'd love to start one."

"Here?"

"Here or somewhere else outside the city. This seems like a good bet. People come here to relax, and they want relaxing things to do. They want to buy things to take back home to remind them of their vacations. We're not far from the main road. It's a nice detour."

"Then why don't you do it? You're a grown-up. You get to do whatever you want."

Tracy laughed a little. "Do you think so? If you're counting on that, I'd better warn you now. There are always things that get in the way."

"Like what?"

"For one thing, it would cost a lot of money. And take a lot of work."

"You have a lot of money. And you work all the time anyway." This made perfectly good sense to Molly, so she was sorry when it was clear her words had hurt Tracy.

"Hey, I don't work all the time. We're here today, aren't we? And yesterday and the rest of the weekend?"

"I'm sorry."

Tracy ruffled her hair. "Don't be. I do work too much, and so does Mr. Wagner. Before you came, we'd almost forgotten how much fun it is to take some time off."

Molly figured she'd have to think about that. She wasn't sure this was a good thing. She wasn't really used to good things happening just because she was living with somebody.

"Anyway," Tracy said, "this is the big moment, kiddo. Are we going to take your quilt apart and make it bigger with the new fabric we bought last weekend? Or are we just going to try to fix it a little so it won't fall apart as fast?"

Molly had been thinking about what to do ever since Tracy had proposed the idea of expanding her quilt. A new quilt would be great, but it would never be the same. It wouldn't feel the same, look the same. On the other hand, it would last a lot longer, maybe her whole life if she took good care of it.

And the new fabric, more lavender and yellow prints, was awfully pretty.

"I think we ought to do it," Molly said, not without reservations.

"Then let's get this antique threaded and see if it really works."

That night after Molly went to bed, Tracy went in search of Graham. They had dined early on Thanksgiving leftovers, then he had disappeared. She and Molly had hardly noticed since they'd gone right back to work.

The machine had worked surprisingly well, the quilt had come apart with only a little help, and they had been pleasantly surprised to find that most of the original blocks could be used again if they restitched some of the seams. They had made more blocks, following the instructions Tracy had received from the gracious quilters she had consulted. Now, tomorrow, they could sew the blocks back together and begin to add borders.

Meantime, Graham had disappeared.

Tracy thought she knew where she would find her husband, and she was right. He was off in the old woodworking shop where his father, an excellent woodworker himself, had taught his son the basics and beyond.

The shop was compact but well-organized. Graham hadn't used it in a long time, and he kept his tools locked away in the condo's spacious storage area.

This weekend, though, he had brought a few with him, and now they were neatly lined up on a freshly dusted worktable. A space heater warmed the room, and moonlight and two shop lights illuminated it. From the looks of things, there was a project in the offing.

"Don't tell me," Tracy said from the doorway, feigning a heart attack by slapping her hand over her chest. "You're going to make that headboard at last?"

He turned and grinned. "Nope."

"A woman can dream."

"Maybe that'll be the next project."

She joined him at the table and sniffed the air. "Cedar, right?"

"A couple of good-size trees up on the hill keeled over in a storm a few years ago, so I had them sawed into boards. They've been curing in the garage ever since. I almost forgot they were there."

"What are you making?"

"Well, I thought if you and Molly get into quilting, there might be more quilts down the road a piece. She'll need a place to store them. So I'm making her a cedar chest. I thought I'd give it to her for Christmas."

Tracy was so surprised she blurted out the first thought she had. "What if she's not with us at Christmas? What if she's been moved by then?"

She hadn't wanted to squelch Graham's enthusiasm, but Tracy realized by the way his expression hardened that she had. "And how is she going to take it to her new home?"

"I thought of that." His next comment had a pronounced edge. "Or does that surprise you?"

"I'm sorry. I just hate… Well, you're going to so much trouble, and she's going to be so disappointed if she has to leave it behind…."

"If she's not allowed to bring the chest with her, we'll keep it for her. She'll know that she can have it the moment she has a place of her own. We're not going to just let her vanish from our lives, are we? We're going to stay in touch. She'll be able to visit, I'm sure."

"I'm not. Social services will probably want us to back off and let her get adjusted to the new family. We've only had her a couple of months. We won't have much in the way of rights."

He faced her, arms folded over his chest. "So what would you like me to do?"

She wished they had never started this conversation, but clearly it had been hanging at the edges of their lives, waiting for this moment. This wasn't about a cedar chest. Nor was it only about Molly. A lot of it was about the two of them.

"Our lives have changed since Molly came," Tracy said. "And I think we've been good for her. She's been good for us, too. We've started taking a little time off, working fewer evenings and weekends. We talk more…"

"Right now I wish that part wasn't true."

She winced at his tone. "I didn't mean to rain on your parade. The cedar chest is a thoughtful gift. You're right. We'll find a way to make sure Molly can keep it. But this is about more than the cedar chest. It's about asking Darla if we can go from being emergency foster parents to long-term ones. Isn't it?"

He didn't nod. His shrug was almost undetectable.

"There's a lot more to that decision than meets the eye," she pointed out. "Has the extra time you've taken off made your job as difficult as it's made mine? Are you working twice as fast every day to try to make up for it? Have you thought about summer vacation and how we'll manage when Molly's home full-time?"

"Kids get jobs. They go to camp or summer school."

"Why keep her if our solution is to find ways to dump her somewhere else as often as possible?"

"You know that's not how I meant it."

"But that would be the upshot. My job speeds up in the summer, and I work even harder. You can't afford to take up my slack. Doesn't she deserve a family with parents who are home more? Who don't have to rearrange schedules and juggle clients just to take the whole Thanksgiving holiday off? Who have nine-to-five jobs they can let go of when the day ends?"

"Don't you think half the families in this country have those kinds of problems? They manage."

"And what about the day Darla comes to us and says she's found a family that wants to adopt Molly? We put our careers in second gear, rearrange our priorities and suddenly she's gone anyway? And we're left with a hole in our lives and our hearts?"

Graham was silent. Outside the workshop, the country night was still except for an owl hooting somewhere on the hillside.

"So that's what this is about," he said at last.

"I never lied to you. I told you I wasn't sure I'd ever want kids."

"Trace, it's not about wanting a kid, it's about letting a kid go. You're afraid you're going to fall in love with her."

She gestured to the cedar planks. "And what is that about?"

He didn't answer. She took a deep breath. "I'm trying to be level-headed. I'm looking at our lives and what we *don't* have to offer Molly. I'm looking at the very distinct possibility that someone else will have more, and we'll have to say goodbye. I'm warning you not to get too attached."

Graham waited a moment before he spoke. Tracy wasn't sure he was going to say anything at all, but at last he did.

"You know what?" This shrug was obvious. "I'm willing to take my chances. I'd rather give Molly a piece of my heart when she leaves than keep my heart sealed away for no good reason. That's the chance you take when you care about somebody."

He turned back to his project, leaving her to wonder what chances she was willing to take.

CHAPTER
SIX

MOLLY DIDN'T REALLY LIKE Jennifer Carvelli. Jennifer was *sooo* positive there wasn't anybody else in the world as wonderful as she was. But through the years Molly had learned to be practical. In her short life she'd been stuck with a lot of people she had to get along with, whether she liked them or not. Compared with the girl in one of her foster homes who had cut up all Molly's clothes with their foster father's hedge trimmer, Jennifer wore a halo.

Jennifer had been pretty cool after the cheating episode. Everybody knew Jennifer cheated, lied and cut classes. She couldn't be bothered studying when there were so many better things to do. But she was very grateful when other people took the blame for her indiscretions. After Molly lied to save her, Jennifer made sure Molly was welcome at the lunch table where the most popular kids sat. No one talked to her much, but it was better than sitting alone, which had happened too often in the past.

Even now, on the first day after the Christmas break, Jennifer's group still made room for her. And Jennifer asked if she could go home with Molly after school to work on an English report. Molly knew what that meant. She would write most of Jennifer's report while Jennifer tied up the Wagners's phone or watched HBO, but Molly's cooperation would buy her more days at the lunch table.

Molly didn't feel good about this, but she was no dummy. She would feel much worse in the long run if she refused. Jennifer would make sure of that.

She felt especially bad calling Mrs. Thaeler on Jennifer's cell phone to tell her she couldn't baby-sit that afternoon. Even though

Mrs. Thaeler said it was fine, Molly still felt bad. But now that she and Jennifer were at the Wagners's condo after a high-school friend of Jennifer's dropped them at the door, the guilt was disappearing.

"Hey, this is tight!" Jennifer threw her books on the sofa and didn't pick them up when two fell to the floor. "How'd you end up in a place like this?"

Molly examined the question and figured that what Jennifer really meant was how did a complete reject like Molly end up somewhere other than an institution straight out of *Oliver Twist*.

"I don't know," Molly said with a carefully nonchalant shrug. "The Wagners are okay."

"What's it like being a foster kid? Who buys your clothes? Do they give you money and stuff?" Jennifer picked up a pottery statue of a Mayan god sitting on an end table and turned it over, as if looking for a price tag.

"It's not too bad," Molly said carefully. "I get to be on my own when I turn eighteen."

Jennifer set the statue down too hard and Molly winced at the thud.

"What happened to your real parents?" Jennifer asked. "They die or something?"

Molly could just imagine how much mileage Jennifer would get from the truth. "Uh-huh."

"Sometimes I wish mine would die. Honestly. They treat me like a baby."

"Do you have brothers and sisters?"

"You're kidding, right? My mom says that one kid was too many. Every time I do something she doesn't like, she fixes herself a martini. She'd be sprawled out on the street somewhere if she'd had another kid on top of me."

It was hard for Molly to imagine the sophisticated Mrs. Carvelli facedown in the gutter. "Maybe we ought to get to that paper. I'm not sure the Wagners want me to have friends over while they're gone."

"Do they lock up the liquor?"

"I don't know. I never checked."

"Find out. This could be a great place to party."

Molly could just picture how fast she'd get booted out if that happened. "What's the subject for your report? I've got a computer in my room. We can check out the Internet just to get some ideas."

"Just don't try to copy one. Mrs. Oakley checks Google to see what's out there. Somebody I know got busted. It's got to be *o-rig-i-nal!* She's a fat cow, isn't she?"

Molly liked their English teacher. She wished she could tell Mrs. Oakley the truth about that test, but she knew the woman would not understand. "My paper's on Wordsworth," she prompted.

"Mine's supposed to be on Colgate or Coldhearted or something like that."

"Coleridge. Samuel Taylor Coleridge."

"Why do you pay attention to that stuff? Do you like it?"

"Yeah," Molly said without thinking. "I'd like to be a writer someday. I figure with everything I've seen, I'd have something to say."

Jennifer looked up. She'd been busily draping one of the handwoven afghans on the sofa around her. "You probably would. You're smart that way."

Molly was warmed by the other girl's reaction. She felt a little better about "helping" Jennifer with her report. "You want to get started?"

"I guess. I got a book on poetry from the library. That might help."

Slightly encouraged, Molly wondered if the afternoon might not be as bad as she'd feared. Jennifer left the afghan in a heap on the coffee table and Molly led the way to her room.

"Not bad." Jennifer glanced around. "But mine's a lot bigger and I have my own bathroom." She wandered to the window and looked out at the incomparable view. "Wow, you can see all the way to Alaska...or wherever."

Molly was beginning to relax. She watched Jennifer examine everything. She seemed to approve. Molly was sure she would not have approved of most of the places she had lived. Jennifer would most certainly not approve of the farmhouse in Alsea. Molly tried to imagine Jennifer in a house without central heating, with limited hot water and the nighttime rustling of mice or bats in the walls and ceilings.

Flopping down on the bed, Jennifer drew Molly's new quilt around her. Molly loved the quilt, even if it would not, even now, win a prize at the State Fair. She and Tracy had laboriously sewn the top, adding strips of fabric in pleasing designs, then Tracy had taken it somewhere to have it quilted on a machine as a Christmas present. Now the entire quilt was covered with little hearts in bright yellow thread. Molly wasn't sure which gift she'd liked better, the finished quilt or the beautiful cedar chest Graham had made for her.

Nor was she sure what either gift had meant.

"What's this?" Jennifer tapped the toe of her leather boot against the chest.

"It's a cedar chest," Molly said, pulling herself back to the present. "To keep blankets and stuff in."

Jennifer stuck her toe under the lid and tried to raise it. "Nice…"

Molly didn't want Jennifer's foot on her chest. She watched Jennifer lift the lid halfway, then drop it. The resounding thunk made her uneasy. "Do you want me to get on the Internet so you can look up Coleridge?"

"I don't care." Jennifer lifted the lid again. Higher this time. This thunk was louder.

"Okay. That's what I'll do." Molly knew enough about human nature to realize if she asked Jennifer not to play with the chest, she would either make fun of her or keep doing it anyway. She hoped to distract her.

At the desk, Molly could hear Jennifer dropping the lid, over and over. She prayed for the computer to boot up quickly and for the Internet connection to be instantaneous.

"Okay, here we go," Molly said. She turned, just in time to see Jennifer give the lid one particularly hard kick. The little chest, with nothing inside to weight it, tilted backward and fell over. Molly heard a crack as the lid hit first, then folded back with a snap as the chest turned over. She was afraid to look.

"Whoops," Jennifer said.

Reluctantly Molly got up and went over to the bed. The top of the chest had come free of one of the brass hinges and lay at an angle. She stared at the gift that had been made with loving hands, just for her, then she stared at Jennifer.

To her credit, Jennifer looked apologetic. "Sorry."

"Sorry?" Molly shook her head. "Mr. Wagner made that for me."

"Then it's no big deal. He can probably fix it."

"It's no big deal to you!" Molly hadn't known she could get so angry, but suddenly a white-hot rage filled her. She wanted to tear out every strand of Jennifer's carefully highlighted hair. "You have everything! You don't know what it's like *not* to be you. You don't care, either. Do you think it's anything except luck that you're not me? Can you even *try* to imagine what it's like not to have everything you want?"

Jennifer stared at her. "It's no big deal. What's wrong with you?"

"Get out." Molly pointed to the door. "Write your own stupid paper."

Jennifer's eyes narrowed. "You think you can talk to me like that?"

"I just did. But don't worry, I don't ever want to talk to you again. We're finished talking."

"Where do you think you'll be eating lunch tomorrow?"

"Maybe I'll be eating it in Mrs. Oakley's classroom, while I tell her what a miserable cheat you are!"

Jennifer gave a short laugh. "You wish." She stood, and Molly's quilt slid to the floor. "I can make your life hell."

"You'll have to stand in line," Molly said.

Tracy's day had been awful. She had risen early to get into the office for two crack-of-dawn appointments. Neither set of clients had liked any of her ideas. The first couple insisted the bathroom tile they had chosen two months before was unacceptable and had to be replaced with something other than the vast array of samples Tracy had on hand. The next couple could not agree on a shade of paint between vanilla and linen. They had left after threatening to find a designer with a better eye for subtleties.

The drapes she had ordered for a new home were five inches

too short. The wallpaper mural of mountains her developer had asked for in his office turned out to be a city skyline instead. Six clients called to demand after-hours appointments that week, and three more called to cancel orders already in progress.

By the time she got home, she was ready for a glass of wine, painkillers, a back rub and half an hour of soothing music. In any order.

The house seemed oddly still when she opened the front door. "Molly?" she called as she hung up her coat.

Normally she picked up Molly from Janet's, but this month Janet's oldest son was in a late-afternoon gymnastics class, and Janet had begun dropping Molly off on her way to the gym. Tracy wondered if there had been a change of plans today.

"Molly?" When there was no response, she muttered to herself and went in search.

She stopped at Molly's door and stared. The chest that Graham had so carefully crafted for the girl was lying on its back on the floor, the lid at an odd angle. The closet door was wide-open, and there were no longer any clothes hanging inside.

The quilt had been stripped from Molly's bed. But nothing else appeared to be missing.

"Molly?" she said softly.

The front door slammed and she whirled and ran out into the hall. "Molly?"

Graham appeared, loosening his tie as he moved toward her. "Hey, Trace." When he saw her expression, he frowned. "What's going on?"

"I…I'm not sure. I think Molly's run away."

"What?" He looked as if she'd lost her mind. "What do you mean?"

She stood aside and gestured toward the door of Molly's room. "See for yourself."

He walked over and glanced inside. Then he turned. "Tell me everything you know."

There was so little, she covered it in one run-on sentence. His mouth drew into a grim line.

"Did she say anything to you this morning when you dropped

her off at school?" Tracy demanded. "Maybe it's some activity there? A class sleep-over?" She knew she was grasping at straws. All Molly's clothes were gone, not just an extra pair of jeans and pajamas. And the chest, obviously damaged, was still lying on the floor, as if Molly had knocked it over in a fury.

"She told me Janet would bring her home," Graham said.

"Janet." Tracy felt a rush of relief. "I'll call Janet. Maybe she knows something. Molly was there." She hesitated. "She was *supposed* to be there."

He joined her in the kitchen after wandering the living room like a detective looking for clues. Tracy wedged the phone between her ear and shoulder and scrambled for a notepad and pen, although she had no reason to think she might need them.

The phone rang six times, and finally Janet's answering machine picked up.

"I don't believe it!" Tracy told Graham what was happening, then when the beep sounded, she left Janet a message to call her right away.

"I'd go out looking for her, but I don't have any idea where to go," Graham said. "She's either here or she's at school or Janet's. Do you know any of her friends? Is there anybody you can call?"

Tracy had made attempts to get Molly to invite friends to the house, but she hadn't pushed very hard. She knew little about the girl's life outside their walls. With a sinking heart she realized how little she did know. Molly had been with them for four months, and for the most part she was still a stranger.

Graham correctly read her expression. "Don't beat yourself up."

"Why not? I don't have the phone number of even one friend I can call. She's a teenager. They live in packs. What kind of parent am I?"

"For all we know, she doesn't have any friends. She's the lone wolf."

"Yeah, for all we know. And what do we know? Have we made any real attempt to figure that out? We've just been playing at being parents."

"There's Jennifer Carvelli. Molly stuck up for her."

"Yeah, when she shouldn't have." Tracy knew what a long shot

Jennifer was. She was not the kind of girl to hang out with any-body who couldn't add to her own social status. But at least it was a start. Maybe Jennifer could give them phone numbers.

"I'll try their house. It's not a common name. How many Car-vellis will there be?" Graham dug through a bottom drawer for the phone book.

He straightened, found the right page and dialed, tapping his foot while he waited for someone to answer. Tracy motioned to the re-ceiver and he tilted it to share it with her as the phone rang and rang.

Finally a girl's voice answered. "Yeah?"

"Is this Jennifer Carvelli?" he asked.

"Uh-huh. Who wants to know?"

Tracy pantomimed strangling somebody.

"This is Graham Wagner, Molly's foster dad. I'm looking for Molly. Have you seen her this afternoon?"

There was a long pause. For a moment Tracy wondered if the girl had fallen asleep out of spite. Then Jennifer said, "Yeah, I was over there. Sorry about the chest. I didn't mean to break anything."

Graham snatched the receiver to his ear, as if he knew that Tracy was about to give the girl a piece of her mind. "Never mind the chest, Jennifer. We just want to know where Molly is."

"I don't know. She kicked me out. She was really angry, you know? I had to walk about a mile to a phone so I could get a ride home."

"I hope it did you some good." Graham handed the receiver to Tracy so she could hang up.

The phone rang the moment she put it back on the hook. Tracy snatched it up. "Hello!"

Janet was on the line. "Tracy, good grief. It's just me."

"Janet, do you know where Molly is?"

There was a pause, followed by a sigh. "She's here. We were just finishing a heart-to-heart when you phoned."

Tracy went limp. "Oh. I was so afraid something had happened. Her room's all cleaned out, and her chest is broken and—" She lowered her voice. "Why is she *there*? She didn't baby-sit for you today, did she? She was here earlier. She had a friend over."

"No, she didn't sit for me today. And she must have walked over here while I was running Alex to gymnastics. There's no easy way to tell you this. She claims she wants to stay with us until she can move into the group home. She doesn't want to go back to your house. I've tried to get the story out of her, but she just says she doesn't like living with you anymore. She wants to leave. She's going to call the social worker."

"Darla?" Tracy was too confused to think of anything else to say. "She's calling Darla?"

"I asked her not to just yet, to give this a little more thought. But she's determined."

"And she didn't say why? Janet, she's been happy here. We've gotten along, I know we have. There was no sign of trouble…"

Janet lowered her voice even more. "You can figure this out if you try hard enough."

"What's that supposed to mean!"

"I mean, you just answered your own question. She's happy there. Maybe that frightens her."

"No, I think it's got something to do with Jennifer and the chest and—"

"I've got to go. I'll stall her as long as I can." The phone clicked and the line went dead.

"What'd she say?" Graham demanded.

"She's there. She wants to stay with Janet until she can move into the group home. She wants to call Darla and tell her."

"And Janet doesn't know why?"

"She says maybe being happy here scared her." Tracy felt tears welling, and in a moment they were sliding down her cheeks.

Graham didn't reach for her. "What do you think?"

"I think it has something to do with Jennifer breaking the chest."

"So do I."

She looked up. "How?"

"For somebody who understands teenagers as well as you do, you've got a real blind spot about this one."

Graham didn't sound angry, but she heard the challenge in his voice.

"Then enlighten me," she said.

"She loves that chest, Trace. She loves her quilt. Don't you see? She's starting to love us. Jennifer damages the chest, and from experience, Molly is sure we'll kick her out. So she leaves on her own. That way she won't be abandoned by people she cares about. It's easier and safer to abandon us."

It was so simple and yet so complex. But Tracy knew that what Graham said was true.

"We've been playing at this." She wiped her cheeks with her fingertips. "I was right before. We've been doing our good deed for the year by letting her stay with us. We've made a few accommodations to her schedule, taken a little more time off, given her things, but we haven't given any real thought to what's going on inside her."

"And now she's left us."

Maybe it's better this way seemed like the appropriate response, yet it was so far from what Tracy wanted to say, the words wouldn't form. "I don't want her to go," she said softly.

"If she agrees to come back, it'll be even harder next time she leaves. Darla will find her another family eventually, or Molly will run away again the next time she panics. Maybe it's better this way."

She didn't like his tone. He sounded like the financial adviser he was, cool and logical. "No, it's not!"

"You're not thinking straight."

"Who cares! I don't want her to go. I come home in the afternoons now and I look forward to her being here. On the good days, when she shares a little, I feel like somebody's given me a million dollars. And when the three of us are together, we feel like a family. Not just two people pursuing careers they don't really care about, but a *family*. People who are trying to find their way to something better. Don't tell me you don't feel the same way."

He relaxed visibly. She hadn't realized until then how tense his posture had been. "Then I won't," he said.

"Why didn't you say something before?"

"Trace, you're the one who's resisted falling in love with Molly. You've refused to recognize it. I wasn't sure you could see it."

She thought about the Friday night after Thanksgiving. She'd

stood in his workshop and cautioned him against getting too attached to Molly. And all the time her attachment had been growing and strengthening, until now she felt as if her beloved daughter
had been torn from her arms.

"I didn't want to be a mother," she said, her voice cracking.

"Trace, you've been one for months, and you've loved every
minute of it. Taking Molly was your idea, remember?"

"We can't go on the way we have been."

He wrapped his arms around her and pulled her against his
chest. He kissed her hair.

"I'm getting your shirt wet," she said in a muffled voice.

"Don't worry. I won't be needing white shirts much longer."

She pulled away just a little to see his face. "Why not?"

"Honey, come on. Don't you see where this is going?"

She sighed and relaxed, hugging him tighter. Because sometimes, when life was taking a one hundred and eighty degree turn,
all a person could do was let it happen.

Tracy decided to enjoy the ride.

CHAPTER
SEVEN

MOLLY HOPED that the Wagners would not show up at the Thaeler house, either to yell at her for the broken cedar chest or to talk her into going back home with them. *Their* home, of course. Never hers, although a few times she'd thought about it that way.

Those thoughts should have been a clue. Little by little she had slipped into feeling like she was part of something there. But she knew better. She was the Wagners's charity project, the poor orphan girl who needed a place to live. She'd seen *Annie* on television. She knew all about Daddy Warbucks.

Of course, Daddy Warbucks had never crafted a cedar chest for Annie. And there'd been no Mommy Warbucks in the movie who helped her make a new quilt, or took her shopping for better jeans, or understood why she had lied about cheating on a stupid English test.

She felt sick about the cedar chest, sick that she had let Jennifer break it. Because Molly knew she was the one who'd really screwed up. She'd been so worried that Jennifer would make her life miserable that she had allowed her to kick the chest again and again.

She didn't *want* to see the Wagners…but she wondered a little why they hadn't tried harder to find out what was wrong.

"Molly?"

Mrs. Thaeler was standing in the bedroom doorway. Molly had agreed to sleep in the nursery with Liza on a fold-out bed in the corner. Liza had gone to sleep hours ago, giggling until her eyes finally closed for good, but Molly hadn't been able to sleep a wink.

"What?" Molly whispered.

"I need you in the living room."

Molly didn't know what to say. Was she being kicked out in the middle of the night? Had Darla come to get her tonight instead of waiting until morning, like she'd said when Molly called her?

"Molly?" Mrs. Thaeler asked in that pleasant tone of voice that still meant Molly had better move quickly.

"I'll put on my jeans."

Once she was alone with Liza again, Molly got dressed. She supposed this wasn't the end of the world, even if it felt like it. Maybe the group home would be okay after all. At least she wouldn't have to be perfect all the time, no matter how she felt. Where else could they send her after that?

She touched her quilt, then picked it up and smoothed one corner along her cheek. It was old and new, past and present. She wondered if it would be safe at the group home. Sighing, she dropped it back on the bed and walked down the hall.

After too many hours had passed, she'd convinced herself that the Wagners weren't coming to see her. When she saw them sitting on the Thaelers's sofa, she nearly fled.

Mrs. Wagner looked like she wanted to cry. Something clenched inside her. Was Mrs. Wagner upset because of her? That made her uneasy. That made her feel a little sick. She really liked Mrs. Wagner as much as she'd tried not to. She hated to think she could make her cry.

"Hi, Molly." Mr. Wagner stood, like she was a grown-up and he wanted to do the polite thing. It seemed so odd, so formal that she wasn't sure what to do. He didn't look comfortable, either.

She wondered what they were going to say to her. She thought of the chest that he'd worked on so hard, just for her, and she felt even sicker. She looked away.

"I'm sorry about the cedar chest," she mumbled, eyes focused on a plastic dump truck in the corner. "It was an accident. Sort of."

"Jennifer Carvelli already apologized."

That surprised her. She glanced up briefly, then turned back to the truck. She heard a noise behind her and realized that Mrs. Thaeler had brushed past on her way out of the room. Molly was alone with the Wagners.

"I shouldn't have let her come over," Molly said.

"Probably not," Graham agreed. "But that's not why we're here."

She knew better, but she glanced up because now she was curious.

"Molly, come here." Tracy patted the sofa. Graham sat down again, but he left a place between the two of them.

She didn't like this. Emotions churned through her, and she didn't even know what they were. She did not want to sit between them like the filling in a sandwich.

"Please?" Tracy asked.

Molly heard the wobble in her voice and knew that she had to go, whether she wanted to or not. She walked the last mile to the sofa and sat between them, perching forward so she could jump up the moment it became necessary.

"We brought you something," Graham said. "Will you open it?" He lifted a rectangular package off the table, wrapped in flowered lavender paper. The paper reminded her of her quilt. She was suspicious immediately, but still, regretfully, intrigued.

"Go ahead," Tracy said.

"It's not my birthday. Christmas is over."

"I know when your birthday is," Tracy said. "August 18. I'm looking forward to it. But sometimes when people care about each other, they give gifts for no good reason."

Molly considered bolting. Cared about each other? But the present was too mysterious. If she didn't open it, she was afraid she'd wonder the rest of her life what it was.

"I can cut the ribbons," Graham said.

"Just like a man," Tracy said. "He's in a hurry, Molly. Can you untie it quickly?"

Molly relaxed just an ounce at the glimmer of humor in Tracy's voice. She began to pick at the ribbons. It took her a moment, but at last both ribbons and paper fell away to reveal a white box. She lifted the top to see a scrapbook with a photo of her with the Wagners on the front cover.

She frowned. "What's this?"

"It's your baby book," Tracy said. "Or, I guess we have to say it's your teenage book."

Molly continued to frown. "What's inside?"

"Look and see," Graham said.

Molly was suspicious, but it was hard to say no. The scrapbook was covered in some sort of shiny blue fabric that changed colors, like the water at Alsea Falls. She liked the photo, too. Mr. Wagner had taken it. He always took these crazy timed photos everywhere they went. He put the camera on a rock or a tree limb and ran back to stand with them before the camera clicked. He'd taken this one on the front porch of the farmhouse with the camera on the railing. They were all making faces.

She looked happy.

She had *been* happy.

She took a deep breath and turned the page.

"What's this?" She leaned closer.

"The prologue to the *Canterbury Tales*—in Middle English," Tracy said. "Remember? You were learning it the day I found out you needed a new family."

Molly thought that was a little weird, but nice. She was surprised Mrs. Wagner had remembered something so silly.

She turned the page and stared. "What's this?"

"A menu from the first restaurant we took you to. Remember? You ordered the Portobello mushroom sandwich?" Tracy pointed. "There it is."

"How can you remember what I ordered?"

"I paid attention," Tracy said simply.

Molly looked at the next page. "A shoe?"

"I traced around yours. That's from the first new shoes we bought you. You left them behind."

Before she'd left that day, Molly had carefully put everything the Wagners had bought her in the bottom drawer of her dresser. She was surprised they'd found out so quickly.

"There's a pocket from those old ratty jeans you used to love, too. I discovered them in the trash a couple of weeks ago." She made a little choking noise, then recovered. "I have to confess, I've been saving stuff of yours ever since you came to live with us. I have a shoebox in my closet. I've been filling it with your stuff.

My mother did that. I guess I inherited more from her than I thought."

Molly thought that was getting weirder by the moment, but she didn't feel weird. She felt warm and softer inside, and she thought she might start crying if this got any stranger.

"What's this?" But the question was stupid. The next six pages were packed with photographs Mr. Wagner had taken of her. Thanksgiving photos, photos at the falls, photos on the hill behind the farmhouse, photos from their Christmas trip to meet Mrs. Wagner's family.

Mrs. Wagner's family had treated her like she belonged. The memory gave her a brand-new pang.

"Darla—Miss Chinn—says she'll call every foster parent you've had and see if they have any photos they can copy," Graham said. "We'll add them later."

Molly was skimming now. There was a page with her progress reports from school, photos of the Thaeler children, a copy of a speech about World War II that she'd gotten an A on in history, ticket stubs from a movie they'd gone to, the tag for the new coat she'd gotten at Christmas. It had been in the cedar chest with the quilt.

And how had they known how badly she wanted that coat?

She stopped on the next to the last filled page, although there were many blank pages beyond it. This was a drawing. No, it was a blueprint, or sort of. House plans.

She pulled the scrapbook a little closer. "What's this?"

"Those are my plans for remodeling the farmhouse," Graham said. "If we're going to live there, we need to modernize the upstairs a little. A new bathroom, a bigger master bedroom—see, we can knock out walls here, add some built-ins in your bedroom. Until we can afford to build a new house on the hillside."

She looked up, then hazarded a glance at him. "The farmhouse?"

Tracy answered. "We're moving there, Molly. We're selling the condo and moving to Alsea. Mr. Wagner's going to build cabinets and furniture, and I'm going to turn the downstairs into a craft gallery. At the very latest we'll have the new house built by the time you're in high school, or maybe we'll build a gallery instead and stay in the farmhouse. You can help us decide. Meantime, you can decorate the room any way you want."

Tracy pointed to the fabric and paint samples on the final page. "We can start with these, but you can do anything you like. Black walls, cardboard furniture—I don't care. It's yours." She sounded enthused. But underneath it all she sounded scared, as if she was afraid Molly might refuse.

Molly took all this in. She hardly knew what to say. Finally she blurted out, "But I'm just your foster kid."

Tracy put her arm around Molly's shoulders. "Not for long."

There was no way Molly could misunderstand. She thought about life with the Wagners. A real life. Pets and barbecues and vacations. Fights and misunderstandings, love and laughter, a place to come home to once she was a grown-up herself, relatives and holidays and knowing secrets about each other.

A family of her own.

"I'm not as perfect as you think I am," she said doubtfully. "You might not like me as much as you think you do."

"Are you trying to give us a way out?" Graham asked.

She realized his arm was around her, too. She nodded, and despite all efforts, tears filled her eyes.

"We'll take you just the way you are," Tracy said. "If you'll take us the same way?"

What else could she do? What else could she possibly want? She was trapped by what she was very afraid might be love.

Molly nodded, too.

MEMORY BOX ARTIST PROGRAM
TERA LEIGH

For award-winning artist and author Tera Leigh, life is all about living one's passion. Tera's passion is creativity—and following her passion led her to found the Memory Box Artist Program. Through the program, Tera has mobilized a community of women to put *their* passion and deep sympathy into creating hand-decorated boxes to hold cherished mementos for mothers grieving the death of an infant. The boxes are a way to acknowledge the baby's brief life and always keep their child close.

The Memory Box Artist Program began with Tera's decision to follow her own passion. Tera had been writing and painting most of her adult life, but her energy was focused on her career as an attorney. Tera was an excellent attorney. She'd followed in her father's footsteps, but it wasn't her dream. Painting was—and inspiring creativity in others. In 1995, feeling a need to connect with other painters, Tera began a Web site for decorative artists. It was a fortuitous first step in unexpected ways. The same day she launched her Web site, she met her future husband online. They married five months later. And it was through her Web site that Tera first heard about the need for Memory Boxes.

About this time, one of Tera's closest friends died of cancer at the age of forty-two. This loss brought home to Tera how precious and fleeting life can be. So Tera decided to follow her dreams. She left her job as an attorney, and she and her husband concentrated on living a life that would make them happy and fulfilled—emotionally and spiritually. Tera realized life wasn't about making money. It was about giving back. "At the end of your life it's all you have," says Tera. "What you did is all that matters—how you lived your life."

Creating Memory Boxes touched Tera on a personal level, too. Because of a medical condition, it's unlikely she and her husband will ever be able to have a child together. Tera understands about the loss of a child—for her, the children she might never have. Tera's mom, Marie Gemmil, who has been instrumental in the program since it began, had lost a baby—the child between Tera and her brother. Her mom says there isn't a day that goes by when she doesn't think of that baby.

Few of us know what to say or how to help when a mother is grieving the loss of her infant, even though we all feel compassion. Mothers want desperately to talk about the child they've lost. Instead we may say, "It's for the best" or "You'll have another one." Tera herself had said those very words to a dear friend who'd lost a child two years before she started the Memory Box program. After that, she was determined to help other women in the way she had not been able to help her grieving friend. A Memory Box holds precious memories—the child's birth and death certificates, footprints, wristband, crib card and other treasured mementos of a tiny life. The boxes become a bridge to allow the mother to discuss the child by beginning with "look what a woman made for me to hold my baby's things."

Tera launched the Memory Box Artist program in June 1998 with the help of her mother and a neonatal nurse, with twenty boxes going to three hospitals. Tera's mom painted the basecoat on the boxes and Tera did the decorating. Other artists and hospitals quickly came into the program. Now, after five years, volunteer artists have donated more than 58,000 boxes to over 600 hospitals around the world for use in neonatal infant bereavement, late-term miscarriage or stillbirth. But the ongoing need for more boxes is a key motivator for Tera. To put it in perspective, there are over 500 hospitals in the state of California *alone*. Every year in the United States, approximately 40,000 infants are stillborn. In 1995 in California, 3,478 children died before reaching the age of eleven months.

Loss of a child is difficult for families, and also for the hospital staff who must cope with these tragic deaths. They, too, mourn the loss of a baby. There is a definite need for a compassionate, nonclinical form of support, and doctors and nurses are grateful for the opportunity to offer grieving mothers the caring touch of a Memory Box. One nurse told Tera about a mother who wanted to take home mementos of her stillborn baby and the only thing the nurse could find to carry them in was a biohazard trash bag. It is Tera's goal, her dream, that one day, no bereaved mother will ever leave the hospital without a Memory Box in hand.

The artists themselves also benefit from the Memory Box program. One of Tera's purposes in starting the program was to give women a way to use their creativity to make a difference. Most volunteers will tell you that their creative work brings them joy. Using their talent to help others provides a double blessing. And many of the women who've lost a child themselves and received a box contribute art to the program, which becomes a form of therapy. Others have lost a child in the past and were unable to acknowledge and grieve the death fully until volunteering for the Memory Box Artist Program. One volunteer is ninety years old. She lost a child over sixty years ago and she dedicates each box she decorates to that baby. Tera points out that the boxes don't have to be works of art to make a difference. The love and caring behind them is what matters.

The Memory Box Artist Program stands for everything Tera believes in. Living life with creativity and passion gives meaning and purpose to our lives, and in turn can enrich and touch the lives of others. Tera believes we are all creative beings…and all of us can make a difference.

More Than Words

BRENDA NOVAK

SMALL
PACKAGES

BRENDA NOVAK

Two-time Golden Heart finalist Brenda Novak grew up thinking she didn't have a creative bone in her body. It wasn't until she was twenty-nine and married with three kids that she discovered writing—and if not for a difficult situation that prompted her to find a way to make money from home, she might not have started even then. It took her five years to teach herself the craft and to finish her first novel. But it introduced her to something she loves to do more than anything else. Now she has five children; three girls and two boys, and juggles her writing career with softball games and carpool runs. She and her family make their home in Sacramento, California.

PROLOGUE

Yuba City, California

THIS WAS HIS DAD. At least that was what his mom had just told him. Two seconds ago, Rosie Ferello had brought their old Buick to a screeching halt, jammed her finger out the open window and said, "There he is, Harrison. You happy now? You've hounded me all your life to meet your pa. Well, *that* rotten son of a bitch is your daddy."

His daddy… A man he couldn't remember…

Harrison scrambled out of the back seat to see a pair of work boots sticking out from beneath an old Chevy pickup sitting on blocks in the driveway across the street. He'd longed for this day, but the shabby house and tall weeds in the yard worried him a little. The place wasn't any nicer than where he and his mom lived….

Hesitating near the back bumper of the Buick, Harrison bit his fingernails into the quick while waiting to see what his father might do.

The stranger beneath the truck slid out and sat up on a wheeled dolly. His gaze locked with Harrison's, then traveled to the car and Rosie. When recognition dawned, he stood up so fast the dolly rolled down the drive and crashed into the gutter.

Rosie stuck her head out and waved Harrison forward. "Go on," she said. His mother was trying to punish him for stealing that candy bar from the Quick Stop a couple of hours ago. He'd known she'd be angry about it. He'd done it to *make* her angry. He was angry, too. *Most* days. He just couldn't explain why….

When Harrison didn't move, she frowned and lit a cigarette. "You've always had so much to say about your beloved daddy.

Well—" the smoke curled from between her lips as she exhaled "—there he is. Let's see what you think of him now."

Obviously he wasn't expected to think much.

Forcing his hands to his sides, Harrison dried his fingertips on his jeans and drew a deep breath. It was June and blistering hot so late in the afternoon, but Harrison couldn't quit shaking inside.

He cast a hesitant glance in his mother's direction. The rumbling engine reminded him that she could drive off any second. He was afraid she would. She threatened to give him to his father every time Harrison caused her any trouble—and Harrison caused her plenty of trouble.

"This is your big chance," she said. "Don't stand there all day."

For the better part of Harrison's nine years, he'd pictured his father to be like his best friend Jimmy's stepdad. Henry Spits wore glasses and suits, and smiled vaguely as he talked on the cell phone. But Harrison's dad didn't look anything like Mr. Spits. Dressed in a pair of grease-covered jeans and a Budweiser T-shirt that barely stretched over his round belly, Duane Ferello was one of the biggest men Harrison had ever seen. He had hair the same toffee-color as Harrison's, thick dark whiskers, and eyes that seemed as cold as a rainy day in January. He smoked, too. Harrison could see a pack of cigarettes rolled up in his sleeve.

"What're you after now, Rosie?" his father called out, squinting at her.

Harrison's heart beat faster as he waited for his mother's response.

Cigarette dangling from her mouth, she ran a hand through the dark roots of her hair and rolled her eyes. "God, it's been eight years since we broke up. Is that all you can say to me, Duane?"

His father grabbed a towel off the top of the red toolbox at his feet and leaned against the truck, making a show of wiping his hands. "What'd you expect? That maybe I'd write you a check?" He spit on the lawn. "Well, you can forget about that. You're not gettin' any more than the state's already takin' out of what I earn."

"You're only givin' me a hundred and fifty bucks a month," Rosie retorted. "Is that the best you can do?"

"I just told you, it's all you're gonna get."

Harrison's mother made a noise of disgust. "I didn't drive out to this dump to get another few bucks from a tight-ass like you. I didn't come for me at all." She hitched her thumb at Harrison. "There's someone here who wants to meet you."

Harrison knew he should speak, show his father that he wasn't as dumb as he probably looked, hovering there on the side of the road. But he couldn't think of a single thing to say. As soon as his father's attention swung back his way, he could've sworn someone had punched him in the chest and knocked the wind out of him.

"What're you starin' at, huh, boy?"

The gruffness of his father's tone did little to invite an answer, but Harrison had waited too long for this moment to let fear get the better of him. Maybe if he showed his dad that he wasn't as small and unimportant as he appeared, Duane would be happier to meet him. Hooking his thumbs in his pockets, he lifted his chin, adopting the tough-guy attitude he'd learned from the older boys in his neighborhood. "So you're my dad?"

His father tossed the towel onto the toolbox. "That depends on what you mean by 'dad.' You're not gonna get another dime out of me, neither."

Harrison hadn't seen Duane since his parents split eight years ago, since he was only a baby…. "I'm not asking for money," he said.

But his father didn't beckon him closer. He didn't tell him he seemed like a fine boy or ask if he played sports. Duane pinched his neck and muttered, "Yeah, right. You think I'm dumb enough to believe it ain't gonna come down to that eventually?"

Suddenly Harrison's stomach hurt. His whole life he'd believed it was Rosie's fault his father never came around. She smoked too much, yelled too much, slept in too late. She bragged about naming him after Harrison Ford, as if that connected them to someone important. She didn't behave like the other mothers. But now he knew she wasn't entirely to blame. His father didn't want him, pure and simple. Probably never had.

A lump the size of a baseball rose in his throat. Hunching into himself, he hurried to get back in the car. He wouldn't let his father see him cry. He wouldn't let *anyone* see him cry.

But he couldn't blink the tears away quickly enough to fool his mother. Craning her head around, she took one look at him and cursed under her breath. Then she got out and called his father every cussword Harrison had ever heard—even more. She told Duane Ferello he was a boil on the butt of humanity and didn't deserve to know his own son. She told him that she and Harrison had never needed him and that they didn't need him now.

When she finished, she got in the car and peeled away, leaving behind only the echo of her words and some flying dust and gravel.

The hot wind from the open window rushed against Harrison's wet cheeks as the miles passed. He sat silently, waiting for his mother to say, "I hope you learned your lesson back there." He was in trouble often enough that she always wanted him to learn a lesson. But today she didn't say anything. She kept glancing at him in the rearview mirror, sniffling as she drove, and strangely enough, Harrison felt as though he *had* learned something. Even if she wasn't perfect, his mother was all he had. And it was time to make some big changes, because he was never going to look himself in the mirror and see a man like his father staring back at him.

CHAPTER
ONE

Sacramento, California
Twenty years later…

WHAT WAS TAKING SO LONG?

Harrison Ferello glanced nervously at his watch, then loosened his tie and continued to pace the length of the room. He'd been waiting almost thirteen hours. Surely Lynnette's mother would come out and tell him—

"Are you waiting for a baby to be born, too?"

Harrison looked over at the stout woman with gray hair who sat in the corner. She smiled kindly, but he didn't want her or anyone else to draw him into a conversation right now. He had too much on his mind, too many decisions to make. Still, he couldn't ignore her. Forcing a pleasant smile, he nodded.

Her grin widened. "I figured that had to be the case, the way you're worrying a hole in the carpet. Who's having the baby? Your sister?"

"Excuse me?" he said, resisting a scowl.

She waved toward the corridor leading to Labor and Delivery. "If you were the father, you'd be inside. So I thought maybe you're expecting a new niece or nephew. Am I right?"

Harrison struggled to come up with an appropriate label for his relationship with Lynnette. After their breakup almost eight months ago, they weren't even friends. They'd scarcely talked to each other since she moved away.

"No," he said abruptly. Any other response would only raise more questions.

"Oh." The woman's smile faded. "My daughter-in-law is having her second child," she said, obviously trying to smooth over the awkwardness. "She's having a girl."

"You must be very excited."

"I'm crocheting this blanket for her." She dug a large half-finished square of pink yarn from her purse.

"That's nice."

Shoving a hand through his hair, he went back to pacing, but after another hour, anxiety got the better of him. "Does it always take this long?" he asked the woman, who was now crocheting quietly.

She pulled off her half-glasses and studied him. "This is your child, isn't it?"

Harrison nodded. What could he say? There wasn't even supposed to be a pregnancy, but Lynnette had lied to him.

"Your first?"

"Yes."

"How long have you been waiting?"

"Thirteen and a half hours."

"That's not unusual," the woman told him. "First babies generally take longer."

He knew that from working in the emergency room this past year, of course, but talking seemed to help. "Thanks."

"Do you know if you're having a boy or a girl?"

"Twins," he said. "Twin boys."

Her eyebrows shot up. "Twins! How wonderful."

Harrison couldn't agree, at least not yet. He was still reeling from the news. When he'd met his father at nine years old, he'd decided he was going to make something of himself. And he'd fought damn hard to do it. He'd avidly avoided anything that could threaten his goal. But he hadn't bargained on meeting a woman like Lynnette....

"I hope you'll have some help," the woman said. "My cousin has twins, and I can tell you, they're a handful."

Help? Lynnette's mother suffered from severe bipolar disorder, her sister, who had an infant of her own, was going through a divorce. Harrison's own mother had recently remarried and moved to Las Vegas. Rosie would be floored to hear that she was about to become a grandmother—almost as shocked as he'd been to learn he would soon be a father.

He opened his mouth to respond, when a nurse appeared and glanced around the waiting room.

"Dr. Ferello?" she said when their eyes met.

"Yes?"

Her expression was somber. "Could I speak with you for a moment, please?"

"Of course." The back of Harrison's neck prickled as he walked over to her. "Is there a problem?" he asked.

She drew him into the corridor.

"I'm Charlene Matheson, the nurse who's been caring for Ms. Donovan. I'm afraid I have bad news."

Lynnette was young and healthy, and the babies were nearly full-term. What could be wrong?

Harrison cleared his throat. "Tell me what's happened."

"There were…complications during delivery. Ms. Donovan's blood pressure skyrocketed and…" Charlene Matheson clamped her hands together in front of her and squeezed until her knuckles turned white. "There wasn't anything we could do. It happened too fast."

He couldn't quite comprehend what she was trying to tell him. "*What* happened too fast?"

"Ms. Donovan had a massive stroke, Dr. Ferello. She died a few minutes ago."

Harrison's heartbeat vibrated through his whole body, radiating outward from his chest to his arms and legs. "Wasn't there any warning?" he asked.

The nurse gently placed a hand on his arm. "Dr. Spring can explain in a few minutes. He's with Ms. Donovan's mother and sister now, or he would've come out to speak with you himself."

Numbly Harrison's brain registered that the woman who'd been so alive when he'd brought her to the hospital that morning was now dead.

Soothing words spilled from the nurse's mouth, something about the hospital offering grief counseling.

"Dr. Spring said he's never seen this happen before," the nurse was saying when he tuned in again. "I'm sorry. I know this has to be a terrible blow."

Harrison nodded. He didn't know what else to do.

"And the babies?" he managed to say. "Did they…did they die, too?"

Her eyes filled with sympathy. "The second baby died moments after he was born. He had spina bifida and several other problems."

Guilt immediately assaulted Harrison. He'd been so consumed with how the pregnancy was going to affect *his* life…. And now both Lynnette and one of the babies were gone. "And the first baby?"

"He's only five pounds and in an incubator, but we have every reason to believe he'll survive."

One out of three… "So what now?" he asked, almost to himself.

"I'm afraid I can't answer that for you. You'll have to speak with Ms. Donovan's family and make plans from there."

"Right," he said. They had to make plans. For two funerals and a new baby. *Lots* of plans. But Harrison didn't know where to begin unraveling such an emotional mess. He'd imagined himself playing a supporting role. Taking the children whenever he could. Paying as much child support as possible. But now…

"Will you be okay?" the nurse asked.

He rubbed the stubble on his chin, vaguely aware of the raspy sound. This had to be a nightmare. Any minute, he'd jerk awake and realize he'd dreamed all this, even the pregnancy. But the clock on the wall kept ticking. The automatic doors in the lobby *whooshed* open and shut. And the nurse stood before him, waiting expectantly…

Finally he hauled in a deep breath. "I'll be fine," he said, because he knew she couldn't stand there with him all day. "Just fine."

She smiled with a degree of relief. "Give me a few minutes, and I'll take you to the nursery to meet your son."

Harrison stared after her as she hurried away. She'd said she would take him to meet his son… *His son!* God, what was he going to do? He hadn't known he'd be having children until three weeks ago.

Now it wasn't children at all but one son.

And it was only the two of them.

Noelle Kane hurried through the hospital toward Labor and Delivery, carrying the Memory Box she'd created under one arm. "What did you say?" she asked, pressing her cell phone tighter to her ear.

Her friend Theresa raised her voice. "I said we'll miss the movie if you don't get here soon. Where are you?"

She tried to shut out the antiseptic smell, hushed voices and white walls of the hospital because they triggered such painful memories, and checked the time on her watch. She should've told Theresa and Eve she'd be late. She would have, except she'd never dreamed traffic would be so bad—and deep down she'd sort of liked knowing they were at the theater not far away and would be standing outside waiting for her when she finished this difficult errand.

"Listen, you two go on without me. We'll have to hook up afterwards."

"But you're the one who wanted to see this picture," Theresa protested. "You've been talking about it for weeks."

A nurse walked by pushing a pregnant woman in a wheelchair, and Noelle couldn't help watching them enviously until they disappeared around the corner. "I know, but…" she blew out a sigh "…I got a message from Charlene Matheson."

"Charlene Who?"

Noelle opened her mouth to answer but Theresa remembered before she could explain.

"Wait a second. That's the nurse from the hospital, right? Noelle, you're not still making Memory Boxes, are you?"

"Of course I am."

"I thought you said you'd quit."

"No, I just quit telling you about them."

"Because you knew what I'd say."

"Because I disagree with you. When I…" The familiar tightness in her chest made it difficult to get the words out. "When I lost Austin, people didn't know what to say to me, so most people said nothing at all. Those who tried to offer some comfort blundered through it with hurtful remarks like, 'You can have another one.'"

"I know, and I'm terribly sorry, but—"

"My baby came and went so fast that it felt as though he didn't matter to anyone but me."

"You're purposely misunderstanding me, and you know it. The Memory Box Artist Program is wonderful. I'm only concerned that—"

"There's nothing wrong with me participating in it," Noelle broke in again.

"There's nothing wrong with constantly poking and prodding at a painful wound? With never allowing your heart to heal?"

"That's not what I'm doing."

"Yes, it is. You're torturing yourself."

Noelle recognized some truth in what her friend said, but she deserved every poke and prod. Theresa just didn't know it and would probably be stunned to learn the real reason Noelle had lost her baby. Not that Noelle planned on telling her—or anyone else, for that matter. "Quit being so melodramatic. I'm simply trying…" *to atone* "…to help others, okay?"

Theresa made an impatient noise. "Then help AIDS patients or the families of cancer victims. Raise money for the Stanford Home for Children. But stay away from the hospital. Going there has got to be hell on you."

"I *want* to do this," Noelle said.

"Then at least let me deliver the boxes."

When she reached the labor and delivery area, Noelle hesitated outside, gathering the emotional strength to walk through those double doors. She would hand her gift to Charlene Matheson, who would in turn give it to the grieving parents of the lost infant. Then Noelle would leave immediately—before she fell back into the depression from which she'd barely escaped six months ago.

"We'll have to talk about it later," she said. "If you don't want to watch the whole movie without me, get some seats and I'll be there as soon as possible."

Without waiting for a response, she pushed the end button and slipped through the doors.

She couldn't see Charlene Matheson, but another nurse she recognized, Fiona Farley, sat at the nurses' station.

Focusing strictly on Fiona, Noelle hurried forward. *This won't take long, only a minute....*

"Noelle!" Fiona smiled the moment she glanced up. "Charlene mentioned you were coming, and I'm so glad. Someone has stored the Memory Boxes you brought us last month in such a safe place that we can't find them, and we're dealing with a really sad situation."

"I heard." Noelle set the silver papier-mâché box she carried down on the counter. She'd put her whole heart into painting the serene lake and pine trees on the lid and sides. "At least now the poor mother will have the prettiest box I could create to store the baby's personal effects in."

Fiona blinked at her. "The *mother?* Didn't Charlene tell you?"

"I got a message on my machine saying you needed another box, that's it."

"So you don't know that the mother died, too. Only one baby survived. There were twins."

"Oh, no!"

"It's been rough," Fiona said. "Especially on the father. He wasn't married to the babies' mother, but he seems pretty affected. He's been walking around here looking shell-shocked."

Noelle's palms began to sweat. Theresa was right. She shouldn't have come. These situations upset her too much. "I'm so sorry."

"Me, too."

Noelle turned the Memory Box in a circle. "So this is for the father?"

"Yes. Charlene said he was here all night, standing near the nursery window, staring inside."

The memories, and the pain that went with them, rolled over

Noelle like a suffocating blanket. She needed to go, right away. She needed to get out....

"Well, good luck." She forced herself to think of Theresa and Eve waiting for her at the movie theater. The sadness of this tragedy would lift as soon as she left the hospital and let the routine of life swallow her again.

Intending to do exactly that, she said goodbye to Fiona and headed out. But as she passed the hall leading to the nursery, Noelle couldn't help lingering. She knew it was a bad idea, but she had to stop by and see the baby that had survived.

CHAPTER
TWO

HARRISON PROPPED ONE HAND against the glass of the nursery window and rubbed his burning eyes with the other. He hadn't gotten any sleep in the past forty-eight hours. After the first nine months of his residency, he was used to living on willpower and adrenaline, but the stress of his current dilemma seemed to have zapped his usual resiliency. He'd gone home this morning and tried to rest for a few hours, only to lie awake and stare at the ceiling, wondering what to do. He owed more than $120,000 in student loans, was working nearly eighty hours a week at the UC Davis Medical Center, earning barely $30,000 a year, and he had another twenty-seven months before he could practice medicine on his own. Even then, his career would demand the better part of his time and focus for several years. If he kept the child, how would he care for it?

Maybe the baby wasn't even his…. He planned to get a paternity test, just to be sure, but deep down he had little real doubt. Lynnette had been absolutely unwavering when she promised him she'd slept with no one else in over a year. Considering how single-minded she'd been where he was concerned, how hopeful that they'd marry, she was probably telling the truth.

But even if the baby *was* his, he should let the child be adopted by parents who were eager and excited to have a newborn, right? Harrison's own mother, when he finally broke down and called her before returning to the hospital a few hours ago, had said as much. *What does it matter whether he's your son or not? You're not ready to be a father. Give him to someone who wants him.*

Unfortunately he couldn't really rely on her opinion. Rosie didn't have much of a track record for making good decisions. She'd messed up her life over and over again, usually because she was attracted to the wrong kind of man. And she didn't understand how he felt about his father. Harrison could easily imagine Duane walking away from the hospital without a backward glance, which was partly why he couldn't do it himself.

He smiled vaguely at the nurse who waved at him from inside the nursery and shoved off the glass. He should go. He wasn't doing himself or anyone else any good standing here, stewing. But...

Jamming his hands in his pockets, he continued to watch his tiny, dark-headed baby sleep, so oblivious to the tides of fate. So innocent. So dependent...

Dependent on Harrison to make a decision as to what his future would hold. And soon.

The nursery door cracked open and the nurse poked her head out. "It's time for your baby to eat. Do you want to give him his bottle?"

Harrison knew he shouldn't say yes. He'd held his son once, earlier, and the weight of that small body in his arms had only added to the desperation he felt to find a solution they could both live with. But he couldn't refuse to feed him. This poor child—*his* child—didn't even have a mother.

"Sure." He blanked his mind while he waited, but like before, a flood of emotion welled up inside him as the nurse placed his son in his arms.

"Have you picked out a name for him yet?" she asked, passing him the bottle.

The moment the rubber nipple brushed his cheek, the baby turned his head and opened his mouth. "No, not yet."

"There are books with lists and lists of names, if you're having trouble thinking of one."

Harrison didn't want to look through any books. Until he made up his mind about the role he wanted to play in this child's life, he sure as hell knew better than to name him. "Thanks," he said, so she wouldn't press him further.

"Let me know what you come up with so we can fill out the birth certificate." With that, she disappeared into the nursery.

Harrison knew she'd return for the baby in just a few minutes, and was grateful for the time alone. But the solitude didn't last long. A tall slender woman with olive-colored skin approached the nursery. She was wearing a pair of snug-fitting jeans and a red sweater, and was so intent on staring beyond the glass at the new babies that she didn't seem to notice him sitting in the small alcove to her right.

Spotting her, the nurse waved and hurried to the door. "Hi, Noelle. Good to see you."

"Good to see you, too, Lana."

The woman named Noelle was so attractive, Harrison normally would've figured out a way to meet her. She wasn't wearing a ring. But in the process of one day, *this* day, dating had fallen completely off his list of priorities.

"Did you already find Charlene?" the nurse asked her. "I know she was asking if you'd been in."

"I didn't see Charlene, but Fiona was at the nurses' station."

"Great. So, what brings you by the nursery?"

"I wanted to see the baby boy who lost his mother and brother. Is he in there?"

Harrison sat up straighter, wondering how word of his predicament had spread to this elegant stranger.

The nurse immediately dropped her voice and jerked her head subtly in Harrison's direction. "He's with his father, over there."

Noelle turned and blushed to the roots of her shiny dark hair. "I'm so sorry," she said. "I didn't notice you. And I…I wanted to…"

"What?" he prompted curiously when she hesitated.

"I wanted to offer my silent support to the baby, I guess. But since you're here, I'll tell you how terrible I feel about what's happened. I know you're dealing with a very difficult situation. If there's anything I can do—"

"Do I know you?" he asked, confused. This woman had almond-shaped green eyes and a touch of the exotic in her face and bearing. Harrison felt pretty certain he would have remembered her if—

"No, we've never met."

"She helps us out here at the hospital," the nurse interjected.

"So you're in the medical profession?"

"No." Noelle hitched her purse higher on her shoulder and slid the fingers of one hand into the pocket of her jeans. "I'm an artist."

He didn't get the connection. "Are you also a grief counselor?"

"Definitely not. I—"

"Noelle heads up some of our community projects," the nurse explained. "We're all very grateful to her."

So how did that apply to him? He was about to ask, but the baby started to cry and Noelle didn't give him the chance. She'd been rummaging through her purse while the nurse talked. Now she stuck a card under his nose.

"I'd like to leave this with you just in case…in case you ever feel the need to talk. I may not be a counselor, but I've been where you're at now. I know it's not easy." As soon as he accepted her card, she left.

Harrison finally got the baby to take the bottle again and stared after her before turning questioning eyes on the nurse.

"I'm sorry if Noelle put you on the spot," she said gently. "But she really is a very caring person. If you ever need someone to talk to, I'd give her a call."

After leaving the hospital, Noelle sat in her car for several minutes, watching drop after drop of rain splatter on her windshield. She knew her friends were waiting for her, that it was rude not to hurry to the theater. But she couldn't seem to make herself put the key in the ignition. She didn't want to be around anyone tonight. She was too busy feeling sorry for the father and baby she'd seen in the nursery—and wondering why the heck she'd given the man her card. There really wasn't anything she could do for him.

Her cell phone rang. She stared down at the caller ID, saw that it was Theresa, and was tempted to ignore the call. She didn't want to talk right now. But Theresa wouldn't give up. The ringing stopped, only to start up again a few seconds later.

Finally Noelle answered.

"Where are you?" Theresa whispered. "You've missed half the show."

"I just got in the car. I'm coming."

"How'd it go?"

Noelle once again pictured the father she'd seen in the nursery. He'd looked rumpled and dazed, but if possible, he was even more handsome than her ex-husband. Steven was a bit shorter and stockier, perhaps—it was difficult to tell, because the man in the hospital had never stood up—but they both had very short blond hair, blue eyes and a confident air that worked a lot like gravity, constantly drawing hapless souls closer.

Hapless souls like her….

"Fine."

"Truly?"

"Truly," she said, and decided to forget about the man in the hospital. She'd just met him. What were the chances he'd ever really call her?

CHAPTER
THREE

HARRISON SAT in his spare bedroom, which he used as an office, and stared at the Memory Box the nurses at the hospital had cautiously presented to him. A card bearing the foot impression of the twin who'd died, the baby's photograph, a slip of paper with his birth statistics, and Lynnette's hospital bracelet were arranged neatly inside. Those items were all that remained to signify that his other child had even existed.

Harrison could see that, in a normal situation, the nurses' gesture would bring significant comfort to bereft parents. But he didn't know how to feel—about the baby who had died or the baby who had lived. His need to cut free from anything that might hold him back from the life he'd planned was waging war with his sense of duty, and he doubted he'd be the same person when it was all over, no matter which side prevailed. To make matters worse, he didn't have time to get his head together. The pediatrician had indicated that the baby who'd lived would be released from the hospital in a few days. A decision had to be made.

With a frustrated groan, he set the Memory Box on his desk and picked up his pocket planner. Lynnette's funeral was the day after tomorrow. They'd have a small service for Tyler Brent—who'd been named by Lynnette's sister—at the same time. It was tough to face Lynnette's mother. She was taking her daughter's death hard and seemed to blame him, but he wanted to attend the funeral. If only he could make arrangements at the Medical Center. They were having trouble covering his shifts.

Glancing at the Memory Box again, he remembered Nurse Matheson telling him that Noelle Kane, the woman he'd met in the nursery, had painted it. She was also the one who'd planted the thought that talking through his dilemma might help him arrive at a resolution. But he couldn't think of anyone close enough to call. His best friend Jimmy, who'd more or less stuck by him growing up even though their lives had taken very different paths, was in jail for getting into a bar fight and nearly beating a man to death. Most of the other people he knew were professional associates, except for the guys on his softball team. Occasionally they went out for a beer after the game, but he doubted any of them would appreciate hearing from him at three in the morning.

He remembered the card Noelle had handed him and began to dig through his pockets. *I've been where you're at.* Obviously she didn't completely understand his situation, but the empathy in her eyes, along with the nurse's recommendation, seemed hopeful. And why not talk to a stranger? Noelle Kane didn't have any expectations where he was concerned. She would be less prone to make value judgments and had no reason to sway him one way or the other.

Finding her card jammed into his billfold, he stared at her personal information. Judging by the address, she lived twenty minutes away from him in Sacramento's Fabulous Forties, a neighborhood to the east of downtown that was made up of unique old homes. It was an expensive area, but it wasn't ostentatious. He could easily picture the woman he'd met living there. That section of town generally appealed to artists and other creative types.

Fleetingly he wondered if Noelle had a husband or boyfriend who might object to his call. But she hadn't been wearing a ring, and calling *had* been her suggestion....

With a sigh, he dialed the number in the bottom right-hand corner.

Three rings went unanswered. He almost hung up. Surely when she'd said he could call, she'd never imagined he'd do it in the middle of the night—

"Hello?"

He winced at the muffled sound of her voice. He'd awakened her all right. "Noelle?"

"Yes?"

"This is Harrison Ferello."

A confused silence settled over the line.

"The guy you met at the hospital nursery tonight," he clarified.

"Oh!" He heard some rustling, and when she continued, she spoke more clearly. "Are you okay, Harrison?"

Despite the fact that he'd called her for help, he almost gave her the habitual, "I'm fine." Because his mother hadn't been capable of holding down a job or keeping a roof over their heads for more than a few months at a time, he'd grown up very fast. To admit weakness or need felt awkward, unmanly. But he reminded himself that he didn't know this woman, that he'd likely never see her again, and forced out the truth. "No."

Another pause. "What's going on?"

"Are you married?" he blurted out.

"Why do you ask?"

Wariness had entered her voice, making him realize she might think he was coming on to her. "My call could be…unwelcome, especially so late," he explained. "If you're with someone, I'll let you go, maybe call back at a decent hour." *Or maybe not…*

She seemed to relax. "We don't always need others according to a convenient schedule."

He wasn't very well-versed at needing anyone, anytime. He liked companionship, but dependence, especially any kind of *emotional* dependence, scared the hell out of him. "Still, I don't want to cause a problem for you—"

"You're not causing a problem. I'm not with anyone. I'm divorced."

"Do you have children?"

"No, but let's talk about you," she said firmly.

He'd called to talk about him, but now that he had her on the line, he didn't know where to start. "To be honest, I'm not sure what I expect you to do."

"Maybe you just need someone to listen. If you're like I was, you're drowning in grief and despair and there doesn't seem to be anything to stop the pain."

"I'm not sure what I'm feeling." He carried the cordless phone from his office to the living room. "Confusion. Anger. Resentment. Take your pick." He slouched onto the couch and stared at the television he'd left on earlier.

"Who or what are you angry at?" she asked. "God? Fate?"

"Lynnette." He blinked when he said that, surprised by his own admission. How could he be angry with Lynnette? She'd left him in the lurch, but at least *he* was still around. Sadly, she'd lost her life.

"Who's Lynnette?"

"She's the woman who died in the hospital yesterday." He knew he must sound callous, stating it so baldly. But he was so overwhelmed by everything that had happened, he couldn't face Lynnette's death right now, not in addition to the decisions about the baby.

Somehow, Noelle didn't seem put off. "A lot of people are angry when their loved ones pass away. It's part of the grieving process."

He laughed bitterly as understanding dawned. She thought he was upset with Lynnette for *leaving* him. She thought he was the brokenhearted husband or lover. "I'm afraid my feelings aren't that noble."

Her response came slowly. "They're not?"

"No." Leaning his head on the couch, he closed his eyes and rubbed his temples. "I'm angry at her for—" he struggled to be specific "—for ever loving me, I guess. I never really wanted her to, especially after the first few weeks."

"Does that mean you didn't return her feelings?"

"I might have loved her a little. I don't know. Things got crazy pretty fast."

"Do you want to explain that?"

Harrison generally wasn't one to share the details of his relationships. He was busy and driven and knew he didn't focus on them as much as he should. But tonight, talking seemed to shove *the big decision*, the decision that would affect him and his child for

the rest of their lives, into the background, bringing him temporary relief. "She became so…obsessive," he explained.

"In what way?"

"In every way. She hated it when I spent time with anyone else,
resented the hours I studied or worked. She even tried to get me
to give up softball so we could be together more often."

"Did you?"

Somehow Noelle Kane was beginning to seem less like a real
person than a voice coming out of thin air to help him spill the
torturous thoughts bottled up inside his head. "For a while. I
wanted to make her happy. But enough was never enough. I decided I needed to create some space between us. Not long after
that, I caught her following me around, checking up on me."

"Did she have reason to distrust you?"

"None." He propped his feet up on the coffee table and muted
the television because the low hum he'd found comforting before
now seemed too loud. "Anyway, it got to the point where I didn't
want to see her at all. She'd pout if I couldn't come over. Or if we
did get together, she'd beg me to stay longer, even though I had
to work or get my laundry done or whatever. Pretty soon she
started hinting that she wanted to get married."

"To be honest, it doesn't sound as though she was very stable."

"She seemed normal to everyone else."

"*That* doesn't mean anything."

He detected a note of bitterness in her voice but didn't give it
much thought. Now that he was finally opening up, the words inside him seemed to be battling each other in their hurry to get
out. "I tried to be as honest and up-front as possible. She knew I
wasn't in the market for a wife, that I've never wanted kids."

"You don't want a family?"

"No."

"Why not?"

He was probably afraid he'd fail as badly as his father. "I don't
know."

"Then, what *do* you want?" she asked.

He could tell his sentiment toward marriage and children hadn't endeared him to her, but he'd already committed himself to being ruthlessly honest. "I want to devote myself to medicine."

"You're a doctor?"

"Yes, but I'm in the first year of a three-year residency."

"What's your specialty?"

"Emergency Medicine."

"My ex-husband is the administrator at Wilheim General so I know how difficult it is to get into the medical profession."

That was a whole other subject. Med school had been beyond grueling, and his internship wasn't much easier. But he didn't have any complaints. He'd known from the beginning that his career path wouldn't be an easy one. Dealing with Lynnette had been a bigger challenge because the relationship had so quickly become one-sided. "I'd be fine if developing my career was all I had to worry about. But this..." He shook his head.

"I'm sure you wish you'd broken up with her long ago."

"I *did* break up with her," he said. "It's been eight months since we were together. After we quit seeing each other, she gave up her job at the sandwich shop where I met her and moved forty minutes away. I thought our relationship was over. Then, out of the blue, she contacted me."

"When?"

He leaned over to reach the remote and started flipping aimlessly through stations as a way to siphon off some of his nervous energy. "Three weeks ago. She called and asked me to meet her for lunch. And that's when I learned about the twins."

"You're kidding."

"No."

"Why didn't she contact you sooner?"

The outrage in that question validated his own reaction and goaded him to continue. "That's what I wanted to know. She said she was afraid I'd try to talk her into having an abortion."

"So, was the pregnancy an accident, or..."

He rested his elbows on his knees, tossed the remote away and forgot about the television as he stared down at the carpet. "I don't know. She claimed it was, but I can't imagine how that could be true. She told me she had polycystic ovarian syndrome and prob-ably couldn't get pregnant. She was on the pill to regulate her pe-riods, and I *still* used a condom." Fleetingly he realized this was a rather personal conversation to be having with a woman he'd barely met, especially such a beautiful woman. But he didn't care. He was in so far over his head that he couldn't consider anything except how to get out of the mess he was in.

"It wouldn't be the first time a girl got pregnant on purpose," she said.

Harrison was almost positive Lynnette had been hoping he'd break down and marry her, but now that she was gone, he wanted to give her the benefit of the doubt. "I guess it doesn't matter any-more. Knowing isn't going to help me."

"But do you think she was capable of that kind of deception?"

He picked up the ball and glove on his coffee table. "She was making me pretty uncomfortable there at the end," he admitted. "Right after I broke off with her, she paged me at the hospital. When I called her back, she started sobbing and saying she'd rather die than live without me."

"So that's what you meant by crazy. Well, I wish I could say I'm surprised, but it actually makes sense in a twisted way. You were backing off, she was feeling desperate. And you were so careful to use protection when you had sex, it probably gave her the impres-sion that a baby was the one thing that could hold you."

If so, his concern with preventing pregnancy had actually *caused* his current predicament.

There was more rustling on the other end of the phone, and Harrison imagined Noelle trying to get comfortable in bed. "I'm sorry for interrupting your sleep," he said, suddenly aware that she was a living, breathing human being and not the disembodied voice he'd imagined earlier. "I should let you go."

"No, I'm okay."

He hesitated. He was reluctant to take advantage of her, but he had to admit that talking to her made a difference.

"What I can't figure out is why she waited so long to make you aware of the pregnancy," she went on. "If she meant to get pregnant but was afraid you'd push for an abortion, I'd expect her to call you somewhere in the fourth or fifth month, not right before the babies were due."

He tossed the ball into his mitt with a satisfying *thwump.* "When I never called after she moved away, she knew I was serious about the breakup and said she'd decided to keep the news from me indefinitely. But her conscience finally got the better of her."

Noelle's response was a small but honest, "Wow."

Growing agitated again, Harrison stood up. *Thwump.* The impact of the ball felt good as it hit the pocket of his glove. "And now there's a newborn lying in the hospital who…" He didn't know what ending to put on that sentence. Who had no mother. Who deserved a real chance in life. Who was tiny and perfect and yet—

"Who what?" she prompted.

Harrison could hear the wind driving rain against his living room window. The rest of the leaves on the trees would probably be in the parking lot by morning. It had been a wet November. "Who has no one but me," he finished.

Silence reigned for several seconds. He forgot about tossing the ball while he waited for her response.

"And from what you've told me, you don't want him," she said at last.

Scowling, he stretched his neck muscles and tried to explain. "It's not that simple. I don't have anything to give a baby. And I'm not sure I'd be the best person to raise him, even if I did. I was an only child. We moved around a lot. I was never around younger kids." Considering his relationship with Rosie and how they'd taken care of each other almost like equals, he felt as though he'd never really *been* a kid.

"Do you have anyone who might be able to help you?"

"No."

"Then why not put the baby up for adoption?" she asked. "Surely you've thought of that."

"I've thought of it, sure. But…" *Thwump.* The ball hit the glove again. "I can't be certain he'd go to a good home," he said, although he knew there had to be people, couples, who were far better equipped for a baby than he was.

"You could try to find a family with whom you feel comfortable," Noelle responded. "Depending on the type of adoption you choose, you might even be able to maintain a relationship with him."

He couldn't imagine passing his son off to complete strangers. Shirking his duty was something Duane would do, wasn't it? What Duane *did* do?

Somehow the important decisions in Harrison's life always came back to his father. Duane seemed to be standing in the corner of Harrison's apartment, glaring at him, taunting him. *You think you're different, boy? Better? Look at you. You're scrambling to get out of this one, huh?*

"How involved could I be?" he asked.

"That would depend, but there've got to be options."

"I'll have to do some research." As if he had the time… *Thwump.* "Or…"

Her tone held the promise of a resolution. "Or?" he repeated hopefully, trying to banish Duane from his mind.

"I don't know if you'd ever consider this, but…I'd be happy to take him."

Harrison froze with the ball in his hand. "*Take* him? What do you mean by that?"

She sounded more than a little hesitant when she answered. "I haven't considered all the ramifications yet, but…I'd love to have a baby. *This* baby."

Her? He'd met Noelle only once. And yet he knew several important facts about her already, all of which seemed to recommend her. She was about his age, not too young or too old, obviously kind, definitely intelligent, and she came highly recommended by the nursing staff at the hospital.

"Are you talking day care or adoption or…what?"

"Not day care."

"Then adoption?"

"Yes," she said, almost defiantly. "I'm talking adoption. My heart. My home."

He froze, surprised that he wasn't more relieved to have someone ready to step in for him. "That sounds pretty permanent."

"If I'm going to care for him, I should have legal rights, don't you think?"

"But you're single. If I give him up, why not make sure he goes to a couple or maybe even a family?"

"Because you won't find anyone who will take better care of him than me. And I'll be flexible about letting you be part of his life."

"How big a part would you let me play?"

"How big a part do you *want* to play?"

He pinched the bridge of his nose, trying to answer the one question he'd found unanswerable so far.

"You say you don't want children, but at the same time, you seem reluctant to give him up," she said when he didn't respond right away.

Because he was torn. Before he'd left the hospital tonight, he'd decided his son looked like pictures of his mother's father, who'd died when Harrison was barely five. Ever since that moment, his baby hadn't been a nameless entity to him anymore. His baby had suddenly become Jeremy Ferello.

"Why don't we sleep on the idea and talk about it some more tomorrow," he said. "In person. Can we get together?"

"Of course. Is tomorrow afternoon okay?"

The day before the funeral. "Fine. Where?"

"We could meet here at my place."

Closing his eyes, he tried to envision handing his baby over to this woman. Could he do it? He wasn't sure, but he had to do something.

"Sounds good," he said. Then he set up a time, jotted down directions and hung up.

Noelle sat on the edge of the bed and dropped her head in her hands. Had she lost her mind? What had she been thinking? Basically she'd just offered to raise someone else's child. The son of a man she scarcely knew. And she'd promised Harrison he could be part of his son's life, which meant he'd be part of *her* life.

"I'll never learn," she groaned, and fell back on the bed. Harrison was handsome and seemed intelligent, successful. But Steven had been handsome and intelligent, too. Marrying him had been like biting into a creamy, delicious-looking truffle, only to get a mouthful of salt. She wasn't likely to forget the experience, or be tricked by another smooth-talking man.

Smooth-talking... Harrison definitely knew how to handle himself with a woman. She'd sensed that immediately.

She glanced at the phone. She should call him back and tell him she'd changed her mind. Except she wasn't sure she *had* changed her mind. She wanted a baby. She wanted a second chance to be a good mother, to protect the innocent. Nothing meant more to her than that.

And deep down, she doubted Harrison Ferello would stick around very long, anyway.

CHAPTER
FOUR

"TELL ME YOU'RE NOT really going to do this," Theresa said, trailing Noelle into the house.

They'd been together all morning, shopping. Noelle hadn't mentioned anything about Harrison's call last night, or his baby, until Theresa was about to drop her off. Why she'd broken down in the end, she didn't know. She should've kept her mouth shut.

"Can't you be positive for once?" she asked, hanging her suede jacket on the antique hall tree in her small entry and stashing her purse right below it. "If Harrison and I can come to some sort of agreement, I have a chance to get a baby…*a newborn baby*…right away. That's a miracle!"

"A miracle?" Theresa didn't bother removing her coat. Until Noelle told her about Harrison and their meeting this afternoon, she hadn't been planning on coming in. She had to take her niece to the orthodontist in fifteen minutes, but she wasn't about to let that stop her from trying to dissuade Noelle from making what she termed "a big mistake."

"The question is why you'd want to take on a baby right now," Theresa said, following Noelle so closely as they made their way into the kitchen that she nearly stepped on her heel.

Sometimes Theresa seemed to take Austin's death far too lightly. Her attitude triggered a rush of anger in Noelle, but she beat it back by reminding herself that Theresa didn't really understand. "In case you've forgotten, they gave me a hysterectomy when I lost Austin," she said. "I can't have children of my own, and babies don't grow on trees. I can't pass up an opportunity like this."

"Think about the risks!"

Theresa tried to get in front of her to capture her complete attention, and Noelle finally whipped around and propped a hand on her hip. "The only risks I'm thinking about are what might happen to the baby if I don't take him."

"For all you know, the baby could go to an ideal family. You can't say for sure that he won't."

Noelle had been up half the night, worrying about her decision, but she wasn't about to admit that to Theresa. "I'll feel more assured of his safety and well-being if *I'm* taking care of him."

"What if this Harrison guy makes your life miserable?"

"I told you, he doesn't really want the baby. He's reacting to a sense of obligation. Once he realizes I've got everything under control, that the baby doesn't need him, he'll go on about his business. After a few weeks, I doubt I'll hear from him more than twice a year."

"And the baby will be yours."

"And the baby will be mine."

"What if it doesn't work out that way? What if Harrison changes his mind in a few years and wants to take his baby away from you? What will you do then?"

"A private open adoption is still an adoption. He can't do that. Besides, this baby's mother tricked Harrison into getting her pregnant. As I said, he's just looking for a good way out."

Theresa shook her head. "Haven't you ever heard of Murphy's Law?"

With an exaggerated sigh, Noelle circumvented her friend to start the coffeemaker. After her sleepless night, she needed a strong jolt of caffeine to get her through the rest of the afternoon. "What are my other options?" she asked. "I can't use an adoption agency. They'd put me on a list, a *long* list, and because I'm single, I have no doubt I'd be at the very bottom of it. And this baby needs me."

"Lots of babies need loving parents," Theresa said. "This isn't the only one. Why not wait until later to adopt—like when you meet someone else and remarry?"

Noelle doubted she'd remarry anytime soon. She still hadn't recovered from her divorce. But Theresa hadn't heard the extenuating circumstances, didn't know about Steven's dark side. Noelle had kept his "little problem" to herself after he'd promised that he'd seek help—and because she didn't want to face the questions it'd raise among her friends and family. *Why didn't you say something sooner? Why didn't you get away from him? How could you let him treat you like that?* Asking herself those questions was painful enough.

"I'll just have to hope for the best," she said, and filled the coffeepot with water.

"That's a cop-out. You're telling me you're not willing to consider all the dangers."

Noelle understood the dangers. She just couldn't think beyond getting her arms securely around the tiny bundle in the hospital. "Maybe I'm not."

"I think you should. Harrison Ferello might be unsafe."

"He's a doctor. He's highly educated and driven, not dangerous." After her experience with Steven, she cringed at her own words, but she knew it was an argument Theresa would understand.

"You don't even know this guy," Theresa insisted.

"Harrison won't stick around!"

Theresa threw up her hands. "Steven said you could be stubborn, but this is ridiculous."

The note of familiarity in Theresa's voice when she mentioned Noelle's ex-husband was new—and nearly caused Noelle to drop the coffeepot. "What'd you say?"

A flash of something—Guilt? Alarm? Regret?—passed through Theresa's eyes, and she turned away. "Nothing. I've got to go. I'm late."

It was Noelle's turn to follow Theresa through the house. "Wait a minute. When did you talk to Steven?"

Theresa finally turned at the door. "A week or so ago."

"Where?"

She glanced down at her car keys as she opened the door, appearing more eager to leave by the second. "I bumped into him at the movies."

"Why didn't you mention it to me?"

"Because it was nothing. We said, 'Hello, how are you?' You know, the usual."

"That's it?"

"Yeah."

They stared at each other for a second, then Theresa mumbled goodbye and left.

Noelle leaned against the door. Something with Theresa didn't sit right. She suspected it had to do with Steven but couldn't imagine what or why. Steven and Theresa had always hated each other.

With a sigh, Noelle decided to let it go. The stress of what was going on in her own life right now was making her jumpy.

Harrison slowed so he could compare the numbers painted on the curb with the address on Noelle's card. This was it. He'd found her house, and it was everything he'd anticipated. A small English Tudor made of red burnished brick, with an arched entry covered in climbing ivy, it sat in the middle of a classy neighborhood of equally stylish homes and looked as clean as it was well-maintained.

Was it the perfect place to raise a child?

He couldn't answer that now, but he was hoping his meeting with Noelle would give him a better idea.

Parking his old truck out front so he wouldn't block the rather narrow driveway leading to a new Volvo and a detached garage, he got out and strode up a walkway littered with red and gold leaves. After hanging up with Noelle last night, he'd fallen into a troubled sleep, but what rest he'd managed to grab, combined with a hot shower and shave and a pair of comfortable jeans, made him feel almost new again.

Noelle answered the door before he could knock. "Hi," she said, a polite smile on her face. "Did you find the house okay?"

Wearing a black sweater and a pair of gray slacks, she was even prettier than Harrison remembered, but he told himself to ignore that. Looks didn't make a mother. His own mother was more than moderately attractive, but as much as he loved Rosie, he wouldn't wish her style of parenting on any child. "Your directions were easy to follow," he said.

"I'm glad." She opened the door wider. "Come in."

The interior of the house smelled slightly of fresh paint and was stylish yet warm and homey. Harrison could see Noelle had a knack for decorating, although he probably didn't have the most discerning eye. Anything was better than the stained Goodwill couches and tattered drapes he'd grown up with. "Nice place."

"Thanks."

"Is this where you lived when you were married?" he asked.

"Steven purchased the house while we were engaged. I moved in after we married. When we divorced, I bought him out." She waved to a picture window overlooking a well-tended garden. "My workshop is out there, to the left. I didn't want to lose it."

Harrison had come here determined to view everything from its worst possible angle, just to be safe. But he didn't see much to be leery about. "Your ex is the hospital administrator you mentioned last night, right?"

"Right. Can I get you a drink?"

"No, thanks."

She waved him into a living room with hardwood floors, overstuffed green sofas, a circular area rug, distressed pine tables and plenty of candles. But it was the artwork covering the walls and the large sculptures blending in with the furniture that caught his attention.

"This is nice," he said, carefully studying the painting of a rocky cove over the fireplace.

"Thank you."

He recognized the style from the painting on his Memory Box and verified that it was her work by checking the name scribbled in the bottom corner. "So this is what you do for a living?"

"No. Painting's only my hobby."

He cocked an eyebrow at her. "Then…"

She motioned to a life-size sculpture of a small child doing a cartwheel between the sofa and chair. "This is what I do for a living."

He couldn't help being impressed. "You created this?"

She nodded. "Right now I'm doing a whole group of teenagers for the lobby of a new office building on J Street."

"No kidding." She was obviously talented. Her work looked worthy of the best galleries in New York and San Francisco— which lent her even more credibility. "You're good," he said.

"Thank you." She waved him toward the couch. "Please, sit down."

He did as she asked, but refused to let his reservations disappear too quickly. She seemed normal, almost ideal, but there was so much to raising a child, and he had to take every precaution. He'd never be able to live with himself if she abused or neglected Jeremy. From working in the emergency room, he'd seen what some adults were capable of doing to children.

"Where do you want to start?" she asked, folding one knee beneath her and perching on the leather ottoman across from him.

"Maybe you can explain to me why you want a baby."

He'd been hoping to begin with something simple, but he could tell by the expression that flitted across her face that this question wasn't particularly easy. "Because I lost my own baby," she said shortly. "A year ago."

Of course. She'd mentioned grief and despair. He should have anticipated a tragedy in her recent past. But with postpartum depression, bipolar disorder, and a host of other maladies that sometimes compelled a mother to hurt her own child, this information ended up worrying him more rather than creating any kind of kinship between them. "I'm sorry to hear that."

Her gaze remained steady despite his scrutiny, but she didn't elaborate.

"How old was the baby when…"

"He was stillborn."

Harrison allowed himself a mental sigh of relief. If she was telling the truth—and he'd have to make sure, of course—her response ruled out his worst fears, including Shaken Baby Syndrome. "Were you married at the time?"

"Yes. But my husband and I split up right after I got out of the hospital."

"Losing a child is difficult on a marriage," he said.

Finely arched brows gathered above clear green eyes. "My marriage was in trouble before that, Mr.—"

"Call me Harrison." They'd been so informal with each other last night, but that was before they were considering some type of on-going relationship. Now they both seemed to have taken several steps away from each other.

"Harrison, then," she said. "I was trying to make my marriage work. I didn't realize until I lost the baby that I'd been stupid to hang on for the five years that I did."

"I see." He rested his hands on his knees. He was curious to hear the reasons behind the divorce, but he didn't feel justified in asking, at least not yet. The possibility of a future marriage, however, was a different story. "You know, I hate to pose such personal questions, but—"

She held up a hand. "I understand. You have to do what you can to protect the baby."

"Exactly."

She gave him a brittle smile. Maybe she didn't mind him *asking*, but anything that involved the loss of her baby was obviously a sensitive subject. "What else do you want to know?" she asked.

He searched his mind for a question that didn't pertain to her marriage or her lost child. That way she could relax a bit before he returned to the hard stuff. "Do you know CPR?"

"No, but I'd happily take a class."

He knew this was coming off like a job interview, but wasn't sure how else to approach it. He couldn't make a decision without feeling reasonably secure that it was a good one. "Tell me a little about your background."

"I grew up in Chicago with three younger brothers. My parents divorced when I was starting high school, which is probably why I tried so hard to save my own marriage. I don't think I ever really forgave my mother for kicking my father out."

"You were close to him?"

"My life just wasn't the same afterward, especially once he remarried. My stepmother had two children of her own, and my brothers were such a handful, she didn't like having us over, so we rarely got to see my father."

"Unfortunately I think that happens all too often. Where is your family now?"

"Still in Chicago. Two of my brothers have married. The youngest is in high school."

"What brought you to Sacramento?"

"I went to UCLA. While I was there, I roomed with a girl who was born in Granite Bay. After graduation, Senator Rodriguez offered her a job here in Sacramento and she talked me into moving north with her."

"And you like it well enough to stay?"

"It's not as cold as Chicago or as crowded as L.A."

He rubbed his chin, trying to think of a delicate way to ask his next question. But there *was* no delicate way. "Have you—" He cleared his throat. "Have you ever been sexually molested, Noelle?"

Her jaw dropped. "*What?*"

"I'm sorry, but that kind of trauma would definitely affect your core values and beliefs, which might carry over into how you treat a child. I want my son to have a healthy view of human intimacy. It's an important part of life."

"I guess I can understand that," she said, but she spoke with some reservation and he got the impression she was evaluating him as much as he was evaluating her. "I've never been molested." She met his gaze more directly. "Have you?"

He recognized the flare of spirit that had motivated her to return the question. "No."

"Well, that settles that, I hope."

Not quite. "How would you handle the subject of sex when raising my son?"

She lifted her chin as if to say she could answer any question he thought to pose. "I'd teach him that sex is normal and enjoyable."

Their gazes locked, and an unexpected frisson of awareness zipped through Harrison. It had been eight months since he'd been with a woman. He was beginning to feel deprived—and Noelle was more than a little appealing. But now wasn't the time to experience any kind of arousal. If she was the decent person he thought she was, he needed her too badly to risk a romantic entanglement that could easily end badly.

"I'd also teach him to respect himself and the women he gets involved with," she continued. Her voice held just enough challenge to make him believe she'd felt the change in chemistry between them but was resisting any type of acknowledgment. "He needs to be aware of the dangers, both physical and emotional. And he should know that sex is never better than when two people are *fully committed and in love.*"

Had she emphasized that last point, or had he imagined it? He wasn't sure. Regardless, he felt his desire wane. After Lynnette, commitment equated with obsession and didn't rate high on his personal list of "must haves."

But what Noelle had said sounded excellent from a parenting perspective. Perfect, as a matter of fact. "That's a healthy response."

"I'm glad you think so."

"What about your future love life?"

"What about it?"

"Do you think there's any chance you might marry soon?"

"None whatsoever."

That had been stated strongly enough. "In a few years?"

"I can't predict something like that, can you?"

Even without a crystal ball, he felt fairly safe saying he wouldn't marry in the next ten years. But he took her point.

"Is there anything else?" she asked.

He had at least a million questions, but he was quickly coming to the conclusion that he wasn't going to find a better candidate to take care of Jeremy. Because he didn't want to scare her off, he decided to ask just a few more. "What type of discipline would you use if Jeremy—"

"Jeremy?" she said.

"That's what I've named him."

"I see. Jeremy what?"

"I don't know. I haven't decided on a middle name. I thought, if we came to some type of agreement about his future, that maybe I'd let you do that."

Another distracting, sexy smile curved her lips. "Okay."

He shifted to the edge of his seat and forced himself to regain his focus. "Anyway, about your style of discipline…"

"My methods would depend on the age of the child and what he's doing wrong," she said. "Time out, if he were younger. Loss of privileges if he were older."

Harrison remembered his mother beating him with a vacuum cord when he was eight years old. Rosie hadn't been particularly violent, but she'd been ill-equipped to raise a child, especially alone, and he'd pushed her too far once or twice. "Jeremy could do much worse," he said. "Are you ever planning to work outside the house?"

"As long as business is good, probably not. But situations change. I can't make you any promises there, either. Only that I'll do my best no matter what comes."

He liked her. She was honest and talented and intelligent. Could he have actually found a solution to his dilemma? "I believe you would."

She seemed to relax. "Great. Any more questions?"

"Don't you have a few?"

She rubbed her palms on her pants as if suddenly nervous again. "You indicated last night that you'd prefer to be involved in your son's life in some capacity. I'm still wondering *how* involved. Are we talking about weekend visits? Or a yearly Christmas gift?"

A yearly Christmas gift? She was obviously offering him the chance to play a very minimal role in Jeremy's life. But just because she seemed like the perfect caregiver didn't mean she was. And he hated the thought that one day there might be a little nine-year-old boy lying awake as he once had, wondering why his father hadn't cared enough to know him.

He took a deep breath. "I'm not sure how involved I want to be…yet. My schedule is pretty demanding. Can we play it by ear for a while?"

Her smile widened considerably. "Of course. I know you're in a difficult situation, especially with the pressure of your residency and everything."

"Exactly." She seemed a little *too* accommodating in this area, but it was the first thing about Noelle that made Harrison the least bit uncomfortable, so he chose to believe she was only trying to be agreeable. "What about child support?" he asked.

"Child support?" She blinked at him as though she'd never heard of the concept.

"Surely you expect some kind of financial help from me."

"Actually, I hadn't considered it. I don't think parents who adopt a child get support, even if it's an open adoption."

What had sounded so ideal just moments before now seemed so...*permanent*. He wouldn't owe any child support, but he wouldn't have any parental rights, either. He'd be like a visiting uncle. "Is that the only arrangement you're willing to consider?" he asked, feeling conflicted again.

Her eyes narrowed. "What other type of arrangement did you have in mind?"

He raked a hand through his hair. "I guess for right now, I was hoping for something less formal."

She stiffened. "If we don't do a legal adoption, I'll have no protection. You could change your mind in a year or two and decide to cut me out of Jeremy's life. And I've already lost one baby, Harrison…." She didn't finish, but she didn't have to. She'd lost one, and she wasn't willing to risk losing another. He could understand her reluctance to trust him, especially on this, and yet he wasn't ready to give up his parental rights, not until he felt more confident in his decision and in her.

"Then we need some sort of trial period," he said. "I can't sign Jeremy over until I know you better."

Clearly not pleased, she frowned. "How long of a trial period?"

"Three months?" he offered hopefully.

She sank her teeth into her bottom lip. "I'll give you one month," she said at last. "But you *have* to be willing to make a decision by then."

CHAPTER
FIVE

A ONE-MONTH TRIAL period. Noelle had known right away she'd made a mistake bending on that issue. Once again she'd been too empathetic for her own good. But how could she expect Harrison to trust her with his child before he really knew her?

Besides, a month wasn't unreasonable, she decided as she headed in to Wee Ones, a shop specializing in baby furniture that was located a few blocks from her house. Thirty days would allow the shock of the situation to wear off and give Harrison a chance to recover, which was only fair. And Noelle didn't have too much to fear. He was in the first year of his residency, which meant he was as busy as he'd probably ever be. Chances were he wouldn't be able to come around much. If he did show up a lot, he'd learn just how needy a newborn was and how ill-equipped he was to deal with it; if he didn't visit very often, he'd quickly grow accustomed to letting her care for Jeremy while he devoted himself to his career, which was what he really wanted to do anyway. Soon he'd realize he was better off letting his son go. Then it would simply be a matter of filling out the paperwork.

Noelle's cell phone chirped as the Wee Ones saleswoman approached with a polite, "Can I help you?"

Noelle offered her an apologetic smile before glancing down to see who was trying to reach her.

Her screen read, "Unknown caller."

"I'll be with you in a second," she said, and pressed the talk button. "Hello?"

"There you are."

She gritted her teeth the moment she recognized her ex-husband's voice, frustrated that his name hadn't popped up on her screen so she could have let the call go to voice mail. "You've been looking for me?"

"I tried the house first. So how's my beautiful ex?"

The charm meant Steven wanted something. When he was this nice, he always wanted something, and he generally knew how to get it—at least from everyone else.

"My phone said 'unknown caller,'" she told him.

"I'm at a restaurant, using a pay phone. I lost my cell this morning and it hasn't turned up yet."

Lowering her voice, she pivoted away to spare the saleswoman their conversation. "What do you need?"

"Jeez, you're abrupt. Is it always going to be this antagonistic between us?"

He was trying to disarm her, but she wasn't willing to be duped by his salesman-like tactics. "I'm busy right now, Steven. I can't talk."

"Come on, this will only take a second."

"What is it?"

"I want to quit counseling."

She didn't even need to think about it. "No."

"Come on, Noelle. It's been a year—*a year!* I'm better now. If you'd ever agree to let me come around, you might see that."

Noelle knew he couldn't have changed so fast. "Sorry. You promised to get me a letter from your therapist before you quit seeing her."

"So?"

"I haven't received anything."

"Are you kidding me? You're going to hold me to that? She makes a hundred bucks every time I show up. She'll never admit that I don't have a problem…anymore," he quickly added, but Noelle knew it was only for her benefit. Steven took no responsibility for his violent temper. When he'd caused her to lose their child a year ago, he'd actually had the nerve to tell her it wouldn't have happened if she hadn't made him so angry.

"We already agreed on this, Steven," she said, fighting to keep calm.

"I don't want to go back to that therapist."

"Then find a new one."

"Therapy is a total waste."

"I don't know of a better option."

"People at work are beginning to wonder where I disappear to every Monday afternoon."

"Then let them wonder."

"Screw you! I'm not going anymore."

Noelle clenched her jaw. "If I don't receive a copy of your canceled check for this month, as usual, you know what will happen."

"You're bluffing. You don't have any pictures. I never hit you hard enough for pictures to show anything."

"You're deluding yourself again, Steven."

He started shouting obscenities.

"I'm going to hang up," she said.

"Go ahead! You're the biggest bitch I've ever met. I should've knocked some sense into you when I had the chance—"

Noelle disconnected. Shaking, she stared down at her phone as the memories of her many altercations with Steven washed over her. There had been times when he'd knocked her around and, fortunately, she did have the photographs to prove it….

"Are you okay?" Noelle turned to see the saleswoman hovering behind her, wearing a concerned expression. "You look a little pale."

"I'm fine." She forced a quick smile, but her mind was still on Steven. She was tempted to give up and let him quit counseling. She wanted him out of her life once and for all. But she was afraid of what he might do to the next woman to fall for his handsome face.

Biting back a groan, she realized, once again, that she had to remain strong. If only she'd been stronger a year ago and left him as she should have, as she almost did, she could have saved her baby. "I'm okay," she said.

"Can I get you a glass of water?"

"No." Noelle pumped up the wattage of her smile. "I just need to see your nursery furniture."

★ ★ ★

The following day, the pediatrician's office called Harrison to say he could come down and pick up his son, and he rushed off to buy diapers and other supplies first thing. Jeremy's release had come a day earlier than expected. Harrison wasn't prepared and had never been more scared of anything in his life. Jeremy seemed so small, so fragile....

"I can't believe they're going to let someone like me walk off with a baby," he told his mother, shifting his cell phone to the opposite ear as he pulled into the hospital parking lot.

"What do you mean *someone like you?* You're a doctor, for Pete's sake," she laughed. "What type of training do you think a parent should require?"

He was too nervous to appreciate her confidence in him. "Some sort of basic baby care course would be a start."

"Oh, quit worrying. It's easier than you think."

It hadn't been easy for her. He could still remember all the mornings she hadn't been able to make herself get up and help him off to school. After he'd met his father and decided to change before he wound up just like him, he would pull on clothes from the discarded pile on his bedroom floor, eat potato chips, pretzels, or anything else he could find in the kitchen cupboards and hurry outside to catch a ride with Jimmy's mother. If he didn't make it to the corner by eight o'clock, he wouldn't reach school until noon, when his own mother finally dragged herself out of bed. Then she'd get into an argument with his teacher because he'd been late so many times already, and he'd have to miss his recess to catch up on his schoolwork.

But he didn't point Rosie's failings out to her. He didn't want to do anything to wreck her recent happiness. His life could have been worse. At least she'd always loved him and stuck by him. He couldn't say that much for his father.

"Why didn't you have that woman who will be helping out come with you if you're so nervous about picking up the baby?" Rosie asked. "You told me you already checked her character references."

Harrison had checked as many as he could in one afternoon.

Not only had Noelle's friends and neighbors confirmed how her baby had died, they'd each said they'd trust her with a child of their own. One person he hadn't been able to reach was a woman named Theresa. But Noelle had said Theresa was her best friend, so he doubted Theresa would tell him anything different. "I did. She seems ideal. But she's gone for the day. I wasn't expecting the pediatrician to call until tomorrow."

"Where'd she go?"

"She has an appointment to show her sculptures to some commercial developers in Stockton."

"Sounds fancy."

Juggling his purchases and his phone, he locked the truck and strode toward the entrance. "She's talented."

"Are you still planning to attend Lynnette's funeral?" his mother asked.

He shifted the car seat he was carrying so he could see his watch. When he realized it was already noon, he frowned. The funeral started in an hour. "I'm trying, but I'll be late if I make it at all."

"That won't reflect well on you."

Light drops of rain began to fall, and Harrison picked up his pace. "Since when have you cared about appearances? Or being late, for that matter."

"I don't, but neither do I like anyone saying anything bad about my boy."

Harrison smiled despite his preoccupation with the funeral and the fact that he wanted to be there for Jeremy's mother and his twin, Tyler. He wanted to have that memory in addition to the small articles in the box Noelle had painted for him. "Lynnette's family isn't going to approve of me no matter what I do. They blame me for her unhappiness this past year, maybe even her death."

"What'd you have to do with her death?"

"She died giving birth to my children, remember?"

"She got pregnant on purpose, against your wishes!"

He entered the lobby and quickly moved off to one side, out of the footpath of the other visitors. "You and I know that, but we're talking about *her* family here." He put his packages down until he could finish his conversation. "They see the situation a little differently than we do."

"Has her mother or anyone else in the family offered to help you with the baby?"

"No."

"Have they even been to the hospital to see him?"

"Winona, her sister, came by when I was here last night. She said her mother's relapsed into depression and isn't up to visiting. She wanted to know what I planned to do with the baby."

"Did you tell her you're putting him up for adoption?"

Harrison fought the reluctance that gripped him at mention of the adoption, reminding himself of all Noelle could offer his son. She had more time *and* money than he did. Everyone he'd spoken to had given her a glowing report. And she wanted a baby. "I told her that I've found a good home for him."

"Does Winona think you're doing the right thing?"

"She didn't say, but she seemed relieved I'm handling the situation. From what I can tell, Lynnette's family isn't in a position to do anything for Jeremy and—"

"You named him?" his mother broke in.

Harrison adjusted the tie he'd put on in anticipation of the funeral. "Yeah, actually I did."

"After my *dad?*"

"He looks like Grandpa."

"You didn't tell me."

"I didn't see the point. You're emotionally unattached right now. Why make this hard on you?"

There was a long pause. "Is it hard on you?"

"No," he lied.

"But if you've named him after my dad, you must really believe he's yours."

A large group of people came into the lobby, several carrying flowers. Harrison could smell the carnations as he moved the car seat off to one side. "I'm pretty sure he is, but I still ordered a paternity test. I can't spend the rest of my life with that 'what if' in the back of my mind."

"Isn't a paternity test expensive?"

"It cost three hundred bucks, but I found a lab online that's overnighting me a tester kit. I'll do the cheek swabs myself, then send the DNA samples back."

"How long will it take after that?"

"A few days."

"It happens even quicker in the movies."

"Unfortunately this is real life, and the hospital lab, at least *this* hospital lab, doesn't do them." He peered through the window as the sky darkened and the rain fell harder. "I'd better go," he said. "It's starting to storm outside, and I don't want it to get too ugly before I buckle Jeremy into the truck."

"Okay. Call me later and let me know how it goes."

Harrison picked up the bag containing the diapers, diaper-wipes, undershirts and fuzzy sleepers he'd bought, but before he hung up, he had one last question. "Mom?"

"Yeah?"

"Did you ever hear from Duane after that day we...after we went to his house that summer?"

"God, you haven't mentioned Duane for twenty years. What makes you ask about him now?"

"I was just wondering what became of him."

"He worked at the same auto shop until you turned eighteen. I know that much because of his child-support payments. But since then..." She released a long sigh. "He could've left Yuba City. I sent him a notice of your college graduation and included a note that you'd been accepted into med school, but never got any response. It's been so long now, I guess he could be anywhere."

"Of course he could."

"Why? You don't want to see him again, do you?"

"No, I was only curious."

"He was the one who missed out, Harrison."

"Was he?" Harrison remembered how badly he'd longed for a father and found that very difficult to believe.

"Of course he was. Maybe I wasn't the best parent in the world, but now that I'm older and at least a little wiser—" her normally strident voice faltered "—I realize you were the best thing to ever happen to me. And you're the best thing I'll leave behind when I go."

"Thanks, Mom," he said. But her words—and the strong emotion they evoked—did nothing to make his decision easier.

If he let Noelle adopt Jeremy, he'd be the one missing out.

CHAPTER
SIX

THE RINGING of the cordless phone woke Harrison from a deep sleep. He was startled for a second, blinking against the darkness, wondering where he was and how he'd gotten there. Then something squirmed in the crook of his arm and he realized he was lying on the couch, holding a baby.

The full reality of the situation—the fact that this was *his* baby—connected in his brain a second later. But he still couldn't believe it.

Using his free hand, he fumbled under the pillows and between the seat cushions, but didn't reach the phone in time.

It was probably Rosie, checking up on him. Earlier, Jeremy had cried so much that Harrison had placed three distress calls to his mother and two to the nurses at the hospital. He'd been positive there was something critically wrong, even though, from a medical standpoint, he couldn't figure out what that might be.

Fortunately the nurses he'd spoken to had confirmed what he thought—that sometimes babies cried for no apparent reason—and that everything was probably okay. Odd how different it was being on the receiving end of medical advice.

Thank God Jeremy had settled down at last. He was sleeping peacefully now, so peacefully that Harrison couldn't imagine how he'd caused so much trouble in the first place.

He considered calling his mother back to tell her the situation had improved, but he decided to let it go until morning. He was so tired….

He let his eyelids drift closed once more, only to have the

phone drag him to consciousness again. Evidently Rosie couldn't wait until morning.

A new search yielded the handset before the ringing could subside. "Hello?"

"Harrison?"

"Yes?" It was a woman's voice, but not his mother's, and Harrison was too groggy to place it.

"It's Noelle."

Noelle! Clutching the baby, he sat up, trying to gather his senses. He hadn't expected her to call so late. "Are you home?"

"I'm in my car. I just went by the hospital. Nurse Matheson told me they released Jeremy today."

He gazed down at the bundle in his arms. "I picked him up this morning."

The baby began to stretch, causing Harrison's stomach to knot in dismay. Would he start crying again? The past few hours had been harrowing. Harrison had never felt so helpless or inadequate. He needed Noelle even more than he'd thought.

Leaning closer to the table beside him, he squinted at the bottle he'd left there, trying to see if there was any milk in it. But between the darkness and the kind of bottle it was—the one with the plastic liners designed to keep the air out—he couldn't really tell. *Don't cry, kid. Come on, don't cry....*

"I left a message on your answering machine," he said, lowering his voice.

"I don't know how to check it remotely. Where's the baby now?"

"Here with me."

"I'm sorry I wasn't around to help. Are the two of you okay?"

For the moment, they were. But whether or not Harrison remained okay depended on what Jeremy did next. "I think so." Still tense, he watched the baby squirm and yawn and squirm some more.

Finally, Jeremy seemed to settle once more, and Harrison released his breath. "He's going back to sleep."

She laughed softly. "Don't worry, I can take him now. Or would you rather I wait until morning?"

Harrison remembered the mess in the kitchen he'd made when he'd sterilized the nipples and rings and bottles; the bedding and clothes he'd washed, with a gentle detergent, that still needed to be moved into the dryer; the dirty diaper waiting by the door for a trip to the garbage; and the packaging he'd discarded as he opened the different items he needed, including the alcohol pads to clean around Jeremy's umbilical cord. The car seat sat over-turned in the middle of the living room, where he'd stumbled over it, and the diaper bag was tossed to one side, its contents strewn across the floor because Harrison had been in such a hurry to get Jeremy changed in case that might stop the crying. He'd had his son only one day, and already his apartment had been transformed into a place he barely recognized.

Taking care of a newborn was every bit as difficult as he'd imagined. "I'll bring him over to you right now," he said.

"No, I'm already in the car and you sound tired. Tell me where you live and I'll come get him."

"Are you sure you don't mind?"

"Positive."

Harrison envisioned his father chuckling over the relief he felt that Noelle was on her way, but he was too tired to let it get to him. At least he'd picked Jeremy up from the hospital and cared for him all day. That was a step in the right direction—and a lot more than Duane would've done.

Noelle had trouble finding Harrison's apartment. By the time she arrived it was nearly one o'clock and raining again. Opening her compact umbrella, she stepped out of her Volvo, quickly surveyed the garden-style complex, and hurried across the puddle-ridden lot, moving as fast as she dared in high heels. It hadn't made sense to go home and change. She'd been too excited to get Jeremy.

Jeremy... She liked that name. She'd been searching her brain for a good middle name to go with it ever since Harrison had mentioned he'd let her choose one. She had yet to come up with anything. But she was sure she'd have better luck once she had a chance to get to know her baby.

Her baby... She could hardly believe the twist of fate that had given her this opportunity.

Or was it an opportunity? Was she being stupid to get involved?

She didn't think so. Maybe it would be different if she could have more children of her own, but Steven had made that impossible.

A little damp and definitely cold, she lowered her umbrella before knocking softly on Unit #31. She waited several long seconds, then knocked again. Finally she tried the door and found it unlocked.

"Harrison?" she called, poking her head inside.

"Noelle?"

The thickness of Harrison's voice indicated that he'd fallen back asleep, just as she'd suspected he might.

"Sorry to barge in on you," she said, "but you didn't answer my knock." Leaving her umbrella on the stoop, she stepped inside a utilitarian family room and kitchen area, lit only by the flicker of an old console-style television. A bike stood in the corner, and some shelves held several books, a few photographs and the Memory Box she'd made.

Harrison was lying on the couch, wearing socks, a T-shirt and faded jeans and holding the baby. "I thought I was dreaming." He yawned and scrubbed a hand over his face, then his gaze ran down to her feet and back up again. "You look nice."

"Thank you."

"What time is it?"

"Late. I got lost."

"Why didn't you call me?"

"I wanted to let you rest." She stared down at the baby in his lap and felt her pulse leap. "Looks like Jeremy's doing okay."

"You say that as though he's sweet. He's been a nightmare."

A flash of white teeth told her Harrison wasn't really upset, and Noelle couldn't help returning his smile. For someone who didn't want children, he'd taken his role as a father pretty seriously. His apartment was in shambles, but from what she could see, the mess was all baby-related.

The television changed colors, allowing Noelle a better glimpse of Harrison's clean, strong features. Stubble darkened his square jaw, but the thick blond hair sticking up on his head and his sleepy blue eyes gave his face a disarming, boyish look.

Jeremy could certainly have inherited worse genes, she thought. If he took after Harrison, he had every chance of being tall, well-built and too handsome for his own good.

"Did you make it to the funeral today?" she asked. She was eager to get Jeremy in her arms, but she was afraid, too—afraid she'd melt down the moment she touched him. Sometimes she felt completely recovered from the loss of her baby a year earlier. But there were other times when it seemed as though the passing months had only camouflaged the hurt.

Harrison shook his head. "I would've been *really* late, and I had Jeremy by then. I decided it might be better for Lynnette's family if we said our own prayers for her and Tyler—"

"Tyler?"

"Lynnette's sister named the other baby."

"I see."

"Anyway, I decided it might be better for them if we just faded away."

"They're not interested in seeing the baby?"

"It isn't that so much. Her mother suffers from depression and isn't doing well, and her sister's involved in a custody battle for her own child. They can't do anything for Jeremy. I was afraid it'd just make them feel worse to have a reminder that the entire situation didn't end with Lynnette's and Tyler's deaths."

Noelle was mildly surprised by Harrison's sensitivity. Lynnette had tried to trap him, yet he was doing his best to shield her family from the consequences?

"Can I hold him?" she asked at last, unable to wait any longer.

"Sure." Harrison sat up and motioned to the space beside him. "Have a seat."

Noelle could feel his residual body heat when she perched on the couch. But that had nothing to do with the warmth that rolled through her when he handed her the baby. This warmth came from somewhere deep inside, like a candle burning in her heart.

Closing her eyes, she rubbed her lips across the baby's cheek. He smelled so good, so…familiar. She'd known this moment might be difficult for her. But she'd had no idea that Jeremy would evoke such vivid memories of the day she'd had her own baby. Although she'd held Austin only briefly, her arms had ached for him ever since. And now, after so long, it felt almost as if she had him back.

She could sense Harrison watching her and tried to say, "He's so soft," to cover the depth of her reaction. But she couldn't speak. Tears welled in her eyes almost instantly, and her chest constricted until she could scarcely breathe. Her only escape was to bury her face in the baby's terry-cloth sleeper before she came apart.

Mommy's so sorry, Austin, so terribly, terribly sorry….

"Noelle?" Harrison said softly, unsure how to react.

She didn't move.

"Noelle, are you okay?"

She said nothing, but she didn't need to. He knew she was not okay. She was crying—if he had his guess, for the baby she'd lost.

Harrison hesitated, knowing she probably wished she were alone. But the sight of her bowed head made him want to protect her, to comfort her.

Moving closer, he put his arm around her. "You're going to be okay," he murmured.

Only the wind answered him. It howled outside, tossing rain against the large front window in great gusts that made Harrison feel isolated from the rest of the world—from everyone except this lovely woman who was struggling so hard with her inner demons. He understood her fight, understood how memories, experiences and losses of the past could sneak up in a dark moment.

Her shoulders shook beneath his arm as she cried silently. Rubbing his hand up and down her spine, he turned her slightly so he could draw her and Jeremy into a loose embrace. "Let it go," he said. "There's no one here but me."

He thought she might pull away and insist on coping alone, or even leave, but she didn't. "Do you want to talk about it?"

"No."

"It might make things easier."

"It's nothing."

"It doesn't seem like nothing."

Her eyes finally lifted. "I—I should've left him sooner, that's all," she said, her expression tortured. "It would have changed everything."

Harrison took Jeremy from her and put him in his car seat. Crouching before her, he covered her cold hands with his. "Who?"

"My ex-husband."

"Why?"

"It was my fault," she said.

Her fingers felt dainty, almost fragile beneath his touch. "What was your fault?"

Her next words seemed to require significant effort. "The baby's death."

Chills cascaded down Harrison's spine, and he couldn't help glancing at Jeremy. "How?"

"My ex-husband was…"

"What?" he prompted.

She closed her eyes. "A bastard."

A bastard didn't tell him much. "What'd he do?"

No response.

"Noelle?"

Her face suddenly seemed chalky white in the darkness.

"Did he hurt you?"

She nodded as the possibilities poured through Harrison's mind.

"Physically?"

As she opened her eyes, her large pupils reflected the light of the TV, but she didn't seem to see him.

"Noelle?" He lifted her hand to his mouth, brushed his lips across her knuckles to gain her attention. "Did he hit you?"

Drawing a ragged breath, she suppressed a shudder, and it was enough to confirm what he'd guessed already.

"Damn him."

Finally she spoke, but her voice sounded flat, unnatural. "He made me lose my baby. And…after that, I had to have a hysterectomy, which of course means…"

She didn't finish, but she didn't need to. Harrison finally understood why she might want a stranger's baby, why she might be willing to take Jeremy on almost any terms.

Reaching up, he wiped a tear from her cheek. "How is that your fault?" he asked.

Her forehead rumpled as she fought the emotions coursing through her, but another tear escaped her thick lashes. "I told you. I should've left him."

"You didn't know what he was going to do."

"I knew he wasn't what he appeared to be. I thought…I thought I could help him, that he'd try harder, that the baby would make a difference, but—"

"It didn't," Harrison said shortly.

"No." The word was barely a whisper.

"Then it was *his* fault, Noelle, not yours."

She started to shake her head, but he gripped her shoulders to make sure she'd listen. "If he struck you, he *is* a bastard, and it's *all* his fault."

She blinked at him with those large green eyes of hers, as though she longed to accept what he said, and he hoped she'd be able to. She was carrying a burden that was far too heavy for her.

"I wish I'd never married him."

"You can't change the past," Harrison told her. "You have to forget and go on."

"I can't forget."

"Sure you can, in time." He lifted her hand and rubbed her knuckles against his lips once again, trying to ignore the fact that his desire to comfort her was beginning to mix with other desires—like the desire to kiss her, to replace the pain she was feeling with powerful, positive sensation.

He knew they were experiencing an unusual emotional connection, enhanced by the darkness in his apartment and the late hour. But he doubted she felt the same arousal that snaked through his blood. Letting go of her, he stood up, and she wiped her eyes with quick, impatient strokes.

"It's late—I'd better get going," she said. "I'm sorry for unloading on you. It was just…holding Jeremy for the first time—"

"Noelle…"

She looked up at him.

"I understand."

She nodded mutely, then stood and started gathering Jeremy's things, but he caught her arm. "Is there any chance I could convince you to stay the night?"

Evidently he hadn't done a very good job of concealing the sexual awareness he felt. Suspicion entered her eyes, and the color immediately returned to her face. "You can have my bed," he hurried to add. "I'll sleep on the couch. It's just that the storm's getting worse by the minute, and I'd rather not have you and Jeremy driving in these conditions."

"Right, the storm." She glanced at the window, as if she were only now aware of the slashing rain.

"It'd be better to get some sleep and leave in the morning, don't you think?"

She met his gaze and that intangible *something* he'd sensed in her living room arced between them again. "Sure, better safe than sorry," she said, then cleared her throat and looked quickly away.

Crying woke Noelle only a few hours later. At first she couldn't grasp the significance of it. It was just noise. Loud. Foreign. Intrusive. And she couldn't figure out where the heck she was. The bed was comfortable, but the room was strange, sparsely furnished. No pictures on the walls. Nothing but a blind on the only window.

Suddenly she remembered. She was sleeping in Harrison's bed, she was wearing Harrison's clothes, and his baby, Jeremy—no, *her* baby—was crying. He needed her.

Springing out of the tangle she'd made of the blankets, she fumbled through the darkness to where she'd left Jeremy wrapped warmly in his infant seat. "I'm coming, sweetheart…I'm here," she cooed.

His cries quieted to a whimper as soon as she scooped him to her. "You're okay, honey. I'm right here." She settled him in the crook of her arm. "Better late than never, huh?"

The moment she kissed his soft cheek, he twisted toward her, innocent, trusting, searching for food. The solid feel of him in her arms seemed to fill the massive emptiness in her chest that had been there since her own baby's death. And the pain she'd experienced earlier when she'd held Jeremy drained out of her, at least for tonight. Now she was actually able to smile. "Don't fuss. I'll get you a bottle."

She opened the bedroom door to head out into the hall and bumped into Harrison coming from the other direction. It was too dark to see him, but her arm had definitely grazed the warm bare skin of a flat, tightly muscled stomach.

"Sorry, I didn't mean to frighten you," he said, steadying her when she let out a startled gasp. "I thought I'd get the baby so you could sleep."

"I should have gotten up sooner. For some reason his crying didn't wake me right away."

"You haven't had much sleep."

"What time is it?"

"Four o'clock."

"The door was shut. How did he manage to wake you?"

"I'm a light sleeper. It comes from working through the night at the hospital."

"Then you probably need your sleep more than I do."

"I'm getting used to the hours."

It *would* be hard for a single person in his situation to raise a baby, she thought.

"I already made a bottle," he said. "Do you want me to take Jeremy?"

"No, I've got him."

Harrison's hand slipped down her arm. He was only guiding the bottle, but his touch, the darkness, his scent on the clothes she was wearing and the knowledge that she was sleeping where he slept every night caused a giddy, breathless sensation to shimmy through her.

"Here you go."

She thanked him, but she didn't turn back to the bedroom. For the moment, she stood transfixed between the bed at her back and the man standing in front of her.

Finally Harrison muttered, "See you in the morning," and the floor creaked as he moved away.

CHAPTER
SEVEN

HARRISON HAD TO WORK hard not to stare. Noelle was wearing
the gym shorts he'd given her last night to sleep in, only she'd
rolled them up at the waist so they wouldn't slip down over her
hips. Now they revealed a pair of the shapeliest legs he'd ever seen.

After washing and drying her bowl, she put it in the cupboard
and came toward the table. Harrison dragged his attention back
to his cereal.

"Did the pediatrician say when I'm supposed to bring Jeremy
in for a checkup?" she asked, adding another spoonful of sugar to
her coffee as she sat down.

Jeremy was sleeping again. Fortunately he did that quite often.
But Harrison thought it would be nice if the baby would wake
up, so he'd have something more demanding than cereal to distract him from Noelle's nicely sculpted legs. "In two weeks."

"Do you have his name and address?"

Legs… What was wrong with him? He had other problems to
worry about, *big* problems that were never going to go away. And
here he was, watching every move she made and fairly salivating.
The male sex drive sometimes surprised even him. "I'll call you
with it later."

She took a sip of coffee. "Would you also let them know of our
arrangement so I don't surprise anybody when I show up instead
of you?"

"Of course."

When she finished her coffee and got up, he allowed himself another admiring glance at her legs. "When can I see you again?"

She pivoted to face him, her eyebrows arched in apparent surprise. "What?"

He cleared his throat. "I mean, when can I see *Jeremy* again?"

She glanced at the baby as if she hadn't done so a million times already this morning, and Harrison hid a smile. She couldn't keep her eyes off Jeremy; Harrison couldn't keep his eyes off her. It was almost laughable.

The moment she saw that Jeremy was still sleeping peacefully, she turned to Harrison. "When would you like to?"

"I have six twelve-hour shifts at the hospital this week, but I'm off on Wednesday. Will that work?"

She started making a bottle, presumably for the road. "That's fine, but…"

"But?" he echoed.

"I understand how stressful a residency can be, so if it doesn't work out, don't worry. Work, sleep, play softball. We'll be fine on our own."

Play softball? She sounded as though she didn't care if she ever heard from him again. And of course she probably didn't. Then she'd have the baby all to herself. "It'll work out," he said.

"Well, if something comes up and you can't get away for a while, I hope you know it'll be okay. I'll love Jeremy as my own, give him everything he needs—"

"Noelle."

She ignored him and checked her watch. "Oh boy, is it that late already? I'd better get changed." She started for the bedroom, but he stood up and cut her off.

"I'll see you on Wednesday," he repeated, more pointedly.

She stood only inches away. His clothes fell baggy and shapeless on her smaller frame, and her mascara was slightly smudged, but she looked more beautiful than she had the night he'd first seen her at the hospital. Fresh, casual, warm and real…

The hand he'd placed on her arm itched to explore the warm skin beneath his touch—and elsewhere. But he let go of her and merely allowed himself to run a finger along her jaw. "I'm going to be part of Jeremy's life, Noelle," he said softly. "That was our agreement."

Her neck muscles worked as she swallowed, and if he wasn't imagining it, her breathing grew shallow. "Of course. I was just letting you know that I have no expectations. Visit only when you want to," she said, then slipped past him.

"You wanted to *what?*"

Noelle held the phone a little farther from her ear, cringing at the shock in Theresa's voice. "You heard me. I wanted to sleep with him. If he'd come back into the bedroom with me when he brought me Jeremy's bottle, or when I was getting changed to leave, I'm honestly not sure I would have sent him away."

"But you'd barely met him!"

"I know. It's crazy, but also…exciting, hopeful. It's the first time I've felt anything like that since my divorce." Noelle hugged Jeremy closer and continued to rock him gently in her arms while he slept. She'd scarcely gone out in the two weeks since she'd brought him home, but she didn't mind being cooped up. She loved having a new baby, and that night at Harrison's—and the nights she'd seen him since—had given her a lot to think about. Now she knew she could desire a man again, that after the hysterectomy, her body wasn't the numb, empty shell she sometimes feared it was.

"Why didn't you tell me about this before?" Theresa asked.

"You haven't really been by, except that once when you came to see the baby."

"Sorry, I've been…busy lately." Noelle wondered what was suddenly taking up so much of her time, but Theresa rushed on before she could ask. "I've called you a few times. You could have mentioned it then."

Before, Noelle hadn't wanted to talk about that night at Harrison's. "I don't know why I didn't tell you. I was embarrassed, I guess, wasn't sure *what* I thought of my reaction."

"And now?"

Noelle laughed. "I still don't know what to think, but like I said, I'm happy that I seem to be healing."

"Do you ever feel that way when you're with him now?"

"Sometimes," Noelle admitted.

"You should let him know," Theresa stated bluntly.

"I can't. What if he feels the same way? We'll wind up in bed together."

"Then you'll have what you want."

"You think I should sleep with him?"

"You bet I do. Since you and Steven split up, you've been walking around like the living dead. As far as I'm concerned, it would be good therapy."

"That's some kind of therapy, Theresa."

"Besides, he's not much of a stranger anymore."

That was true. Harrison had spent several evenings with her since she'd brought Jeremy home. He was usually on his way home from work or, if he was working graveyard, just heading back to the hospital after trying to grab a few hours' sleep in the afternoon, but they'd spent a lot of time talking, watching TV and eating dinner together.

"At least the tension between you would have an outlet," Theresa added. "Once it's over, maybe you can concentrate on other things. This way—"

"I can't risk getting involved with Harrison," Noelle interrupted briskly. "If the relationship didn't work out, I couldn't very well expect him to walk away and leave me his son. And you know this baby is more important to me than anything."

"I agree that Jeremy is wonderful. But love and desire are an important part of a woman's life, too."

"Thank God I'm beginning to believe that again. I'm thrilled just to *want* to feel a man's hands on me."

"So…the attraction's merely physical, or—"

"Oh yeah," Noelle said, but she knew that wasn't true. Harrison had been the only person capable of reaching that cold dark place where she harbored her feelings about her lost baby and her divorce. His support had helped her deal with some of the debilitating guilt, and because of that, she'd been tempted to trust him to bring her body back to life, too. That night, at his place, she'd felt healthy and normal for the first time in twelve months. She was grateful to him and liked him a great deal. But she didn't want to make Theresa feel like less of a friend for not being the one to help her through Austin's death.

"How do you think *he* feels?" Theresa asked.

"I don't know. It's been two weeks since that night and he hasn't even touched me."

"How many times have you seen him?"

"At least ten. He comes over for dinner whenever he can. Sometimes I cook, sometimes he brings takeout." She went to lay Jeremy down because she needed to do a load of laundry. "What about you?" she asked. "Your love life must be hopping, considering how scarce you've been around here. Are you still seeing that guy from work?"

"Not anymore."

Noelle turned on the mobile over Jeremy's head while waiting for Theresa to expand on her answer—but she didn't. "So what happened?"

"The attraction fizzled out before it got off the ground. And…"

"And?"

"I've met someone else."

"Really?" Noelle straightened in surprise. "When?"

"I've known him for a while, actually."

A strange tension sprang up that hadn't been there just moments before, but Noelle couldn't figure out what, exactly, had changed. "And you think *I've* been keeping secrets?"

"I wasn't expecting the relationship to come to much, but I…I think I really like him," Theresa admitted.

"So who is he?"

A strained pause. "Noelle…"

"What?"

The doorbell rang in the background. "Never mind. He's here. I've got to go, okay? I'll call you later."

The phone clicked in her ear, and Noelle sank into the rocker near Jeremy's crib. She wasn't sure what was going on with her best friend, but she had a feeling it wasn't good.

Exhaustion weighed heavily on Harrison's back and shoulders. He'd just spent one of the longest days of his life. His shift at the Med Center had seemed to drag on for an eternity. He had a headache, his nerves were on edge, and he felt like he wanted to sleep for a month. Yet here he was, calling Noelle the moment he walked into his apartment. It had been two weeks since he'd let her take Jeremy home with her, but he thought of her when he was at work, late at night, first thing in the morning.

What was going on? He'd never been so preoccupied with a woman.

It was because of Jeremy, he told himself. He hadn't been able to stop thinking of his son, either. He'd gotten the results back from the paternity test a week ago, and they'd been positive, just as he'd expected.

When the fourth ring went unanswered, Harrison figured the answering machine would kick in. He was about to hang up when he heard a breathy, "Hello?"

"Noelle? It's Harrison."

"Oh…hi."

He glanced at the Memory Box she'd painted for him, which had come to represent Noelle as much as his lost son, and smiled. "How's Jeremy?"

"Good. I just bathed him and was drying him off when the phone rang. That's what took me so long to pick up."

"Do you need me to call you back?"

"No, he's here in my arms."

"Can I see him tonight?" Harrison asked the same question almost every night. He wanted to see his son, but he wanted to see Noelle, too. There was something comforting about her home and the way she took care of his baby. And sometimes, when he looked up at her, he could imagine taking her in his arms and—

"Can I fix you some dinner?"

He forced his wandering mind back to the conversation. What

had he eaten so far today? A package of Pop-Tarts he'd found in the employee lounge and a gallon of coffee. But she'd cooked last night. "Why don't I bring pizza?"

"I've already defrosted a couple of pork chops."

He smiled. She was beginning to expect him. "Are you sure you'd rather cook?"

"I'm sure."

"Okay, I'd appreciate it." He hung up and immediately started giving himself the usual pep talk about continuing to keep things impersonal with Noelle. He didn't want to blow what seemed like a perfect situation for Jeremy. But where Noelle was concerned, he was finding it more and more difficult to keep his hands to himself.

Harrison stopped at the closest convenience store for a bottle of wine to take to dinner and a cup of coffee so he wouldn't nod off on the way. Then he hurried onto the freeway. He had a fifteen-minute drive. He wanted to enjoy being away from the Med Center and relax to some good jazz on the radio while he anticipated seeing Noelle and Jeremy. But Lynnette's mother hadn't returned his call when he'd tried to apologize for missing the funeral, and he thought he should let her know the results of the paternity test.

Setting his coffee cup in its holder, he retrieved his cell phone.

"Hello?"

Harrison didn't recognize the voice of the person who'd answered. "Is Connie there?"

"One minute."

A few seconds later, Lynnette's mother came on the line. Harrison wasn't surprised to find that she sounded extremely subdued.

"Connie?"

"Yes?"

"It's Harrison."

A long pause. "What do you want?" she asked at last.

He couldn't put a name to the emotion in her voice but the undercurrent wasn't positive. "I wanted to tell you…the baby's mine."

"I thought so."

Ignoring the vindication in her voice, he forged on. "I also wanted to say…" What? How could anything he said make the smallest difference to her? She'd lost her daughter three weeks ago. "I'm sorry about Lynnette. I never meant to hurt her. I hope you'll believe me."

Silence followed, then he thought he heard her sniffle.

"I know you're going through a miserable time," he went on, "but I wanted to put your mind to rest about the baby. I'll make sure he has everything he needs, and…if you ever want to see him, just give me a call."

"You're keeping him?" she asked in surprise.

Harrison's heart jumped against his chest. He hadn't meant that he was keeping him. He couldn't keep him. With his hours, Jeremy would be raised by day-care personnel.

But if Noelle insisted on adoption, he wasn't sure he could live with scheduled visits and no real involvement, either.

"Um…I'm not sure exactly what'll happen. At least not yet. But whatever I do, I'll make arrangements so that we can both be part of his life."

"Thank you, Harrison," she said softly. "I have to admit that I'm starting to see why Lynnette loved you so much."

Harrison smiled and hung up. His call had made a difference, at least to Connie. But *he* was feeling more unsettled than ever. He hadn't chosen to have Jeremy; he wasn't the best person to raise him. Yet the moment Connie had asked if he was keeping his son, he'd suddenly known, in a bone-deep way, that he could never give him up. Not completely. Not even to Noelle. Which meant he had to tell her…tonight.

CHAPTER
EIGHT

NOELLE WATCHED Harrison park from her kitchen window, then drew a steadying breath as he dodged a soggy pile of leaves in the gutter and strode up the walkway. She'd thought of him far too much since she'd seen him last, and it had only been one day.

She waited for him to knock before she answered the door. Although she'd told herself she wasn't dressing up for him, she'd pulled her hair back, applied makeup and changed into a nice pair of jeans, a black sweater and leather boots with heels high enough that she and Harrison were almost at eye level.

"That was quick," she told him as she stood in the doorway.

"I'm getting pretty familiar with the trip." He grinned, looking great in a brown sweater and chinos. But small lines at his eyes and mouth showed fatigue.

"Come in." She held the door for him. "Jeremy's getting fussy. I think he wants to be fed."

Harrison turned his shoulders so he could fit past her, bringing him close enough that she could smell his cologne. The scent immediately carried her back to the night she was in his clothes and his bed, and all the nights she'd spent with him since then.

"Smells good," he said.

She'd been thinking the same thing, but not about the food. "Dinner's almost ready. Why don't you sit in the living room and feed Jeremy while I finish up?"

"Sure, no problem."

While he settled in with the baby, she turned off the stereo in favor of ESPN so he'd have something to watch. But when she returned from the kitchen fifteen minutes later, she found both Harrison and the baby asleep.

Harrison had dozed off a time or two in the past, but never *before* dinner. She was disappointed they wouldn't be eating together, but she was also relieved to see he was finally getting some rest. He needed to slow down. And he looked perfect on her couch.

Lifting Jeremy from his lap, she put the baby in his crib, turned on the monitor and closed the door. Then she brought a blanket and a pillow from her bedroom.

Harrison opened his eyes when she pressed him to lie down. "We need to talk," he mumbled.

"We'll talk in the morning. Get some sleep."

She thought he might argue, but the doorbell interrupted.

"Are you expecting someone?" he asked, coming more awake.

She checked her watch to see that it was only seven o'clock. "No, but I'm sure it's Theresa. She said she might drop by tonight."

He started to sit up, but she nudged him back down and covered him with the blanket. "Relax. I'll talk to her in the kitchen."

"This isn't going to work, you know that, don't you?" he said before she could leave the room.

"What isn't going to work?"

"Keeping everything so…polite and formal between us."

"It has to work," she said.

He shook his head but closed his eyes, and she went to answer the door.

She was so sure it was Theresa that she didn't bother checking the peephole, something she immediately regretted when she saw Steven standing on her front porch.

"What are you doing here?" she asked before he could say hello.

He put a hand on the door so she couldn't close it. "I've come for the pictures."

"Steven—"

"Get them. I won't let you blackmail me any longer."

"Blackmail you! I'm trying to make sure you get some help, you ungrateful jerk."

"I don't need any help."

"You need lots of help, Steven. You caused me to lose a baby—and the chance of ever having another one."

"That's bullshit. I'm tired of you blaming me. It was an accident."

"An accident that wouldn't have happened if not for your violent temper!"

"You'll see the meaning of violent if you don't get me those damn pictures."

"What I have are only copies. They won't do you any good."

"Bullshit." He started shoving his way into the house but came to an abrupt halt when he realized that Harrison had just blocked his way.

"Who's *this?*" Steven's gaze darted suspiciously between the two of them.

"Harrison Ferello, meet my ex-husband," she said.

Harrison didn't bother with any niceties. "I don't remember hearing Noelle invite you in."

Steven's expression turned sulky. "She has something of mine. As soon as she gives it to me, I'll leave."

Harrison raised a questioning eyebrow at Noelle.

"That's not true," she said. "He wants some pictures I have, but they belong to me, and the originals are somewhere else anyway."

"I guess that settles it—now get out," Harrison told him flatly.

Steven's eyes narrowed, but he focused his attention strictly on Noelle. "You'd better shut up your new boyfriend or there'll be hell to pay for this."

Hearing the not-so-subtle threat in his voice, Noelle put a hand on Harrison's arm. "Harrison, don't. When he gets angry, he loses all control, and this isn't your problem—"

"He doesn't scare me," Harrison replied. "As a matter of fact, I'd like to show him what happens when he loses control with someone his own size." He looked Steven up and down, wearing an expression of disgust. "But I don't think he's got the guts."

Noelle saw Steven's hands ball into fists and felt her heart leap into her throat. "Look out!"

Harrison stepped closer instead of backing away, his eyes hard and glittery. He hadn't fisted his own hands, but the tension thrumming through his body told her he was ready for a fight. "Are you thinking about throwing a punch, big man?" he asked, shoving Steven in the chest.

Surprisingly Steven didn't do anything but back up. "I'm just trying to resolve something. It doesn't have anything to do with you."

"It does now," Harrison said. "You ever touch Noelle again, and you'll answer to me, understand?"

Steven glared at Noelle. "And this asshole's the guy you told Theresa you wanted to sleep with? Hell, if you're that hard up, you can come to me." Whirling around, he stomped off, pausing only long enough to throw a few parting words over his shoulder. "This isn't over, Noelle," he shouted, then he got into his car and peeled off.

Noelle stared after him, her knees weak.

"He's gone," Harrison said, once the sound of Steven's car had died on the night air.

Slowly she nodded, but she didn't move. It was more than Steven's threats and the narrowly averted fight that upset her. Theresa had told Steven about Harrison. They were in close contact….

I've met someone else…I've known him for a while, actually….

God, Theresa was seeing her ex-husband.

Noelle continued to stare down the empty street until Harrison pulled her inside and closed the door. "Are you okay?"

She nodded and folded her arms to help her stop shivering. Steven and Theresa. She almost couldn't believe it, not after the many arguments she and Steven had had over Theresa. Steven had been so opposed to the friendship that Noelle had finally tried to distance herself from Theresa just to keep peace. And Theresa had definitely resented it. She'd never had a nice thing to say about Steven….

"Maybe you should show me those pictures," Harrison said, watching her closely.

Steven had just told him she wanted to sleep with him, which made her cheeks blaze hot. But they were both ignoring that, pretending it hadn't happened. Thank God. Noelle couldn't handle the embarrassment along with everything else. The pictures made her look pathetic enough.

She couldn't understand why she hadn't put a stop to what was happening sooner, except that Steven would always start crying and insisting that he was sorry. She'd believe him, believe it would never happen again. It took time to kill the hope. Too much time. But she knew Harrison, or anyone else for that matter, wasn't likely to relate.

"They're humiliating," she said.

He shoved his hands in his pockets and leaned against the opposite wall, watching her. "You've already told me the truth. Seeing the pictures won't change anything."

"I'm not the same person I was," she said. "I'd never let a man do that to me now."

"I'd never let a man do that to you, either," he said softly.

She remembered Harrison holding her while she cried. As humiliated as she was by the past, and by what Steven had blurted out, Noelle realized she was trying to shut out the one person who had really comforted her. He'd been there for her—and he was here for her now, if she'd let him be.

"Just a minute," she said, and went to her bedroom to retrieve the copies she kept in her dresser.

When she returned, she handed Harrison the manila envelope before she could change her mind.

He frowned as he slowly shuffled through date-marked photos that showed her with a split lip, a nasty bruise, a mark on her leg…. "Who took these?" he asked when he'd gone through them all.

"I did. I have a tripod and a time-delay on my camera." She chuckled humorlessly. "I'm surprised I even bothered. I was so heavily into denial that I half-believed the lies I told to cover for him."

"These make me regret that I didn't break his jaw," he said frankly.

Noelle smiled. "Be glad you didn't. He's not worth it."

Harrison tapped the pictures. "So who's he afraid you're going to show these to? The police?"

"No. It's too late to take them to the police. I have no proof that he was the one who caused those injuries. He's worried I'll go to his mother. She'll believe me, even though she's had nothing but praise for him since the day he was born."

"From what I've seen, you should've sent them to her long before now."

"I know, but she's old and sick, and I love her. I'm not out to hurt her by ruining the image she has of her 'perfect' son. I only want to see that he gets help."

"What kind of help?"

"Weekly visits with a therapist."

His eyes ran over her, and suddenly all she could think about was feeling his lips on hers. She was in the middle of a crisis. She needed to protect her relationship with Jeremy. And yet Harrison made her breathless at the thought of one kiss. It was worse now that he *knew*…. "Has he been fighting you on the counseling issue ever since your divorce?" he asked.

"No. At first he felt badly enough about what happened to our baby that he didn't balk. But the past few months he's managed to convince himself that he doesn't have a problem. And now I think he's seeing my best friend."

"Theresa?"

She nodded. "But I won't let him get away with hurting her the way he hurt me. I'll show her the pictures if I have to."

"And you'll keep insisting Steven see this therapist?"

She considered her options. "I have to."

"Why?"

"What if he hurts someone else?"

"God, do you think you have to take care of *everyone?* You're not responsible for his actions, Noelle. You've done your best to help, now let it go so *you* don't get hurt again. And what about the baby?"

"He'd never purposely hurt a baby. He didn't mean to do what he did to Austin."

"Accidents happen."

She knew that, knew what an accident could cost. She rubbed her eyes, feeling tired—tired of worrying about Steven, and tired of fighting her attraction to Harrison. "You're right. Now that I've got Jeremy, I can't risk Steven showing up angry again. I'll have to get a restraining order."

An odd expression crossed Harrison's face, one that sent talons of fear through Noelle. "Don't you think that's enough?" she asked.

"Maybe." He shoved the pictures back into the envelope and handed them to her.

She waited, watching him closely. "Harrison?"

Raking a hand through his hair, he sighed. "What?"

"Earlier you mentioned that we needed to talk."

He didn't respond.

"Steven hasn't changed your mind about Jeremy, has he?" *He might have made me look like a fool, but please say he hasn't changed your mind....*

"No," he said. "I know you'd never let anything happen to the baby."

Noelle's fear eased and she managed a tremulous smile. Maybe he'd forget the part about her wanting to sleep with him. "Then what?"

"Never mind. It's nothing. We can talk about it later."

Home cooking held a special place in Harrison's heart. Probably because his mother had done so little of it. He'd grown up on cold cereal and drive-through, and until he'd met Noelle, he'd still been surviving on anything instant. But as good as Noelle's grilled pork chops probably were, Harrison couldn't taste anything. He was too preoccupied with the images floating through his head—images of Steven standing on Noelle's front porch, saying she wanted to sleep with him, threatening her; images of Noelle in those pictures; images of Noelle at dinner, shyly telling him that she'd decided Jeremy's middle name would be Dane, after a beloved English teacher she'd had in college who had inspired her.

What now? Harrison wondered. Part of him wanted to carry her down the hall. The other part knew he couldn't take advantage of her, then tell her what he'd decided about Jeremy. She'd be better off if he kept his distance. But there was something about Noelle that really got to him. That she could still hope Steven would change told him how deeply she believed in the goodness of others. Being more of a cynic himself, he admired her idealism, especially because she hadn't let Steven harden her, even after all the bumps and bruises. The respect Noelle had for her ex-mother-in-law also impressed him. She wasn't out to hurt others simply because she'd been hurt. She'd borne the brunt of Steven's problem in silence and demanded, on her own, that he seek help. How could he take Jeremy—Jeremy *Dane*—away from her after everything she'd already been through?

He couldn't. But neither could he risk that a restraining order would be enough to keep Steven away, or relinquish his parental rights by going through with a formal adoption. They'd have to figure out how to protect the baby and share him…somehow.

"I can pack the leftovers for you to take home, if you want," she said.

This is the guy you told Theresa you wanted to sleep with? His gaze traveled over her. The later it got, the more difficult it was to ignore the fact that, despite the baby issues and the ex-husband problems and Harrison's fatigue, he felt the same way about her.

"Harrison?" she said when he didn't answer.

"I don't think I'm going home."

"Excuse me?"

His cell phone interrupted. Glancing down, he saw his mother's name on his caller ID.

"Just a sec," he said, and answered.

"How's it going?" his mother wanted to know.

Harrison thought of the mess he was in, which had only worsened over the past two weeks. "Fine."

"You don't sound fine."

Because he wasn't. He was sexually frustrated and exhausted and his orderly, ambitious life was spinning more and more out of control. "I've got a headache."

"You need to get more rest."

"That's easier said than done."

"So have you seen him lately?"

"Who?"

"The baby, of course."

"I saw him an hour or so ago, when he was awake. I'm at Noelle's right now."

"Again?"

"Yeah."

"But if he's been asleep for an hour, what are you still doing there?"

A very good question. Except, as he'd been about to tell Noelle, he couldn't leave. Not when there was a chance that Steven might return. "Noelle's ex-husband is causing some trouble. I'm hanging out to make sure he understands that playtime is over."

"What do you have to do with Noelle's ex-husband?"

Harrison recalled his hastily uttered promise. *You ever touch Noelle again and you'll answer to me.* Where had *that* come from? He'd said it as though he had a stake in her life, in her future....

"Remember Vince Boyd from around the corner?" he said.

"How can I forget? You knocked out his front tooth, and when his mother came crying to me to pay the dental bill, I had to tell her—"

"I remember what you told her," he interrupted, chuckling. Half the people in their old neighborhood could probably recite what his mother had told Mrs. Boyd, because Rosie had chased Mrs. Boyd out of their house and screamed it down the street.

"At least he quit trying to stir up trouble with you after that," she said. "And Mrs. Boyd never had the nerve to contact me again."

"Exactly."

"You're saying Noelle's ex-husband's a bully?"

"More or less."

"And you're taking care of it."

"Someone has to."

"Normally you can't be bothered with anything that isn't a patient or a textbook...."

He glanced at Noelle, who'd gotten up and started the dishes.

He considered denying what his mother was implying—that he had deeper motives for protecting Noelle—but he didn't dare. Rosie knew him too well, had hinted about it before. And he had to admit, as crazy as things were, he wanted Noelle badly enough to let them get a little worse....

CHAPTER
NINE

"So what are you trying to say?" Theresa snapped.

"I'm not *trying* to say anything," Noelle replied, curling her hand more tightly around the phone. "I'm telling you that I know something is going on between you and Steven."

"He called you?"

"He came over."

"What for?"

Noelle could hear the jealousy and confusion in Theresa's voice and felt sorry for her. Theresa dated a lot, but for some reason, she had trouble establishing serious relationships. "He wants something I have."

"Which is…"

Noelle craned her head to see down the hall. Harrison had disappeared while she was feeding Jeremy, and she suspected he was sleeping in her spare bedroom. Fortunately, he hadn't said anything about what her ex-husband had announced to him at the door.

"Some pictures," she said, heading from the baby's room back toward the kitchen.

"So give them to him. You don't care about him anymore. You haven't had one nice thing to say about him since the two of you broke up."

"There's a reason for that," Noelle said.

"Yeah, you don't love him anymore. Which means he should be fair game, and you shouldn't be upset if we go out."

Noelle frowned at the defensiveness in Theresa's voice. "Theresa, I don't love him anymore, I love you."

A long pause. "So you're doing me a favor."

Sarcasm. "I'm warning you not to get involved with him. He's got serious problems."

"Everyone says that about their ex-husband," Theresa said. "So what if he leaves the cap off the toothpaste or doesn't pick up his boxers? I don't care. I think Steven's someone I could love, and he seems just as interested in me."

Noelle took down the pictures she'd stashed on top of the fridge before dinner and started going through them. With each photo came a memory she'd rather forget, but she had to save Theresa from making the same mistake. "He's abusive, Theresa."

"Oh, come on. Maybe he's a little aloof emotionally, but I don't think I'd call that abusive—"

"I mean *physically*."

Silence. Then, "I don't believe it. You would've told me."

Noelle released the breath she'd been holding. "I was ashamed, embarrassed. Beyond that, I was planning to get our relationship straightened out and didn't want everyone I know to hate my husband. I knew I could probably forgive him, but I was afraid it would be asking too much of the people who care about me to do the same."

"I'm your best friend."

"I didn't tell *anyone*."

"Probably because it wasn't that bad."

"It *was* bad." Noelle opened her mouth to explain what had really happened to their baby, but in the end she couldn't do it. She'd finally put her pain over Austin to rest. She was working on forgiving herself and moving on, and she had a fresh start with Jeremy Dane. She wouldn't dredge up her most painful memory again. Fortunately she didn't feel as though she needed to. If Theresa would only lower her defenses enough to listen, Noelle had all the proof she needed. "I have pictures."

"What? I don't believe it. You're just jealous. You don't like it that I've found value in someone you've tossed away."

"Theresa—"

"Don't ruin this for me, Noelle," she said vehemently, and hung up before Noelle could respond.

Closing her eyes, Noelle pressed her forehead to the refrigerator door. Theresa wasn't listening....

The moon filtered through the blinds, outlining Harrison's profile in silver. After what Steven had said, Noelle knew she was crazy to be standing in the open door of her spare bedroom, admiring Jeremy's father. She should try to get some sleep, too. There was no telling how many times Jeremy might get up in the night. But she couldn't quit worrying about Theresa or wondering if Steven would come back, and she wanted Harrison to wake up and be with her. His support changed everything.

Telling herself not to succumb to her need for a little more solace, she turned to go, but his voice stopped her. "Don't tell me you're chickening out."

"What?" she said, surprised that he wasn't asleep after all.

"You've been standing there for ten minutes."

Noelle clung to the shadows so he couldn't see her blush. "So?"

"So now you're leaving?"

"Don't you think that's a good idea?"

"I think it's a better idea for you to stay, or I wouldn't have left the door open."

She smiled. "Said the spider to the fly."

"How do you know *I'm* the spider?"

"Because I can't seem to move from this spot."

He chuckled softly. "Fighting only makes it worse." He fell silent for a few seconds. "So, did you mean it?" he asked at last.

"Mean what?"

"You told your best friend that you wanted to sleep with me."

What a mess. Theresa, Steven, Harrison... "Our situation is difficult enough already, don't you think?" she said.

"Definitely."

"My climbing into bed with you won't make our lives any easier."

"That may be true, but at this point, I'm not sure it'll hurt anything, either."

After the year she'd spent, she was beginning to agree. How terrible could it be to feel good for a change?

"We'd be taking a chance."

"On what, specifically?"

"On each other."

"Maybe I'm not as bad a gamble as you think."

Folding her arms tightly, she leaned against the door frame. "Or maybe you're even worse."

"Come on. Life is full of unknowns. That's what makes it fun."

"You wore a condom even when you thought Lynnette couldn't have children. You don't appear to be a big risk-taker to me, Dr. Ferello."

"Regardless, my life is veering out of control, and I don't seem to mind as long as you're around. Can you explain that?"

"Um—" she pretended to think "—you like my cooking?"

"I like more than your cooking." He sat up and patted the bed beside him. "Come here."

Noelle stared at the empty spot he indicated. Her heart was pounding in her ears, egging her on, and her body was growing warm, responsive, reminding her that she was still very much alive.

Tentatively, she stepped closer. "This is crazy."

"Some things are meant to be crazy," he said, and captured her elbow, pulling her down on top of him as he fell back on the bed.

"I like the way you smell," he said, sweeping his nose up her neck and kissing the indentation below her ear. "And..."

Noelle shivered at the sensation. "And?"

He slipped his hands beneath her shirt and touched the bare skin of her waist. "And I like the way you feel."

Bracing her hands on the pillow at either side of his head, she stared down at him. The huskiness in his voice and the expectant glimmer in his eyes seemed to curl through her veins like smoke. "And?"

"And I want to make love to you. I've wanted to since you were in my apartment—no, since I first saw you in the hospital."

Even when she was married to Steven, their problems had loomed so large that Noelle had experienced little passion. She couldn't remember the last time she'd felt like this, the last time she could actually say she burned for a man.

Maybe it wouldn't last, but she'd at least have this night.

"Then, what are you waiting for?" she breathed.

She felt his hand slip up her shirt, over her bare back as he rolled her beneath him. Yes! This was what she wanted. She could quit worrying, let go. One night with Harrison couldn't hurt anything. She couldn't even get pregnant anymore. She was normal, healthy….

"Harrison?" she whispered.

He'd just fisted his hand in her hair. "Hmm?"

She gazed up at his face, inches from hers. "Just promise me you won't change your mind about Jeremy. I can risk everything else, but I can't risk losing him."

He'd been about to kiss her. Now he froze. Noelle could smell a hint of the wine they'd had with dinner on his breath, could almost feel his soft, warm lips moving over hers. She wanted to taste him, to finish what they'd started. But her words had thrown up an unexpected barrier. "Noelle, I…"

"What?"

His forehead creased in a pained expression, he rolled off her, and sat up. "I don't know how to say this, but I have to tell you the truth, especially now."

That hesitancy she'd noted earlier was back, and so was her fear. She couldn't look at him; she could scarcely breathe. "What truth?" she said softly.

He took her hand, which suddenly seemed cold and foreign to her body. "I'm sorry. I can't let you adopt Jeremy."

She felt as though he'd slugged her. The confrontation with Steven ran through her mind, along with the meals and late-night talks she'd shared with Harrison over the past two weeks. What had changed his mind?

Finally she managed to speak. "Because of Steven?"

"Not just Steven. I can't let him go. I'm afraid I'd regret it the rest of my life." He shot her a troubled glance. "I hope you can understand."

Of all reasons, she could understand that one best. But it didn't make the reality any easier. She'd lost another baby, just when she'd found hope.

Numbly, she nodded. "Okay."

"I'm sorry."

She blinked back the tears that threatened. She would *not* cry. She would not make him feel guilty for making a decision he had every right to make—for making essentially the same decision she would have made in his shoes. "Don't be sorry," she said. "You're his father."

"Maybe if you're willing to explore other options, we can—"

"No." She held up a hand. "I—I can't. Not right now."

He sat on the edge of the bed and hung his head. "I feel terrible about this."

"Don't. Jeremy's a beautiful baby." Her voice wobbled in spite of her attempt to control it. Gritting her teeth, she fought against the crushing pain in her chest. She'd come so close.... "You can raise him just fine," she continued. "You don't need me. Find someone you can trust to look after him while you work, and spend every minute you're not at the Med Center with him, loving him. You won't regret it."

He seemed encouraged by her words. "It'll be a challenge, probably the biggest one of my life."

She forced a smile. "But you're good at challenges. Look what you've accomplished already."

The decision had been made. There was no turning back.

Harrison took a deep breath as he packed up Jeremy's belongings. He was sure he was doing the right thing. The peace he felt inside told him so. He was keeping his son because he wanted to—even though he knew the future wouldn't be easy.

"What about all this...baby stuff?" he asked, motioning to the crib and changing table and rocker she'd purchased.

She hovered at the entrance to the nursery she'd created as

though she didn't dare venture inside. "You can buy it from me, if you want. Or I can take it back. It doesn't matter."

He needed baby furniture, but he was pretty sure he should visit Goodwill to get it. With his student loans and the added expense of caring for a baby, he needed to be frugal. He still wasn't sure how he was going to pay for childcare. He might have to start tutoring Med Students on the side. "You should probably try and take it back. If the store won't return your money, let me know. I'll reimburse you." *Somehow....*

"I don't think that'll be a problem. I still have my receipt and it hasn't been thirty days."

"Okay."

Noelle folded her arms as if she had to physically hold herself together or she'd come apart. Harrison wished he'd been able to make a decision sooner so he could have saved her the false hope. He'd put what she wanted most inside her grasp, only to snatch it away again. But he'd come to terms with fatherhood as quickly as he possibly could.

"Are you sure I should leave you here alone?" he asked when he had the baby buckled in his car seat. "I'm afraid your ex-husband might—"

"With the baby gone, there's nothing to worry about," she interrupted quickly. "If Steven comes back, I can handle him. This time I'll know better than to open my door to him, and if he tries to force his way in, I'll call the police."

"That's good," Harrison said, but her words hardly made him feel better. He was only leaving because he knew the night wouldn't be any easier on her if he stayed. She was obviously trying to deal with his decision the best way she could, but it had affected her deeply and he suspected she'd crumble the moment she had some privacy.

He winced as he remembered her reaction when she'd first held Jeremy...Jeremy Dane. He decided right then that he'd keep the middle name, in honor of her.

"I guess that's it, then," he said.

"I guess so."

"Thanks for everything."

"You bet."

He started out with the baby, but his feet grew heavier and heavier as he neared the front door. Finally he turned back. "Maybe we can get together and grab a bite to eat this weekend, or—"

"No," she said firmly. "But thanks for the offer."

Jeremy let out a squall and Harrison couldn't help noticing how quickly Noelle's gaze dropped to him.

"Do you want to hold him one more time?" he asked.

She shook her head in an abrupt movement that told him she couldn't handle it.

"Okay. Well…" He wanted to get his arms around *her* one more time, but knew she'd rebuff him. "Dinner was great, by the way."

"Be careful driving home," she said, then he stepped out into the cold and she closed the door behind him.

CHAPTER
TEN

HARRISON GLANCED OVER at his sleeping son as he drove home. He was just as frightened as when he'd retrieved Jeremy from the hospital, but he swore that, regardless of the problems he encountered in the future, he wouldn't give up on being a father. That's all he had to offer—his determination to stick around, as Rosie had, and do his best.

Unfortunately all the determination in the world couldn't make him feel better about Noelle. He'd only known her a few weeks, but he'd felt a spark the moment he laid eyes on her in the hospital nursery. When he imagined making love to a woman, *she* was the one he pictured. The one he wanted....

But Harrison didn't believe in love-at-first-sight. He wasn't even sure he believed in plain old "love," at least not the kind depicted in the movies, where two people became so enthralled with each other that nothing and no one else mattered. Other things always mattered to Harrison. His freedom, his work, staying in control of his emotions and protecting—

He cut off his thoughts because he didn't want to look quite that closely. He was simply feeling a sense of obligation, along with compassion for Noelle's loss, and guilt for his part in making that loss worse. Even his mother would tell him that.

He decided to call Rosie immediately, before his doubts could undermine his intentions any further.

"Is everything okay?" Rosie asked as soon as she picked up.

The worry that resonated in her voice nearly elicited the truth: *Yes and no. I know I'm doing the right thing by Jeremy, but I still feel as though someone has blown a hole right through my chest.* But he managed to catch himself. "Fine."

"You're fine," she repeated, her tone going flat.

"Yes, of course."

"Then do you think you could call me in the middle of the day next time?"

He'd been thinking so much about Noelle that he hadn't realized it was after midnight. "Sure. Sorry. I just wanted to let you know…I called to tell you that I'm taking Jeremy home."

She hesitated. "You mean for the night, right?"

"No, I mean forever."

The silence grew strained.

"Mom?"

"It won't be easy," she said softly.

"I know that."

"How will you get by?"

"I'll figure out a way. You did, right?"

Another long silence. "Okay," she said at last. "I'm coming home."

Harrison turned down the radio. "You are? For how long?"

"Forever, if that's how long you need me."

Harrison's eyes began to burn, and a lump so large it nearly choked him rose in his throat. "Mom, don't. You deserve a life of your own. You're newly married and happy in Vegas. You own a home for the first time. I don't want to be responsible for—"

"Harrison," she interrupted.

"What?"

"You mean more to me than this home, and Bill and I will be just as newly married and happy in Sacramento, where we can help take care of our grandson."

Harrison remembered all the days his mother hadn't climbed out of bed to help him get off to school, the way she'd embarrassed him by cussing like a sailor in front of the other PTA moms, the fast-food wrappers that had stacked up on their kitchen table and the general mess in their house. Maybe Rosie hadn't done an exemplary job of raising him, but she'd always been there when it mattered most.

Noelle sat in the nursery she'd created for Jeremy, gently rocking in the wooden rocker. The silence felt profound. She knew she needed to pack up the baby furniture and return it. She couldn't let herself dwell on another loss. For one thing, she had to get back to work or she'd blow her deadline on the ceramic teenagers she was under contract to create for the J Street office building. For another, she knew from experience that focusing on the pain didn't help. Life would go on, eventually.

Yet even though she knew all of that, she couldn't make herself get up. She'd been sitting there for hours; it was nearly midmorning.

The cordless phone that rested in her lap rang. Noelle turned it over to view the screen, hoping it was Theresa. She'd left several messages, begging her friend to come over and talk, but the Caller ID read, "Grantham Hospital." Noelle almost let it go to voice mail. She didn't want to talk to anyone, especially someone who might have bad news—until a terrible thought crossed her mind.

"Hello?" she said.

"Noelle, this is Charlene Matheson."

Fear clutched at Noelle's stomach. "Is something wrong with Jeremy?"

"With who?"

Noelle reminded herself that Charlene and the other nurses had no idea she'd been involved with Harrison or Jeremy. "The baby who lost his mother. He's okay, isn't he?"

"As far as I know. I'm calling about something else."

Noelle closed her eyes and sank deeper into the chair as the tension drained out of her. *Thank God.* "What's that?"

"Good news. Sutter General across town called earlier, asking about our infant bereavement program. I told them about the Memory Boxes, and they want to be included. Do you know how to get them on the list?"

"Of course. They can call the coordinator or log on to the Web site to add their information."

"Do you have the URL?"

"It's www.memoryboxes.org," Noelle said and nearly let the conversation go. Another artist could supply the boxes Sutter General required. Noelle couldn't do it. Without Jeremy, she wanted to crawl in a hole and hide from the world again, just as she had when she'd lost Austin.

She stiffened. Wait a minute… The reason she'd become involved with the Memory Box Artist Program in the first place was to forget about her own problems by helping others. How could she let herself backslide now?

Standing up, she let her eyes sweep the nursery one final time. Then she walked out in the hall and closed the door behind her. One day would lead to the next….

"Never mind," she said. "I'll give them a call and take care of it myself."

Theresa held her breath as she knocked on Steven's door. Noelle had to be lying. Sure, Steven had been a jerk when he was married to her. Theresa would be the last person to argue that point. But Noelle and Steven were split up now, and he seemed to have changed for the better. He was educated, had lots of friends, his family adored him, and he had a high-powered, well-paying job. A person like that didn't beat his wife. If he was violent, she would have known by now. Noelle would have told her. She wouldn't have kept something like that from her best friend.

Surprise registered on Steven's face when he finally opened the door. "Theresa? I thought we were planning to hook up later."

"I couldn't wait."

His eyebrows shot up at the urgency in her voice, but Theresa couldn't hide her concern. She'd been stewing about this all night and all day, wondering what to do.

"Is something wrong?" he asked.

"Tell me it isn't true."

"I don't know what you're talking about."

"Tell me you didn't hit Noelle. Ever."

Disgust swept across his face. "She's telling you I caused her to lose the baby, isn't she?"

Theresa's heart thumped heavily in her chest. Noelle hadn't mentioned the baby…. "Tell me what happened," she said. "I want to hear it from you."

"Nothing happened. We argued, I tried to leave, she got in the way of the car, that's all. Accidents happen, you know?"

Accidents happen? Noelle had been suffering over the loss of her son for a year, and Steven could stand there and act as though it was nothing?

"So you never struck her with your fist or—"

"Of course not," he interrupted.

Theresa longed to believe him. For a second, she told herself she *did* believe him. But there was a slight tic in his cheek and something else, something in his eyes, that betrayed him. Deep down, she knew that Noelle was telling the truth.

"What about the pictures?" she asked, her anger growing at the thought that Noelle had suffered in silence while this man—this man Theresa had thought she was beginning to care about— showed no remorse.

His face grew mottled. "Did you see them? Did she show them to you?"

Theresa briefly closed her eyes and shook her head. "She didn't need to," she said, and turned away.

"So what's going on?" he called after her. "You're not cutting things off between us just because I lost my temper a few times with my ex-wife. She's the one who caused it. She provoked me."

Theresa couldn't believe her ears. How could she have almost fallen in love with this man?

"You're pathetic—don't ever call me again," she shouted back. Then she walked away, swiping at the tears she hadn't realized were falling.

The next morning, Harrison stood in the supervisor's office of A-B-C Daycare. He'd managed to survive his first day as a full-time father without too much trouble. He'd wanted to pass his second day sleeping as much as possible, but Jeremy had other ideas. And since Harrison had to work tomorrow, that left only today to make arrangements for his son. Rosie wouldn't be arriving for another few weeks, and even after she moved back to town, he'd need some type of fall-back baby-sitting for the times she wasn't available.

Painted in bright primary colors, the day care had looked nice enough from the outside. It was located in an upscale part of town. But Harrison didn't like it any better than the other four he'd already visited—at least not for a newborn. There were too many kids, some with runny noses and coughs, and the place *smelled,* even though it appeared clean. He couldn't imagine leaving Jeremy here with strangers. Jeremy was too young.

"Dr. Ferello?"

He blinked and returned his attention to the woman who'd been telling him all about A-B-C's child-care philosophy.

"What do you think?" she asked, obviously at the end of her spiel. "Would you care to fill out the paperwork?"

She'd assured him that the new babies were separated from the older children, but that placed Jeremy in a tiny room with three cribs. Was that where he wanted his son to spend a good portion of his first year? Had he taken him out of Noelle's cozy home for this?

Noelle…. He pictured her smiling down at him when they were on the bed together—just before he'd delivered the news that must have ripped her heart out again. He'd almost called her a dozen times since he'd left her house, but unless he could give her Jeremy Dane, he knew he'd only wind up hurting her more.

"Dr. Ferello?" the young woman repeated. "Did you want to fill out the paperwork?"

"Sure." With a sigh, he sank into the chair she'd offered him once before and set Jeremy on the floor in his infant seat. What other choice did Harrison have? He had to work tomorrow, and this day care wasn't any worse than the rest. In any case, beyond gut instinct, he had no way of telling which one would be best for his son.

"It doesn't take long," she said, obviously pleased. "Here are the first forms. There's actually a couple more, but it looks like I'm running low. I'll make a few copies while you get started."

She handed him a pen and a clipboard from her desk, then went into a small back room where he could soon hear the hum of a copier.

Harrison started filling out the first form but hesitated once again when he saw the financial commitment he was making. Day care was outrageously expensive. He'd be spending nearly one-third of his total income to put Jeremy in a place he didn't want him to be. But it wasn't the expense that bothered him so much. What he was doing just wasn't right. He could feel it.

He looked down at Jeremy to find his son wide-awake and gazing up at him.

"What do you think?" he murmured, running a finger over his baby's downy head.

Jeremy continued to stare up at him as though transfixed, and Harrison finally attached his pen to the clipboard. He wasn't going to put Jeremy in day care. He wasn't going to let his mother watch him day after day, either. Jeremy belonged with Noelle, and Harrison belonged with Jeremy. Which meant there was really only one answer—and outlandish though it was, Harrison liked it.

Harrison's heart pounded as he carried Jeremy through Noelle's gate, then made his way along the garden path to her workshop. He'd knocked at the front door several times and received no answer, but her car sat in the driveway, so he knew she was home.

Leaving Jeremy around the corner of the little building, where Harrison could see him, but Noelle couldn't, he knocked on the workshop door.

"Who is it?"

Harrison drew a deep breath. "It's me."

The door opened slowly. Noelle had her hair pulled back in a ponytail and wasn't wearing any makeup or even a bra. Just an old

T-shirt, a pair of faded jeans and slippers. Silver paint was smudged on her hands and one cheek, but she looked absolutely beautiful to him.

"Hi," he said, and had to work to convince himself that he wasn't about to have a heart attack. After all, he should know the symptoms.

"Harrison. What are you doing here?" She glanced around, obviously looking for Jeremy. Harrison knew that if Noelle agreed to his proposal, she'd be doing it largely for Jeremy. But he needed to feel as though at least a little part of her cared about him, too. Or that she was *open* to caring about him.

Clearing his throat, he jammed his hands in his pockets. "I have something I want to ask you."

In his mind, this whole exchange had gone much smoother. But now that he was here, facing her, he felt awkward, and very nervous. His future—and Jeremy's—hinged on his next question.

She eyed him suspiciously. "I can't baby-sit for you, Harrison. I'm sorry. I—"

"I know. That's not it. I—" He took her hand and met her gaze. Now that he'd made his decision, he was going to do this right. "Will you marry me, Noelle?"

Her jaw dropped and so did his stomach. He'd expected to feel a flood of remorse at this point. He'd never taken such a daring emotional plunge before. But he felt fear instead—fear that she might not say "yes."

She blinked several times before answering. "Harrison, you can't be serious. There are easier ways to get the help you need."

As if that was her last word on the subject, she tried to pull away, but he wasn't finished yet. "There's no other way to get Jeremy a mother."

"So this is for Jeremy?"

"Not just Jeremy."

"Think about your goals, Harrison. If you marry me, you'll have a wife *and* a child. That pretty much constitutes a family, which is something you've told me you *don't* want."

"I know what a family is."

"Well, I can't have any more children. If you've changed your mind, you'd be better off to find someone—"

Harrison had heard enough. Stepping closer, he gripped her shoulders and drew her to him. She lifted her paint-speckled hands as if she might protest, but her resistance disappeared the moment he bent his head and kissed her. Then she molded herself to him the way he'd dreamed she would, and let him deepen the kiss. She stirred his blood, made him forget how to be passive or indifferent about love or life. "I want *you,*" he said.

Noelle was drowning in a sea of muscle and warmth and titillating sensation—and didn't want to come up, even for air. A moment before Harrison had shown up at her door, she'd thought it was all over. No Harrison. No Jeremy.

"What do you say?" he murmured, trailing kisses down her neck. "Will you marry me, Noelle?"

She didn't know how to respond. Harrison and Jeremy were everything she'd ever wanted, which meant there had to be some reason she couldn't have them. "Where will we live?" she asked.

"Here, for now. I don't make a lot of money yet, but in a few years I'm hoping I'll be able to buy you the house of your dreams."

In a few years… He was serious about making a life with her.

A startled sound drew Noelle's attention before she could respond. Glancing over Harrison's shoulder, she saw Theresa standing just inside the back gate.

"I'm sorry to interrupt," she said, twisting the strap of her purse.

Harrison kept one arm around Noelle's waist but turned as Noelle made the introductions. "Harrison, this is Theresa."

"Your best friend?" he said.

Noelle studied Theresa, wondering what she'd come to say. Their last conversation hadn't ended well, and Theresa hadn't returned any of her calls. "She used to be my best friend, but I'm not so sure how she feels anymore."

A tear rolled down Theresa's cheek and she quickly wiped it away. "I'm still your best friend."

"What happened with Steven?"

"I told him to hit the highway."

"How did he take the news?"

She chuckled shakily. "He's left me some pretty angry voice mails, calling us both all sorts of nasty names."

Noelle slipped away from Harrison long enough to hug Theresa. "It's better to find out now," she said. "There'll be someone else for you."

"I know." As Noelle stepped back, Theresa sniffed and jerked her head toward the side of the workshop. "What's your baby doing over there?" she asked Harrison.

He gave Noelle a sheepish look. "Waiting for Noelle to say yes."

"To what?"

He grinned and pulled a small box from his pocket, which he held out to her.

The sight swept Noelle's breath away. She took it and opened the velvety lid. He'd bought her a *ring*.

"Oh, my gosh!" Theresa cried. "You two aren't…you're not getting *married,* are you?"

Noelle couldn't take her eyes off the ring. She knew Harrison didn't have a lot of money. That he'd taken such a chance where she was concerned touched her. "I don't know. I really need some advice from my best friend."

A broad smile split Theresa's face. "Do it."

Noelle glanced up at Harrison to find him watching her closely. "But we've only known each other a few weeks."

Theresa laughed and shrugged. "So? That baby was meant to be with both of you, and you know it."

Noelle did know it. Even better, she knew she was already in love with Jeremy's father. Sliding the ring on her finger, she rose on her tiptoes to give Harrison a kiss. "When should we have the wedding?" she asked.

EPILOGUE

THERE WAS SOMETHING familiar about the old guy in the gas station. Harrison hesitated the moment he caught sight of him, wondering where they'd met before. Had he seen him as a patient? If so, Harrison doubted it was during the past five years since he'd started his own practice. He knew most of his patients pretty well. It might have been during his residency....

"Dad, can I have this?"

Harrison turned to see Jeremy holding up a candy bar. "That doesn't look like a very healthy snack," he said.

"Aw, come on. You and Mom make me eat too many vegetables. We're going to the cabin for a whole week. One candy bar won't hurt, will it? *Pleez?*" He screwed his face up into the pleading expression Harrison and Noelle both had such a hard time refusing. They were planning to roast marshmallows later, which would be treat enough, but Harrison knew he might as well give in. He would in the end, anyway.

"I guess so. But you'd better eat your dinner tonight...and brush your teeth a little longer before bed."

Jeremy grinned, revealing the gap in his smile where he'd lost his two front teeth. "What teeth?"

"You know what I mean."

"Okay, I promise."

Harrison followed his son to the cashier and ruffled the boy's dark hair before letting his gaze stray back to the man pulling a six-pack of beer out of the cooler. The old guy straightened and came toward them, and suddenly Harrison knew exactly where they'd met.

"Those cars are cool, aren't they, Dad?"

Harrison didn't know what Jeremy was talking about, and couldn't bring himself to glance away long enough to find out.

"I bet they can go two-hundred-thousand miles an hour. They have a book at the library—" Jeremy finally seemed to realize that Harrison wasn't paying attention because he paused to look behind him—and followed Harrison's line of vision to Duane Ferello. "Who's that, Dad?"

Harrison wasn't sure how to respond. This man was a stranger; this man was also his father.

Duane scowled when he found himself the object of their attention. Keeping his eyes fastened mostly on the floor, he shuffled down the aisle to get in line behind them.

The bell jingled over the door as the person in front of them left.

"That'll be $33.75," the clerk said.

Jeremy pulled on Harrison's shirt. "Dad? It's $33.75."

"Oh, right." Harrison fumbled in his pocket for his cash and set the whole wad on the counter.

"Wow, look at all that money," Jeremy said. "That's too much, isn't it, Dad?"

Harrison was vaguely aware of the cashier counting out his change. Jeremy collected the money and the receipt and started for the door, but Harrison couldn't bring himself to move.

Duane reached around him to put his beer on the counter. "Excuse me," he said gruffly. When Harrison *still* didn't move, Duane drew his eyebrows together. "Do you *mind?*"

"Duane?" Harrison said.

Jeremy stood at the door, waiting for him. "You know that guy, Dad?"

Duane stiffened. "That's my name," he said, "but I don't think I know you, do I?"

Harrison felt Jeremy move closer to him. He put his arm around his son's shoulders and squeezed. Since he'd had Jeremy and married Noelle, he hadn't thought much about his father. His life had been too full to worry about Duane anymore, to bother accounting for old losses. But now he realized that there was more to his peace than the love he received from his wife and son. He no longer felt any anger. The difficult decision he'd made eight years ago had helped him understand the fear a man might have about taking on a child. Harrison was finally able to forgive and know that Rosie was right: Duane was the one who had missed out. He was still missing out because of Jeremy, who had to be the greatest kid on earth.

"No, you don't know me." Harrison offered his hand and Duane tentatively took it. "But I wish you well."

With a smile at the bewildered expression on his father's face, Harrison walked out with Jeremy. Noelle was waiting for them in their Ford Expedition, along with Theresa, Theresa's husband, Ben, and their new baby. Glancing up, Noelle caught his eye and mouthed, "I love you." And not for the first time, Harrison thanked God that he'd chosen differently than his father.

THE MOTHEREAD/FATHEREAD®
LITERACY PROGRAM
DENA WORTZEL

More Than Words could very well describe Dena Wortzel's beliefs about books and literacy. For Dena, books truly *are* more than the words on the page—they're a way for us to learn about ourselves, and to help us develop passion and empathy. Reading has a healing quality that can transform lives and, most importantly for Dena, transform families.

Ninety million adults in the United States have limited literacy skills. Many of them are parents. Motheread/Fatheread® is a literacy program that focuses on *family* literacy. Established in 1987 in North Carolina by Nancye Gaj, Motheread/Fatheread® has gained national recognition for its innovation and effectiveness. Its emphasis on literacy in the context of people's lives inspired Dena to spearhead the program in Wisconsin through the nonprofit Wisconsin Humanities Council. Motheread/Fatheread® helps parents improve their own literacy skills and also strengthen their family communication and relationships. Parents are helped to do the one thing that's been proven to lead to children's success in school: read with them daily.

When she was a little girl, Dena's mother read to her every day. And as soon as Dena learned to read books herself, she read constantly. Dena describes herself as having been "a bookish child." She was always sitting in a corner reading, and she'd take a duffel bag full of books on family trips. Books were definitely part of her life growing up, part of her. And they still are.

Dena has always been strongly committed to helping people in need—to helping the poor and the powerless change their lives. She was involved in international development in third world countries, working in Sri Lanka before moving back to Wisconsin and joining the Wisconsin Humanities Council. Dena is deeply concerned with issues of social justice and people living in lesser circumstances—*and* she has this love of literature. It all comes together in Motheread/Fatheread®.

Dena doesn't divide the world into readers and nonreaders. One of the main ways we understand our world is through storytelling, which is often an oral tradition. But people who did not grow up reading latch on to reading when the stories and the books are meaningful to their lives. And as Dena points out, the reading material in Motheread/Fatheread® reflects what matters most in all our lives…our family relationships.

Motheread/Fatheread® doesn't address literacy as a skills deficit, and this is important to Dena. She emphasizes to parents in the program that they are their children's caregivers and are there out of concern and love for their kids. They'd like their children to have a better time in school than they might have had.

The act of reading together is important in itself. "It's a way for parents and children to spend time together and communicate about things that matter," says Dena, "rather than daily interactions like eat your peas. In this reading time, parents and children are actually asking each other questions about what they think and feel. Parents are listening to their children." Many parents didn't know how to read to their kids because they were never read to as kids. Now they can sit with their children and read to them— even initiate play around the reading of books. Children and parents both benefit.

Teaching is what Dena most looks forward to in her week. She teaches inmates in the Wisconsin correctional system using the materials of Motheread/Fatheread®. But Dena says she learns as much from the participants as they learn from her. "It's an extraordinary experience to meet with a group of adults, and within an hour or two of meeting, see them develop meaningful relationships, have meaningful conversations. They understand one another, share concern for one another—and their children—through books. It's miraculous. Simple, yet miraculous. And it is the power of stories that has brought on this miracle. Books are the entryway." By talking about characters and stories, the participants are identifying with the material and with each other. "Without books," Dena says, "they just wouldn't be having these conversations, these connections." Dena is working with a member of the Wisconsin state assembly and representatives from the state's Department of Corrections in an effort to implement classes in more prisons around the state.

As the director of Motheread/Fatheread®, Dena works with a vast network of social service workers, librarians, teachers, and others throughout the state who want to use this nationally recognized program to help families in their communities. Dena organizes the training of at least forty people a year to teach the Motheread/Fatheread® program—and those forty instructors can reach at least eight hundred families throughout Wisconsin annually. Many of the professionals Dena trains are swept up with the same enthusiasm she has for the program, often saying it is the most exciting educational experience in their careers. One instructor was teaching a group of new immigrants using an African folktale about a village threatened by monsters. This opened up a discussion of what "monsters" have come into their lives, and the participants shared incredible stories of personal tragedy and strength.

Dena's desire to help those in need also extends to animals. She and her husband live on a horse farm where they specialize in rehabilitating horses with behavioral problems that others have given up on. Their efforts are saving the lives of horses that might otherwise be destroyed.

Dena really feels grateful that she has been able to use her education, the privilege and opportunities she's had to better people's lives. Motheread/Fatheread® brings together two of her passions—her love of literature and her desire to help those in need—in a way that inspires students and colleagues. Now Dena and her work with Motheread/Fatheread® have become an inspiration for this book…and for others to reach out with the healing power of words.

More Than Words

SUSAN MALLERY

BUILT
TO LAST

SUSAN MALLERY

Susan Mallery is the bestselling author of over sixty books for Harlequin and Silhouette. She is a reader favorite who publishes in the Harlequin Historicals, Silhouette Intimate Moments and Silhouette Special Edition lines, and is excited about writing for HQN Books. Susan and her husband live in sunny Southern California, where the weather is always perfect and the eccentricities of a writer are considered almost normal. She has two beautiful but not very bright cats, and the world's greatest stepson.

CHAPTER
ONE

MARISSA SPENCER liked to think she preferred quiet, average men who were kind and funny, and that she never found herself attracted to brooding hunks. But in this case, she was willing to make an exception.

Aaron Cross had the body of a male centerfold, the face of an angel—fallen, of course—and dark eyes so filled with pain they could rip out her heart at fifty paces. Her friend Ruby would say that a man like Aaron was nothing but trouble, and in this case Marissa would have to agree. Still, she indulged herself in a look-fest while he completed his phone call.

She'd arrived a few minutes early for their 10:00 a.m. appointment. Based on what she'd heard about the amazingly talented and reclusive Mr. Cross, she'd expected a cranky old man. Sometimes surprise was a good thing, she thought when he hung up and turned to face her.

"Ms. Spencer," he said as he moved toward her, holding out his hand.

He was tall and she was a woman used to looking men in the eye. He wore his dark hair long and shaggy and walked with a grace that nearly took her breath away.

When she shook hands with him, she felt sparks that were so predictable, she nearly giggled. Of course, she thought, holding in a grin. With Joe, the sensible guy who ran the hardware store and kept asking her out, she felt nothing. But with danger-guy, she was all aquiver. So went her life.

"Marissa," she said when she could catch her breath to speak. "Thanks for seeing me."

He glanced at her, taking in the long wool skirt, cropped jacket and boots. It might be spring in the rest of the country, but here in Wisconsin, there was still snow on the ground.

"You said you had something unusual to discuss with me," he said, motioning to a leather chair in the corner of his showroom.

She'd already looked around and admired the amazing furniture he made. The hand-carved pieces were both strong and elegant. The fabrics he chose were distinctive, while much of the leather was reworked from older pieces.

As she sank into the seat, she wished her budget allowed for this kind of indulgence. But alas, her needs were more easily met at the local thrift store.

He perched on a stool, forcing her to look up to meet his gaze. As their eyes locked, she felt a definite shiver low in her belly. Was her attraction to this stranger really that intense, or was it just her second Danish of the morning talking back to her?

"I'm here to beg," Marissa said happily. "I could pretty it up for you, but that's the unvarnished truth. I'm on the acquisitions committee for a charity auction. We're raising money to buy books for our Motheread/Fatheread® program."

Aaron didn't blink as she spoke, which made it hard for her to judge his reaction.

"Are you horrified?" she asked.

"I'm listening."

She supposed that was something.

"I shouldn't really be here," she confessed with a grin. "While everyone agrees that your furniture is so amazing as to be brilliant, apparently you don't have a reputation as a joiner."

"I keep to myself," he admitted.

"That's what I heard. Everyone told me I was crazy to even ask, but hey, what's the worst that could happen? You say no. Which would be sad, because the program is amazing. We're teaching people to read—mostly parents."

She leaned forward and clasped her hands together. "You can't imagine how a person changes when he or she learns to read. There's such pride. Watching parents read a story to their children for the first time would totally break your heart. Reading gives them a chance to participate in their children's education—to be better parents. The purpose of the auction is to raise money to buy books."

The woman kept on talking. Her energy filled the showroom until Aaron half expected to see mini bolts of lightning bounce off the ceiling and walls. Most of the locals knew enough to leave him alone, but not this one. She showed no signs of stopping.

"Who are you?" he asked, interrupting her in midsentence.

She frowned slightly. "I told you. Marissa Spencer."

"Not your name. Who you are. Why are you doing this?"

"Oh." She shimmied a little in her seat and smiled. "I moved here about two years ago. I'm a part-time bookkeeper, part-time librarian, and I volunteer a lot."

"So you think you can change the world?"

"Of course."

Figured. He knew the type. Those who still believed in happy endings and miracles.

"I don't think so," he said, standing.

She bounced to her feet. She was tall, blond. Pretty.

"If this isn't a good time, I can come back."

He saw it then, what he'd missed at first glance. Behind the long hair and the easy smile was a spine of steel.

"What can I say to make you go away?" he asked.

"Aside from a donation?"

He nodded.

"We could reschedule."

He was only a few years older than her, but he felt tired and worn by comparison.

"You're going to keep coming back, aren't you?"

She shrugged. "Sorry, but yes. I'm determined. It's a flaw."

She made the statement with a cheerfulness that told him she didn't consider it a flaw at all. Which meant the quickest way back to his solitude was to give her what she wanted and get her out of his life.

"What did you have in mind?" he asked.

Her blue eyes widened. "You mean you'll donate something?"

"Sure."

"Wow. That's great. Really. I don't know how to thank you."

"Pick something."

He motioned to the contents of the showroom. She walked to a small upright chair and ran her fingers over the carved wood.

He liked the way she took her time to study the piece. She noticed the little details and then stepped back to look at it from a distance. When she turned over the price tag, she went pale, and for a second he thought she was going to pass out.

"Okay, then," she said, straightening. "Maybe something smaller?"

He realized she had no idea who he was. To her he was a local recluse who made furniture. Not a man with a waiting list a year long and thousands of people willing to pay exorbitant prices for something made by him.

"I mean, it's all lovely, but we're talking a charity auction. We thought your piece would go for maybe five hundred dollars."

"I have some shavings out back," he said, holding in a smile.

She pretended to consider the possibility. "If we put them in containers, maybe. How about kindling from your workshop? I could sew up little bags and label them or something."

She was so earnest, he thought, amused for the first time in ages.

"I'll make a bookcase. It's not the sort of work I usually do, so there's no way to compare prices. It will be simple, but a good piece. How's that?"

Marissa clapped her hands together and spun in a circle. "That would be amazingly cool. I don't know what to say." She stopped the twirling and grinned at him. "You'll get a letter for tax purposes, of course."

"I thought I might."

"Maybe I'll bid on the bookcase myself."

He doubted that. She struck him as the type who never had two cents to rub together. No doubt she spent her spare time helping in a soup kitchen or working with sick kids at a hospital.

"Tell me when you need it by," he said, ready to end the conversation.

She pulled a small notebook out of her purse and read off a date. "And then there's the picnic next Saturday."

His gaze narrowed. "What picnic?"

"The one where we thank all the donors. You'll have to come because you're the grand prize, so to speak. The last item to be auctioned. Everyone is very excited to meet you." She bit her lower lip. "I sort of said you would be there."

Events like that were his idea of pure torture. "I'm making the bookcase. Isn't that enough?"

She sighed. "You'd think it would be, wouldn't you? But there will be a lot of families at the picnic. You know, people who have completed the program, along with those just starting. And lots of kids. You're a real inspiration to them."

He doubted that. "Does anyone ever tell you no?"

"Oh, sure. Lots of times. At first anyway. It means I have to keep coming back and asking."

Which sounded a lot like a threat to him.

He wanted to swear. He wanted to complain he didn't have time and, more important, didn't want to make time. He wanted to tell her to get out of his life and never come back.

She looked at him with her big blue eyes and trusting expression. As if she believed down to her bones that there was nothing in the world he wanted more than to go to her picnic. In the past he'd always found it easy to tell people no, but for some reason, right now he couldn't seem to speak the word.

"What time?" he asked.

Marissa beamed at him. "Eleven. You don't have to bring anything. We're providing the food. I'm making brownies and the Main Street deli is donating sandwiches. You'll have a great time. I can't wait."

"Yeah. Me, too."

Her gaze slipped past him to settle on something over his shoulder. She opened her mouth, then closed it.

He turned and saw Buddy standing in the doorway of the showroom.

The coyote still had much of his winter coat, making him seem bigger than usual. His dark eyes never left Marissa as he sniffed the air to catch her scent.

"A friend of yours?" she asked.

He liked the fact she didn't call Buddy a pet. "He hangs out around here. When he was young, he got caught in a trap. I rescued him. He healed, but he's got a bum leg and can't survive on his own."

"Is he tame?"

"Sometimes."

She turned her attention from the coyote back to him. "Why do I suddenly think you're not as mean and tough as you want the world to believe?"

"Think what you want."

"I will." She smiled. "Thank you, Aaron. For the donation and for spending time with me. I look forward to seeing you at the picnic." She glanced again at Buddy, then left the showroom.

Aaron and Buddy watched her go. When they were alone, the coyote approached and Aaron rubbed his ears.

"What do you think?" he asked the silent creature. "Women like that are trouble."

Buddy sniffed and Aaron grinned. "You're right. She sure did smell good."

CHAPTER
TWO

"HE'S TOTALLY HOT," Ruby said as she unpacked supplies for the picnic.

"Maybe, but that doesn't make him my type." As Marissa spoke, she was careful to keep her left hand—and her crossed fingers—out of sight. She didn't want to actually be *lying*.

"But he's wounded," Ruby said, her expression knowing. "You love that. Lord knows you can't seem to avoid a broken man. Show you someone normal, successful and interested in settling down, and you run screaming in the opposite direction. But if there's a battered soul within fifty miles, you're trembling with desire."

Marissa wrinkled her nose. "I do not tremble with desire."

"You do something, girlfriend, and it's not healthy."

Marissa knew better than to argue. Her track record with men bordered on pathetic. Unfortunately she *was* attracted to men with issues—men who tended to move on after solving their issues. Wasn't that just the way of it?

"Aaron's not like that," she said as she opened packages of paper plates. "He's very successful and normal."

Ruby snorted. "Sure. That's why he keeps to himself all the time. And what's up with that wolf of his?"

"I think Buddy's a coyote."

"Whatever. Can't the man get a lab or golden retriever like the rest of the world?"

"He rescued Buddy."

"Maybe. All I'm saying is you've been acting goofy ever since you met the guy. I can read the signs. You're already crazy about him, and from what I've heard, he's going to break your heart. Why don't you try staying safe for once?"

Good advice, Marissa thought as she watched her friend toss her long braids back over her shoulder and start setting out the wrapped sandwiches.

"I'm not crazy about him," Marissa said as she put out containers of fruit salad. "I think he's interesting."

"Uh-huh. You did five minutes on his butt two days ago. Before that it was his face, and then how beautiful his furniture is."

Marissa felt the heat of a blush on her cheeks. Had she really been that bad?

"His furniture *is* beautiful. You should go to his showroom sometime."

"And be a nice juicy replacement for coyote chow? No thanks. Besides, I don't have a spare twenty thousand for an original Aaron Cross table."

Marissa thought about the price tag on the simple chair she'd seen. "Yeah, he does make the big bucks."

Ruby grinned. "At least that's a change. Usually you go for guys who are dead broke. This time you won't be making his car payments."

Marissa put her hands on her hips. "That happened once, and you promised to never mention it again."

"You're right. Sorry. I just want to see you happy. With someone who'll treat you right."

That was exactly what Marissa wanted, too. She tried not to be envious of Ruby's great husband and her two kids, but sometimes it was tough. Why couldn't she find the same?

She had to admit her usually lousy taste in men complicated the issue. She did attract those in need of rescuing. Unfortunately she found it difficult to say no to anyone in need.

"So when does Mr. Tall, Dark and Weird arrive?" Ruby asked.

"He's not weird, and he didn't say what time he'd be here."

"Want to bet he's not going to show?"

"He'll be here," Marissa said with an assurance she didn't feel. As much as she wanted to believe Aaron would come, she was starting to have doubts. Somehow he didn't strike her as the picnic type.

★ ★ ★

Aaron sat in his truck a full five minutes after he'd parked. He could see the crowd of people gathered around the wooden table. To the left, kids chased a couple of soccer balls; to the right, someone had started a fire in one of the pits. Altogether too much life for his liking. He was about to put the truck in Reverse when he saw a tall blond woman pick up a toddler, swing the child around and laugh.

He recognized Marissa even as he refused to acknowledge the ache that seeing her had started. Yeah, she was attractive and he liked her smile, and maybe he appreciated that she still saw the best in people when he'd long since given up hope. But that didn't mean he wanted anything to do with her. Or her causes.

Still, he found himself opening the door and stepping out into the sunny April afternoon. Spring had arrived in Madison and everyone seemed to appreciate the fact. Sounds carried to him—the laughter and shrieks of children, the conversation of adults. In the distance, a couple of dogs barked. Still, for him, the world narrowed as Marissa glanced up. She held the child, but her attention was on him. Their gazes locked in a moment of pure connection.

The ache intensified. He walked toward her, telling himself he was a fool for bothering. He'd never thought to check for a wedding ring when she'd been in his shop. It figured that the only woman to catch his interest in the past five years might be married.

"You came," she said with a smile that lit up her whole face. "Of course, I knew you would, but you hadn't exactly said so."

She was lying, he thought, and doing a piss-poor job of it. "I didn't know I was coming until I got here," he told her. He nodded at the kid. "Yours?"

"What? No. No husband, no kids. This is Tamara, my friend Ruby's daughter. Tamara, this is Mr. Cross."

The toddler buried her face in Marissa's shoulder.

"That age," Marissa said. "She's shy. Come on. I'll return this little sweetie to her mom, then introduce you around. Or do you know everyone?"

Aaron glanced at the crowd. He might have made his home here for the past five years, but he'd never been one to socialize.

"Can't say that I do."

"You will after today."

Marissa was as good as her word. He met everyone associated with the Motheread/Fatheread® program, along with town dignitaries, several local business owners and dozens of program graduates. People were lining up for sandwiches when a teenage girl rushed toward him.

"You're Aaron Cross," she shrieked, clutching a thick magazine to her chest. "Oh, I knew it! My friend Heather called me so I found the magazine with your picture. Can you sign it for me?"

She thrust out a trendy magazine that had done a spread on his furniture a couple of months ago.

"I don't have a pen," Aaron said, wishing he'd never bothered to show up.

The girl handed him one as she danced from foot to foot. "I can't believe you're really here. Someone said you live in town. Is that true?"

"I, uh—"

"Jenny, why don't you let Mr. Cross get some lunch," Marissa said. "We don't want to scare him off, now do we?"

She gently led the teenager away, then urged Aaron into line for lunch. He glanced longingly toward his truck but knew he needed to wait until he wasn't the center of attention before bolting.

Even as he berated himself for showing up in the first place, he made conversation with the people in line. They were friendly enough, and none of them were holding magazines for him to sign. When he'd collected his food, he made his way to a dry spot a few yards from the picnic tables and settled against a tree. Marissa had been called away by one of the organizers, which meant if Aaron timed it right, he could be out of here in about fifteen minutes.

He bit into his sandwich, then reached down for his can of soda.

"Hi."

He turned toward the speaker. "Hi, yourself."

A young boy stood next to him. The kid was maybe six or seven, with tousled dark hair and a big red car on the front of his sweatshirt. He held a large picture book on cars in both hands.

"Whatcha got there?" Aaron asked when the boy didn't speak again.

"Is that your truck?" the boy asked, pointing to Aaron's large vehicle.

"Uh-huh. Do you like trucks?"

The boy nodded. He held up his book. "I like cars, too. They go fast."

"So I've heard."

Aaron felt torn. Part of him still wanted to escape to the solitude of his shop, but he wasn't willing to simply walk away from the kid.

"Is your mom here?" he asked.

The boy pointed to a group of adults laughing at one of the tables.

"I can read," the boy said. "Want me to read you this story?"

Aaron felt the weight of the inevitable drop onto his shoulders. He wrapped up his sandwich and moved it to one side before patting the ground next to him.

"Sure. What's your name?"

"Christopher."

The boy dropped to his knees and held the book out in front of him. It was already open to the first page.

"'Look at the cars,'" he said, reading slowly. "'Many, many cars. Some are red. Some are green. Some go fast.'" He glanced at Aaron, then pointed to the page. "That's the red one."

"I see that."

Aaron gave his truck one last, longing look before turning his attention to the boy. "What happens next?"

"I don't know what to say," Ruby admitted in a low voice.

Marissa shared her confusion. While she was delighted that Aaron had showed up at the picnic, she'd never expected him to stick around for very long. And if someone had asked her if he liked kids, she would have put her meager savings on a definite no!

But there he sat, under a tree, surrounded by at least six little kids. They all had new books they'd earned for their excellent reading skills and were taking turns reading aloud to him.

"The man has the patience of a saint or else he's touched in the head," Ruby told her.

"I don't think he's a saint," Marissa said, watching him laugh with a little girl as she pointed out a picture of a mouse dressed up like a princess. "I guess I should rescue him."

"Seems to me he's big enough to rescue himself."

Marissa wasn't so sure.

"At least he's not like the usual guys you get involved with," Ruby said. "That's something. I was doubtful, I'll admit it, but now I give him a big thumbs-up."

Marissa shook her head. "We're not dating."

Ruby smiled. "Maybe not, but you will be. Mark my words."

CHAPTER
THREE

"You didn't have to stay and help me clean up," Marissa said as she collected leftover sandwiches and put them into a basket.

"No problem."

Aaron's low voice rumbled through the late afternoon and made her want to shiver. Not from cold, but from, well, him.

She knew she shouldn't keep looking at him, but she couldn't help darting quick glances every couple of seconds, as if to confirm he was still there, picking up empty soda cans and dropping them into the recycling bins.

"Besides, I owe you," he said with a smile. "You saved me."

She laughed. "I was afraid those kids were going to wear you out. All that reading."

"It wasn't so bad. Were they all part of the Motheread/Fatheread® program?"

"Their parents are."

"Those kids sure loved their books."

"It's fun to watch them pick out their first book. They treat the decision with such seriousness." She glanced up again and found him watching her. "What?"

"Just you." He jerked his chin toward the basket of leftover food. "Let me guess. You're taking it to a shelter."

"Of course. I couldn't just throw it out."

"Right. And these?" He pointed to the cans.

"We collect them all month, then take them in to the recycling center and use the money for an emergency fund."

"There's something wrong with you," he said.

"Because I care?"

"Because you care too much."

He stood there, lean and tall and ultramasculine. He might not approve of her, but she couldn't help approving of him. Strength radiated from him. His handsome, chiseled features made her want to trace the lines of his face. He looked like the kind of man who could withstand whatever life had to offer and still come out ahead.

He bent down to tie off the last of the trash bags, then leaned against a picnic table.

"Tell me, Marissa Spencer, have you ever done anything wrong in your entire life?" he asked.

She closed the basket and slipped on her sweater. "Silly question. Of course I have."

"Name it."

"I got into fights, brought a knife to school and set fire to the girls' locker room."

He frowned. "Not you."

"Yes, me." She slid onto the picnic table and put her feet on the bench seat. "I was nothing but trouble all the way through school."

"I don't believe you."

"Amazingly enough, that doesn't change what happened. Once I spent an entire summer locked up in juvenile detention."

She had the satisfaction of seeing the usually emotionless Aaron look shocked.

"But you're a goody-goody," he told her.

"Not exactly. I'm a person who wants to change the world. There's a difference."

"Explain it to me."

Marissa thought about her past. So much had changed for her that those troubled days seemed to belong to another lifetime.

"I used to frustrate my teachers because they knew I was smart enough to do the work, but I simply wouldn't bother. One day I'd done something—I can't remember what—and one of my teachers had had enough. She told me I had a choice. I could be suspended or I could work off my punishment in another way." She smiled. "There was this cute guy I liked, so I didn't want to get kicked out of school. I took Plan B."

"Which was?"

"Helping another student with his reading. I had to work with him every day after school. At first it was torture. I couldn't stand it. But after a while, I really started to like it." She smiled. "Then his reading improved, and I felt as if I'd just done something amazing. I offered to help someone else, and within a few weeks I realized that I could make a difference in a person's life. It was a liberating thought and it changed me completely."

"In what way?"

"I'd been bounced around in various foster homes from the time I was twelve. I didn't have a clue what I wanted to do with my life, I just wanted to be on my own. After the reading experience, I decided to go to college, where I majored in library science and sociology. I received my master's in social work and then settled here."

"Where you help everyone and volunteer in your free time."

"It's not like that," she told him. "I'm not perfect. I'm not a goody-goody, as you claimed. What I learned when I was sixteen was that I can make a difference. I can change someone's life for the better with only a little effort and time. Why wouldn't I want to do that? People ask me why I give so much. What I want to ask them is why they aren't getting involved."

He folded his arms over his chest. "Some people don't see the point."

Was he speaking about himself? "Maybe they haven't tried."

"Maybe they think no good deed goes unpunished."

"Ouch." She winced. "You don't actually believe that."

He shrugged. "There are a lot of things in this world we can't control."

"All the more reason to improve what we can."

"You're naive."

"You're a cynic."

He surprised her by smiling. "You left out grumpy."

She laughed. "Okay, a grumpy cynic. How can someone who doesn't believe in the world create such beauty? Your furniture gives pleasure to people."

"They also pay dearly for the privilege of owning it."

"So you're only in it for the money?"

"Sure."

She studied his dark eyes. "I don't believe you. I think you create such beautiful things because they matter to you."

"Believe what you want—it's the truth." His humor faded. "I'm not some project you can take on, Marissa. Don't try to save me."

"I wouldn't do that."

His gaze never left her face. "You're not a very good liar."

She hadn't actually planned on saving him, but maybe she had considered bringing him out of his self-imposed isolation.

"You shouldn't shut yourself away," she told him. "It's not healthy."

"Neither is running around worrying about everyone else so you don't have time to worry about yourself. Who looks after you?"

Interesting question. Even more intriguing, how had he figured her out so quickly?

"I can take care of myself," she said firmly.

"Something you've been doing since you were a kid."

"Exactly. I've had lots of practice and I'm good at it."

Pushing away from his table and walking toward hers, he moved closer. With every step he took, her breath hitched a little.

"Like I said, you're not a good liar."

She stared at him. "I'm telling the truth. I handle things just fine on my own."

"Uh-huh." He didn't sound convinced.

He stopped scant inches from her. He was close enough that she had to tilt her head to meet his dark gaze. Something flashed in his eyes, but she couldn't read it—probably because she couldn't think.

He put one hand on her shoulder. The heavy weight was warm and comforting, but also…exciting.

"Sometimes it's best to leave things as they are," he said, right before he lowered his head and kissed her.

Marissa had less than a second to brace herself for the impact of his mouth on hers. She wasn't sure what to expect, but it wasn't the light, tender brush of firm lips against her own.

He didn't claim her or push her, instead he gently kissed her, as if she were special and easily frightened. The hand on her shoulder moved to the back of her neck, where he rubbed her skin. His other hand cupped her chin.

Heat rushed through her, dousing her in need. Her stomach

constricted, her chest got tight, and suddenly it was difficult to catch her breath.

When he stepped away, she had a feeling she looked as stunned as she felt.

"Why did you do that?" she asked.

He raised one eyebrow. "Hell if I know."

Aaron helped Marissa load her car with the leftover food and bagged aluminum cans. He waited until she was safely out of the parking lot before making his way home.

The sun had set by the time he pulled into the long road that led to his driveway. The automatic outside lights had already clicked on. After he parked he went into the house, but didn't bother turning on lamps. For some reason he wanted to stay in the darkness. As if hiding would help.

None of this should have happened, he thought as he set out food for Buddy, then grabbed a beer and walked into the family room. He sat in his favorite chair and stared out through the curtainless windows into the night. Not the day spent at the picnic or the kiss. He'd been telling Marissa the truth when he said he didn't know why he'd done it.

She wasn't what he'd expected, he admitted to himself. He would have guessed she'd been raised with money and a guilty conscience. Instead she'd learned her lessons the hard way. Her intelligence and humor appealed to him, and Lord knows, she was plenty easy on the eyes.

But not for him.

Darkness invaded his house. Even so, he turned his head toward the chest that sat tucked in the corner. He knew what lay inside. Talismans and memories. He'd been through the contents so many times, he knew them by heart.

Thinking about what had been, what he had lost, made him ache. If only...

Aaron drank down his beer, then set the bottle on a table. He closed his eyes and waited for the ghosts.

They came sometime before dawn. He'd retreated to bed around midnight and had tossed and turned for an hour. But now he slept, trapped by exhaustion. At first everything in the dream was fine. He saw Jilly as she'd looked when they'd first met. So young, he thought—had she really been that young? Barely eighteen and laughing. Always laughing. He saw her father's stern face—the old man had never approved of Aaron. No daughter of a colonel should be dating an enlisted man, even a Marine. But Jilly had stood firm against her father. She'd proclaimed her love for Aaron for all the world to hear. And the colonel had given in.

Next, he saw the wedding. The men in uniform, the toasts, the cake. He heard bits of conversation, the recitation of the vows and Jilly's laughter. Always her laughter.

Time moved forward again, to her knowing smile as she handed him the small, flat package containing a baby blanket. Deep in his sleep, he smiled as the feeling of elation rushed back to him.

He saw the ultrasound and the promise of their son. And then the orders came that sent him far away.

He'd been home for the happy birth, but had left again only a few weeks later.

The dream turned, shifted, got dark and cold. Pain swept through Aaron, immobilizing him. He knew what was coming, reached out to stop it, but he couldn't. Not then and certainly not now.

A rainy street. That dangerous time between day and night. Shadows. Too many shadows. He might have been half a world away, but he saw it as if he rode in the car with them. Jilly and little Matt. She was singing. He shouldn't have known that, but he felt it deep in his gut. She'd been singing as the drunk swerved through the stop sign and plowed into her small car.

Then the singing stopped.

Aaron came awake in a single breath. Sweat drenched his body and made him shiver, but he didn't reach for the covers. He heard the light clicking of Buddy walking toward him. Something had alerted the coyote. Had he cried out, or did Buddy simply sense his pain?

The ghosts turned to mist and faded. He watched them go, knowing he couldn't make them stay. When they were gone, it was as if he'd lost Jilly and Matt all over again.

★ ★ ★

Aaron didn't bother trying to go back to sleep. By five-thirty he was in his workshop. Buddy lay curled up on his bed in the corner, although he kept a watchful eye on Aaron.

"I'm all right," he told the coyote as he sipped coffee. "As all right as I'm going to get."

It had been six years since the car accident that had killed his wife and son. He'd left the Marines and had wandered around the country, looking for something he could never find. Eventually he'd settled here and started making furniture.

At first the ghosts had come every night. Eventually they'd haunted him weekly, then monthly. Now they rarely came. But he'd known they would be there last night.

What had called them? His time with those children? Or Marissa?

Did it matter? In the end, he only had to remember not to get involved. Caring, wanting, needing—they all led to pain. When he'd lost his family, he'd vowed never to love again. Keeping that promise had been a whole lot easier than he'd figured it would be.

CHAPTER
FOUR

MARISSA STOPPED the car in front of the woodshop and drew in a deep breath. She couldn't seem to make the nerves in her stomach stop dancing. The weird tingling sensation that filled her whenever she thought about Aaron had only intensified since she'd driven onto his property. Telling herself she was here for a really good reason and not just because he'd kissed her didn't help.

"It didn't mean anything," she muttered under her breath. "It was just one of those things." Except she didn't know which thing.

"Did you say something, Marissa?" Tim Evans asked from the back seat.

"No. Just mumbling things. Old people do that from time to time."

Tom, Tim's twin brother, turned in his seat and patted her arm. "You're getting senile, aren't you? Should we be thinking about medication?"

"Very funny," she said with a grin. "Okay, you guys give me a second. I'm going to go talk to Mr. Cross."

Tim, the serious one of the two, met her gaze in the rearview mirror. "You didn't tell him we were coming, did you."

"Nope. But Mr. Cross loves surprises."

As she spoke, she carefully crossed her fingers, then she opened her door and stepped out into the warm Saturday morning.

The air smelled fresh and clean from the rain two days ago. Spring was showing off with new leaves and plenty of late daffodils and tulips. Marissa paused to admire the beauty of the rural setting, ignoring the voice in her head reminding her that putting off the inevitable wouldn't make it go away.

"Maybe Aaron really *does* like surprises," she whispered to herself as she made her way to his workshop and pushed open the door. And maybe next week Buddy would take to flying across the night sky.

"Hi," she yelled as she stepped inside the noisy room. "It's Marissa. Anybody home?"

She hadn't seen him since the picnic the previous weekend, and though she'd been thinking about him almost constantly, there was no excuse for the sudden thrill that shot through her at the sight of him now.

Aaron stood behind some woodworking tool that was nearly as tall as he. He wore goggles and something over his ears. Wood chips covered him, but somehow they only added to his charm.

He moved the equipment with a confidence that came from familiarity. A half-finished chair sat on the table next to him. From where she stood, she saw an open door leading to the woods behind the property. Buddy was lying in a patch of sun, watching her anxiously.

Aaron obviously hadn't heard her enter. He continued to work for several seconds before he looked up and she waved. When he clicked off the machine, a rush of silence filled the room.

"Hi," she said, hoping she sounded more cheerful than anxious. "How's it going? Did you have a good week? Isn't the weather great?"

He pulled off his goggles and brushed back his dark hair. His gaze narrowed. "What's wrong?" he asked.

"Nothing. Why?"

"You're nervous. You've done something. What is it?"

"Me? No." She went for a smile, then sighed. "Okay. So, maybe. See, I brought Tim and Tom Evans with me. I thought they could spend the afternoon out here and you could show them what you do."

"No." He slid on his goggles and reached for the switch on the machine.

"Aaron, please."

He glared at her. "Marissa, you don't have the right to invade my life."

"I know. It's just…"

"I'm not interested in saving the world. That's your job."

They'd talked about that before. Was that why he hadn't called her to get together again? But he'd kissed her. Hadn't that meant anything? She nearly stomped her foot on the cement floor. Questions like that had haunted her for the past week. She should just come out and ask what had happened, except that would require a level of maturity she'd yet to master.

She drew courage from the fact that he hadn't restarted the machine.

"Their mother has cancer," she said quietly. "She's dying. It's just a matter of a couple of weeks or maybe even days. They're only fifteen, scared, and their dad is a wreck. Both sets of grandparents are hovering. I had to get them out of the house, but then I didn't know what to do with them. They need a distraction. Something physical."

Aaron silently ran through every swearword he knew.

"You don't play fair, do you?" he asked.

"This isn't a game. Not to them."

At the picnic she'd worn jeans and a long-sleeved T-shirt that had hugged her curves in a way designed to make a man go slowly mad. Today she'd dressed in another long skirt, with boots and a loose blouse. He'd spent the better part of a week doing his best *not* to think about her, which was pretty much the same as thinking about her all the time.

"Why me?" he asked.

"I didn't have anywhere else to go."

He knew what she wanted—to drag him into her "heal the world, one good deed at a time" philosophy. She wanted him to be a true believer, like her.

Well, that wasn't going to happen. He didn't need her or anyone else to get by.

The door to the shop opened slowly and two boys walked in.

"Marissa, is everything okay?" one of them asked.

They looked enough alike to be able to get away with murder, he thought. Young. All arms and legs, awkward, lanky. Scared.

Instead of answering the question, she looked at him. He felt her silent pleading. He should be furious with her for putting him on the spot like this, and he would be. Later.

"I'm Aaron Cross," he said as he tossed the goggles onto the table and walked toward the boys.

One of the twins moved toward him. "Hi. I'm Tom. That's Tim." Tom looked around. "You really make all your furniture here?"

"Every stick of it."

"That's so cool. What's that?" He pointed at a lathe. "What does it do?"

"Come on. I'll give you the grand tour." He turned to Tim. "Interested?" he asked.

The quieter twin nodded and moved closer. "Yes, Mr. Cross. Thanks for letting us stop by."

"Aaron," he said. "I'm not old enough to be Mr. Cross, yet."

Tom smiled. Tim still looked out of place. Aaron frowned as he realized the boys were identical, yet he knew exactly who was who. What was up with that?

"So what time should I come back?" Marissa asked. "I said I'd take the boys home around four, but I can come sooner and we can go to the mall or something."

Aaron glanced at the clock. It was barely after ten.

"Three-thirty is fine."

Marissa's eyes widened. "Are you sure?"

"Yeah." He glanced at the boys. "You two up for sandwiches for lunch? That's about all I have around here."

The twins glanced at each other and smiled. "That sounds good," Tom said. Tim nodded.

Marissa beamed. "Great. I'll see you guys later."

"You can't just show up like that," Aaron said two days later when Marissa dropped by with some banana bread as a thank-you for what he'd done for the twins.

"I know." She sat curled up in a corner chair in his workshop while he paced and looked fierce.

"It's not right. It's not fair to me or them."

"I'll agree that it's not fair to you," she said, hoping he wasn't as annoyed as he seemed. "But the boys were transformed. They talked about their day with you the whole way home. Besides, it can't have been that bad. You invited them back."

He turned to glare at her. "They're making some shelves for their room and they're not done. What was I supposed to do? Leave the project unfinished?"

"Of course not. That would have been horrible."

His gaze narrowed. "Are you making fun of me?"

"Me? Never. I'm simply pointing out that you had a good time, too."

He folded his arms over his chest. "That doesn't give you the right to do things like that."

She knew he had a point. "I'm sorry. It was sort of an emergency."

"You're the kind of person who always has emergencies. Don't involve me in the next one."

"Okay. I promise."

"Do you mean that?"

She nodded, careful to keep her crossed fingers out of sight. "You look really cute when you're mad," she said.

"Marissa!"

Her name came out as a growl. The low, forceful sound made her all quivery inside. She wondered if he wanted to kiss her as much as she wanted him to.

"Do we have an understanding?" he asked.

"Sure. There's a spaghetti dinner at the Methodist church tonight. Usually those things are a bust because it's only five dollars and how good could the food be? But this is different. I know the lady who makes the sauce, and I have to tell you, it's fabulous. Plus there's garlic bread, and the money raised is for the new roof. Want to go?"

"No."

"Oh."

Suddenly she felt small and foolish. As if he really meant what he said. "Okay." She stood. "I need to get back to work. Thanks again for helping with Tim and Tom. You were terrific. I'll try not to bother you again."

She crossed to the door. Behind her, Aaron sighed.

"What time?"

She spun back to face him. "For dinner?"

He sighed again. "Yeah. What time should I pick you up?"

Her heart did a little happy dance and her insides did a shimmy. "Six-thirty."

★ ★ ★

Aaron was willing to accept the twins hanging around all the time, and the spaghetti dinner at the church, and the newspaper interview about his work in support of the auction. He didn't mind that he was asked to clean out his closets for the women's shelter rummage sale or the sixteen boxes of cookies he bought from the marching band kids who "just happened to stop by" with Marissa one afternoon. But when the vice principal of the local middle school wanted him to come in and talk on career day, he knew things had gone too far. Despite her promise to the contrary, Marissa was taking over his life and she had to be stopped.

He drove out one evening, intending to catch her before she started her Tuesday night Motheread/Fatheread® class.

"The woman is nuts," he muttered as he drove through the quiet streets toward the library. "Certifiably insane."

He could understand her need to change the world. Fine. That was *her* decision. He didn't want any part of it.

He was going to tell her that, along with a few other choice things. He had a mental list.

The library parking lot was nearly full. He found a spot near the back and headed inside toward the classrooms.

When he reached Marissa's, he stopped just outside the open door. The room was already filled with her students. He checked his watch and realized there were still fifteen minutes until the class officially began, but apparently these students didn't want to be late.

Nor did they stay in their seats. He glanced inside and saw several crowding around her desk. One middle-aged woman held up a single sheet of paper.

"From my Joe's teacher," she said proudly. "He is doing so good in his English class. She says it right here." The woman pointed to the paper. "I can read it, Miss Marissa. I can read it!"

Aaron knew there was a time to stand strong and a time for a strategic retreat. No way could he win tonight. Not here. Not like this. But soon he would find a way to get through to her and get her out of his life.

CHAPTER
FIVE

"SAFETY FIRST," Aaron said. "No goggles, no class."

The half dozen teenagers crowded around his largest work-table nodded vigorously.

"Okay. See you next week," he told them.

"Thanks, Aaron," Tom Evans said as he and his brother headed for the exit. Two girls trailed after them, with the last couple of guys bringing up the rear.

Aaron waved, then dropped his own goggles to the bench and shook his head. How had this happened? He'd gone from help-ing grieving twins build a shelf to teaching an entire class. It was Marissa, he thought grimly. Somehow she'd sucked him into her world when he'd been so determined to stay out of it.

"You're looking serious about something," she said, stepping into the workshop.

Her unexpected appearance surprised him. Had he conjured her just by thinking about her? He wouldn't put it past her to fig-ure out how to crawl into his brain.

"I wasn't expecting you," he said.

"I know. I was in the neighborhood."

He raised one eyebrow. "I'm the only one who lives on this road."

She smiled. "Maybe I got lost."

He doubted that. She always knew exactly where she was going. He eyed the foil-wrapped package she held.

"Okay, what is it?" he asked. "Somebody's having a baby and you want me to build the crib."

"Not at all."

"You need me to buy a printing press for the high school newspaper."

"Not even close." She tilted her head so her long blond hair tumbled over her shoulder. "What makes you think I want anything at all?"

"You're bringing me food. That's usually a sign. You bribe me with sugar."

"Not in this case."

Spring had arrived in full force, and with it came sunny days and warm temperatures. Marissa had traded in her long heavy skirts for shorter, softer ones that flirted with her knees and outlined her hips. Gone were the thick sweaters, and in their place were snug little T-shirts. If he were given the choice between whatever she'd brought on that foil-wrapped plate and the woman herself, there'd be no contest.

Still, he didn't move toward her or try to touch her. She might have found a way into his life, but he was careful to keep his emotions out of reach. He would admit to liking her, but nothing more. Nothing dangerous.

She set the plate on a worktable. "This is a freebee. Mostly me thanking you for everything."

Why didn't he trust that? "You *always* want something."

"This time I don't."

"Show me your hands."

He'd caught on to her finger-crossing trick, the one she used when she didn't want the lie to count.

Holding up both hands, she wiggled her fingers. "I'm not here because I want you to do something or buy something. I just came by to say hi."

"Huh."

She grinned. "Trust is an important part of our relationship. You really need to stop assuming the worst about me."

"It's only because I know you."

She laughed.

The sound washed over him, seeping inside and awakening things better left sleeping. When they were apart, he knew that being strong was best for both of them, but when they were together, sometimes he wanted more.

Buddy walked into the workshop and glanced around. Marissa went very still, waiting to see if the coyote would finally accept her. So far, he'd kept to himself, but this afternoon, he approached cautiously.

He paused about two feet away and sniffed.

"Hey, big guy," she said in a low voice. "You've lost the rest of your winter coat. You're gorgeous. Such a pretty face, too, although what with you being a guy, I should probably say you're handsome."

Buddy took another step toward her and pressed his nose close to her hand. Then he turned and bolted from the workshop.

Marissa laughed. "That was pretty cool. I think he's starting to accept me."

"He's cautious."

"As he should be. He's also amazing. I've always wanted a pet. Unfortunately my hours are crazy and it wouldn't be right to leave an animal alone for so long. Unless I got fish. But they're hard to cuddle."

He didn't want to think about that. "How's the auction going?"

"Good. We have less than a month to go. Donations are pouring in. People have heard about your bookcase and they're excited. We're going to start the bidding at four hundred dollars."

She sounded delighted. Aaron didn't burst her bubble by telling her that even a simple end table of his usually went for several thousand dollars. In an odd way, he liked the fact she had no idea how successful he was.

"Four hundred is great," he said.

"I think so. We get our books wholesale, so that's a lot of reading. Makes me happy." She pulled up a stool and plopped down. "How long have you been making furniture?"

"About five years."

"And why are you famous?" She winced. "I didn't mean that exactly how it came out. Your stuff is beautiful and all, but why are your pieces in magazines and not some other guy's?" She winced again. "I'm putting my foot in it here, but you know what I mean."

He chuckled. "Yeah, I know. Why did I get struck by lightning and not someone else?"

"Exactly."

He'd started making the furniture as a way to heal. Somehow working with wood seemed to ease the ache inside after losing his family.

"I was looking for a place to settle and this was as good as any," he said. "I started making tables and chairs. I'd always played around with this kind of thing, but I'd never done it seriously. One day I went to an auction to buy some old leather. I had this idea for a padded chair. There was a kid there, a photographer. We got to talking. It turned out he wanted to build a portfolio and I wanted some pictures taken of my work so I could start to sell it. We worked out a trade."

He settled on a stool. "In the process of showing the pictures around New York, he gave them to a designer who was helping a friend dress a movie set. So they bought a couple of pieces, and when the stars were interviewed to publicize the movie, they used my furniture. A decorator for an upscale hotel chain saw the piece and called me, along with several of the cast members."

Her eyes widened. "Talk about a chain of events."

"You're right. In a year I went from barely paying the bills to having more work than I knew what to do with."

"It's amazing how a single event can make such a difference," she said, glancing at him from under her lashes.

He stared at her. "You're going somewhere with that."

"Not at all. I think it's great that your life was changed for the better. I had a similar thing happen. It didn't make me rich, but I'm successful." She leaned forward. "One moment, one person can make a difference."

He groaned. "You're killing me, you know that?"

"No, I'm not. I'm showing you the possibilities."

"Isn't teaching the woodworking class enough?"

"I don't know. That's for you to decide."

If only he could believe that. Marissa had a way of working her will on people that was nothing short of a gift. He just wasn't sure he wanted to be on the receiving end of her largess.

"Didn't you promise to leave me alone?" he asked.

"Not that I can recall. Besides, even though you'd rather eat glass than admit it, you like being part of the world. You're more comfortable on the fringes, but this is really okay with you."

He glared at her. "You don't know that."

"Am I wrong?"

Three simple words. An easy question. Aaron could answer it in his sleep. He preferred solitude and quiet and not being involved. He liked a day without surprises.

She watched him, her blue eyes bright with confidence and humor. He knew what she wanted him to say, what she *needed* to hear. It was as if her heart would wither and die without someone, somewhere, to save.

"Why are you doing this?" he asked. "Why aren't you married with a dozen kids to occupy your time?"

"I'm really busy. It's hard to establish a relationship because of that."

"Uh-huh. Now let's hear the real story."

She laughed. "You could at least pretend to believe me."

"I could, but I don't. Now talk."

She tucked her hair behind her ears. "I have horrible taste in men." She held up a hand to stop him from speaking. "I'm not kidding. I mean truly dreadful. I pick broken men and once they're mended, they dump me."

She sounded surprisingly cheerful, as if she accepted her destiny. At least this explained her attraction to him, though he wondered when she was going to figure out he couldn't be healed.

"Why?" he asked. "Why not regular guys who will make your life better?"

"I haven't a clue. Show me someone with a real job, a steady temperament and no serious baggage, and my heart barely beats. But put me in the path of someone in recovery, or a guy who's flirted with the law or is just an all-around loser, and I'm in heaven."

"Former bad girl seeks former bad guy?" he asked.

She frowned. "I hadn't thought of it that way. Maybe. I've done all the self-help books. I don't think it's a self-esteem issue, which still leaves an assortment of potential reasons. Growing up in foster care. Searching for a flawed partner so I can be the superior one. Or my personal favorite, which is my friend Ruby's theory."

"Which is?"

"I'm an idiot."

"I doubt that."

She was too smart. Which made him wonder why she'd avoided anyone who could make her happy.

"Just so we're clear," he said, "you know I'm past saving."

She smiled. "Gee, Aaron, is that an invitation?"

"Just the opposite."

"Your way of saying there's nothing between us?"

"There isn't."

But even as he spoke, he felt the attraction crackling in the air. It was like standing in an open area right before lightning struck. The air seemed charged; even the silence pulsed with anticipation.

"I mean it, Marissa. I'm not looking to get involved."

"Why?"

No way was he going there. "I have my reasons."

"I know. Deep, dark secrets and those wounded eyes. Anyone else would run screaming in the opposite direction. A smart woman would."

"You're plenty smart."

"Not about men like you."

He felt buffeted by need. It came out of nowhere and consumed him. He couldn't think, couldn't speak, he could only want. She was so different from anyone he'd ever known. Fearless and vulnerable in equal measures. If he were any kind of gentleman, he would send her packing. But he'd always been something of a bastard.

Standing up, he moved toward her. He walked deliberately, giving her plenty of warning, plenty of time to bolt. Instead she swayed toward him in an erotic invitation he could no more deny than he could stop the tide.

He grabbed her shoulders and held her.

"This isn't a good idea," he growled.

"Tell me about it."

Then he kissed her.

CHAPTER
SIX

MARISSA KNEW THAT kissing Aaron wasn't likely to appear as one of her ten most intelligent moves of the year, but she couldn't resist him. Not when he was so close to her and the heat of his body was searing her down to her bones.

She liked everything about him, especially the way he pulled her close and claimed her mouth. This wasn't like the last time. There was nothing delicate about his touch. He wasn't patient or seductive. Instead, he claimed her with an intensity that bordered on ravishment, and she found that suited her just fine.

His lips demanded even as he pressed his fingers into her back. She found herself grateful for the stool—it kept her from falling too hard and too fast, at least physically. She couldn't speak to the rest of her being.

He tilted his head and she did the same. When he nipped on her lower lip, her breath caught and her thighs began to tremble. When he swept his tongue across the place he'd nibbled, she parted her lips instantly.

He slipped inside with the practiced ease of a man intent on pleasing a woman. It was too much, she thought hazily; it would never be enough.

Wanting filled her. Wanting and need and desire and all those other delicious emotions she rarely allowed herself to feel. She wanted to beg him to take her right there on the workbench. She wanted to run out into the sunlight and pound her head against a tree until she forced some sense back into her brain. She wanted this moment to go on forever.

Instead she wrapped her arms around his waist and indulged

herself by pressing her palms against his powerful muscles. She memorized the scent of his body and the way he tasted and how he moaned when she slid her own tongue into his mouth and stroked him.

Need grew, as did a sense of the inevitable. But just when she thought he would suggest taking things to the next level, he pulled back.

He rested his forehead against hers. At least he was breathing hard, she thought, pleased she wasn't the only one affected by what had just happened. When he cupped her cheek, she turned her head so she could kiss his palm. Finally he stepped back.

"This is crazy," he said.

"Probably."

He raised his eyebrows.

"Okay, definitely," she amended.

He turned to the window, then crossed to the open rear door and stared out at the forest.

"There are complications," he said. "Things you don't understand."

Her stomach took a quick and painful journey to her feet. "You're married."

He shook his head. "No. It's not like that."

"Then what's it like?"

He was silent for a long time. So long she began to think he wouldn't answer. Her mind raced with a thousand possibilities. He was sick. He was dying. He was gay.

"You're not gay, are you?"

That made him turn around and face her. He smiled slightly. "No. I'm not gay. But I can't do this."

"What?"

He motioned to her. "This."

Us. Them. A relationship. She wanted to ask why. She wanted to say that with chemistry like theirs, they were insane to ignore the possibilities. But for once, her nearly legendary courage failed her. She felt awkward and scared and more than a little off balance.

"Then what happens now?" she asked.

"I don't know."

"Want to come to my place for dinner one night this week?"

He stared at her. "Didn't I explain—"

"Actually, you didn't. You were very mysterious and woo-woo, but you didn't give me anything close to a reason."

He blinked. "Woo-woo?"

"You know what I mean."

"Not really."

"So?"

He drew in a deep breath. Her heart froze. She desperately wanted him to agree, even knowing that if he did, she would be entering into dangerous territory. All that pain in his eyes might make him incredibly appealing to her, but it didn't make him a good candidate for a healthy relationship.

"What day is good for you?" he asked.

"Dinner, huh?" Ruby asked in a tone that said she thought the evening would be about a whole lot more.

"Yes. And just dinner. I want to take things slow with Aaron."

Her friend didn't look convinced. "You don't know fast from slow when it comes to men who are bad for you. So what's the guy's problem?"

Marissa looked up from the box of books she'd just opened—a donation from a former literacy student of hers. "Why does he have to have a problem?"

"Because you're interested in him," Ruby said wryly. "Come on. Spill. What is it? A prison record? Unpaid taxes? Six current wives?"

"It's not money and he says he's not married." Marissa stacked the books on the desk. "He's fine. Just a little reclusive."

"But?"

Marissa thought about bluffing her way through, but she'd never lied to Ruby and she was honestly confused.

"I don't know. I think he likes me." If his kisses were anything to go by, he liked her a lot. "He says he doesn't want a relationship, but then he accepted an invitation to dinner. He pulls back and moves forward in the same conversation."

"Commitment issues," Ruby said wearily. "The man's afraid love is a prison."

"I don't think so. There's something in his eyes. Something dark and sad. Like he's been seriously hurt."

Ruby set down a handful of picture books. "Girl, when are you going to get it? Pain in a man's eyes isn't a *good* thing. Run. Run now, while you still can. He's going to rip your heart out and chop it up into little pieces."

"No. I'm maintaining emotional distance. I'll be fine."

Her friend shook her head. "You call inviting him over to dinner, then mooning about him all week emotional distance?"

"I can still see him without having to worry about falling for him."

Ruby's brown eyes turned knowing. "Oh, it's like that, is it?"

Marissa frowned. "What do you mean?"

"It's too late. You're already crazy about this guy." She sighed. "You do like to lead with your heart."

"I don't…" Marissa was too surprised to do much more than stare. "I haven't fallen for him. I think he's nice and interesting and sexy, but that doesn't mean anything."

"Of course not."

"I'm serious."

"So am I. You're a goner." Ruby circled around the table in the library until she stood next to Marissa. "I hope he's all you want him to be," she said quietly. "I hope he makes you happy. But if he doesn't, you know I'll be here for you, right?"

Marissa was still too shocked to do much more than nod. No way had she fallen for Aaron. Not in such a short period of time. Of course she liked him. Who wouldn't? But serious feelings were something else. Besides, she'd promised herself she wouldn't make another bad choice. She was tired of giving and giving, only to end up alone.

But the white-hot burning in her heart warned her that it might be too late to be making rational decisions where her feelings were concerned. Sometime, when she hadn't been paying attention, she'd started falling for a guy who went out of his way to tell her he wasn't interested.

"I wanted someone nice and normal," she said quietly.

Ruby shrugged. "Girl, you wouldn't know normal if it bit you on the butt. Look on the bright side. Maybe we're both wrong about Aaron. Maybe he's just a regular guy with a little history in his eyes. Maybe he's been dying to meet a woman just like you and settle down."

Marissa brightened. "You think?"

"It could happen."

Aaron arrived for his dinner with Marissa fifteen minutes late. He almost hadn't come. On the way over he'd nearly turned around twice, but in the end, he'd decided to keep the date, if only to tell her that he couldn't see her anymore.

She made him crazy, he thought as he pulled up to her small duplex and parked behind her battered import. She didn't have the good sense God gave a turnip, what with her running around and trying to rescue everyone. She wanted to make the world better and he wanted to be left alone. He was determined to make her understand things would never work out between them.

But first he wanted to see her. He wanted to breathe in the sweet scent of her body and listen to her laugh. He wanted to hear her explanation for a thousand different oddities of nature and whatever crazy plan she'd come up with for peace in the Middle East.

He wanted to touch her and taste her, which made him ache with guilt. Whenever those images filled his brain, he pushed them away. Liking was acceptable, but not wanting. Never that. He was only ever supposed to want Jilly.

Determined to get things cleared up once and for all, he slammed the truck's door closed and walked up the path. When he rang the bell, the sound seemed to echo.

A few seconds passed, then nearly a minute. He pushed the bell again. Nothing.

Aaron stepped back to make sure there were lights on in her side of the duplex. He knew he had the right house. Not only did he recognize the car, but there were crystals and sun catchers hanging from all the windows. Everything about the place screamed Marissa.

He knocked loudly and thought he heard a faint noise from within. Worry gripped him. When he tried the door, it was open, so he stepped inside and called out her name.

"In here," she said, her voice coming from the back of the house. "I'm sorry I'm not ready. I just need a little more time."

He followed the sound of her words through a cheerfully decorated living room into a bright kitchen. Children's artwork covered most of the walls. Something bubbled on the stove and delicious smells filled the room. But what most caught his attention was Marissa herself, sitting at a round table. Her skin was pale and damp, her eyes unfocused.

"What happened?" he asked as he crossed to her and touched her face. She was burning up with fever.

"I don't know. I started to feel a little tired earlier today and it's just been getting worse. Maybe I should have canceled. I'm kind of hot, but chilly, too, and I couldn't keep down lunch."

"The flu," he said as he walked to the stove and turned off all the burners. "We need to get you into bed."

She blinked at him. "I think it would be better to take things more slowly than that, you know? Not that I don't think you're incredibly sexy and everything. But until I figure out why you have all that pain in your eyes, I have to be sensible."

When she finished talking, she put her head on the table. "I'm okay."

"I can see that."

He moved close and picked her up in his arms. She shrieked. "What are you doing?"

"Making sure you don't pass out in the pasta." He started toward the stairs.

"But we're supposed to have dinner. I cooked."

"I'm sure it's delicious. I'll take a rain check."

She wrapped one arm around his neck and leaned her head against his shoulder. "What does that mean? Rain check. Why is there rain involved? Is it raining? I thought it was nice earlier. Did you think it was nice?"

There were two rooms at the top of the stairs. One seemed to be a home office and the other was a bedroom—pure girl. Pale colors, lots of flowers and frills and a four poster bed fit for a princess.

He set her on the edge of the mattress. "Where are your nightgowns?"

"Huh?" She blinked at him. "In the dresser." She pointed. "But I'm not really tired."

With that she collapsed back onto the mattress.

CHAPTER
SEVEN

"I'M SAYING THAT MAYBE I was wrong," Ruby said as she sat on the sofa beside Marissa.

Marissa half expected the roof to fall in. Not only was Ruby never one to admit that sort of thing, but what her friend was saying meant that Aaron wasn't like all the other men in her life. "The whole time?" she asked again.

"Every minute. You were out of it for nearly three days and the man never left your side. And let me tell you, you were doing some serious puking. It was gross."

Marissa didn't want to think about that. Her bout with the flu had laid her low for nearly ten days, but the first three had been the worst. She had few memories beyond feeling as if she'd already died and hearing Aaron's gentle voice promising her that things would get better.

"He ducked out twice a day to go check on that coyote of his and that was it," Ruby said. "He was worried, too."

"Wow." Despite still being a little weak and wobbly on her legs, Marissa couldn't help grinning. "So…"

Her friend smiled back. "He's got it bad. I can't believe after all this time, you finally picked someone right. He's smart and successful and easy on the eye. Plus, when the going gets rough, or in your case, when the going is some pretty nasty green stuff, he was right there. That's what I call a catch."

Marissa felt so happy, she wanted to float. "I should go see him. You know, to thank him."

"Uh-huh." Ruby looked amused. "I'm sure that's all you have on your mind. But a little advice. Wait until morning. For one thing, I don't want you driving at night just yet. You need to build your strength back up. For another, you're in some serious need of personal grooming."

Marissa fingered her lank hair. "You're right. I haven't had a shower in days. But I'll take care of all that in the morning, then go see him."

Her heart fluttered with excitement and the potential for finally finding her own happily ever after.

Aaron sat alone in the darkness, staring out the window. The promised storm had arrived and lightning cut through the inky blackness. He waited for the accompanying thunder, and when it came, he heard the angry judgment in the sound.

They were gone. The ghosts he'd come to count on as the last remaining tether to the life he'd once had faded. Two nights of drinking had done nothing to bring them back.

Pain cut through him. It was as if he'd lost Jilly and the baby all over again. They were gone, and he'd been the one to chase them away this time. They'd disappeared because of Marissa.

He closed his eyes and gave himself over to the recriminations. He should have left, he told himself for what must be the thousandth time. He should have called her friend and just walked away. But she'd been sick and he'd felt...worried.

No, he thought, opening his eyes and staring out into the storm. More than worried. He'd been frantic. When she'd passed out, he'd tasted terror. So he'd been right there with her for three days. He'd thought of nothing but getting her better. He'd forgotten, and that's what the ghosts couldn't forgive.

He turned his head, and when the next bolt of lightning illuminated the heavens, he saw the framed picture of his late wife. Jilly was laughing. She'd rarely been without a smile. He'd tried to comfort himself with that thought in the first year after her death. That she would have been smiling right up until the end. Singing to their baby and telling a story. She wouldn't have thought to imagine the worst. In her world, bad things never happened.

Bitter betrayal tightened around his chest like a tourniquet. He could barely breathe. He prayed for a stray bolt of lightning to crash through the roof of the house and strike him right then.

Bracing himself, he waited for the relief, but instead there was only the sound of the rain, then a cold dampness as Buddy sniffed his hand.

Aaron rubbed the coyote's ears. That's right, he told himself. He had Buddy to take care of. The animal would die without him, and he hadn't rescued him for that to happen. Reason returned, and with it, the list of his obligations. The woodworking class, the bookshelf he still had to finish.

He opened both hands. Buddy rested his head on one. Aaron closed the other in a fist.

Two worlds, he thought. What could have been and what was. The animal's fur was warm, and Aaron felt the steady beat of his blood pulsing through his body.

It was wrong to throw all this away because he'd lost his ghosts, he told himself. But he wanted to—he wanted to down to his soul.

Marissa washed her hair twice the next morning. She went through her wardrobe for the right outfit to wear to Aaron's. The man had spent three days with her while she looked like cat gack. She was determined to make a better impression when she showed up to thank him.

She still couldn't believe what had happened—that he'd stayed with her while she'd been so sick. Her heart told her that meant something important, something with the potential to change her life forever.

She couldn't seem to stop smiling as she walked into his shop later that morning. The open area looked much as she remembered—various pieces of furniture in different stages of assembly. The scent of spring and wood shavings filled the air. The heavy sliding doors at the back of the shop were open and she saw Buddy stretched out in a patch of sunshine.

Aaron stood by a bench. He wore safety goggles and was working some kind of sander. When he saw her, he flicked off the machine and pushed up his protective eyewear.

"Hi," she said, suddenly feeling shy and a little awkward.

"You're back on your feet," he said. "How do you feel?"

"About ninety percent. I still get a little tired by late afternoon, but otherwise I'm fine."

He nodded to the overstuffed chair in the corner. "Have a seat."

"Thanks."

Once she sat down, she let herself drink in his appearance. Man, oh man, did he look good. Worn jeans that hugged narrow hips and long legs, a long-sleeved shirt rolled up to the elbow. He moved with that same easy grace that left her breathless.

"I wanted to thank you," she said, tucking her skirt around her knees. "For taking care of me. You didn't have to."

"You scared me," he admitted as he pulled up a stool across from her and sat. "You were pretty sick."

"It was going around the schools. I guess one of the parents in the reading program got it from her kids and gave it to me."

"Next time, look for a gift you can return."

She smiled. "Good point."

His dark gaze settled on her face and the contact was as potent as a touch. Her heartbeat increased, as did her breathing. Tension charged the air.

"Aaron," she began, but he cut her off with a shake of his head.

He stood and returned to the workbench, where he picked up a rag and began rubbing the legs of a half-built chair.

"Don't," he said, not looking at her anymore.

"Don't what?"

"Say whatever it is you're thinking."

"But I'm not…"

"Yes, you are." He kept his attention on his work. "I was married before. While I was in the service."

Marissa's breath caught as her muscles tensed. Married. She hadn't considered the possibility. She certainly didn't want to now, but if this was the reason for the shadows in his eyes, she had to know.

"What happened?" she asked. "Did you split up?"

He looked at her then, his expression both weary and heartsick. "No. I was away on deployment. She'd had our first child a couple of months before. Their car was hit by a drunk driver. The crash killed them both."

She didn't know what to think, what to say. What words could make any difference?

"I'm so sorry," she murmured at last. "You must have been devastated."

"More than that," he told her. "Destroyed. What I lost still haunts me. I never want to forget her…them." He swallowed. "I was overseas and I was supposed to go home the following week. I was getting out of the military, heading back to the States for good."

She ached for him and quickly rose. "Aaron."

He stepped back. "Don't. Don't touch me, don't try to fix this. You can't, and I don't want you to."

She nodded, even though she didn't understand. "How long?"

"Six years. But it could have been yesterday." He tossed the rag onto the bench. "I still love her. I'll always love her."

Marissa frowned. "Of course you will. What does that have to do with anything?"

"I don't want this," he said. "Not you or the kids or the town. I want to be left alone. I want you to go away and never come back."

His words hovered in the air like sawdust, then slowly filtered into her brain. At first the shock was so great that she didn't feel any pain.

"I don't understand," she whispered, even though she did.

"I won't betray what we had. I won't betray my family."

"By living? By caring about someone else?"

"You don't understand."

"Right. Because I've never lost anything and been left alone. We'll ignore the death of my parents when I was twelve. I'm sure my pain was wildly insignificant compared with yours," she said sarcastically. She didn't want to believe what he was saying, but he wasn't giving her a choice. She walked closer and put her hands on her hips.

"How dare you," she accused, feeling the anger fill her. Anger was safe, she thought. Anger would keep her breathing and moving and surviving. "How dare you retreat into your workshop and turn your back on the world. You have a responsibility."

He glared at her. "The hell I do."

"You're alive. That makes you a member of this society. Where do you get off retreating? Isn't it easy, just you and Buddy out here alone. Nothing to worry about except your next big fat check and getting the wood you need. All the time the rest of us are struggling to make a difference."

"Get out of here," he told her.

"I'm leaving. You bet. And if you really don't want to be a part of anything, I'll make sure it happens." She dropped her hands to her side. "I thought you were different. I thought you were one of the good guys. You claim to love your wife and child, but you certainly haven't honored them in their death. What does it say about your life with them that the only thing you want to do now they're gone is hide? Loving someone means opening your heart, and once you've done that, you can't ever close it again. Oh, sure, there's pain and a time of mourning, but eventually you're sup-posed to heal and move on."

She rubbed her hands along the chair leg. "It's perfect, Aaron. I'll give you that. But it's also cold and lifeless. Do you think your wife would be proud of you and what you've become? Do you think this is what she'd want as her legacy?"

He took a step toward her. "Don't you dare speak about my wife. You didn't know her."

"You're right. I didn't. But I imagine her to be beautiful and loving and someone I'd really like. That person would hate what you've become."

He leaned against the bench. "I told you not to try to save me. You should have listened."

"I'm listening now," she said. "I'm listening, and all I can say is that I feel sorry for you."

"Do you?" he asked, turning his attention back to her. "That's funny, because we're not all that different. I might hide in the dark, but you're also hiding. Only you do it in plain sight behind your projects and your loser guys."

She wanted to tell him he was wrong, that it wasn't like that. But when she opened her mouth, she found she couldn't speak. The pain she'd been avoiding crashed into her and nearly sent her to her knees. There was nothing to say, nothing to do but run.

CHAPTER
EIGHT

MARISSA WAS AS GOOD as her word. The following week no one showed up for Aaron's woodworking class, and when he finished the bookcase for the auction, a man he'd never met came to pick it up.

No one visited him, no one called to ask him to speak anywhere or help with any cause. His life returned to the way it had been before—perfect solitude.

Even the ghosts came back. Nearly a week after Marissa had left, Aaron worked through the night, only to fall into an uneasy sleep just before dawn. He saw Jilly again. She was laughing. He heard the sound and it filled him with joy. He watched as she picked up their baby and danced with him across the small bedroom, but when he put out his hands to touch them both, they disappeared into the mist.

He awoke suddenly, his fingers grasping at air, and he knew then that the ghosts weren't real, and he was truly alone.

That night he drove to the library and stood outside Marissa's class. He heard her patient voice going over the night's lesson with her eager students. Adults read haltingly, stumbling over difficult words, but never giving up. She praised them and he heard the pride in their voices.

He returned to his large house on his isolated plot of land. Even Buddy had disappeared into the spring darkness.

Aaron walked from room to room, looking for something that wasn't there.

Around midnight, he heard a sound in the distance. The faraway wail of sirens made the hair on the back of his neck stand up. He walked to the big windows in his living room and stared toward the town. Flames licked up into the night.

Without thinking, he grabbed his truck keys and hurried outside. Ten minutes later, he found himself parking at the edge of a massive fire.

Two apartment buildings seemed to be going up in flames. Firefighters swarmed around, dragging hoses and pulling people away from the danger. The smoke and heat were living creatures, sucking the oxygen from Aaron's lungs. People screamed, children cried. In the middle of the cacophony, he heard a young voice calling, "Mommy? Mommy, where are you?"

Turning, he saw a young boy dressed in pajamas. His hair stuck out in all directions, soot smudged one cheek, and he held a large picture book in his hand.

Recognition slammed into Aaron. "Christopher?" he asked, remembering the boy from the picnic.

At the sound of his name, the child looked up at him. "Who... Who are you?" he said with a sniff as he wiped the tears from his eyes.

"Aaron Cross. You read to me about a month ago. At the literacy picnic."

"My mommy hit her head. When she carried me out of the building. She fell down and didn't move and they took her away."

Aaron swore under his breath. How had the kid gotten separated from his mother?

"Do you have any brothers or sisters?" he asked. "Where's your dad?"

More tears spilled down the boy's cheeks. "I just have Mommy."

Without thinking, Aaron bent down and scooped the boy up in his arms. "Hey, it's going to be okay," he promised. "I'll help you find out what's going on."

He walked around the milling crowd looking for someone in authority. The firefighters were all too busy with battling the fire, and everyone from the apartment building seemed to be in a panic. Finally he located someone who would know exactly what to do.

Marissa stood at the edge of the disaster scene. She spoke into a cell phone while she gave directions to those around her.

"Maybe fifty families," she said into the phone. "The high

school gym has the most space, plus there are showers and the home ec kitchens. Right. No. I've called them already. They're delivering cots and blankets. We'll have to get the word out for other supplies. I think most of these people have lost everything. Hold on."

She turned her attention to a couple of teens with clipboards.

"Start collecting names," she told the kids. "Find out who is missing and what family members need to be reunited. We'll have an information hotline up within the hour."

"You're kidding," the sleepy teenaged boy said. "How can you do that?"

She gave him a quick smile. "Practice. Now git."

The kids took off. Marissa completed her phone call, and as she hung up, he approached.

She looked tired, he thought. Dark circles shaded the area under her eyes and he had a feeling her weariness had nothing to do with the fire. He'd hurt her badly. First by making her think there was a possibility for the two of them to have a relationship, then by dismissing her in the cruelest way possible.

"What are you doing here?" she asked.

"I saw the fire." He paused. What *had* compelled him out into the night? "I wanted to help. Christopher here seems to have lost his mom." He briefly recounted the child's story.

Marissa shook her head. "At least there aren't that many hospitals to check. Can you take care of him until I can find out how she is?"

"Sure."

She looked more wary than pleased, which made sense. He thought of a thousand things he would like to say to her, but this wasn't the time. Instead he carried Christopher over to a relatively quiet grassy area by the parking lot and sat down.

The boy stared at him, and Aaron realized he didn't have a clue what to do.

"How you doing, sport?" he asked, feeling foolish even as he spoke the words.

The boy shrugged. Aaron struggled to think of something to say that wasn't frightening or stupid or a lie.

"I want my mom," Christopher said.

"I know you do, and I want to take you to her. But first my friend Marissa is going to find out where she is. Okay? That may take a little while. But I'm going to stay right here next to you. I'm going to keep you safe."

Big blue eyes stared at him. "Promise?"

Aaron made an X on his chest. "Cross my heart."

Christopher nodded, and at the same time he started to cry again. Not knowing what else to do, Aaron pulled him close and wrapped his arms around him.

"It's okay," he said, not sure if the words were true.

The tiny body shook. Aaron closed his eyes against the madness around them. For some reason, he thought of Jilly and their son and how he'd held the baby after he was born. Holding Christopher reminded him of all that he'd missed, but oddly enough, the pain wasn't as bad as he would have thought. Oh, sure, there was a sharpness to it, but he could survive.

He looked at the book the boy had dropped and reached for it.

"I remember this," he said. "It's all about cars. Boy, do I like cars. Always did." He opened the book and began to read.

Two hours later, the fire had been put out. About half the apartments had been destroyed and the rest were smoke and water damaged. Surprisingly, there had only been two injuries, and both had proved minor, which was why Marissa was looking for Aaron. She'd finally located Christopher's mother at a local hospital. The woman had a slight head injury and was expected to make a full recovery. The doctor wanted her to stay the night for observation, but he planned to release her in the morning.

Marissa had been relieved. Christopher would be happy and she could take him to the hospital on her way home. She would keep him overnight and then reunite him with his mother in the morning.

Everything had worked out better than she'd dared to hope. A fire in a crowded apartment building at night could have meant a devastating loss of life. Instead, everyone was going to be just fine.

Donations from the community had started to pour in and

would continue. Once again, she'd made a difference and that felt really good.

Of course it wasn't enough to fill the gaping hole where her heart used to be, but she was getting used to that empty feeling in her chest. In time, she would stop loving Aaron and move on. Until then, she would put one foot in front of the other to carry on.

She rounded a corner and stumbled to a stop. Disbelief swept through her as she stared at the tall handsome man sitting on the damp grass, reading to several children by the emergency light from a nearby fire truck.

"You are the best baby kitten in the whole world," he read. "Your soft fur feels nice against my hand and your purr always makes me smile."

Christopher and a little girl were both snuggled up on Aaron's lap. Two slightly older kids leaned against him. Several teens were sitting around, holding younger children. And around them, dazed parents looked on with gratitude.

She must have made a sound because they all turned to look at her. She cleared her throat.

"The, uh, buses are here to take everyone to the shelter," she said. "If you have pets, animal control is offering foster care for as long as you need it."

The children scrambled up and headed toward their parents, except for Christopher, who clung to Aaron.

"I can take him," she said when the three of them were alone. She crouched down in front of the boy. "I talked to your mom. She's feeling just fine. I'm going to drive you to the hospital so you can see her, then we'll have a sleepover. In the morning, she'll come get you. How does that sound?"

"No!" Christopher buried his head in Aaron's shoulder. "Don't let her take me."

"I won't." Aaron hugged him close. "But I know you want to see your mom. What do you say the three of us go to the hospital together."

The boy sniffed. "Okay. Don't forget my book."

"I won't."

Aaron stood. "Does that work for you?"

She nodded as she rose. "Sure. But I don't understand. What are you doing here?"

"Helping."

"I got that. But why? I thought you wanted to be alone."

"I did." His beautiful dark eyes seemed to see into her soul. "I thought the ghosts were enough, but you were right. Jilly wouldn't be very proud of me right now."

Jilly. A beautiful name, she thought.

"I'm done hiding," he said. "I want to make a difference."

Good news, she told herself, refusing to hope. "That's great. There are a lot of local organizations looking for volunteers. I could hook you up with—"

He pressed his fingers over her lips. "I'll start up my wood-working class again and help out wherever you want, but that's not what I meant. I want to make a difference here. With you."

Marissa wanted to believe him, but she still hurt so much. "I guess we can talk about it later," she said.

The morning of the auction dawned perfectly clear. Marissa knew, because she'd been awake to see it. Nerves had kept her from sleeping. Nerves and anticipation.

This was the biggest event she'd ever planned. So much was riding on the success of the day. She was supposed to give a big speech right before they auctioned off Aaron's bookcase and she'd rewritten her text about four million times. As of ten minutes ago, she still didn't have it right.

"I need to concentrate," she told herself as she waited for the second pot of coffee to brew. How could she? Between all the last-minute details occupying her mind and the way Aaron kept popping up in her brain, she felt as scattered as a balloon in a twister.

Aaron. He'd been as good as his word. Two weeks ago he'd started up his classes once again, had shown up for literacy training and invited her out to dinner three times. The impending auction meant she hadn't been able to accept, but she'd been tempted.

Even knowing how he'd hurt her, she'd wanted to see him again, be alone with him. She'd longed to hear him say she mattered, that they belonged together. But would he? Was his transformation about his need to heal the world, or was it about them?

374 SUSAN MALLERY

She was willing to admit to more than a little fear on that front. On her good days, she told herself it was important to know where they stood. On her bad days, she wanted to run away and hide.

Promptly at seven-fifteen the phone began to ring as people called with questions about setup and deliveries. She got out of the house at nine and by noon was fighting panic and a headache.

By two, the high school auditorium was standing room only. By four, they'd sold everything but Aaron's bookcase. Marissa checked her makeup in the tiny cracked mirror backstage as she prepared to head out to deliver her speech on the Motheread/Fatheread® program.

"It's not here." Ruby ran up to Marissa and grabbed her arm. "Aaron's bookcase. It's not here."

"What? I saw it this morning."

"Maybe, but it's gone now."

Marissa stared at her friend. "Stolen? But who would do that? I don't…"

The auctioneer began his introduction.

"You're on," Ruby said, pushing her toward the front of the stage. "You're going to have to stall them while we figure out what we're going to do."

"Don't stall anything," Aaron said as he approached.

Marissa turned and stared at him. "Did you hear? Your bookcase is missing."

He smiled a warm, sexy smile that made her heart flutter and her mouth go dry. "I took it home. It wasn't right."

"I don't understand."

"This program is worth a whole lot more than just a bookcase."

He jerked his head over his shoulder. Behind him, men were carrying in chairs, tables and sofas. She couldn't believe it.

"Aaron, I appreciate the gesture, but we can't possibly sell all that. The people around here don't have enough money."

"I know. I'm holding back a couple of chairs for local bidders only, but the rest of it will go onto the Internet auction."

She blinked. "The what?"

"I've been setting it up all week. I sent a mailing to my clients, informing them of the auction. Most of them are sitting in front of their computers, ready to start buying. I'm figuring we'll get close to five hundred thousand for the lot."

Ruby gasped. "That's going to buy a lot of books."

"My thoughts exactly," he said.

Marissa didn't know what to think. "Why are you doing this?"

"Because someone I care about very much once told me that even a single individual can make a difference. I finally figured out she's right." He touched her cheek. "That's your cue."

"What? Oh." Marissa smoothed the front of her dress and stepped onto the stage. Everyone in the auditorium applauded her entrance.

"Without this little lady here, we wouldn't have much of a program at all," the auctioneer said.

Marissa walked to the microphone and smiled. "Thank you all so much. I've just found out there's going to be a change in the program. There's no Aaron Cross bookcase to bid on."

Several people groaned.

"Instead we're going to auction off an entire collection."

As the furniture was carried on stage, she explained about the online bidding.

"This all goes for a good cause," she said. "Most of you know how the Motheread/Fatheread® program has changed so many lives in our community. What you may not know is that we're reaching beyond our community to men and women in desperate need of a second chance. Volunteers are working with parents in prison. Most of those incarcerated can't read very well, if at all. They're away from their children and they don't know how to be good parents. Our program gives them the opportunity to learn a valuable skill—reading—and to use that skill to become better mothers and fathers. We're teaching them to communicate, to understand what their children need from them. For many, the love of a child is incentive enough to find a new and better life after being released."

She looked around at the familiar faces in front of her. "I didn't grow up in a big family. I was raised in foster care, where no one had the time to read me a story. So I know what it's like to wish for that connection. For all of you who are willing to give just a little so others can know the pleasure and wonder of reading to their children, I thank you."

Applause filled the auditorium. One by one, the people rose until they were all standing. Suddenly the stage filled as the volunteers joined her, clapping and cheering.

Marissa didn't know what to say, where to go. Gratitude filled her. She glanced around and saw Aaron joining in the applause.

As she looked at him, she saw that the pain was gone from his eyes. She'd spent the last two weeks pushing him away and he'd continued to show up. That had to mean something.

Without thinking about the thousand or so people watching, she walked over to him.

"Why are you still here?" she asked.

"Because there's nowhere else I'd rather be."

"Than at the auction?"

He smiled. "Than with you. I meant what I said, Marissa. You got it exactly right. I've been living my life the easy way. Staying alone, mourning. What kind of a legacy is that? I'll always love Jilly and my son, but that doesn't mean my heart is closed. There's plenty more love in there for a wonderful woman who constantly pushes me to be my best. I want to be there for you. I want to be the one person you're willing to lean on. I want to love you and look after you—if you'll have me."

He moved closer. "You're so busy taking care of others, you don't bother taking care of yourself. The way I see it, you're in need of a good rescuing, and I'm just the man to do it."

She was too stunned to speak. This was everything she'd ever dreamed of Aaron saying to her, and yet she couldn't seem to form any words for a response.

"Kiss him!" somebody yelled.

"What?"

She turned and saw they were the center of attention. Even the auctioneer watched eagerly.

"You heard the nice man," Aaron said with a grin. "Kiss me."

"Why should I?"

"Because you love me nearly as much as I love you. Because you've spent your whole life falling for the wrong guy, and this time you've got it right. And because you want to."

She started to laugh. "When did you get so smart?"

He picked her up and swung her around. "The day you walked into my shop and started taking over my life."

She sighed as he set her back on the ground. "That was a good day," she said, wrapping her arms around him.

"This one's better."

He dropped his head and kissed her. Marissa heard cheering in the background, but she couldn't be bothered to see who it was. Not when Aaron was there, holding her, wanting her. Loving her.

She drew back. "Did I tell you I love you?"

He cupped her cheek. "With everything you do."

"All right, you two," Ruby ordered. "Let's get off this stage so they can finish up the auction."

Once they were backstage, Aaron pulled Marissa into a corner. "I want to marry you," he said. "Let me take care of you, love you. For always."

She nodded, her throat too tight to speak. He wasn't just offering her his heart—he was offering the one thing she'd been looking for all her life.

Home.